Last Known Address

ALSO BY ELIZABETH WRENN
FROM CLIPPER LARGE PRINT

Second Chance

Last Known Address

Elizabeth Wrenn

W F HOWES LTD

This large print edition published in 2009 by
W F Howes Ltd
Unit 4, Rearsby Business Park, Gaddesby Lane,
Rearsby, Leicester LE7 4YH

1   3   5   7   9   10   8   6   4   2

First published in the United Kingdom in 2008
by HarperCollins*Publishers*

A CIP catalogue record for this book is available
from the British Library

ISBN 978 1 40743 655 5

Typeset by Palimpsest Book Production Limited,
Grangemouth, Stirlingshire

Printed and bound in Great Britain
by TJ International Ltd, Padstow, Cornwall

ACKNOWLEDGMENTS

Thanks to Marcy, girlfriend from the get-go. And to Maxine, Keshini, Sammia, Yvonne and Caroline at Avon: thanks for all your work and support. Thanks to the following for sharing medical expertise and/or experience: Dr John Fleagle, MD, Jean Scott, and Georgia Robertson. I endeavored to be accurate with their input, but any medical errors in the story are mine, either out of ignorance or poetic license. Thanks and love to dear friends Terry Johnson and Paul Nelson: Terry for being the best letter-writer I know, and to Paul for carrying them, and to you both for decades of friendship. Love and thanks also to Margaret Ruttenber, my Catholic connection, wonderful neighbor and great girlfriend. Thanks also to: Det. Larry Gibson of the Boulder Police Dept. for advising me on the Amber Alert law; Sally Ham Govan for being my southern go-to gal for this book; Serena & Gary Galloway of Ankhu Italian Greyhounds for literally immersing me in the wonderful ways of Iggys; Roxanne Hawn, who also loves and writes about dogs; thank you for all your support, and for sharing your experience with the dog psychic with me. And much love and gratitude to Ella: for this book and in life, I am grateful for your wonderful insight and ideas. The best thing about you flying the nest? We get to be girlfriends! And finally, to Stuart: my best friend, first editor and favorite co-conspirator. Thank you for *everything*, from hours of listening and being a sounding board, to drawing me blueprints of Dogs' Wood, to construction and URPL advice, to that all-important man's point of view. And, of course, for the love letters. T T EOT E.

To *all* my girlfriends; you know who you are!
With special love to my first and most enduring
girlfriends: Ali, Peggy and Jenny. And to
girlfriends everywhere, of every age.

PART I

LEAVING

CHAPTER 1

C.C.

C C.'s huge suitcase lay open on her bed, looking like a collapsed buffet guest. It was already too full to close, primarily due to the brand-new velour sweatsuits, tags still on, neatly folded and fanned on top of the bulging mound. Even so, C.C. turned a slow circle, scanning for anything she might have forgotten. She could tuck an item or two into the trunk of Meg's car.

Should she take the third of a bottle of Happiness perfume on her dresser? No. One orange foam earplug on the bedside table? She tossed it over the bed toward the wastebasket. When it arced right in, she grinned. 'That's a good omen!' She bent to pick up an old paper bookmark lying forlornly on the floor. She walked over and dropped it directly in with the earplug. Bookmarks didn't fly well, and if she missed the wastebasket, well . . . Best not to tempt the fates.

Looking around the room, she mostly saw what *wasn't* there. The other earplug. The rest of the perfume. And most of all, Lenny, who had bought her the perfume, for whom she'd worn the perfume. And whose snoring had made her reach for the earplugs each night.

She stepped to her dresser, picked up the picture of the two of them, its chrome frame glinting in the stark light of the nearly empty room. She had already packed the smaller picture, the one of Lenny and Kathryn and Lucy on the couch on Christmas morning, Lenny's long arms embracing both her girls amid a litter of colorful paper and ribbons. She'd wrapped it in a short-sleeve cotton top, placed it in the middle of her suitcase, safely tucking it away, ready for the trip.

The trip. That seemed too small a word for this big . . . adventure. She laughed a little, all by herself there in her quiet bedroom. C.C. and Shelly and Meg's Big Adventure.

She stared at the picture in her hands. It wasn't a great picture, but it was the last one taken of just the two of them, at the Iowa Accountants Labor Day picnic two years ago. They were in front of a big oak tree, had their arms around each other, hers on Len's thin waist, his hanging over her shoulder like a friendly snake. The light around them was peach-colored, and lovely, but they were both squinting into the setting sun. Like they were trying to see into the future or something. She'd left this picture out of the boxes till the last possible moment, to keep her company, and give her resolve. She touched Lenny's smile. She could imagine him telling her, *Go ahead, be brave.*

Her eyes moist, C.C. allowed herself half a

moment to hug the frame to her chest, then hurriedly pulled the nearest unsealed box across the carpet toward her. But when she saw the contents of the box, she laughed. Her extra slips, lingerie and other 'unmentionables'. She wouldn't be needing those. She didn't fit into most anyway. She tucked the frame in, burrowing it into the slinky depths.

'How's that, darlin'?'

Eighteen months after his funeral, she could now finally talk to him without bawling. She'd considered bringing his sealed urn down south, but realized it wasn't practical; she'd be devastated if something happened to it while they were on the road, or after. Where would she put it, after all? There would be painting, construction – mess throughout the house down there. So, months ago, before her house even went on the market, Kathryn had taken it, checking with Lucy first to make sure it was okay with her to have the urn in their apartment. Kathryn had told C.C. that, every night, Lucy blew Lenny a kiss; she called him 'Papaw-on-the-bookcase'. Blood may be thicker than water, C.C. thought, but sometimes love was thicker than blood.

The sound of a car pulling into the driveway drew her to the window. She knew without lifting the blind, from the glub-glub motorboat sound, that it was Kathryn's old Pontiac. The engine cut as C.C. glanced at her watch. They were early. Meg and Shelly wouldn't be here till six thirty for the 'clean your fridge out potluck', as Shelly called it. C.C.

5

sucked in a breath. This dinner would be it, the big goodbye, to Kathryn and Lucy. And C.C.'s last chance to make things right with her daughter, which she had little hope of achieving.

They could have said their goodbyes in the morning, Meg having pointed out that they might as well wait till after rush hour to head out of town. But Kathryn had to work the early shift at the store, and Lucy had school, although C.C. knew both would like to have a reason not to go. But C.C. needed to say her goodbyes the night before; she didn't want to be sitting in the back seat crying for the first hundred miles.

She stood, massaging her lower back. If fifty was the new forty, it still came with the old aches and pains of fifty. She reached up toward the ceiling, stretching, muttering a Hail Mary, but thinking it wasn't quite fair that she *felt* fifty, six months before she *turned* fifty.

C.C. lowered her arms, found herself staring out the bedroom door, down the hall, at the blank wall, the nails and hooks poking forlornly out of the wall where the family pictures had hung. She'd decided to leave them; maybe the new family would use them. How odd it had felt, padding about her nearly empty house these last few days, knowing it wasn't hers anymore. Most of the proceeds from the sale had gone directly into an account that, God willing, would be enough to buy a small place outright, when she returned. There wasn't nearly as much as she had hoped;

they didn't have a lot of equity, and she'd gotten caught in a down market. If the housing market recovered before she was ready to buy, she'd be in a real pickle. Yet again, her security seemed inexorably linked to Dogs' Wood, Aunt Georgie's house – *her* house, now – in Tennessee.

The closing on her Iowa house had been weeks ago, but Shelly – real-estate agent extraordinaire – had put a clause in the contract for C.C. to rent it back till they left, and a few days beyond so that Kathryn could come to collect the bed and dresser for her apartment, and take the remaining boxes to storage. C.C. had had a flare of excitement when Kathryn had mentioned the new guy at work, Matt, who had a truck and was going to help her move the things. The maternal delight had once again been too obvious on C.C.'s face. Kathryn had quickly informed her, with stern emphasis on the words she clearly felt her mother needed to hear, that Matt was over ten years younger than she, a *kid*, *nineteen*, and she was going to *pay* him to help her on his day off from his job as *sacker* at the store. C.C., determinedly cheerful, had put her arm around her daughter and told her (not for the first time), 'Your true love will come, darlin', just you wait.' But Kathryn had angrily shrugged her arm off. It helped not at all that C.C. knew that Kathryn's anger was really frustration that she too could not leave town, have an adventure.

C.C. sat on the bed, her eyes closed. If only she

hadn't made things so much worse with what Kathryn called 'the mall incident'. C.C. did regret what she'd done at the mall. But at the time, it had seemed nothing more than a mother's pride spilling over. Helpful, even. She and Meg had been having lunch after doing some clothes shopping for the trip. When Meg had excused herself to the restroom, C.C. had felt conspicuously alone at her table, so had started chatting with the two handsome young businessmen lunching nearby. It seemed only natural, in the context of their conversation, to show them the picture in her wallet of her beautiful, single, very available daughter.

'Let me ask your opinion on something,' she'd said, and they'd both been very willing. 'Honest, now, don't you think she looks like a young Meg Ryan?' They'd nodded, smiling, good-natured. And C.C. had told them with unreserved pride that it was her daughter. Immediately one had said that she, C.C., didn't look old enough to be that woman's mother, always the hoped-for response. C.C. had blushed and beamed and given her usual reply: 'I'm *not* old enough to be her mother. But I am!' And when she found out that both men were single, what was she supposed to do? C.C. had only wanted to give Kathryn's number to the lawyer, the one with the steady job, not the one who was starting an adventure travel business. But how could she politely exclude the entrepreneur?

She'd realized almost immediately afterward that

she'd overstepped, confirmed by Meg on the drive home. It was just that C.C.'s heart broke for her daughter. Kathryn was hardly *old* at twenty-nine, but she wasn't exactly prime dating age, either. And she had what that lowlife Jordan had called 'the genetic ball and chain'. Imagine calling a child that! Especially, darling Lucy. C.C. knew she would have to tell Kathryn what she'd done, just in case one (or both!) of the men called. But despite her numerous apologies to her daughter, Kathryn had been madder than a swatted-at hornet. She'd been giving C.C. the silent treatment ever since.

C.C. clicked the lamp off, then peeked out the blinds again, wondering why they hadn't come in yet. Down below, mother and daughter were sitting in the car, illuminated by the glare from the floodlight above the garage. Lucy was slumped far down in her seat, the heels of her hands on the cushion on either side of her. Her head was tucked turtle-like into her shoulders, her chin down. C.C.'s heart twisted. She hoped something hadn't happened at school again. She watched through the crack, keeping herself hidden behind the blind. Kathryn took Lucy's small hand, kissed it, held it to her chest. Lucy wiped at her cheeks with her other hand. C.C. let go of the blind, wanting them to have their private mother–daughter moment.

Until recently, she and Kathryn had always been close too, for much the same reason: they were just twenty years apart in age. Of all the ways C.C.

would have wanted her daughter to emulate her, getting pregnant unmarried at twenty was not one of them. For one, it had made C.C. a grandmother at age forty. But she would never call sweet Lucy a mistake, unlike that fool Jordan. He and Kathryn had been dating only two months, but it was two months too long, in C.C.'s opinion. How she wished Kathryn would show that leather-clad lowlife the north end of her boot, send him out of town on that noisy motorcycle of his.

The front door opened, then slammed shut. 'Meemaw? We're here! Where are you?'

'Be right down, Lovebucket!' C.C. yelled as she headed across her bedroom. She stepped quickly into the bathroom, to the only remaining mirror, to check her hair. It was up, as always, curled, pinned, sprayed and clipped into not quite a beehive, but close. She tucked a curl in, then pushed her palm under it admiringly. Her hair was, and always had been, her best feature. Though she didn't mind telling people that she now achieved her naturally light blonde color unnaturally.

'Where are you, Piece-a-pie?' C.C. called out as she reached the bottom of the stairs.

'Coming!' Lucy ran from the living room into C.C.'s outstretched arms. They hugged and C.C. kissed the top of her head, inhaling the child's sweet scent. Kathryn took a long time hanging their coats among the empty hangers in the hall closet.

Lucy pulled back, beaming. 'We brought you a present!' Whatever she'd been crying about in the car was forgotten. At least for the moment. C.C.'s heart gladdened at Lucy's words, specifically 'we'. She glanced at Kathryn, but Kathryn spoke only to Lucy.

'Shhh!' she gently admonished. 'We were going to do that at the end, remember?' Kathryn had not, and would not, look at C.C.

'Oh. Yeah. I forgot,' said Lucy, lifting her shoulders apologetically.

'It's okay,' said Kathryn. She at least gave Lucy a smile. 'You want to go get it? It's on the back seat.'

Lucy rushed outside without answering, or donning her coat, leaving the wooden door wide open. The storm door slammed behind her and the frigid air blew in through the screen. Lenny had been the one to put the glass panes in each fall. C.C. hadn't even found them till last week, bringing the last of the boxes from the basement. She'd decided to just leave them there. The new family wouldn't want them in now anyway. It was almost April, nearly spring.

C.C. smiled, closing the big wooden door. 'Land, that girl can't remember to shut a door to save her life!'

'You and your doors, Mother. She'll be *right* back in.' Kathryn looked past her, her jaw tense.

C.C. nodded, wondering if she should open the door again. She didn't know how to get off these eggshells with Kathryn.

'Sweetheart,' began C.C., 'I'm glad we have a quick minute alone here. I just want to say, again, that I shouldn't have given those men—'

'No! You shouldn't have. But I don't want to discuss it anymore.' Kathryn looked out the small window of the door. 'So, this present?'

'Yes?' C.C. said hopefully.

'It's not really a present for you. It's for Lucy. Mrs Diamont suggested it. I had to go in for another conference and—' Kathryn caught her breath. 'She's way behind in spelling, writing in general. And she can't – *read.*' Her voice cracked, she placed a hand over her mouth briefly, then removed it, placing her palm on the door. 'Mrs Diamont thinks she's going to have to be held back, repeat second grade.'

'Oh, darlin',' said C.C., stepping toward her daughter, her arms open. But Kathryn spoke without turning. 'Mother, no. Please. Just – leave it. I don't want this to come up. With Lucy. But that's all this present is about.'

'Of course.' She got it. She'd gotten it at 'Mother'. Kathryn called her that only if she was angry, inaccessible. She called her 'Mom' casually, 'Momma' in a tender moment or when she most needed her. It had been a while since she had heard the tender moniker. C.C. lowered her arms to her sides, then clasped her hands in front of her, then put them back at her sides, suddenly wishing that arms came with some proper storage system. The doorbell rang. C.C. looked at her

12

daughter, asking with her eyes if she could open the door. Kathryn nodded, stepped away, and C.C. pulled the door open.

'Trick or treat!' Lucy burst into giggles as she stood outside, her hands behind her back.

'Land sakes, child! It's only the end of March. Y'all come back in October!' C.C. pretended to close the door.

'It's a treat for *you*, Meemaw!' Lucy laughed, pushed the door open with one hand and brought the gift from behind her back. She jumped up over the threshold. C.C. gently closed the door behind her.

The gift was wrapped in colorful Sunday comics and had an inordinate amount of tape on it. It also had an impressive amount of pink ribbon, wrapped around several times, tied into several floppy bows, all with curly ends. Lucy handed it to C.C. 'Here. We got me one that—' She clapped her hand over her mouth, glanced up at her mother.

Kathryn gathered her in her arms, kissed the top of her head. 'Good catch.'

'Shall I open it now, or wait till your aunties arrive?' asked C.C.

'Wait for Aunt Meg and Shelly,' said Lucy. 'But you have to guess what it is now!' She bobbed up and down on her toes.

C.C. looked at the box, hefting it. 'Let's see . . . It could be a big, fat book, but it's too light. And I guess we can rule out a basketball, huh?' She grinned at Lucy, who grinned back, almost filling C.C. up. She held the box near her ear, shook it gently. There was a soft rattle. 'Umm, is it a goldfish?' She sucked in her cheeks and crossed her eyes, giving Lucy her fish face. Lucy dissolved in giggles.

'Nooo, Meemaw! Guess again!'

'Knock, knock,' said a voice, as the door pushed open.

'Auntie Meg! Shelly!' Shelly had long ago told Lucy to just call her Shelly, but Meg liked being an unofficial auntie, as long as there was never a 'great' or 'grand' in front.

Both women bent, Meg setting a heavy-looking tote bag on the floor. Shelly gave Lucy a quick but sturdy hug. Meg, however, kneeled, wrapped her arms around Lucy. Her eyes closed as she held her, as if feeding on the life force all little girls have to spare. A small smile appeared on Meg's thin, pale face as Lucy grunted happily, her little arms squeezing Meg back. C.C. didn't know whether to smile or cry. What that little girl lacks in males in her life, she makes up for in maternal love, she thought.

'Scooch back, please, you two, so I can close the door,' said Shelly. When Meg and Lucy had moved, she pushed the door closed with a thud. 'Don't want to let the cold air in.'

C.C. smiled at Kathryn, gesturing with her hands to say, 'See? I'm not the only one.' Kathryn quickly moved to embrace Shelly, then Meg.

14

'Look!' said C.C., holding up her gift, trying another tack. She winked at Meg and Shelly. 'Lucy gave me a goldfish!'

Lucy fell to the floor, laughing. Kathryn exhaled in a way that only her mother would hear.

'Oh, a goldfish is just the ticket!' said Shelly. 'He'll come in handy on our road trip. He can point the way.' Shelly shrugged off her coat, threw it over the banister. She wiggled her hand like a fish in front of Lucy, alternately swimming and pointing. Then she gave her a little poke in the belly, eliciting more giggles.

They all made their way into the kitchen, with C.C. bringing up the rear, her gift in her hands, but a heaviness in her heart, too aware for days now of 'the last time' they'd be doing one thing or another. *The last time we'll all walk into the kitchen together. Their last meal in this house.* It made it feel like she was never coming back to Wisataukee, which she was. She just didn't know when. But not to this house. She'd likely buy a condo or something. A condo for one. She saw herself with a cat, tending too many plants, eating baked beans out of the can, standing over the sink. She didn't even like cats much. A little sigh escaped as she joined the others in the kitchen. How often had the five of them gathered like this, for an impromptu meal, or a trip to the museum, or shopping? All happy events. But like the cold wind circling outside, a chill pulled at the edges of the group tonight.

Meg set the bag on the counter, began to

unpack. 'Shelly's contributing caviar, believe it or not. How old is this, Shel?' Meg stared at the small round container, intently studying the lettering of the black and red label, an uncertain look on her face. 'Is this *Russian?*'

'Yes. It was a gift from Sergei.'

'Who?' asked C.C.

'Ah, yes,' said Meg knowingly. She turned to C.C. 'You know, tall, dark and handsome, in a pointy kind of way? The one before the one before . . . the last one.' She bobbed the caviar through the air as she counted.

Shelly shoved Meg's hand playfully out of the air, grabbing the caviar from her. 'I don't know, maybe six months,' she said, studying it. 'A year?' She lifted the top and sniffed, made a face. 'How do you tell when smelly fish eggs have gone bad?' She pushed an errant, graying bang back behind her ear. C.C. knew Shelly had stopped coloring her hair for budgetary reasons, and had told them she wanted to try long hair again. The poor thing had gone from being the most well-off of the three of them, to avoiding creditors, all by way of one disastrous, overreaching business deal.

'Have you ever had caviar, Lucy? Little fish eggs?' Kathryn asked. Lucy had her back against her mother's legs and Kathryn held her with criss-crossed arms over Lucy's chest. Lucy made a face, shaking her head and sticking out her tongue. Kathryn laughed. 'I think we'll pass on the caviar, thanks. What else you got in there?'

16

'Bagels . . . cream cheese . . . Cheddar cheese . . .' Meg lifted containers and bags out, one by one, but stopped on a large round one. 'Some, um . . .' She held it to the light, tipping it this way and that, the bright red, lumpy contents slopping back and forth inside, '. . . Jell-O. With fruit, one would hope.' She set it on the counter and dug back into the bag. 'Pickles, an apple . . .' She paused for a fraction of a second, her hand still in the bag. 'Some fried chicken . . .' She set the container on the counter, as if it were a small wounded creature she'd been caring for. She stared at it for a few seconds, then dug back in the bag. '. . . A box of crackers . . . and . . . some leftover wild rice.' Meg set the last items on the counter. Shelly rearranged everything.

'My stuff's right here,' said C.C., pulling several containers out of the refrigerator. 'Some leftover tuna casserole, some cheese, bread, watermelon pickles and tapioca pudding.'

'Let's eat!' said Shelly, grabbing the stack of paper plates and handing one to Lucy.

'Can Meemaw open the present first? Please?' Lucy handed her plate back to Shelly.

'Oh, yes!' said C.C., lifting the box from the counter again. 'I want to open my present!' She undid the ribbon, handing it to Lucy, then tore off the paper, revealing a creamy yellow box with bright illustrations on the top. 'Butterflies! What could this be?' She set the box on the counter and lifted the lid. Inside, was a thick stack of pale yellow stationery bound up in a bright yellow silk ribbon. C.C. fingered

17

the soft, ragged upper edge of the sheets as she tried to swallow the lump in her throat.

'Look under!' shouted Lucy.

C.C. did, finding two neat stacks of matching envelopes, also tied with yellow ribbons. In the middle were two long strips of colorful butterfly stickers.

'Look at this envelope!' said Lucy, pulling one from the stack. She held it in front of C.C., her small hands gripping either edge. 'See? We already addressed it!'

C.C. read Lucy's uneven scrawl aloud. 'Lucy Prentiss. Thirty-one twenty Clemmons Way, Wisataukee, Iowa.'

'And read the other, up here!' said Lucy, pointing excitedly to the upper corner.

'Meemaw Byrd, seven thirteen Raven Road, Fleurville, Tennessee.'

Damn. C.C. could feel her eyes welling up. Something about seeing that address printed on an envelope, especially in Lucy's labor-intensive hand, took her aback. That address was both more than and less than home; it was the place she had landed, the place that had caught her, after a long, hard fall. She felt like her body was being stretched forward and back in time, all at once.

'You have to send the first one to me!' said Lucy, putting her finger on her chest. 'And we got another box for me! Mine has dolphin stickers and it's blue and I already wrote to you!'

C.C. kneeled, quickly gathering Lucy up in

a hug, hiding her tears behind her granddaughter's head. 'Oh, my darlin' girl.' C.C. swallowed again, hearing her southern accent creep into her words. Emotion always brought it out of her. 'I *will* write to you. And I can hardly wait till I get my first letter from you!' She had to struggle to get her words out. 'I am going t'miss you, Lovee.'

'Will you fill me up with brave, Meemaw?' asked Lucy softly.

'Well, of course I will!' Shelly gave her a hand, helped her stand, as Meg retrieved a small empty ceramic pitcher from the sill above her sink. She handed it to C.C., who held it above Lucy's head, and began to pour. 'Show me where your fill-line is, Lovee.' Lucy held her hand near her stomach, then let it rise. C.C. poured till Lucy's hand was at the top of her head. 'Full of brave?' C.C. asked her. Lucy nodded, and they hugged again.

Still clutching Lucy, C.C. looked up at Kathryn, then at her two best friends, all of whom were teary. But Kathryn turned away from her. C.C. could hear her daughter's sharp intake of breath, but she didn't know how to read it. Kathryn held her hand out to Shelly for a plate.

Only her granddaughter enjoyed the picnic dinner on an old sheet on the floor of the empty living room. For C.C., and she suspected for the others as well, all the leftovers of their lives made for an odd and bittersweet meal.

CHAPTER 2

MEG

'I spy with my little eye, something blue.'

'*Blue*?' said Shelly. 'It can't be inside the car, Ceece!'

'It's not! Look! On the bottom of that silo.'

'Well, don't show me, for God's sakes! Now you have to pick something else!'

Meg smiled at them, Shelly riding shotgun, C.C. in the back, where she would be the entire trip because she didn't drive a stick. Meg wasn't playing the I Spy game; she was too worried about her car. The windshield wipers had done it again, a sort of hiccup. As she watched, they stalled mid-swipe and finally slid down and lay there, as if exhausted. Meg stared at them; she could relate.

At least it had nearly stopped raining. She glanced over at Shelly, then caught C.C. staring at her in the rear-view mirror. Both of them had that flicker of alarm in their eyes, their lively chatting abruptly stopped. It was clear to all of them now, the car was unwell. But it kept on going. Good ole Rosie, Meg thought. But she wondered again if the full load – all their suitcases, the cooler and the three of them – wasn't too much for her ancient Honda.

'I think your old car is having mid-life issues too, Meg.' Shelly was fanning herself with the map again. She laughed, and C.C. chortled in the back.

Meg turned the radio off, then the headlights. She flipped the wiper switch off, then on, and the blades reluctantly picked up. But then the car surged and sputtered, and the wipers flopped spasmodically again.

As long as the car is moving, I'll be damned if I'm going to pull over here, in Middle-of-Nowhere, Illinois. Meg stared up at the gray sky, not to God, because she'd long ago dismissed that notion, but rather in the same way Eeyore would look at his personal rain cloud, not questioning, but with a somber acceptance. *Hello there, Rain cloud. I knew you'd stay with me.*

'Those wipers look about as useful as goose doo on a pump handle,' said C.C., matter-of-factly.

Meg smiled, finally. She was always grateful for C.C.'s take on things, and now it seemed their every mile southward was bringing out a little more of her latent accent and homespun sayings.

Meg looked at the trip odometer: 212. *And they had nearly four hundred miles to go!*

She tried the wipers again. 'C'mon, you worthless things!' They sprang to life, as if to mock her.

'Yay!' said C.C., and she and Shelly resumed their conversation.

Meg straightened in her seat again, able to see

now through the cleared arcs. They rolled past another mile marker and Meg flinched when she saw it: 32. Her upcoming wedding anniversary. She said nothing, fearing that C.C. would interpret it as a bad omen.

Was it her imagination or were the wipers slowing again? Her fingers tightened on the steering wheel. They were. They stuttered, then refused to rise. Again. She glared at the blades, black and crisp-looking – she'd bought new ones just for this trip – but utterly useless on their metal arms. Involuntarily, she glanced down at her new pants, loden-green corduroys, also purchased just for this trip; she'd been shocked to find that she had to buy a size six. She'd been a fit ten her whole married life, except for when she was pregnant. A deep and audible sigh of empathy with the wipers slipped out as she decided she really couldn't see. She carefully steered the car toward the side of the road.

Suddenly the wipers picked up again and the engine hummed to life. 'Make up your friggin' mind!' Meg growled. She steered the car back onto the paved but unlined country road.

'What the hell's wrong with the wipers?' asked Shelly.

'Yeah, what's wrong?' C.C. asked.

Meg felt a surge of irritation that she was expected to know what was wrong, just because it was her car. She was a high-school English teacher; her mechanical aptitude wouldn't fill a thimble. She tried the wiper switch again as rustling sounds came from the back seat.

'Here, hon.' C.C.'s chubby pale hand appeared between the seats, holding four squares of a Hershey bar. 'Have some chocolate.' C.C.'s panacea.

'No, thanks. I'm okay,' said Meg, though she realized her posture, hunched over the steering wheel, hands clenched and bloodless on the wheel, belied her claim. C.C.'s hand silently retracted, followed by soft sounds of smacking from the back seat.

Meg touched the accelerator with her toe again. The speedometer registered a lethargic twenty-seven miles per hour. She pressed again and there was a small roar, so she tried the wipers; they started up again, at a galloping beat. But they seemed . . . untrustworthy. But both Shelly and C.C. gave dramatic sighs of relief and resumed chatting.

Did they not notice that they were crawling along? Could they not hear the engine? Meg continued to breathe as if through a cocktail straw. The car was fine, she told herself; it was *her*. Hadn't nearly everything become *untrustworthy* since—

Even the bucolic rural Illinois farmland had become foreboding. The country scene, the broad sky, the rich, chocolatey soil of the newly plowed fields, the red barns with their big white Xs on the doors, they had all always been a salve to her, harking back to another era. She had such nostalgia for a slower pace and a gentler time that

Meg thought reincarnation seemed a more distinct possibility than heaven or hell. But at the moment, the somber gray sky and the sodden fields felt not calming, but remote and desolate.

They were down to ten miles per hour. Should she pull over again? A sudden stillness announced that there was no question for her to ponder anymore. The wipers slid one final arc. The quiet settled into the car like a morose fourth passenger. On momentum alone, Meg steered the car to the edge of the road.

No one spoke, but she knew the other two were looking at her. She exhaled finally; she hadn't even realized she'd been holding her breath. She took one hand off the steering wheel, turned the key in the ignition to off, then turned it back. Nothing. She tried it again, with the same result.

She leaned back hard in her seat. 'Shit. I'm sorry, you guys.' She massaged the red marks on her otherwise white palms. 'It was my stupid literary fantasy, to take the scenic small roads, emulate John Steinbeck. Now we're stuck in the middle of nowhere,' she said morosely, staring out her window. There was not a house, barn or even another car in sight. Just acres and acres of wet farmland.

Meg closed her eyes, too tired to remember C.C.'s cardinal rule never to tempt the fates when things were going wrong. As she rubbed her hands she thought: This can't get any worse. They were stuck in the middle of their lives, in middle

America, in the middle of life crises, and now, in the middle of nowhere. 'So much for our Great Escape,' she said with a small, unconvincing laugh.

How many decades had they fantasized about 'the Great Escape'? To just up and leave their kids, husbands, jobs, *lives* for a week or two, head for the horizon, free of the myriad burdens of being something to someone, other than friend. They'd long ago agreed that their friendship was what held them together, reminded them of who they were as women, whole identities unto themselves, not defined by their roles of work, mothering or marriage. Even when the demands of young children and escalating careers had meant their conversations were carried out more on the phone than in person, especially with Shelly's stint in New York, their friendship had kept them all afloat in hard times, held firm the sails in high winds.

Meg silently recounted all the reasons the trip had never happened till now: someone's kid got sick, or was in the playoffs, or was graduating. Or someone got a promotion, or four new clients, or school was ending late because of snow days. Or someone's husband had the flu, or suddenly had to go out of town that week, or was turning forty, or fifty, or was just too busy, depressed or tired to be left alone with the household responsibilities. Once, it was Meg's dog. He'd cut his leg on some garden edging and the vet bill had wiped out her entire vacation budget. Meg had always thought all the reasons were valid. Disappointing, but valid. But now, at this gray moment, on this gray day, they seemed like so many excuses strung together. Even Buster.

Oh my God! She turned, wide-eyed, looked back at C.C., then over at Shelly. 'How ironic is this? You know all those reasons that kept coming up that we never did the Great Escape? It just occurred to me that the only reason we're on this trip now is because . . .' she had to take a breath, '. . . all those reasons left us first.'

She looked at her friends again and they looked at her.

'Fuck.' Shelly leaned back against her door. 'That's true. First Len dies, then I lose most of my life savings in that damn mall development deal, having the added side benefit of making every man run to the other side of the street when they see me.' She turned to Meg, her expression still incredulous. 'Then your old dog dies and Grant takes off. You'd think The Trio had a curse thrown down on us.'

C.C. made three neat spitting sounds in the back seat. 'Don't even say that!'

'Relax,' said Meg. 'It's merely the curse of middle age.'

No one spoke for a minute, then C.C.'s voice floated up from the back seat, quiet, tentative. 'So, I guess we're broken down, huh?'

'Of course we are,' said Shelly. 'And the *car* is broken down too.' Shelly cracked up, but no one else did.

26

'This isn't a good sign,' said C.C. softly, ominously.

And, there it is! Not with the signs again. Meg thought the words just a half-beat before Shelly barked them out.

'Not with the signs again, C.C.!'

Meg felt that surge of anger again: at C.C. for perpetually seeing everything, good or bad, as a sign, and at Shelly for castigating C.C. for it. It occurred to Meg that their friendship had stood the test of time, but never had they put it to the test of the Road Trip. Not to mention: Remodeling a House. Which necessarily also meant: Going into Business Together. And, most dangerous of all, Living Together.

Meg's breathing grew tight and rapid, her heart pounding. The nausea, the headache. The weather. *Migraine.* As if the universe was saying: This is *but one* way things can get worse. She forced herself to inhale deeply. Don't say it, she told herself, at the insistent thought in her head. But the words came out anyway. 'She's right. I think this whole trip may have been a mistake.'

'Now, c'mon,' said Shelly, lightly punching Meg in the arm. 'We are three competent women. This is nothing.' She made a 'pbllth' sound. 'A mere blip on the radar. We've been through way more than a measly old car breakdown together.'

That was true. Birth, marriage, divorce, death, financial problems.

Abandonment.

27

Shit happens. And it seemed especially to happen when you turned fifty, thought Meg. Your kids leave. And then the dog dies. She'd had other friends who'd lost their old dogs or cats just before or after their last kid went off to college. No coincidence. They'd all waited till their youngest kid was five or six before they relented to the incessant begging and got a puppy or kitten. So all those animals simply came to the end of their natural lives at the exact time when many of the moms were feeling like a significant part of their own lives was ending. But Meg had been *looking forward* to the empty nest, that's why she'd taken early retirement. She would not have if she'd known her husband, too, was going to leave her.

She reached down with her left hand, found the lever and reclined her seat; she couldn't go far because the cooler and jackets and pillows were on the back seat behind her. She covered her eyes with her hands, massaging her forehead and temples with her fingertips. Her lower back ached, and her underwear was threatening to bisect her. But she didn't have the energy to rearrange anything.

She longed for the safety and comfort of her living room, to be stretched out on her blue velvet couch, facing the big picture window that overlooked the slope of the hill. In her imagination, Buster was taking up half the couch, but keeping her feet warm. Dear old Buster. Her last act before leaving home had been to sprinkle that dear, dumb dog's ashes on the hillside behind their house, saying prayers for him, and for herself, to no one at all.

Home. The purple and white crocuses would soon be dotting that hillside, not quite the cheerleaders of spring that tulips or even daffodils are, but maybe the junior varsity squad, smaller, less popular, but still cute and perky. Every year, just when she needed it most, they had cheered her into believing that spring would once again be victorious over the long, northern Iowa winter. But maybe not this year. Her life had been so turned upside down that now even the spinning of the earth on its axis seemed to be in question.

She was vaguely aware of C.C. and Shelly quietly talking, the kind of softly urgent exchanges between upright people around a prone person, in a coma maybe, or discovered inert on the sidewalk. But Meg drifted away, backing out of reality, which she did so often lately.

But reality, as it always does, followed. The familiar image of her husband, not her, ensconced on the couch with Buster sent a dull ache through her. Then a thought made her heart skip and race in a way that was both invigorating and life-threatening, all at once. Maybe Grant was there now! She put a hand to her chest, unconsciously spreading her fingers wide, like a net over her sternum. Maybe he had come back, was even now reading one of the letters she'd written and left for him, just in case, on the kitchen table.

A weak groan escaped from deep within her. She knew all too well that her house was empty – empty of children, empty of Buster, empty of Grant, and most of all empty of herself, because even when she'd been living there, alone, the past few weeks, she'd felt barely a shell of herself. And maybe even before Grant had left. In her heart of hearts, she'd known that their marriage had been leaking air for years, invisibly, like a balloon forgotten in the corner of the living room long after the party is over. Wizened, sinking almost imperceptibly, but undeniably, weighted down now by the very ribbon that was supposed to keep it from floating away.

'Meg-legs?' C.C. enquired again. Meg held up a finger, asking for another minute before anything was required of her. 'Okay, honey, take your time. We're warm and toasty in here. And we've got food.'

Good ol' C.C. She would sit quietly in the back for days, munching her chocolate bars, supporting Meg in her fragility. In fact, it wasn't her own but C.C.'s situation that had finally made this trip happen, first with Lenny's death, then Aunt Georgie's and the inheritance of Dogs' Wood, the house in Tennessee.

So much change. Wasn't life supposed to be *less* full of change, not more, with age? She wasn't sure where she'd gotten that idea, but it was dead wrong.

A noisy clatter startled her. She abruptly sat up,

bringing her seatback forward with the flip of the lever. The rain had suddenly intensified, the fat drops making a chaotic drumbeat on the car.

'Oh, yay. *That's* what we needed. A percussive soundtrack to our . . . situation,' said Shelly, looking out her window, her enthusiasm of a moment ago gone.

Meg looked at her friends; they were both gazing skyward, hunched down into themselves as if they expected the roof to fall in. Meg grasped the key again, her mouth set. She felt both women's rapt attention on her. C.C. began muttering a prayer.

'C'mon, baby. You can do it,' Meg said loudly, over the rain and over the prayer, deciding that talking directly to the car would be more productive than to a God she no longer believed in. 'You can *do* it.'

It pulled at her throat to hear her words, exactly the way she'd urged on her kids, especially for all their firsts: letting go of her fingers and taking those first robotic steps on stubby legs across the living room; or when they were learning to dive off the edge of the pool, their little toes curled tightly around the cement edge, bony knees knocking from chill and fear, arms plastered against ears, fingers tight, hands laid perfectly, one over the other, a prayer pose if ever there was one, with Meg treading water, waiting, saying, 'You can do it! I know you can!'; or as they wobbled off on their little bikes with the small, fat tires but, for the first time, no training wheels, defying both

31

gravity and Meg's own death-grip on their bicycle seat till she had to let go; or when they first merged into rush-hour traffic on the freeway with their still-crisp learner's permit tucked proudly into their purse or wallet, both child and mother's knuckles white; or when they were sitting on their overstuffed college suitcase, finally succeeding in zippering it closed, and then the child who had been so irritable and distant all summer, nearly bursting with the need to leave home, suddenly burst into tears at the prospect. 'C'mon, you can do it,' she'd said each and every time, until they had.

'C'mon, you can do it,' she said again, louder, to her car and to herself. But when she turned the key, the solitary and forlorn click of the ignition could barely be heard above the rain. She looked right, saw Shelly studying her, overly sympathetically.

'Damn cars,' she told Meg. 'They're like men. You can't live with 'em, and you can't live without 'em.'

Meg nodded, although it was Shelly's mantra, not hers. Meg had never wanted to be alone. Never.

She sighed, reached forward, patted the dashboard. 'What's wrong, little Rosie?'

She felt a gaze pierce the side of her head. Shelly again. This time, mouth and eyes wide open. 'You *named* your car?' she asked. 'I did not know this about you. How could I not know this? Did you name your lawn mower too?' Shelly snickered. C.C. chuckled in the back seat. Meg tried to look indignant, but she couldn't completely stifle a smile.

'And your cheese grater?' asked Shelly. There was just a fraction of a moment of silence, then the car seemed to explode with laughter. Their fatigue and predicament was taking its toll, all of them laughing so hard they could barely breathe, tears streaming down their cheeks, the kind of uncontrollable laughter that was pure, emotional release.

'And your . . . *carrot peeler*?' Shelly wheezed.

'Oh, wait! I know, I know!' said Meg, breathlessly. 'Together, they could be Larry, Moe and Curly!' She fell onto the steering wheel in silent, shaking laughter.

Shelly shrieked, then caught her breath enough to squeeze out, 'Perhaps we should change from The Trio, to the Three Stooges!' More uncontrollable laughter. 'Oh! I've got it!' Shelly was almost screaming now. 'The lawn mower is . . . *Moe!*'

C.C.'s distinct laugh, an almost maniacal giggle when she really got going, made Meg laugh even harder. They were all beside themselves, hardly able to breathe.

Shelly was wheezing, talking in gasps. 'And the . . . carrot . . . peeler is . . . *Curly,*' more shrieks of laughter, 'and the . . . the . . .'

Meg and C.C., still laughing but more controlled, waited for Shelly.

But Shelly had stopped laughing. She looked truly frightened. '*Oh shit!*' she said, pressing her palms to her cheeks. Meg glanced back at C.C., who looked worriedly at Shelly, then at Meg.

'Shell?' asked Meg, placing her hand on Shelly's knee. Meg's mind raced with what the problem could be – a suddenly remembered stove left on at home? Sudden pain?

'*I forgot the third thing!*' said Shelly.

There was just the briefest pause, then all three screamed with laughter again.

'I don't remember it either!' C.C. squealed.

'Oh my God,' Meg said flatly, catching her breath, looking side to side, blinking. 'I can't remember it either! This is so pathetic.' She burst out laughing along with the other two and inadvertently snorted, making them all dissolve again.

'Stop! *Stop!* Or you'll make me pee!' C.C. gasped from the back seat.

They slowly regained control. C.C.'s worry, a frequent one of late, quickly brought some sobriety into the car.

'Oh my,' said Meg, inhaling deeply. She pulled a tissue from the center console and dabbed at her eyes, sighing. 'Golly. Just look at us here, all broken down and stranded, not doing a darned thing about it.'

'Well, why the hell are we just sitting here, girls?' said Shelly, digging through her purse. She pulled out a pack of tissues, which she handed back to C.C., then her bright red reading glasses, then her gem-studded cellphone. 'You're a member of Triple A, right, Meg?' she asked.

Meg shook her head, pointed to a small sticker on the corner of the windshield. 'No, but we've got –' she sucked in a breath – '*I've* got towing coverage. With our insurance.' She held out her hand. 'May I use your phone?' Shelly handed it to her.

'Ceece?' Shelly said, twisting in her seat. 'You'd better get an urgent delivery prayer up that we can get a signal out here.'

Meg turned and watched as C.C. closed her eyes, crossed herself quickly, then put her forehead against her clasped hands. Meg turned back around. She looked at the sticker, blinked, pressed her head back into the headrest, then looked at Shelly again. 'I can't read the numbers. Hand the specs over too, please.' She punched in the number, and when it rang, Meg gave the other two a thumbs-up.

'Yay, Jesus!' shouted Shelly, the recalcitrant but loyal Jew, pumping her fist. Meg could hear C.C. clapping, saying, 'Thank you, Jesus.' Meg waved her hand for them to quiet.

'Hello? Hello? Can you hear me? Yes? Great. Hi. This is Meg Bartholomew. We, uh, need a little help, I guess.'

Shelly leaned over, nearly in Meg's lap, and yelled toward the phone, 'We need a *lot* of help!' Meg swatted her off, grinning.

Meg listened, then said, 'Well, actually, I *did*

35

happen to notice the last mile marker we passed. Number thirty-two.' Whether C.C. hadn't heard, or didn't remember the significance of the number, or simply decided to keep quiet, Meg didn't know. But she was grateful.

When she had relayed the rest of the information, Meg closed the phone and handed it back to Shelly. 'Well, I guess there's nothing left to do but wait for someone to rescue us.'

The rain, which had been slowly letting up, had now finally stopped altogether, as if it too were worn out. Meg looked up, hopeful for a rainbow that she could point out to C.C. But there was no rainbow, no fingers of sunlight breaking through, not even a parting in the clouds.

No one spoke. Meg looked out at the soggy patchwork of farmland, most of it fallow still, even late March being too early and – untrustworthy – for planting. She stared at the barbed-wire fence, watched the drops clinging to the bottom of the wires, like tiny, upside-down birds, until they grew fat and heavy, and gravity made them plunge to the ground. She rested her head on the cool glass and wondered where Grant was. She closed her eyes, picturing him in his ubiquitous Yankees cap, driving his orange BMW. But where? She willed him to write to her, tried even to make herself picture a letter already waiting for her in Tennessee. He had the address; she'd dictated it to him that day he was sitting at the kitchen table making some sort of list and— She had a sudden pang. What had he been writing that day? He'd been sitting at the kitchen table, writing a list on a legal pad, and listening to that awful sports radio where the men seemed to yell all the time. She'd hesitated briefly, then she'd asked to speak to him. 'What's up?' he said, neither looking up nor turning down the radio. The conversation that had followed, like all their conversations, was stilted, awkward. But somehow Meg had worked in how much she'd loved his letters to her in college, and that maybe they could write to each other while she was away. She thought, but didn't say, that if they could write to each other, maybe they could find a way to talk to each other. 'I really don't need the address,' he'd said. 'I'll call you if I need you.' 'Well, the phone may not work when we get there. C.C. thinks it's been turned off. Just write it down. Please?' Meg remembered the tired anger of having to cajole. 'It can't hurt to have it. If only for emergencies.' Only then had he torn a small corner off the bottom of the page, hastily scrawled the address on it as she dictated. But she could tell he was, from habit, more attuned to what was being said on the radio than by her.

Sitting in the car now, Meg realized she should have looked at whatever it was he was writing. Probably his own list of things to take. He had known. Even then. Maybe he'd been planning to leave her for months. Years.

She gazed out at the expanse of emptiness again. She looked at the barbed-wire fence across the

37

road, looking sharp and certain of its responsibilities. On one post was a small, metal 'No
Trespassing' sign, a bullet hole just above the circle
of the o. She wondered if the shooter had been
aiming for the o, or had just taken a pot shot.

Sitting there, just past mile marker 32, Meg stared
at the sign through the wet glass, and wondered if,
in the end, aiming made any difference.

CHAPTER 3

C.C.

The small restaurant was dimly lit, but warm and cozy. Just what they all needed, C.C. decided. But she was worried when Meg and Shelly headed toward one of the three small booths along the wall. She didn't think she'd fit. But, happily, the benches slid out. C.C. decided two things on the spot; one, that, like Meg was always telling her, she was not as fat as she thought she was; and two, that she liked this little place.

Two hours after the tow truck had rescued them, they were sitting in Purdy's Restaurant and Bar in the tiny burg of Tupper, Illinois. Showers in their motel room (number three, like the three of them – a good omen!) had taken the worst of the chill out of them. Now, as dusk fell outside, they were warming their insides with what Shelly called Sleeping Irish – Irish coffees made with decaf. C.C. was so tired that she hadn't realized till two sips into her very strong drink that they were staying at Purdy's Motel, and just down the road was Purdy's Grocery. Purdy himself had checked them in to their room. There were only four rooms;

one of these Purdy had indicated he lived in ('should you need anything, night or day'). Then he had insisted on carrying all their luggage from Mick's Garage and Auto Sales, across and down the dirt Main Street to their room. By the time all of their luggage, mostly C.C.'s, had been delivered, the portly Purdy was red-faced and puffing, but strangely beaming. C.C. had tried to offer him a tip, but he had refused, just stood there, looking every which way but at her. Finally, he'd said that maybe they'd like to freshen up and then come over to his restaurant for dinner. Slightly embarrassed at the looks the other two gave her, C.C. had replied yes, they would probably do that. She refrained from pointing out that there didn't seem to be anywhere else in Tupper that they could get dinner.

Purdy now appeared at their booth, bearing a small cast-iron pan of hot cornbread, and three small plates. 'The bread's on the house, ladies. Sorry your trip down south got detoured, but we're very glad to have you here.' That's odd, thought C.C., as Purdy set everything on the table. They hadn't mentioned anything about their destination when they'd checked in. Evidently Mick had told him. Mick and Purdy probably constituted the entire business district of Tupper.

'S'cuse me, uh, ma'am . . .' Purdy reached across the table and picked up a squeeze bottle of honey from between the napkin holder and a small glass pitcher of syrup. C.C. felt her cheeks redden, though she wasn't sure why. He held the bottle up so they could all see the label:

Minding Our Bees' Nests
Fresh Illinois Honey

'I can personally recommend this honey for my cornbread,' he said. 'We – uh, I, tend the hives myself.' He looks like a TV pitchman, thought C.C., quickly hiding her smile. Not quickly enough, she realized when Purdy darted a quick smile back at her, then looked away.

Not that kind of smile. Was it? No, of course not. She looked at her hands, wrapped around the ceramic mug. The warmth on her palms matched the warmth in her cheeks. Oh, she was just being silly, was all.

'This's real good on the cornbread,' said Purdy. C.C. glanced up, relieved to see he was looking at Meg. His ruddy cheeks formed small balls under his blue eyes, a disarming dimple in his left cheek. He turned toward her again. Dimples in both cheeks, she saw. He held the honey before her like a maître d' holding a bottle of wine for inspection. 'See, it's got a touch of cinnamon in it,' he said, tapping his finger on the label. 'But you got your syrup too,' he added, pointing it out on the table, next to the napkin holder. 'If you prefer that route. My wife, may she rest in peace, was partial to syrup. But I myself like the honey. Ma'am?' He offered C.C. the honey, his eyebrows held aloft expectantly, wiry white caterpillars stopped mid-march.

C.C. looked down again, gingerly touched her hair. She then looked at the honey, keeping her eyes focused on the little bees on the label. 'Well, being from the south originally, I do like syrup on cornbread. But I'll give the honey a try. The cinnamon sounds good.' She couldn't help a quick glance across the table. Meg was doing that cheek-chewing thing she did when she was trying not to smile. Shelly was not so restrained; she had a smirk a mile wide and was staring right at her. C.C. was deathly afraid Shelly would make some wisecrack. But, bless her heart, she kept mum.

Oh, you're acting crazier than a sprayed roach! It was all C.C. could do not to slap herself. Mum about what? Really. C.C. took the bottom of the honey bottle in her hand, looking at the cute illustrations of happy bees on the label. But Purdy still held the top of the bottle, his eyes locked on hers.

'Thank you,' said C.C., pulling slightly on the bottle. Purdy didn't let go. 'Um . . .'

He must have thought she didn't remember his name, because he stuck out his free hand, still holding the bottle in the other. C.C. gave him her free hand, not releasing the bottle either, since he hadn't. It was an awkward shake, her hand too warm from being wrapped around her coffee mug, his cool and a little clammy.

'I'm Purdy. Everyone calls me Purdy,' he said, still holding her hand.

'C.C.,' said C.C., wondering what in the hell was going on. They sat there, neither letting go of the honey, and Purdy not letting go of her hand. The bell on the front door rang and two men, laughing loudly, stepped in. Purdy startled visibly, and gasped. He let go of her hand, but appeared not to realize he still held the honey.

''S'okay, Purdy. Just us,' said a tall, thin man dressed in overalls, a younger man with him, who had to be his son, dressed alike, hair combed with grease alike. They quieted immediately and looked contrite. Purdy gave the men a slight wave. C.C. saw that Meg and Shelly were also looking back and forth between the men and Purdy. Those men acted as if they'd walked too noisily into a library, rather than a restaurant.

She looked at Purdy. He was pale. He slowly turned his attention back to the table, his face quickly pinking. But he still hadn't let go of the bottle of honey. In fact, if anything, he had a tighter hold on it. And now C.C. too had been holding on for so long that she wasn't sure how to let go. Plus, she wanted it. On her cornbread. She was feeling rather possessive of it.

Not knowing what else to do, too embarrassed to look at either of her friends or this odd, jumpy man standing there at the other end of her honey bottle, she studied each letter of 'Minding Our Bees' Nests'. She smiled, realizing for the first time the pun in the name. 'That's a cute name,' she said, still mulling over her options – letting go of the honey bottle that had been, after all, offered to her. Or pull again, harder. But she immediately felt the blush rising in her cheeks as she realized with a cringe that the last thing spoken before she'd made her comment, was Purdy telling them his name. *Oh, Jesus, Mary and Joseph!* She'd just sounded like she'd said *Purdy* was a cute name! She saw Meg and Shelly stifling laughs.

'I, I mean the honey. "Minding Our Bees' Nests",' she added hastily, adding too many Ss at the end. She had a bit of a lisp, which seemed to be getting worse in the past couple of years (she'd even wondered if her tongue had gained weight). But it *was* a hard combination to say. Suddenly the bottle was in her hand.

'I hope you enjoy it, uh . . . uh, ma'am,' Purdy said kindly.

'Yum,' said C.C., setting the honey down close to her. Was he asking for her name again? It would be so embarrassing if she gave it to him, and it wasn't what he was stuttering about. She felt like she was thirteen! But Purdy nodded and, if she wasn't mistaken, gave a slight wink. Not in a flirty way, C.C. was sure. Just excited about his honey. She was glad she hadn't blurted out her name.

He gestured toward the pan, still steaming on the table. 'Lemme know what you think. That's my own cornbread recipe. Secret ingredient.'

C.C. feigned adjusting the band of her watch.

'Just wave if you need anything,' said Purdy.

C.C. nodded without looking up, not until she

44

heard the other two say thank you and Purdy's footsteps heading off.

'*Well!*' exclaimed Shelly. 'My, my. My, my, my, my, *my*!' She lifted her mug toward C.C. 'Ya still got it, babe!' Meg giggled and lifted her mug too, clinking against Shelly's. C.C. felt herself turning about four shades of red as the two intertwined arms and gave each other doe eyes, then sipped their drinks.

'Oh, now, stop that. *What!*' They were just being silly. What man would choose to flirt with *her* over the other two? Of *course* he wasn't flirting. He was just . . . odd, frankly. And he just really believed in his honey. And cornbread. She shook her head dismissively and sipped her drink. 'Wow! These puppies are strong,' she said, desperate to change the subject. Shelly and Meg both set their mugs on the table, doe eyes gone, puzzlement in their place.

'Mine sure isn't. Is yours?' Shelly asked Meg.

Meg shook her head. 'No. In fact, I was just going to say that I'm not sure there's any kick in there at all. It's good coffee and all, but—'

C.C. shoved her mug across the table. 'Here. Taste this.'

Meg took a sip, recoiled. 'Holy cow!' She handed it to Shelly.

Shelly sipped, then slapped the table. '*Hee-heeee!* Either he's trying to get you drunk on your first date or he's so distracted by your beauty that he poured all three shots of booze into your mug!'

45

'Oh, *please*. You're nuts, Shelly,' said C.C., batting the air between them dismissively, and trying hard not to look as embarrassed as she felt.

'No, I think she's right,' whispered Meg, leaning in, smiling. 'The man is obviously smitten.'

'And you're the kitten with whom he's smitten!' said Shelly, too loudly.

'Shhhh!' hissed both Meg and C.C. Shelly slapped her hand over her mouth, but snickered underneath it. Removing her hand, she turned to Meg, whispering now, but with just as much animation. 'Hey! I guess we each get our own bed tonight if Purdy makes his move on C.C.'

C.C. kicked her under the table, feeling Meg's foot doing the same.

'Ow! OWW!' yelped Shelly.

'I'm not *you*, Shelly,' said C.C. 'I don't sleep with every Tom, Dick and Harry. Now, give me your mugs.' She poured the three drinks back and forth from mug to mug, till they were mixed, giving the lion's share to Meg and Shelly. She figured she was several sips ahead of them. She pushed their mugs across the table. 'Besides, I'm sure it was just an accident. The booze, I mean.'

'Of course it was,' said Shelly. 'An accident caused by your bewitching beauty.' Grinning, Shelly served them each a thick slice of the cornbread.

C.C. couldn't help the small smile that slipped across her own lips. Could it be? *Really?* She hadn't had a man flirt with her in a long time, maybe even since . . . When? High school? Lenny had certainly not been the flirty type. She wondered if he had *ever* flirted with her. Surely he must have when they'd met. But for three years he was just the guy at Byrd and Franholz, doing her taxes. Unless asking if she had a receipt for the high-school band wreath she'd bought was flirting. Come to think of it, his laborious explanation had grown longer and more cumbersome each year: that she 'could only deduct the amount over the cost of an average Christmas wreath because the wreath itself was considered a benefit of having bought the wreath and only the remainder could be considered a charitable deduction to the band'. Was *that* flirting? She'd thought at the time, and still thought, that if a tax guy wanted to impress a girl he probably shouldn't even tell her that he was a tax guy, much less go on and on about the tax code. But from the beginning, Lenny was always polite, albeit quiet, and somewhat narrowly focused. If he was reading an article in a magazine, she could walk into the room naked, with a bowl of fruit on her head, and he would not notice. And that wasn't just a guess; she had tried it. But when he was focused on her, it was all about her. And Len didn't have a dishonest bone in his body, unlike her first husband, Billy, whose entire skeletal system was the lying bone connected to the deceitful bone connected to the cockamamie bone (Shelly would say 'the bullshit' bone). There had been something so fresh and clean and, all right, maybe *boring*, about Lenny. But thank God by the time he'd gathered his courage to ask her out, she'd gotten past the stage in her life when she found 'bad boys' attractive. (Kathryn was still in that phase, she thought morosely, picturing Jordan.) But C.C. had been much younger than Kathryn was now when she'd finally learned that hard-won lesson, that the other side of a dull, black piece of glass was the shiny, beautifully reflective mirror. The flip side of boring was sincerity. Right after Lenny's third explanation about the band wreath, on his third year of doing her taxes, after he'd spent ten minutes telling her about 501Cs and benefit versus cost versus donation, he had nervously asked her out. Six months later, she'd become Mrs Leonard Byrd.

Now Billy, on the other hand, was a world-class flirt. He was a charmer, that boy. A constant flirt. And what good had come of that, in the end? None. None at all. Except Kathryn, of course. Who had Billy's genes, but Lenny's fathering.

C.C. finished her drink and took another slice of cornbread from Shelly, and the honey from Meg.

But this man – Purdy. Was it his first name, she wondered. He was just being kind to them. All of them. And even if he had sort of singled her out, and even if she did find him charming, jumpiness notwithstanding, what could possibly come of it? They'd be back on the road tomorrow, gone for good, heading south again.

She stared at her breasts. Heading south, indeed. Shelly and Meg must be wrong about Purdy. If he was looking for a woman to – well, *date* – he would certainly be more attracted to one of them, not her. Meg was almost eight years older than she was, but Meg was so trim and petite, an impeccable dresser, right out of J. Crew. And perky breasts, too. Even though she was too thin now, and her hair mostly gray. But it was an attractive silver on her. And Shelly, so funny and wild and seductive, with her sexy thick, red hair, though now with that troubling gray, unlike Meg's attractive silvery hair. Back in the day, a man might have preferred C.C., when she was young, blonde and her body unaltered by either calories or gravity. But what man would be attracted to her now? Maybe a dairy farmer. She was a cow. She stared at her hands, her chubby fingers, especially her left ring finger. The indentation from her wedding ring still deep. She'd removed the ring not because she was a widow, or because it 'was time', but rather because she'd gained so much weight that she was worried they'd have to cut it off her.

She sighed, picked up the bottle, and squeezed a generous stream of cinnamon honey back and forth over her second slice of cornbread.

After they'd finished all the bread (they agreed, it was exceptional, deep and nutty-tasting, especially good with the honey), they'd decided to go ahead and order dinner, then get to bed early. C.C. stared at her menu: Meatloaf? Fried chicken? Maybe chicken fried steak.

'Ahem.'

She looked up. Mick stood at their table. He'd pulled off his grease-stained cap, holding it to his chest, as if about to deliver a eulogy. 'Evenin', ladies.' All three women put down their menus. 'Well, I've got good news and bad news. The good news is it's just the alternator. Oh. And battery. I tested it and it's pretty low on juice. If I was you, I'd replace it too. 'Specially before a road trip. Now, it's easy enough t'plop another of each in there. But the bad news is that I don't have the right kind of alternator in stock. That's a pretty old model car you got there. But the other good news is that I found one in Sash County, and it'll be here tomorrow morning first thing. I can prolly get you ladies on the road again before noon. You're headed down south, right? Kentucky?'

'Uh, Tennessee,' said Meg. 'Can you tell us about how much this will cost?'

'Well, I'm gonna give you the battery and alternator at cost, and a discount on the labor.' He put his thumb over his shoulder. 'Dad's orders.' They all glanced at Purdy, who, his complexion suddenly ruddier than ever, was wiping a spot on the wooden bar with such vigor one would think he held sandpaper, not a clean white towel. Then he disappeared below the counter, and they heard glassware being moved around.

'Well, isn't that *lovely* of him!' said Shelly, clasping her hands together and grinning. Meg discreetly smiled at C.C. C.C. fidgeted with her watch again.

'So, it'll be around two fifty, maybe three,' said Mick. 'I'll have to pay Kirby for bringing it over here.'

The levity was suddenly gone from the table. C.C. added it up in her head: that plus the motel bill would wipe out most of what they'd allotted for their entire travel budget to Tennessee. They'd each pooled all they felt they could afford to the Dogs' Wood Investment Group, the name they'd given themselves, and had agreed to scrimp and save so that they could afford materials and the unexpected. They hadn't planned on the unexpected being the first day of their trip.

This was another sign. This trip was a mistake. They should probably just head back home, once the car was fixed. C.C. hung her head. The other two wouldn't be in this mess if not for her.

'Well, if you ladies will excuse me now,' said Mick. 'I gotta get Joe Spurn's truck off the blocks.' He nodded to one then the next, bobbing his head like a pigeon. 'G'night, ma'am. Ma'am. Ma'am.' He put his cap back on, pulling it snug with both hands before he turned and walked away. C.C. watched as he reached up and held the little bell quiet as he opened and closed the door.

Feeling adrift, C.C. looked at her friends. Shelly was pulling little bits off her paper napkin, already

51

a small pile forming on her bread plate. Meg looked like she might burst into tears again. Poor Meg. She couldn't control the breakdowns yet. But she would. Eventually. It was only recently that C.C. trusted herself not to break down in public. Right after Lenny died she couldn't even speak, much less go out. It had taken weeks before she did anything besides go to the grocery store. And here Meg was, 'the event' still so recent, and she was on a road trip, of all things. In a way, Grant leaving was worse than Lenny dying. Grant had made a choice to leave Meg. Lenny had simply been called by God. Though she had doubted many times, C.C. still preferred to think there was some sort of intention somewhere in the universe. If not God, then . . . C.C. sighed. Something. Surely there had to be something.

She looked up, waved at Purdy till she got his attention, circling her finger around the table and lifting her mug. Purdy nodded, grinned, and bustled into action behind the bar.

'This round's on me,' she said to her friends, her mug still in the air. 'I'm sorry. I got us into this mess.' As she said 'mess', she gestured broadly with the mug, which slipped from her grasp, and shattered on the hard floor.

'DOWN!'

C.C. looked up, her heart pounding, first from the mug breaking, then from the shout. Purdy was cowering on the floor, at the end of the bar, his dishtowel wadded and held protectively near his head. Nobody moved for several seconds. Purdy suddenly stood, red-faced, and rapidly disappeared behind the swinging kitchen door.

C.C. had thought he was yelling at her. But clearly he was not. Still, she felt the heat of embarrassment. Then confusion.

'Wow. What do you suppose that was about?' asked Shelly.

Meg looked wan, said nothing. C.C. stared at the black, swinging kitchen door, then at the jagged pieces of mug littering the floor. 'We should just turn around, go home. This is another very bad omen.'

'*C.C.!*' Shelly and Meg said in unison.

'Well, it is! Look, I *did* get us into this. When I inherited Aunt Georgie's old house, I was just going to sell it, you know, just get rid of it, take that pittance the real-estate agent was offering and be done with it. But then Shelly told me about flip investments, and, then, well, Meg's situation and all . . .' C.C. hesitated, then went ahead and said it: 'Well, it just seemed like a sign, like maybe we could all finally really do the Great Escape. I thought it'd be fun, all of us getting away, work on the house together, maybe all make a little money on it . . .' Her voice trailed off. Quietly, she added, 'But so far, it's just costing us.'

The kitchen door flapped open again. Purdy was walking slowly toward them with a broom and dustpan. He didn't look at them as he squatted and began to sweep up the pieces.

'I'm so sorry,' said C.C., scooting to the edge of the bench. 'Here, let me do that. And, of course, please put it on our bill.'

'No, no,' he said gently, but keeping his head down. 'It's really okay. Doesn't matter. These are . . . ancient.' He rose, staring at the dustpan filled with mug pieces. He turned and walked back to the kitchen, his steps tight and uncertain.

C.C. watched him go, feeling at an utter loss in a way she didn't quite understand. She was always interested in people's stories, whether she knew them or not. But she wasn't sure she wanted to know this man's story. She was pretty sure, whatever it was, it was a sad one.

'Well, I'm the one who told you about the whole flip thing,' said Shelly. 'So really, it's because of *me* that we're even here.'

'Look,' said Meg, with a resolve that C.C. hadn't heard in a while, 'the only extra to all of us is going to be the motel. It's my car, so it's *my* repair bill. Plus, if I hadn't wanted to do that little detour onto that country road, we would be farther along by now.'

C.C. opened her mouth to object, but Meg raised her palm, again surprising C.C.

'The alternator and battery didn't go out just because we're on this trip. They went out because they were old, used up. If I'd been driving around Wisataukee, a block from my house, they still would have gone out.'

'Well, then, I agree with Shelly,' said C.C. 'It's all

54

her fault.' She playfully stuck her tongue out at Shelly.

Shelly laughed and put her finger on her chest. 'Yeah. And I'll take the *credit* when we all make a tidy little profit on the deal when we're done. C'mon, show us the pictures again. That'll lift our spirits, seeing the old cash cow.'

Even Meg smiled. But C.C. laughed. Where her own drug of choice was food, Shelly's was money: her moods went up and down with her financial bottom line. She had done well as a real-estate agent, and then better, doing flips and small development projects. But she'd gone into a real depression – of every kind – when that big development deal went south.

C.C. gasped. There was that phrase again. It *had* to be an omen! But she didn't know if it was a good one or a bad one. It didn't seem great at the moment.

'C'mon! You have that little picture book with you, don't you?' prodded Shelly, slapping the table lightly.

C.C. nodded. She opened her huge purse and pulled out a small, white vinyl album with a clear plastic pocket on the front. Before they'd left, she'd placed her wedding present from Lenny in the pocket: a necklace, a tiny, gold horseshoe with dots of green peridot stones set within, on a fine, gold chain. She trusted it: all the confusion and upheaval of her life had seemed to settle right down, everything falling into place, after she'd married Lenny. She touched it now, tenderly, with just her index finger. Then she thought about the car breaking down, the rift between herself and Kathryn, Grant leaving poor Meg like that, Shelly's money woes. She pulled the necklace out and swung it around the table, as if it were a thurible, closing her eyes and silently saying as much of the prayer for travelers (which she'd found on the internet the day before) as she could remember, which was not much. Something about angels flying with them, protecting them.

'For luck,' she said, when she opened her eyes and found Meg and Shelly staring at her.

She poked the necklace back into the pocket, and placed the album sideways in the middle of the table so they could all see. She opened the cover slowly, her heart opening in its own way, right along with it. Meg and Shelly both turned, as did she, the better to see the pictures. The first page contained an old four-inch-by-four-inch black and white photo with scalloped white edges, pulled from her mother's old photo album. C.C. thought that in black and white the house looked even more stately than in the later, color pictures. Or maybe it was just that the photo was old, taken in a time when the house had been maintained. She flipped the page to one that showed the expansive front lawn, in which three dogwoods, each heavily laden with blossoms, stood evenly spaced. She remembered planting those with Aunt Georgie, the weekend after the funerals. One each for her mother, her father and her sister. The dogwood had been her mother's favorite flower. Aunt Georgie had referred to the house as Dogs' Wood ever after, even having stationery made with that name in the address.

The picture was too small to see them clearly, but C.C. knew that between two of the trees stood a small dark metal statue of a dog with a ring in its mouth, and between the other two, a stone birdbath. An old Thunderbird four-seater was parked on the dirt street in front. C.C. touched the edge of the picture. The car had been her mother's, and, like everything else, including C.C. herself, had been bequeathed to Georgie. Her mother had told some wild stories about her escapades with Georgie in that car. Both C.C. and her sister, Theresa, had loved her mother's stories, especially while poring over the old photo albums with her, leaning against her on the big settee, like bookends, C.C.'s knees covered demurely by her skirt, her bobby-socked feet tucked neatly under her, Theresa's knees worn through her dirty jeans, her bare feet on the coffee table, till Momma swatted them off. And they each had their favorite stories. 'Tell us the story about your wedding dress!' C.C. would beg. 'No! Tell us about when you made Aunt Georgie climb a tree to get the bowl of butter and sugar!' Their mother had often said about her two girls that they were like two acorns falling from an oak: if they had landed in the same place they'd grow up in each other's shade, neither one becoming all she was meant to be. 'Nature knows what she's doing,' she'd said, 'and that's why you're so different!' 'Like you and Aunt Georgie,' Theresa would point out, and Momma would smile and nod.

And different they were, and it made for a good balance. Occasionally the girls would argue, but mostly they adored each other, each accepting her sister's different interests. Theresa would protect C.C. any time a bully threatened. C.C. did Theresa's makeup for her when she finally relented and said she'd go to the formal dance with Jerry Happ. That had been Theresa's last date. It was no wonder that C.C. had married Billy so young – too young and too quick – longing to recreate the family she'd lost. C.C. flipped the page.

As the pages turned, the decades flew by, the pictures changing to color. Some of the recent ones had been sent digitally by the estate attorney in Fleurville. Toward the end of the book a grainy and too-yellow color print she'd made when her color cartridge was low, showed the house from the front again. The graceful veranda, with its white slatted railing, had always made the young C.C. think of a toothy smile, the dormers on the roof, shining eyes. Now the smile was missing a few teeth, and the eyes were shut by blinds. Strips of the blue paint peeled in several places, and the white trim seemed dirty and worn. Weeds were marching in on every side of the porch, as if ready to climb on up and enter the house itself.

'It's got great bones, C.C.,' Shelly said again, as she had said months ago on first seeing the pictures. 'It'll be an absolute gem. We'll get a good price for it, once we spiff it up. You'll see.'

'I am *so* looking forward to seeing this place in person,' said Meg. 'After all the stories I've heard about it over the years. Especially about you and Theresa.' C.C. reached across the table and took her hand. Dear Meg. Meg was like her sister, in many ways. In fact, C.C. had first met Meg on Theresa's birthday, an omen to be sure. It was when she worked for Welcome Wagon of Wisataukee. C.C. smiled, remembering. She'd loved the job, greeting new arrivals to town, giving them maps, and samples and coupons from local businesses. And her boss had been very accommodating about giving her only homes on the bus route. But Meg's driveway was so long, and carrying that big basket of goodies had her pretty much winded by the time she knocked on the door. Meg opened it just a crack at first, looking fearful. (Meg later told her it was because she was afraid that C.C. was a Jehovah's Witness or something.) When C.C. introduced herself as the Welcome Wagon of Wisataukee woman, Meg looked amused and relieved. Her first words to C.C. were, 'Nice alliteration. Come on in.' They liked to say it was 'friends at first sight'.

But Meg had actually met Shelly first. She'd been their real-estate agent – hers and Grant's. Meg had invited both C.C. and Shelly to brunch not long after meeting C.C., and brunch had lasted all day, with a walk in the woods, and then drinks on the patio, then dinner. The Trio, as they'd christened themselves, was born.

C.C. flipped the last page of the album. To the only picture not of Dogs' Wood. She'd stuck this one in mere hours ago, a sudden inspiration, just before they'd picked her up from her house. Meg and Shelly hadn't seen it yet. At least not in a long time. She twisted it fully toward them.

'Ohhh . . .' said Meg, her eyes filling immediately.

Even Shelly's face softened. 'Damn. Look how young we were,' she said. She covered her pile of shredded napkin protectively with her cupped palm.

''Cept I look beat from that damn hike you two dragged me on!' said C.C., forcing a smile. No one spoke.

'Grant took this picture of us,' Meg said finally, her voice barely audible.

In the photo, their beaming, sunburned faces nearly matched the Bloody Marys in their raised glasses. Their free arms rested over another's shoulders, an ease and comfort and comraderie already evident. Each face was animated, lips forming words in unison. It had been the first of many times they'd raised their glasses and lustily toasted, 'To friendship!'

Purdy arrived at their table and set the tray down with the new round, just as the bell on the restaurant door jingled again. He seemed to grit

60

his teeth, but continued quickly handing out new napkins, followed by their drinks on top.

'Again,' said C.C., 'I'm so sorry about the mug. Please let me reimburse—'

He lowered his eyes, shook his head, said softly, 'Ma'am – C.C. It's okay. Really.'

'Well, thank you. And thank you for that delicious cornbread! That was about the best I've ever had. And that's saying something, from a southerner!' Without even thinking about it, she touched his forearm lightly with her fingertips as she added, 'I don't suppose you ever share that secret ingredient?' When he finally looked at her, she smiled. And he did. His eyes stayed on hers, just a few seconds, but some considerable something passed between them. He hadn't answered her about the ingredient, but his eyes spoke to her somehow.

As he walked away, C.C. was taken hold by a sudden, unbidden memory, but it came very clearly. It was a day bus tour she and Lenny had taken, just a few years ago. To see fall colors. It was late afternoon and they were headed home, when the bus passed a terrible accident, just as emergency personnel were arriving. Had they been moments earlier, the bus would have been involved. As they were directed slowly past the smoking wreckage, C.C. had quickly turned her head away from the window. When she did, she saw a man across the aisle looking past her, out the window. Then he too looked away, and their eyes met, very briefly. At the terminal, they'd all silently disembarked, and she and Lenny flowed into the mass migration into the station. Later, as they headed out of the terminal, the man from the bus walked past them, the opposite direction. Their eyes met again, locked, a mere second. They'd said nothing, but C.C. knew right away that in both their eyes were the words: 'We're alive. We're alive.'

She watched Purdy talking to a very old woman, helping her to a small table in the middle of the restaurant. The old woman said something and they both laughed. He seemed like such a nice man. Yet, there was something about him that gave C.C. a certain unease.

'Ceece? You okay?' Shelly was snapping her fingers, mid-air. She and Meg were both looking at her.

C.C. nodded, picked up her mug, raised it toward the middle of the table. The other two lifted their mugs. 'Here's to the Great Escape, and –' in unison, they added – 'to friendship,' with a tender clink of their mugs.

CHAPTER 4

SHELLY

S helly pulled the pillow into a tight crescent around her ears, willing herself back to her dream, uncertain what had woken her. She'd been dreaming something about a castle. In England? Ireland? She couldn't remember, but it was fabulous – gold faucets, jeweled chandeliers, thick, pillowy beds with equally thick and pillowy comforters, huge colorful rugs across vast stone floors. She drifted back, sliding into sleep again like Alice down the rabbit hole. *What a beautiful room!* A living room, or maybe a library. For a giant. Huge brocade couches and massive French wingback chairs, all with thick, carved figures in their wood trim, leather-spined books floor to ceiling on the back wall, the furniture circling a roaring fire in a fireplace so big you could park a small car in it. She stepped around the huge, high-backed chair, easily three times her height. Startled, she jumped backward, stumbling. A giant chicken was sitting in the chair, roosting on an enormous egg. Shelly immediately wanted that egg. She couldn't help herself. She knew she shouldn't, knew that this gargantuan bird could really hurt her, peck her to death, or get its claws into her hair, carry her off to its lair. But she was driven by an uncontrollable urge. The chicken crowed. Could hens crow, dream-Shelly wondered, despite her fear. Her heart racing, she stepped toward the chicken, wanting desperately to retreat but feeling possessed. She reached for the egg. The chicken screamed at her, wings flapping, feathers flying. As she jumped back again, she screamed, but no sound came out. All she could hear was the chicken crowing as she fell into blackness.

Her eyes jerked open. Her fingers dug into the mattress. She was caught in the tug of war between dream and adrenalin, both pulling her hard to their reality. Adrenalin won. Her heart pounding, she glanced left and right in the dark room. Nothing looked familiar. Finally, she made out the other bed, Meg and C.C. asleep in it. A loud staccato crowing from outside their window broke the dark morning stillness.

Shelly took a moment to wade mentally through the webby remnants of sleep, weighing what was dream, what was real. Finally, she muttered, 'Is that a fucking *rooster*?'

Somehow, neither the rooster nor her mumbling woke her friends. How she envied their ability to sleep so deeply! She untangled herself from the twisted bedcovers, threw them off and stood, stretching her hands over her head, then rubbing her upper arms vigorously, urging some blood to start circulating through her body. She looked at the red numbers of the digital clock on the bedside table: 5.18. Shit. No normal person should be awake at this hour. She lifted just the edge of the orange window curtain and peered out.

The sun had little more than peeked above the eastern horizon, just enough to streak the few clouds in the sky with shades of purple and pink, casting a hoary light upon the town. Down the road a bit, Shelly saw something moving. It wobbled into a yellow-orange circle of light from a lone streetlamp. A rooster. *How fucking bucolic!* He was strutting down the dirt road, as officious as a rabbi headed to temple. He stopped, ruffled his wings slightly in the light, as if spotlit on a stage. He pointed his beak skyward and let loose again. She would have laughed if she hadn't shuddered. He was nearly exactly in the middle of the circle of light. She surmised that he must have come from the other direction, worked his way past their window, and on down the street. He finished his crow in the spotlight, and strutted off again, same direction. Still holding the corner of the ugly curtain, she wondered if maybe it was his job, waking up the town. That he'd worked out some sort of deal with the Tupper officials that he would walk down Main Street (which, frankly, she was surprised wasn't called Purdy Street) and wake everyone up in exchange for – what? Maybe for being fed and not eaten. And maybe let into the coop with the hens every now and then. Shelly's lip curled as she took a last look at the bird, then shuddered again, as if she'd just swallowed down a particularly vile substance. Birds of all kinds gave her the willies.

She sat heavily back on the edge of the bed, rubbed her face, collapsed sideways onto her pillow. She ached with fatigue. Or cold. Or age. Fifty was not old, Shelly knew (she'd been fifty for almost three years now), and she had spent a lot of breath reminding her two friends of that fact, who you'd think had one foot in the grave the way they complained about their age. Meg was only two years older than she, C.C. was only forty-nine. In Shelly's opinion, it was a bit of a cop-out to succumb to the minor aches and pains of middle age. Wait till old age. There'd be plenty of time for complaining then.

Shelly closed her eyes, but sleep was gone, so she opened them, stared upward. C.C.'s night-light (so she could find the bathroom) provided just enough of a glow for Shelly to make out the brown water stain on one of the ceiling panels above her. She stared at it for a minute, its dark brown edges making her crave a cup of coffee. She looked over at Meg and C.C., still and silent in their bed. They'd said they wanted to share a bed and gotten no argument from her. She knew they were being generous. They were well aware of her need to sleep alone. It was hard enough for her to share a room, let alone a bed. Even with men. Especially with men. Men made too damn much noise at night – snoring, sputtering, farting. Breathing. Then they woke up at some ungodly hour, all bright-eyed and bushy-tailed, snuggling up and grabbing her, ready for some more action, right when she felt like she'd finally just gotten to sleep. No, sir. It'd been years since she'd allowed a man to spend the night in her room. Down the hall, maybe. Better they should go to their own home and sleep. After her second divorce she'd vowed she would remain single and not even cohabit for the remainder of her life. That had been the one vow she'd kept. That, and not speaking to Nina.

Shelly sat up again, looking at her friends. She shook her head in dismay. They were both on their backs, C.C.'s hands neatly on the fold of the sheet over the blanket on her protruding chest, fingertips over fingertips, as if she'd been posed by a mortician. Meg was also on her back, but her hands and arms were under the covers. Probably cold. The poor thing had no meat on her bones anymore. On the table next to Meg's head was an envelope addressed to Grant, at their house. Meg must have written it last night. Yet another letter to the asshole.

Shelly sighed, gazing at her friends. They looked like two pens in an engineer's pocket protector, both of them trained by years of habit to sleep in exactly one-half of the bed. Or less.

Not her, by God. Not Rochelle Hannah Kostens. Never again. She flopped back on her bed, spread-eagled, taking up the whole bed, just because she could.

Twenty minutes later, showered, her curly hair ('salt and cayenne pepper', she called it) pulled back in a short ponytail, her face without makeup, Shelly stepped out into the buttery morning light. The clean smell of moist earth and the slow unfurling of spring made her inhale twice, deeply, relishing the scent of possibility. She admired the sky: the clouds were gone and that dusky blue of dawn, not night but not yet day, domed the earth. She checked her watch: 5.56. She had asked Purdy last night when he would open the restaurant for breakfast; she did not like to wait long for that first cup of coffee. 'Six a.m. sharp, ma'am. Coffee'll be fresh-brewed at six a.m.'

She strode down the street, watching for the rooster, not wanting it to sneak up behind her and crow. She didn't see the bird anywhere but walked faster, feeling like she could be attacked by uncooked poultry at any moment. Her distaste for birds came, like so many things, from her youth. (Funny, she thought, how more and more years now qualified as 'her youth'.) But she really had been young when the Tweety Incident happened. She was ten, at her friend Rachel's house. Rachel had a new parakeet she'd rather uncreatively named Tweety. Extolling his many virtues, Rachel had coaxed Tweety out of his cage onto her finger, then onto Shelly's shoulder. At first, Shelly, though nervous, was charmed. Then Tweety pooped a dribbly grayish blob onto her new green shirt. Shelly screamed and Tweety tried to take flight but became momentarily tangled in her long, curly hair. In her preadolescent panic, her brain locked up and all she could think of was the fire-safety lesson they'd all received at school the day before. So she'd stopped, dropped and rolled, with Tweety flapping madly to free himself through the stop, drop and half the roll. In the nick of time, he liberated himself from Shelly's long locks and flew around the kitchen vocalizing his outrage as Shelly continued to roll. Tweety was completely unharmed. Shelly was not so lucky. She rolled into the corner cabinet of the Goldmans' brand-new kitchen island and cut her forehead, requiring three stitches. After that day, Tweety squawked loudly every time he saw Shelly, till Rachel fed him a bird cookie of some sort to calm him down. Shelly felt *she* deserved a cookie, not the damn bird. But all she'd gotten from the incident was a scar on her forehead, the humiliating nickname of 'Drop and Roll', which lasted all through junior high school, and a phobia for birds that had lasted her whole life.

Shelly quickened her pace down the road into a near-jog, till she came to a white clapboard house. She slowed, caught by its simplicity. It was a little box of a house, with a small cement front stoop, two aluminum lawn chairs on it, their webbing frayed and stringy. A thigh-high, white picket fence rimmed the tiny side and front yards. The ordinariness of the house was somehow extraordinary.

She strode on past two more houses and a one-pump gas station with an unmoving white and red barber pole outside the door. Funny little town, she thought. Not much to it. But thankfully, everything they'd needed yesterday after they'd broken down: a mechanic, a restaurant, an inexpensive but safe place to spend the night. And if any of them were interested in a quick trim, she wagered they could get it while someone filled their gas tank. She wondered what a haircut at the barbershop-cum-gas station might cost. Probably ten or fifteen bucks. Maybe less. A little thrill rippled through her, immediately followed by a horrific image of what a ten-dollar haircut might look like. She'd always gone to the most expensive hair salon in Cedar Rapids, just because she could afford it. She made a little 'tsk' sound. It pained her again to have to think about what everything cost. Like when she was in college or something, for crying out loud. She thought wistfully of her gleaming Italian espresso machine, enough to make any barista drool, and the imported biscotti she had nearly every morning with her first cup. Like so many other things, the machine had been sold, the standing biscotti order cancelled. She jerked open the big glass door to the restaurant, feeling angry about life in general, and birds and budgets in particular.

'Good morning, ma'am,' Purdy said, seeming to hold himself and the coffee pot in his left hand with undue grip as the little bell announced her entry. The aroma of coffee all but physically embraced her. Purdy was already pouring a cup, which he then offered to her, smiling. 'You slept well, I hope?'

'Thank you,' she said, taking it, mustering a smile, leaving it at that. He seemed like a genuinely nice man, but if that little bell bothered him so much, why didn't he just take it down? 'You have no idea how much I have been looking forward to this.' She took a sip. 'Ahhh,' she said, eyes closed. Yes, she would make it.

That's how coffee always made her feel, especially lately. That caffeine alone would somehow propel her through one more day. There was no doubt that this was a drug, and she was addicted. Her new 'budget' (*thinking* the word nearly made her gag on her coffee) demanded that she forgo the double-shot lattes she'd grown accustomed to.

Still standing next to Purdy, she cupped both her hands around the mug, sipped again, and gave another satisfied sigh. She had to admit, there was something to be said for a regular cup of coffee. And in a ceramic mug, not a paper cup with a plastic lid. 'That's pretty good Java, Purdy.'

'Thank you, ma'am.' He had the most adorable smile. If smiles could be marketed, she could make some money on his.

'I'm Shelly,' she said, extending her hand.

71

He switched the coffee pot to his other hand, shook hers, gripping her whole hand, but gently. Old school. 'Good morning, Shelly. Do you want to wait for your friends, or . . . ?'

'They're both still asleep.'

He looked slightly crestfallen, but recovered quickly, then pointed to the wall. 'Booth?'

'Sure. Thanks.' She slid into the same booth from dinner. Purdy, thankfully, stayed behind the bar. She needed a minute. She sipped her coffee, then picked up a menu. Grits. Yuk. Who ate corn mush for breakfast? She read on. Bacon and eggs. Waffles. Pancakes. French toast. C.C. would be in hog heaven here. But Meg was going to have a hard time. Let's see . . . Shelly scanned the columns, found there was both a fruit bowl and cereal listed under 'Side Dishes'. She doubted Purdy had soy milk to go on Meg's bran flakes, but Meg would probably just peck at whatever food she ordered anyway.

Ahh. Lookee there, also under 'Side Dishes'. Perfect. She set the menu down and suddenly Purdy appeared tableside, bearing the coffee pot. He was good. Been at this a while, no doubt.

'And what can I bring you this morning?' he asked as he refilled her mug.

'You know, Purdy, a lightly toasted bagel with a shmear, uh, cream cheese, would absolutely light up my life right now.'

'So be it! The light-up-your-life bagel with cream cheese.'

She wanted to reach up and pinch those bulbous, cherry cheeks. With his belly, and those big graying eyebrows, if he just had a beard and wasn't bald, he'd make a perfect Santa. But he could grow a beard, wear a hat . . .

Purdy headed to the kitchen, leaving Shelly thinking about Santa. And suddenly she was thinking about Nina again. She had battled this in the car yesterday too. She knew why, though she tried to forget it. It had been her one reservation about coming on this trip. She sipped her coffee. As long as she kept her mouth shut, didn't let anything slip to Meg and C.C., she could deal with it. But every thought of Nina stirred that deep well of anger, grown black and thick and viscous after so many years. Talking about it would be that much worse. She picked up the menu and read every word on it till her bagel arrived.

She was washing the last bite of bagel down with her third cup of coffee, when the black wall phone at the bar jangled loudly, an old-fashioned ring. Shelly noted curiously that Purdy didn't seem so jumpy today. He strolled over and picked it up. Being the only two in the place, Shelly couldn't help but listen.

'Purdy here. Mornin', son. Yes. Well, one of them is. Why?' He glanced her way. She watched Purdy's face registering confusion. 'Wait. Who?' Another long pause. 'From where?' Pause. 'Kirby? Well, where'd *he* come across her?' Pause. 'Well, how'd she get *there*? Never mind, I'll just have Shelly come over.' Another short pause, then Purdy turned toward the wall and added quietly, 'No. She's the tall, redheaded one. No. She's not up yet.' He turned, more red-faced than ever and clapped the phone back onto the wall base. Shelly picked up her menu again, using it to hide her smile.

Purdy walked back to the booth. 'My son asked that one of you ladies come over as soon as you can. The part's already been delivered and the guy who brought it, well, he somehow . . . eh, something about a runaway? Not sure what it all has to do with the alternator.' He shrugged, then smiled. 'Well, I'd better let Mick explain it. I don't understand, myself.' He shook his head, shrugged his shoulders and smiled his adorable smile again.

Intrigued, Shelly paid for her breakfast – they were keeping their food separate, but splitting all other bills – then headed out the door, the sound of the tinkling bell in her wake. She fished her large, white sunglasses out of her purse, squinting in the bright light till she had them in place. She unzipped her jacket as she walked across the road. It was warming up nicely. She passed another little Mayberryesque house as she walked toward the mechanic shop. But Mayberry turned Hitchcock as she passed by several rusting hulks of cars, and heard a soft but distinct clucking sound from somewhere within. Shelly quickened her stride, then, hearing or imagining little chicken feet

74

pounding the road behind her, she began running to the door of the shop.

On the side window, as if it was a separate business, were letters too big to miss even at a chicken-escaping pace: 'Mick's Auto Sales'. As she rounded the corner, and reached for the big metal handle of the door, she saw there were different letters there. Not as large but bolder, as if that, in and of itself, delineated it as a separate business: 'Mick's Garage – Mechanic 24 Hr'. Shelly flung open the heavy glass door and almost leaped inside, glancing behind her. No bird. Still, only when the door closed and she felt she was safe did she turn and notice Mick, intently tapping away with two fingers at an old and very dirty computer on a battered wood desk. Shelly smiled, smoothed her hair, composed herself, trying to resemble a woman who hadn't just been fleeing a chicken. Or rooster. Or whatever the hell it was.

She stood smiling, both her hands gripping the strap of her purse, hanging over her shoulder. She waited. Mick continued hunting and pecking with two fingers on the grimy keyboard, intent and focused. She hoped whatever it was he needed to tell them wasn't bad news. Of course, 'runaway' didn't immediately make one think of good news. But she felt she couldn't take more bad news. Maybe there was a runaway car that had crashed, not a bad crash where anyone got hurt, but maybe where someone had left the parking brake off and it had slid down the hill and crashed into – something harmless – a dumpster, maybe, and they had been given its alternator to bring their ailing car back to health. Yes. A sort of automobile organ donation. For free. Sure, why not? Shelly was determined to remain optimistic, even implausibly so. Leave the doubt and worry to the other two. They more than had it covered.

Breathing impatiently, she looked out the window. The rooster strutted by, stopping to peck at something in the grass, not five feet from the door. Shelly shivered, turned away from the window and looked for a place to sit down. But the only other furniture in the tiny office, besides Mick's desk and chair, was an orange plastic chair against the wall, also streaked with grime. She decided she would stand. A sign at the other end of the narrow room caught her eye: the universal man/woman silhouette, thumb-tacked onto the wall next to a closed door. Shelly suddenly felt her three cups of coffee. But, given the lack of cleanliness of the office, she thought it prudent to wait till she got back to their room.

'Ah-hem,' she said, tired of waiting. Mick looked up from the keyboard.

He rose, pulling off his cap. 'Oh! Golly! Sorry. Didn't see you there. Morning, ma'am.'

'Good morning,' said Shelly. 'Your dad said you wanted to see me. Or one of us?'

'Yeah. I got a sorta favor to ask. I wonder if you ladies could give M.J. a ride down south with you?'

Oh crap. No vehicle runaway. No free alternator.

76

Probably some tattooed, preadolescent tart who'd scurried off on a romantic escapade with her much older boyfriend, and now wanted to go home to Momma.

'No,' said Shelly firmly, stepping to the desk. 'I'm sorry but—'

'Before you say no,' Mick interrupted. He clicked at the keyboard for a minute, as Shelly cocked her head in irritation, thinking: but I just *did* say no. 'Ahh! Here it is! And . . .' said Mick, lifting his head and smiling, '. . . there's some money in it for you ladies.'

Money?

He twisted the screen around toward her. Shelly stared at his email inbox as Mick highlighted then clicked on *tailhound@whips4me.com*.

Holy shit. Was this from a porn site? Grimly fascinated, Shelly read the email silently.

Hi Kirby and Mick: I got your email about the ladies driving south! That's fantastic!!!!!! It's a miracle!!!!! It's truly God's work sending those ladies to bring my little girl home to me! now Mary Jo won't have to fly! fingers crossed!!!! well, obviously she's terrified to fly!! LOL!!! ☺ now she won't have to!!! ☺ I'm lighting candles at church tonight for both of you and for the three ladies and praying that they agree to bring MJ home to me!!! please, please please email or call me as soon as you know for sure!! I'll let y'all figure out how to split the reward!!

Candy

Shelly stared, open-mouthed, at Mick. She didn't know where to begin. She didn't have children herself, but even she could tell that this mother's screen name was enough to cast her under deep suspicion as an unfit parent. And kids who ran away usually had a reason. Not to mention this woman's extreme excessive use of exclamation marks. Meg would have a field day with that.

'How old is this M.J.?' she asked, trying to keep her tone level, objective-sounding.

'Uh, I didn't ask. Does it matter? Can you take her? Please?'

Shelly already had the word 'No' formed on her lips again, complete with an exclamation mark of her own, when Mick held up his hand. 'Wait. Before you answer, just meet her. She's a sweet girl. She really is. Just scared, is all.'

She's here? Shelly looked around, then out the window, uncertain what she should do. She could just walk out. But that bird was out there.

'One second!' Mick unclipped a set of keys from his belt loop and jogged toward the closed door at the end of the office. 'I've got her locked in the bathroom so she don't take off again.'

Locked in the bathroom? Forget the ride. Shelly realized they needed to grab this kid and take her

78

as fast as they could to the nearest social services agency.

'You've locked her in the *bathroom*?'

'Yep.' He looked a little sheepish as he put the key in the doorknob and tried to turn it. The key didn't seem to be working. He jiggled it, pulled it out again, shooting a quick and embarrassed smile at her. 'Never usually lock this thing, but sometimes it won't latch tight and I didn't want to take a chance of her taking off again.' Finally, he turned the key in the lock.

Shelly put one hand on the side of the desk, steadying herself. C.C. or Meg should be here, she thought, not her. They're the mothers. She took a deep breath. She was okay with Lucy, but otherwise she didn't really enjoy children. Especially not teenagers. Especially surly, runaway teenagers. Mick fumbled at the door. Shelly lifted her sunglasses off the top of her head, set them on the desk. She tried to assume what she hoped was a maternal smile. Then she had a thought: if the kid ran away from her mom, maybe maternal wasn't the way to go here. Maybe her real-estate agent smile would actually be better. She conjured the words 'pristine' and 'move-in condition' and 'envy of the neighborhood', and the smile slid on, natural, inviting, engaging.

Mick slowly cracked the door, standing in front of the opening. 'Hey, M.J.,' he said sweetly.

Shelly leaned to the side, trying to see around him, but it was impossible. Until he slowly opened the door wider. Then she saw a very worn-looking teddy bear face down on the floor.

Oh God. It was a *little* kid! She still couldn't see her, but this was a whole new ballgame. Mick pushed the door fully open, revealing a small, plastic margarine tub, half full of water under the exposed gooseneck pipe of the sink. *Christ!* What a place to stash a kid. *A little kid!* She shook her head, but then noticed a second plastic tub. Filled with . . . ? Cereal, maybe?

Just as the tired synapses of Shelly's brain tried to process the information, Mick stepped aside. 'I guess she's not gonna make a run for it.'

Shelly scanned the little room, but saw no one. She stepped forward, tentatively. Then, she saw her. Hiding behind the toilet, a small, very thin, trembling . . .

Dog.

Her tired brain, like an old train, slowly but surely picked up steam, and headed through an entirely different information tunnel.

A dog.

Shelly guffawed, her shoulders slumping in relief. '*It's a dog!*' The three words echoed joyfully in her head, relief abundant. The dog appeared to be skin and bones, but Shelly thought that it was one of those breeds that looked that way naturally. But it was shaking like a leaf, the poor thing. 'Well, why the hell didn't you tell me it was *a dog*?' she asked, recovering her equilibrium.

'I thought Dad did.' Mick looked at her blankly.

She laughed, shaking her head. 'No, he sure didn't. Or if he did, I didn't catch it. I thought you'd locked some kid up in here!' She put her hand to her chest, inhaling and exhaling dramatically.

Mick grinned, but his eyes were wide. 'Cripes! I wouldn't do that, ma'am. I felt bad enough locking this poor little thing in here. See? I gave her a towel over there for her t'lay on, and my old bear, Mr Snuppy. But she's still scared silly, poor thing.'

Shelly looked at the dog. 'What did you say her name is? The dog's?'

'M.J. Well, that's what they call her. She's got some fancy long name, but I can't remember it.'

She *was* kind of pretty, but also kind of ugly, thought Shelly. She had a beautiful charcoal-gray coat, with four white paws, each looking like it had been carefully and exactly dipped into a can of white paint, a matching thin blaze of white down her nose. Her best feature, in Shelly's opinion, was the tiny white tip on her tail. But she was so skinny, such a wisp of a thing, her features so pointy and bony, from snout to tail, ears to toenails, that she looked like she was only part dog, the rest of her genes contributed by a lanky rat. The poor thing had plastered herself into the corner, her bony narrowness seeming expressly made to fit neatly into a corner. She had the kind of ears that looked as if they were turned inside out, pushed flat against the back of her long, thin neck. She was hiding behind the porcelain pedestal of the toilet, her feet tightly together under her, her tail wrapped securely around them, every part of her quivering, as if she was experiencing her own personal earthquake.

'C'mere, M.J.' Mick was squatting now, snapping his fingers lightly, which only made the dog turn her head toward the wall.

Shelly's heart constricted. Well, maybe they could take *this* little thing to her owner. Her 'mother'. Shelly chuckled, shaking her head. Candy wasn't a porn star! *Tailhound*, for crying out loud, referred to her love of dogs. *Whips4us.* Of course! Shelly realized that the dog must be a Whippet. But Shelly's neighbor in New York had had Whippets, and this dog seemed too small. She wondered if it was a puppy, or maybe there was a sub-breed, Miniature Whippet. Either way, maybe they could help the little dog out. She was sure Meg and C.C., both being gaa-gaa over babies and animals of all kinds, would be willing.

'So when the suitcase guys finally figured out the kennel door was open, M.J. had skedaddled,' explained Mick to the assembled group in the restaurant. 'She was prolly just so scared, she didn't even know where she was running to. Just ran and ran. Kirby found her in the bushes next to his shop.'

'Kirby is the guy who brought the alternator,' Shelly explained to C.C. and Meg.

By the time she and Mick had brought M.J. over

to the restaurant, the two women were on their second cups of coffee and just starting in on their breakfasts. As Shelly had guessed, a dinner-plate-sized waffle with an egg on the top, both awash in syrup, for C.C., and a small fruit plate for Meg. Shelly was sitting next to C.C., Meg opposite. Mick and Purdy had each pulled up a chair. C.C. pinched off a tiny corner of her waffle and fed it to M.J., who had been on C.C.'s lap from the moment she'd seen her. 'Cookie? Yummy!' C.C. whispered, as the trembling dog tentatively took the treat and ate it.

Shelly continued explaining: 'So when Mick mentioned to Kirby that the three of us needed to get on the road again as soon as possible because we were headed to Tennessee, Kirby offered to bring the part over himself. He figured he'd found a ride home for M.J.'

'Kirby's delivering parts to Coryville today, but says he'll stop back by for M.J. tonight if you ladies can't take her,' said Mick. 'But if you can, he's willing to split the reward, sixty-forty, with you ladies getting the bigger half, since you'll be driving her home. That'd more than cover the cost of the alternator and labor. You'd have half your share left over.'

Shelly caught Meg's teacher's grimace at 'the bigger half'. Meg smiled at being caught, then poked her fork hard into a grape she'd been chasing around her plate. Shelly patted M.J. in C.C.'s lap. The dog was clearly enjoying her perch on C.C.'s ample lap, though Shelly wondered how comfortable she could be in the leash and harness that Mick had fashioned. It appeared he'd used yards of twine, making M.J. look like something on which a very small and very inept cowboy had practiced calf-roping. C.C. held the end of the twine leash tightly in one hand, her fork in the other. No one wanted to take a chance on M.J. running away again. But Shelly winced, looking at the harness. The loops and knots of twine looked scratchy. They would have to stop and buy her a proper harness and leash as soon as they hit civilization again.

'But how did she get loose in the first place?' Meg asked.

'This here explains. Kirby gave me this.' Mick pulled a neatly folded newspaper clipping from his jumpsuit pocket and smoothed it on the table. As Purdy left to tend to some other customers, Mick read the article aloud.

'Greyhound Takes Off Ahead of Schedule.'

'A four-year-old Italian Greyhound [Ah-ha, thought Shelly] dog escaped from her kennel on the tarmac of the Quad City Airport on Saturday afternoon, prior to flying home to Kentucky after a local dog show. The dog, called M.J., but registered under the name of "Mary Josephine Fair Maiden Made-You-Look", belongs to

Candy Suddle of Lexington, Kentucky. Suddle and her dog were returning home after competing in the preliminary rounds of a dog agility competition. The kennel was about to be loaded into the aircraft when employees noticed the dog had somehow escaped. "I checked the door not twenty minutes before that, and she was in there and it was shut tight," said Javon Cutch, an airline employee who was loading cargo that day for Mid-America Air.'

Mick stopped reading to take a sip of his very white coffee, and then bit into his cheese Danish. Shelly reached for the news clipping, asking, 'May I?' Mick nodded, pushing it toward her, and took another slurp of his coffee and another large bite of Danish. Purdy reappeared with the coffee pot, and refilled everyone's cup, starting with C.C.'s.

Shelly continued:

'Suddle owns both Italian Greyhounds and Whippets, and shows them in various competitions around the country. "I can't believe this happened," said Suddle, in a phone interview. "I don't know how she got out if someone didn't let her out. The airline didn't bother to tell me my dog wasn't on the flight till we landed in Lexington." Suddle said she is considering a lawsuit against the airline, and is offering a reward of five hundred dollars for the return of her dog. The airline said it would match her reward. There have been several un-confirmed sightings of the dog, each one at increasing distances from the airport. "It's likely it's her," said Tanya Dean, spokes-woman for the Linn County Sheriff's Office. "The descriptions all match hers, gray with white socks." Dean urged area residents to keep an eye out for the dog, and to call the sheriff's non-emergency number with any possible sightings.'

Shelly looked up. 'And then it gives a phone number.' She looked the little dog in the eye. 'That is one helluva name ya got there, girl.'

'What is it again?' asked Meg, smiling.

Shelly traced her finger over the clipping till she found it. 'Mary Josephine Fair Maiden Made-You-Look. Damn! For a name like that, I'd even consider getting married again.'

Meg laughed. C.C. leaned down, kissed the top of the little dog's head. She spoke in a high-pitched voice. 'Yesh she is, isn't she? She is a verr-wee fair maiden! Aren't you, widdle girl?' The dog's seem-ingly naked little tail thrummed against C.C.'s stomach. M.J. lifted her snout and licked her chin, making C.C. giggle. Still in a baby-voice she added, 'Oooo! Tank you for da kisses, widdle girrr!'

Shelly sighed loudly, placing her palms on the table. 'Well, for six hundred bucks I'm willing to take the dog with us and drop her off in Kentucky.' She wagged her finger playfully at C.C. 'But we're dropping you off too if you talk baby-talk the whole way.' C.C. laughed with everyone else, then stuck her tongue out at her, making them all laugh again.

Shelly knew it was crazy, but she would swear the little dog smiled too. M.J. looked like she'd spent her whole life on C.C.'s lap, and would happily remain there for the rest of it.

CHAPTER 5

PURDY

Purdy smiled, but only after seeing that C.C. was laughing, that she had, in fact, taken Shelly's comment about the baby-talk as a joke. He shifted his weight from one foot to the other, as if his feet knew he should be doing any number of a thousand things right now, but his heart was keeping them firmly rooted to a place near the blonde woman, who seemed to be perpetually smiling. He stood behind his chair, holding the coffee pot at the ready, though he'd just refilled everyone's cup. Except the thin woman's; she'd hastily put her hands over the top as he'd leaned in. He'd forgotten; she'd had tea.

He knew he was hovering, but he couldn't just sit back down. It would look idle. The tall redhead, Shelly, was staring at him. She was a little mouthy, but good-humored, and the other one – what was the thin one's name? He couldn't remember, but she seemed nice enough. Quiet and . . . he wasn't sure what. Heavy-hearted, somehow. But C.C. He even liked her name. C.C. It made him smile.

He cleared his throat, rubbed his hand over his face. He was as tongue-tied and nervous as a teenager around her. There was something really *wrong* with him. But this wrong felt so much better than the other wrong. And aside from that mortifying shout and duck for cover he'd done when the mug had fallen, he'd felt . . . what? Hopeful? Even the bell was starting to bother him less.

Shelly was still staring at him, grinning. Oh, she had his number all right. Feeling the heat in his face, he turned and walked back to the bar.

He'd noticed C.C. right off yesterday, as soon as she had climbed out of the tow truck. Laughing. In spite of their car breaking down, in spite of the gloomy rainy day, in spite of being stranded in Tupper, of all places, she was *laughing* as Mick and the tow truck driver helped her down from the high seat. She looked nothing like his Keppie, who had been tiny and dark-haired and bony. In fact, C.C. was Keppie's exact opposite. Was that why he was all hibbity-jibbity? He didn't think he'd ever felt this kind of attraction before. Not that he had all that much experience. His hibbity-jibbities of his youth came mostly from pictures of girls in magazines, which wasn't the same. Not like this. When he saw her, right away, bam! Like his body got plugged into some big old generator after the power had been off a long time. A long time. He was not a religious man, much to Keppie's dismay, but he would almost believe that some divine power might've had a hand in making that alternator fail when and where it did.

Or maybe it was Keppie herself. He and Kep

had always had that 'first one up' rule: first one up in the morning brought the other one a cup of coffee. Maybe the first one up to the Great Beyond brought the other one a new spouse. He would like to think that Keppie would do that for him. And what about the *dog*! Now that was a coincidence! Here's a little lost dog that needs to go pretty darn close to where these ladies are going . . . Well, it made you wonder. It just made you wonder.

Purdy glanced around the restaurant. It was empty, except for the ladies. And Mick, of course. He tried to think of some reason to go back over there. He'd just refilled their coffee cups. Everyone had eaten breakfast. He'd cleared the plates, delivered the tickets. But even if he just went back over and sat down, he couldn't trust himself not to stare at her like a fool. It was better if he stayed here; he could look at her from behind the bar.

He grabbed the towel that he wore draped over his shoulder and threw it hard onto the bar. He turned, his arms folded, and leaned back against the counter. C.C. wasn't interested in him! How could she be? She didn't know him. And he didn't know her. He had never believed in love at first sight. And he knew this wasn't love. Or was it? How should he know? Was it lust? Much to his amazement, he had gotten . . . excited just thinking about her last night. But he hadn't been thinking about having sex with her. He'd just been thinking about hugging her. Just holding her in his arms. When everything in his life had seemed to become so sharp-edged again after Keppie's death, was it so wrong to wonder what it must feel like to hold a woman like that, so round and soft and full?

He had wanted to ask her out after they'd finished dinner last night, but he'd been too embarrassed by his outburst. He hadn't understood at first how that had happened. He'd thought the panic attacks were under control again. It must have been because he was nervous. Besides, he hadn't been able to answer a simple question: how do you ask out a woman who is stranded at your motel with her two friends for just one night? And out to where? They would have had to drive clear to Bennet to find the nearest movie theater. He'd thought about inviting her to stroll with him, just an old-fashioned date, an evening walk through town. But he'd been struck mute as they'd departed, the three of them together too daunting even to approach.

Silence. His old refuge. He was only able to wave good night to all three. Then, when just the redhead came back and asked what time he opened for breakfast, well, of course *then* he could talk! After he'd locked up the restaurant, he'd walked by their room four times. Back and forth, back and forth, unable to go up and knock. He didn't know how long he'd just stood there, staring at the crevice of light between the curtains on their window.

He picked up the towel, turned and looked at her again. If only he didn't feel like this was somehow meant to be. Or at least a chance in a million. Or was it just his age? He remembered old Cort Smith, who'd tracked down and married a girl from his high school just weeks after his wife had died, when Cort was nearly eighty. 'When you get to be my age, you dasn't dillydally,' Cort had told him. Well, Purdy wasn't nearly Cort's age. But was sixty-one old enough to stop the world when C.C. had climbed out of that tow truck?

Before yesterday, he'd thought he'd just spend the rest of his life alone. There were no single ladies in Tupper, except Mrs D'Blatt, and she was ninety-something. He would be like her, he thought. Grow old alone, and die alone, right here in Tupper. And truth be told, he hadn't thought all that much about it, one way or the other. Until yesterday.

Finally, after the fourth pass by their window last night, he'd gone to bed. He'd hardly slept, feeling all night like he had to do or say something before she left. If only he had more time to court her properly. But what did he know about that? He had never even dated Keppie. Not really. He'd just written letters from Nam, in response to hers. Their letters were how they had gotten acquainted. They barely knew each other before he'd shipped out, just sat next to each other at high-school graduation. Mick Purdy and Katherine Purnell. They hadn't even spoken before, just sat or stood next to each other throughout the school years, each time they were made to line up in alphabetical order. Never given her a second thought. Till that graduation day and she kept staring at him, sitting there in his uniform. Then, as their ragtag high-school orchestra – sounding worse than usual without the seniors – played the graduation exit march, she'd told him she'd like to write to him after he shipped out. He'd said okay.

Always shy by nature, it had actually been easier for him to write those letters than any conversation with her would have been, or ever was after. And the letters, well, he'd only said the things he'd said to her in those because he thought the chances were better than good that he'd be coming home in a body bag. So he'd opened up in those letters, more than he ever could have or would have in person. But he did survive, somehow. Probably because he wasn't one of the brave ones.

When he got home, there was Keppie, waiting for him, right there on the airstrip at Quad City, her black-gloved fingers laced through the chain-link fence like it was the only thing holding her up. She was plainly dressed in a gray blouse and darker gray skirt, her hair pulled back, her only makeup a face full of both fear and hope.

Marrying her had seemed the thing to do. But they'd made it work okay, over the years. No great sparks or anything, but when the PTSD had taken hold of him, Keppie had stuck with him, held on, gotten him help. He was infinitely grateful to her, for her. But he'd often doubted that what he felt was love, as he was sure she had from time to time. But his doubt was erased seven months ago. Holding her in his arms, there on the floor behind the bar where she'd collapsed, her hands clutching her shoulder, he'd felt his own heart under attack. All he could think – he knew it was stupid, but still – all he could think was that it should be him; he was the fat one. How could tough, sturdy, bantam-weight Keppie be having a heart attack? But he knew that's what it was right away, even though there'd never been a single warning sign, other than she'd said she felt a mite under the weather that morning. The flu, she thought. And when she'd dropped to the floor, and he'd gathered her up, her back warm against his knees, her shoulder blades sharp against his arm, he couldn't imagine her leaving him, couldn't imagine life without her. That's when the flashbacks started again. A body in his arms. His wife, so small, nearly the same size as the South Vietnamese woman he'd carried from the burning village. And just as then, he'd felt her leave him the very moment she passed, despite his begging her to hold on.

Keppie never did smile too much. But he would never forget the way she smiled – really smiled – at him before her body let go of this life, and he felt some part of her float upward, and away.

Purdy tapped his arms, the trick he'd learned in

94

therapy to bring him back. He took a deep breath and looked at C.C. again, sitting with her friends and Mick, all of them petting that little dog, and laughing about something else now, and he smiled. He was here. Mick glanced over at him, eyes searching. Purdy knew Mick could not delay putting in that alternator too much longer. And when he did, the women were going to leave, and he'd never see C.C. again, never hear that laugh again, never know if her skin was as soft as it looked. He had to think of something. Cort Smith was right. In youth it was hormones that made a man act; now it was the heart itself having a deeper knowledge of time.

As Mick stood up and excused himself from the table, Purdy pretended to rub the bar down again. As his son walked by him, pulling on his cap, he said out of the corner of his mouth: 'Now or never, Dad. Now or never.'

Shelly and Meg stood up, and Shelly said, louder than necessary, 'We're going to the room to finish packing. C.C., you take the dog for a little walk.' The two women left the restaurant.

Purdy tried to calm himself. C.C. was slowly scooting herself to the end of the bench seat with one hand, the other carefully protecting the dog in her lap. He grabbed the towel and turned away, leaning against the bar, dabbing at his forehead and upper lip. He could see himself in the mirror, above the reflection of the tops of liquor bottles. A pale, bald, fat guy. He turned back and glanced her way; she was standing now, the little dog in her arms. Lucky dog. He turned back around, dabbed the towel on his upper lip again.

'Thank you for that great breakfast.'

He spun around. She was slipping her purse strap onto her shoulder, the dog was snug against her bosom, casually held with her other arm, like a girl might carry her books, like she'd carried that little dog that way for years. He noticed the dog wasn't shaking anymore. He nodded, smiled dumbly. 'We just left the money on the table. Is that all right?' He nodded, even more dumbly.

He watched her walk out of the restaurant, with not a word from him. He stepped around the cash register to watch her. He put his hand over his thumping heart, tried to swallow.

Outside, she stopped in the sun, gave the dog a kiss on its head, then set it on the ground, holding the end of the twine leash. She began rummaging in her purse.

Go out there! He paced back behind the bar. His hand suddenly shot to the squat bottle of brandy at the end of the row of bottles. He grabbed a highball glass from the towel-covered shelf. He wouldn't let himself look at the clock. The neck of the bottle clattered noisily against the glass edge as he poured. He had not had a drink since before Keppie had died. He'd *never* had a breakfast drink. He was an occasional social drinker, was all. Even after Nam, when lots of guys turned to the bottle, he hadn't. Keppie had made sure of that. He took a deep breath and threw the swallow of brandy down his throat. The burn felt good, like it would hold him to consciousness. *Social. That's all he needed to be, was social.*

He headed out the door, suddenly aware of the bar towel on his shoulder. But the damn bell had rung and she was already looking his way, so it was too late to do anything about it. He stopped in his tracks, a happy realization: instead of scaring him, the bell had made him angry. Fitz would say that was an improvement.

'Hello,' he said weakly. She smiled at him, waiting. 'Um,' he said, trying to find his bearings with his voice. He pulled the towel off his shoulder, twisted it in his hands.

She looked concerned. 'Did we leave enough money?'

'Oh!' he said, suddenly pained that he'd caused her concern. 'Plenty! I'm sure. Fine, fine!' He was nodding like a spring had gone loose in his neck somewhere. He felt ridiculous. But he felt good. He was *feeling*.

'Okay. Good.' She smiled, still waiting.

He threw the towel over his shoulder again and jammed his hands in his pockets, nervously scratching his legs with his pocket-covered fingers, till he realized it might appear as though he was doing something else entirely. He quickly pulled his hands out again, pulling a pocket lining out. He shoved it back down, feeling his face redden.

'Well, I'm going to take M.J. for a little walk,'

she said finally. He desperately wanted to ask if he could come, but his tongue, vocal cords, lungs – everything – seemed to be locked up. Damn brandy hadn't helped. She took a step.

'Wait!' he said.

She stopped suddenly, turned, again looking concerned.

'I'm sorry. I didn't mean to startle you.' Well, that was a switch. *Him* startling someone else. 'Uh, mind if I join you on your walk? I . . . I usually take a little stroll about now anyway. For exercise.' He pulled in his big stomach, hoping to look like someone who'd *ever* taken an early morning walk, just for the exercise. Much less *usually*.

'Uh, no. Of course not. You'd be welcome, right, M.J.?' She glanced at the dog. Then she looked past him, over his shoulder. 'But who'll mind the restaurant?'

'Oh, no one. No one in there anyway. If anyone comes in, they'll just help themselves to whatever.'

She nodded warily.

'Mostly regulars around here.' He forced himself to smile.

He marveled at how, when she smiled, her whole face seemed to sparkle. 'Well, sure then. Do you know how long it will take your son to put in the new part?'

'Uh, I'm guessing not more than an hour.' He glanced at his watch. Nearly 7.30. Mick *could* have it done in fifteen minutes, since it was basically already in; he knew Mick could stall only a little longer for him. 'Maybe less.'

She chuckled softly. 'Well, I don't think either one of us would last walking for an hour.' Then she quickly added, 'The dog or me, I mean.' *She* was blushing, and he couldn't imagine anything nicer.

He smiled at her, and this one came naturally. For the first time since Keppie had died, he didn't have to think about smiling, it just appeared on his face, like a finger-drawing on a mirror can show up days later, just by breathing on it. 'Me either. Me either.' He patted his belly.

They stood there a moment, the little dog looking up at them, one then the other, then she sat, waiting. 'Which way would you recommend for a little stroll, then?' C.C. said finally.

'I'd say left. Definitely left. Right takes you to the train tracks and Mento's cow barns. The cows smell a bit, and might scare little, uh . . .'

'M.J.' She smiled again.

'M.J.' He bent, held his fingers toward the dog. 'Do you know how to shake, little one?' Before he'd said 'little one' M.J. had lifted her paw. Both Purdy and C.C. exclaimed, and Purdy took M.J.'s tiny paw delicately in his two fingers, lightly moving it up and down. 'How dee do, ma'am?' C.C. giggled, and Purdy suddenly felt like spring breezes were chasing round his insides. He held out his hand to her. 'I'm Purdy. Mick Purdy, Senior, but everyone just calls me Purdy.'

She took his hand shyly. 'Well, in that case I'm Caroline Camilla Tucker Prentiss Byrd, but everyone calls me C.C. Pleased to meet you, Purdy.'

Her hand. It was as soft as kid leather. He pointed to the left. 'Shall we, then?'

'Okay, let's go, M.J.!' She said it with such energy that the little dog seemed to startle slightly. Then she took off at a brisk trot. 'Whoa! Keep to a pace we can keep up with, girl!'

They walked in silence for a minute, M.J. weaving back and forth in front of them. Their footsteps made little sound on the dirt road, still just moist enough from yesterday's rains to muffle the sounds, but thankfully not muddy. He put his hands back in his pockets again, hastily stuffing one pocket back in, realizing it had probably come out with the other and just been hanging out this whole time. Like a panting tongue. Embarrassment shot up his back again, prickling his neck and scalp. He was careful not to move his hands in his pockets this time.

'Have you always lived here?' she asked.

Bless her for starting a conversation! 'No, grew up over in Platteville. Lived here nearly forty years now, though.'

'My! That's a long time.'

She'd sounded particularly southern just then. He liked it. 'Yes.'

They walked on, till M.J. stopped determinedly, backtracked a few steps, pulling hard on the twine.

She sniffed at a tuft of grass as if she'd picked up the trail of her long-lost kin. Purdy faced C.C. *Ask her a question about her.* He couldn't think.

He pulled his hands out of his pockets and the linings came out again. This time he immediately pushed them back in. But it flustered him. 'And have you lived long?' He closed his eyes. Stupid! *Stupid!* 'I mean, have you lived where you live, wherever that is, for a long time?' Let's see. He could *try* to act like an idiot. But he doubted it would be any better than he was already doing. 'Easy,' Dr Fitzmarin would say, 'don't beat yourself up.'

She smiled, turned and looked at M.J. 'Well, we're all three, me, Shelly and Meg, from Wisataukee, Iowa.' She looked up at him again, her eyes soft under her long lashes. 'I've been there about twenty-five years,' she added. She gave just the slightest sigh, then pulled gently on the dog's leash, encouraging her to move on. M.J. took the lead again, C.C. followed. Purdy fell in step with her as she continued talking. 'This trip we're on, we're going down south to fix up a house I own there. To sell. It's too big to live in. Just me. Though I used to dream about one day maybe finding a small place in Fleurville – that's the name of the town. I grew up there.'

She paused. He waited. They walked. Finally she said, very softly, 'My husband died a year and a half ago, so . . .'

Purdy closed his eyes briefly, giving thanks not

for another man's death, merely for his absence. He looked at her. 'My wife died last September.'

'Just last September? I'm so sorry. Was it sudden?'

'Yeah. Very. Standing there behind the bar cutting lemons, then the next thing I know, she's on the floor in my arms, grabbing at her shoulder. Then, gone.' He looked at the ground, that black feeling every time he said it, grabbing on to him.

C.C. stopped walking again and turned toward him, placing her fingers on his arm again, like she had yesterday. And just like then, her touch sent a current of warmth through him, gentle and comforting, chasing the black. He stared at her fingers, lovely, pale, plump, her small, carefully filed nails, short but clean, with some kind of very pale pink polish on them. Pretty.

'Heart attack?' she asked. He broke his gaze from her hand to her eyes and nodded, the ache and the warmth in him together now. There was complete recognition and empathy in her eyes. He couldn't tell if he was looking at her eyes, into her eyes, or behind her eyes, or she his. 'That's how my Lenny died,' she said. 'No warning at all.'

'None,' he said.

'Lenny was out jogging,' she told him. 'It was his first day of trying to get into shape. He had some crazy notion of running in a race to celebrate his sixtieth birthday.' She looked at Purdy. 'He was over ten years older than me. Anyway, he was thin as a rail, but he was trying to get in shape and . . .'

Neither of them spoke. M.J. had stopped and was circling around a spot. Finally she lowered herself.

'Oh dear. I don't have a bag,' said C.C. quietly.

'Oh. Well. Uh.' He tried not to look at the dog, but wasn't sure what to do. He looked down the road. 'That's okay. I'll come back here later on and . . . take care of it.'

'That's nice of you. Thank you.'

Great. So far they'd talked about death and dog poop. He knew he should offer his condolences on the loss of her husband, but the dog doing its thing there had derailed the conversation.

'Good girl, M.J.! Here's a little cookie!' C.C. bent and fed the dog what looked to be a little piece of waffle that she'd pulled from her pocket. 'Well, now that she's done her deed, I guess we should turn around,' she said. 'I've got a little packing to do myself before we go.' He nodded. They turned around, C.C. tugging gently on the twine to persuade M.J. to head back.

They walked, and still he couldn't think what to say. All he could think was how remarkable it was that their spouses had both died of heart attacks. And they'd pretty much said all there was to say about that. But he knew his mother would roll over in her grave if he let the moment go without commenting on her loss.

'Ma'am? C.C.?' She looked at him. 'I'm terribly

sorry about your loss.' He suddenly felt his eyes welling up with tears. Of all the dadblummed things! He turned away, breathed the emotion out.

When he looked back, she was still looking at him. 'Me too,' she said simply, not explaining whether it was for her loss or his or both. She didn't have to.

After a few seconds of more silent walking, he asked, 'So are your girlfriends married?' He almost smacked himself in the forehead. 'Not that I'm interested,' he blurted out. He stopped walking, winced, hoped she didn't notice. What a bumbling fool he was! You never get a second chance to make a first impression, his dad used to say. 'I mean . . .'

She smiled. 'Meg's married, but her husband just recently, uh . . . left. Walked out on her. After thirty years of marriage. Just – poof! No goodbye. Just left her a note on the kitchen table.' She shook her head, heaved a sigh, looked at him soberly. 'I've never been all that fond of him. And Shelly? Well, she's terminally single. She *was* married. Twice. And divorced twice. She's been single for about fifteen years now, though. She likes it that way.' C.C. smiled, but looked tired.

'And you? You doing okay?' he asked. 'Single, I mean? I, myself, find it kinda like living in an empty can. Kinda echoy, you know?'

She nodded thoughtfully. 'That's a good way of putting it. I'm okay – now – but, yes, it's kind of echoy. Exactly.' She exhaled. 'It gets better, though, with time. A little better.'

Time. Just what he didn't have. They were in front of the restaurant now. Already. They both stopped. He looked at C.C. She was leaning down to pick up the dog.

What did he know about this woman, other than her husband had died? Nothing. So why did he have the feeling, now more than ever, that they were supposed to be together? But he knew if he said that, it'd be too soon, too sudden. She'd head for the horizon. Well, she was heading for the horizon within the hour anyway. Still, this wasn't the time. He looked toward Mick's shop. He was probably playing solitaire on his computer, the car long since finished.

'Well, I'd better go finish packing.' She smiled back at him again, and he suddenly felt taller and thinner, which nearly made him laugh out loud. 'Bye, now,' she said.

His voice seemed caught again, but in a very different way. He lifted his hand and gave her a small salute. She grinned, then turned and walked toward the motel. He watched her go, tried not to think about how, in the movies, it all came down to whether the girl turned around, looked back. He watched her walk away, watched her put her hand on the doorknob, waited breathlessly as she paused. She slowly turned the knob, stepped inside, and closed the door.

Purdy exhaled, only a little disappointed. Those things in the movies weren't real. Besides, it didn't matter. He was just so pleased with himself for having had the courage to walk with her, to speak with her. If this was all he got with C.C., it was enough. She was a breath of fresh air when his life had felt heavy and stagnant. If the gift that someone gives you is merely to see that there is possibility for you, well, that's still a pretty darn good gift.

He was just about to turn and head back into the restaurant when the door reopened a crack. His ridiculous heart flipped. The crack widened, her face appeared. A smile pulled at every part of his face. She was smiling too, as she lifted the little dog's front paw and very gently touched it to its forehead in a small salute. He laughed out loud, she smiled radiantly, and that dog gave a single, happy bark that, for a second, he thought had come from him.

CHAPTER 6

C.C.

C. closed the door, her head inclined toward it still, after it shut. She couldn't .stop smiling. She turned finally, expecting Meg and Shelly to be right there, grinning, or even laughing at her, in a teasing sort of way. Spying, at least. But they were both at the far end of the room, at the bathroom sink area. Meg was fixing her hair, Shelly putting on some lipstick.

Or they were pretending to. C.C. could see both women's reflections in the wide mirror, and Shelly's big grin was making lipstick application nearly impossible. Meg, however, had a great poker face, and was innocently smoothing her short hair behind one ear.

But it was Meg who finally turned and said, 'Well?'

'Well, what?' said C.C., setting M.J. on the floor in front of the TV. The little dog immediately began a sniffing inventory of the orange shag carpeting.

Shelly was warily eyeing the dog. 'She wouldn't pee and poop *again*, right?' C.C. caught Shelly catching herself, the furtive glance toward the window. C.C. turned, looked at the window, saw the curtain pulled to the side, and realized they *had* been watching her. Like little weasels they had obviously scurried to the mirror together so as not to get caught in the act.

'Well, actually, she didn't do either outside.' Two can play at this game, thought C.C., adopting an expression of pure innocence. Shelly eyed her.

'Did you have a nice walk?' Meg asked.

'Yes. Thank you.' C.C. busied herself putting a sweater and her nightgown into her suitcase, open on the bed.

'*Well?*' said Shelly.

'Well, what?' C.C. said, not even looking up, enjoying the moment. She tucked the sweater in, using her fingers to get it just right. Then she lifted the suitcase top over, brought it edge to edge, slowly zippered it shut.

'Oh, come on, Ceece!' whined Shelly. 'We want details! We saw him walking with you. What'd he say?'

She faced the two of them, her fingertips on her chest. '*What?* You two were *spying* on me? I'm shocked!' She held in a giddy laugh.

'Well . . . yes?' said Meg, looking genuinely sheepish.

'Hell, yeah!' said Shelly, proudly.

C.C. couldn't keep up her act, nor could she deny the smile that had been a force unto itself since she'd come back in the room. She'd have been surprised, and maybe even hurt, if they *hadn't* spied on her. She stepped toward them exuber-antly. 'Well, y'all remember when we were talking last week, how we all felt like teenagers, going on this big adventure, so much unknown in our lives?' They nodded, Meg pulling C.C. by the hand to the near bed. They all three tumbled onto the unmade bed, arranging themselves in the standard, juicy-details triangle born of long friendship.

'Well, it's like Aunt Georgie told me after the car accident. "Hon," she said, "your teenage years are pretty much a puzzle to begin with, and you maybe have some of the edges put together, a few pieces in the middle. Then, a tragedy like this happens and it's like a big wind blowing 'em all to Kingdom Come. And when all those pieces drift back down, it takes a while to find them. Then another while to put 'em back together again. And sometimes the picture's a little different. Parts that you were sure were sky, suddenly seem to be ocean. But no matter what, it's your puzzle. Your picture."'

C.C. smiled, remembering how often Aunt Georgie would talk in metaphors of painting or art. But she saw Shelly looking impatient. C.C. knew she had a tendency to go on a mite long with her stories, especially about her southern past, so she tried to speed it up. 'Well, she was really right about that, let me tell you. And I never really imagined my life being blown up a second time. But of course, it was. A bunch more times! There was Billy.' Oh, she could go on about that! But she gulped a breath and went on. 'Then having Kathryn so young, and alone and all . . .' Shelly was circling her finger through the air, hurrying her along, which irritated C.C., but she pressed on. 'Anyway, then when I met and married Lenny, and he took Kathryn on like his own flesh-and-blood daughter, and he was so good . . .' C.C. stopped, looked at them both. 'You know what I used to call him? Lenny?'

They nodded, said in unison, 'Yes, your Steady Eddy.'

C.C. smiled. 'Yeah. I mean, to another woman he might have seemed pretty boring. But to me, he was just pure golden goodness.' She laughed. 'Well, most of the time. We had our little spats.'

M.J. pawed gently at her leg, whining.

'For God's sakes, woman!' Shelly yelled. 'Even the dog wants you to get to the point! Your walk? This morning?'

C.C. laughed, bent and picked M.J. up, settled her on her lap, stroking her palm over the dog's bony back. She remembered her point. 'Well, I guess it's that I feel like a teenager again, in more ways than just going on this trip. This thing with Purdy, I didn't believe it at first, just plum didn't believe it. But I can tell you it's . . . *fun*.' She whispered the last word. 'It makes me feel, I don't know, I guess, alive in a whole new way.' She laughed. 'Or whole *old* way! But I assure you, girls, this is just harmless, a passing fancy. As in, just passing through.' She ran her hand in front of her, then off toward the horizon.

'Did you kiss him?' asked Shelly.

'Of course not! We only just met!' C.C. said, indignant. But then she smiled, pleased that Shelly thought it *could* have happened. 'Purdy is a complete gentleman. And a little shy, I think. Besides, you saw pretty much everything, did you not?' She gestured toward the window. Shelly winked, nodded. But Meg's cheeks pinked, and she stood, began making the bed.

'Meg!' said Shelly. 'What are you doing?'

Meg stopped, the sheet still clutched in both hands.

'They have maids for that,' said Shelly. C.C. wondered if that was true. She bet Purdy did it himself. 'Besides,' continued Shelly, 'they'll just strip the sheets off, y'know.' She pulled her toiletries bag from her suitcase and walked to the sink area and began to gather the unused soap and small bottles of shampoo and lotion, tucking them into her bag.

Meg stared blankly at the headboard, still holding the sheet.

C.C. put M.J. on the floor, stepped next to Meg and put her arm around her thin, hunched shoulders. Poor Meg. She seemed so lost without her routines, her structured life. Her structured home. Her structured classroom. Her structured marriage. And there wasn't one little bitty wisp of her old life left. Except for them.

Meg slowly pulled the sheet back, stripping the bed. C.C. watched as she made a neat pile of the linens on the mattress. She folded both the blanket and bedspread into equal-sized squares, placed them on the chair. She then headed to the second bed.

C.C. dragged her suitcase off, getting out of her way. As Meg pulled the pillows out of their cases, and Shelly tucked her bulging toiletries bag into her suitcase, C.C. wondered how the mood had changed so suddenly. Something about mentioning being a teenager, she thought. She decided a few more details from her walk were in order.

'So, anyway, Purdy is . . . nice,' continued C.C., 'and, well . . .' She put her hands on her large hips, cocked her head to one side, contemplating that which was Purdy: 'Well, I think he's just shy. And his wife died, very recently. *Of a heart attack.*' She looked knowingly at the other two. 'He seems very sweet . . .' She picked up her jacket from the chair and laid it neatly over her suitcase on the floor. 'He's older than me.' She laughed suddenly. 'He kept putting his hands in his pockets, then taking them out again and the pockets kept flopping out.' She felt herself go briefly to a dreamy, distant place, then she abruptly brought herself back. 'But, I mean, *really.* I'm not at all interested. What's the point? Mick should have the car ready in a matter of minutes now. And then,' she snapped her fingers and flung her arm outward, a more dramatic version of the gesture she'd done before. 'We're off! Gone! Byebye, apple pie! Besides, he's not my type. He's very different from Lenny. Umm, physically. And in what he does for a living. He's not my type.'

Shelly, looking incredulous, said loudly, 'What the hell does that mean? It's not like there's only one type of guy for you. For crying out loud! Do you like just one . . . outfit?' C.C. grinned as Shelly stared at her, in her velour pantsuit. 'Or . . . or one flavor of *ice cream*?'

Meg laughed lightly, shaking her head at Shelly. C.C. was delighted by Meg's smile, on two counts: lately, any smile from Meg was to be celebrated; and, it demonstrated yet again that Meg and C.C. were the kind of friends who committed each other's loyal preferences to memory. Shelly didn't commit her own preferences to memory. She said her tastes changed with her hormone fluctuations so sometimes she liked pumpkin ice cream best. Other times mocha cappuccino with fudge chunks. Still others, she was a sucker for rainbow sherbet. Meg and C.C. knew this about her.

Meg looked at Shelly. 'Yes. She *does* only like one flavor. She always, *always* orders pralines and cream. Don't you know that by now?'

Shelly looked stunned. She glanced between the two. 'So, what if they don't have pralines and cream?'

'Then she orders –' Meg looked at C.C. – '*butter pecan*,' they said in unison. C.C., her unrestrained southern accent in full swing again, added, 'And then, mah deah, if they don't have butt-ah-*pee*-can, ah ordah vanilla, with caramel sauce and a heapin' dose a—'

A knock at the door interrupted her. C.C. jumped, her heart pounding. M.J. gave a short bark and ran to the door, ears up, tail high, her body vibrating. C.C. looked at the others. They each smiled reassuringly, Shelly making a 'go on' flick with her hand. C.C. scooped M.J. up, held her close. She wondered if the little dog could feel her heart thumping in her chest. She kissed the top of M.J.'s head, took a deep breath. She put her hand on the doorknob, suddenly feeling as if breathing was something she had to think about in order to do. She thought to check her hair, but the only mirror was behind her, and Meg and Shelly would give her no end of grief. Slowly, she opened the door. Outside, Mick stood, hat off, held against his chest again. C.C. felt her shoulders cave just a little, but she couldn't help but think: this boy was raised right.

'Ma'am.' He nodded in greeting, repeating ma'am and nodding again as Meg joined C.C. at the door. 'You're all set to go, ladies. Just come on over when you're ready, and we'll get you right out on the road again.'

'Thank you, Mick,' said Meg. After another 'ma'am' and nod to each of them, Mick pulled his cap on, then turned and ambled back toward his shop.

'Finally!' said Shelly. She started singing 'On the Road Again', loudly and off-key. M.J., still in C.C.'s arms, raised her little snout in the air and started barking.

'Stop! Stop!' said C.C., laughing, gently holding M.J.'s snout, then letting go and admonishing both the dog and Shelly: 'Saints preserve! You two make *some* choir.' M.J. licked furiously at C.C.'s neck, making C.C. shriek with laughter. Suddenly she stopped laughing. Feeling panicked, she thrust M.J. into Meg's arms. 'Here, hold her, please. I gotta pee!' She ran to the bathroom, lunged inside, slamming the door, barely making it in time.

Sitting in the small, dark room, she shook her head. She probably needed to see a doctor about this. She'd been putting it off for months. It was bad enough going for her 'annual indignity', as she referred to her yearly gynecological exam. She was holding out to do it all at once, and she always scheduled her annual appointment for just after her birthday, in September. Come to think of it, had she had a check-up last year? Or the year before?

There was a gentle knock on the door. 'You okay in there?' Meg words were somewhat muffled by the thick door.

'Yeah! Just the usual problem,' she shouted back. 'That's what comes from having a big baby. And middle age. No going back from either!'

A few minutes later C.C. emerged, washed her hands at the sink. Over the running water she could hear the TV, the SavR King jingle pulsing through the room. C.C. put her hand on the counter, steadying herself, thinking of Kathryn. She felt near tears again. The sounds of a newscast saved her.

'C.C.!' yelled Shelly. 'C'mere! Hurry! We're going to be on the news! Mick phoned while you were peeing, said to turn on channel five.'

They were sitting on the ends of the stripped beds, watching, M.J. in Meg's lap. C.C. sat next to her and M.J. immediately crawled into her lap. C.C. and Meg exchanged quick smiles, an unspoken acknowledgement that M.J. was hook, line and sinker in love with C.C. They turned their attention back to the TV.

A blonde anchorwoman, looking like News Barbie, in a bright, lime-green suit with a large, even brighter and limier rosette on the lapel was speaking. C.C. surmised that it was the local news from Chicago, which she thought was probably as local as Tupper got. Suddenly the newscaster's words grabbed her full attention. '. . . little dog who escaped from her kennel from Quad City Airport and has been on the lam—' Here she turned to her co-anchor, a nicely coiffed man who, C.C. thought, happened to look vaguely like a Ken doll. 'Can a dog be on the *lamb*?' Barbie asked Ken. They each gave a hahaha canned laugh. 'But now, happy day! This is no April Fool joke: we're thrilled to report to all you dog lovers who have been calling in, that little . . .' She started to smile, then giggle. 'Okay. I'm not even going to try that registered name. Anyway, the dog,

M.J. they call her, has finally been found, and will soon be on her way home to Kentucky. And she won't have to fly, thanks to several good Samaritans. Right after this broadcast, I'll be going out myself, to the small town of Tupper, to interview the senior citizens who are on a road trip south, and who have agreed to take the dog back to her home.'

Shelly squawked loudly as she stood, arms akimbo. 'Who is that bitch calling *senior fucking citizens*?' Meg and C.C. both shushed her, but Shelly continued to mutter, just barely under her breath, as the newswoman continued.

'I'll bring you that story today, at *News At Noon* with Marcia and Ralph. I know our viewers will want to tune in for that! This has been quite the story we've been following with this little doggie, hasn't it, Ralph?'

'You bet, Marcia! The whole *country* has been worrying about this little dog.'

Marcia looked into the camera, a big smile directed to her viewers. 'If you've just tuned in, our breaking story this morning is that little M.J., the missing Italian Greyhound, has been found, safe and sound, and is going home to –' she glanced down at her papers – 'her owner, Candy Suddle of Lexington, Kentucky.' She turned again toward Ralph. 'We just love happy endings around here, don't we, Ralph?'

'Yes, indeedy!' said Ralph, looking like he couldn't wait for the happy ending to this newscast.

Ralph moved on to other local news and Shelly

clicked off the TV with the remote. 'Shit. I don't want to be interviewed! TV adds ten pounds! Besides, I don't want to give that little green witch the satisfaction of getting the story. Senior citizens, my ass!' She stepped to the window, peeking nervously, keeping herself hidden behind the curtain. 'Let's get the hell outta here!' she said as if she'd seen gunfighters gathering out front.

'Well, I'm sure the senior citizen thing was just a miscommunication,' Meg said. 'Maybe that Kirby guy said it. Regardless, I'm all for getting out of here. I sure don't want to be on TV. C.C.?'

C.C. couldn't respond, couldn't move. Tears were suddenly rolling down her cheeks. Just when she'd thought she'd gotten past unexpected crying jags, just when she'd thought she'd closed the door yet again on the deep well of grief in her life, here it was again. But these tears weren't for Lenny. Or even Kathryn or Lucy.

'*Hey!* Hey, there,' said Shelly, striding back toward where the other two still sat on the end of the bed. Meg put her arm around C.C. Shelly squatted in front of her, her hand on C.C.'s knee.

'Ceece?' said Meg. A small whimpering cry slipped out of C.C.; she placed her wet cheek on M.J.'s neck, wetting her fur with tears.

'Is this about her calling us senior citizens?' asked Shelly, the anger rising in her voice again.

C.C. laughed, then sniffed. 'No. I don't care about that. I just, well – I realized that we're going to have to . . . *give M.J. back*.' She shook her head miserably. 'I already love this little dog so much.' She rubbed her wet cheek against the top of M.J.'s head. 'It's like I had a little Italian Greyhound-size hole in my life, and I didn't even know it, but she just jumped in and filled it.' C.C. wiped her sleeve across her eyes. 'Like a puzzle piece,' she said, her voice breaking. She took the tissue Meg handed her, wiped her eyes, dabbed at her nose, and looked up at her friends. 'You know?'

Both women nodded. 'Dogs are sneaky, that way,' said Shelly. 'You give them an inch of your love, they'll take a mile.' She rubbed a finger behind M.J.'s ear.

'I hate to rush you when you're feeling low, honey,' said Meg, 'but speaking of miles, I'd like to put as many as possible between us and that TV crew. You okay to get in the car?'

C.C. nodded. 'But I don't want to see Purdy! I'm all – *puffy*! And I'd start crying again and he'd get the wrong idea, and, *oh*! Why is life so complicated?'

Meg stood. 'Don't worry. I'll give him your goodbyes, and settle up the bills.' She grabbed her purse off the desk as she strode across the room, then disappeared out the door.

Shelly gently lifted C.C. by the elbow. 'C'mon, Puffy. We'll take our things out and load up.' C.C. stood, and Shelly grinned at her, rubbing her palms together. 'Come on. Isn't this a *little* fun? It's like a James Bond movie or something. We gotta make a quick getaway before Prissy Galore arrives, a.k.a. Miss Malevolent Marcia.' She cackled. C.C. shook her head, but smiled. Shelly punched her lightly in the arm. 'Ready, Agent Puffy, and her trusty sidekick, M.J.?'

C.C. inhaled deeply, boosted M.J. up in her arms, squared her shoulders, and said, 'Ready.'

Shelly had insisted on loading all the luggage while C.C. sat in the car with the dog. 'You keep M.J. safe and sound in there, and that way you'll also avoid any goodbye scenes with Purdy.' C.C. gratefully slumped down in the back seat, out of view, but none the less feeling at a loss. She *would* have said goodbye to him – wanted to, in fact. If only she hadn't been crying, and gotten all red-eyed and swollen. She would have liked to thank him personally for all his kindnesses. She had imagined maybe even giving him a hug.

But no. She shook her head, telling M.J., 'It's just as well we're in here. He might have gotten the wrong idea.' Men often got the wrong idea about hugs. But she didn't think Purdy would be like that.

Suddenly both front car doors flew open, Shelly on the driver's side and Meg the other, hurling themselves into their seats. 'Hurry! Hurry!' shouted Meg, wrestling with her seat belt. Shelly wasn't taking the time to buckle up, simply started the car, revved the engine once, then threw it into gear and floored the gas pedal, throwing C.C. into the back of the seat, M.J. into C.C. C.C. clawed at her seat belt, but suddenly the centrifugal force of the car careening across the road and turning around, made her instead grab on to the door arm rest and M.J., and hold on for dear life. Meg was dissolved in nervous laughter up front.

'What's going on?' C.C. glanced frantically out every window. 'Is the TV crew here?' They drove past Mick and Kirby, the latter dressed in an ill-fitting suit coat, his hair greased back, small tooth marks from a comb still evident. Kirby turned away from Mick, waved his arm over his head at something in the opposite direction, then pointed toward the women's speedily retreating car. Mick was pushing roughly at Kirby's arm, but Kirby kept waving and shouting and pointing. Finally, Mick pulled his arm down and grabbed a fistful of his shirt and they tussled, till Kirby broke away, running north, heading toward a white SUV with a big dish on the top, a trail of dust behind it.

'It's them!' C.C. shouted, just as Shelly turned the car south, heading toward the interstate.

C.C. breathed a sigh of relief as the SUV turned west, into Tupper, apparently none the wiser from Kirby's efforts. M.J. jumped up, her front paws on the top of the back seat, looking out the back window, now that they weren't careening around or peeling out, just steadily gaining speed to merge onto the interstate. She didn't bark, her tail wasn't wagging, and she wasn't trembling; she appeared just to be watching the retreating scene. C.C. watched too. Kirby was still jogging toward the SUV, with Mick running after him. But something caught C.C.'s eye, the other direction. In front of the restaurant. Purdy. He wore a full, white apron. Maybe he had been cooking lunch, C.C. thought. His arms hung by his sides, his white bar towel hung limply from his left hand as he watched their car drive off.

C.C. lifted her hand, waved. But as she did, Purdy turned, draped the towel over his right shoulder, and walked slowly into the restaurant.

'Whoa! *Big* bump!' Shelly yelled, swerving but not in time. The car bounced mightily over where the asphalt had heaved, making M.J. momentarily airborne. Even C.C. felt the jolt lift all of her, briefly, an absence of gravity for a fraction of a second, like an astronaut, untethered, unmoored. Both she and the dog landed roughly back on the seat. And suddenly C.C. felt the opposite of weightless. She watched the spot where Purdy had been, till Tupper itself disappeared from view. She gathered M.J. into her arms and turned back around in her seat as they merged into the morning rush hour on the interstate, feeling like she, too, had disappeared.

CHAPTER 7

KATHRYN

Kathryn grabbed the phone and angrily punched the intercom, for the second time in as many minutes. She took a deep breath, held the handset to her mouth, earpiece down, and said, 'Can we have another checker up front, please? *Now*?'

She knew she had not succeeded in keeping the irritation out of her voice. She would no doubt be 'having a little chat' with Mr Knelbrecht again about the importance of intercom etiquette, which he infuriatingly pronounced 'eti-kwett'. Chat, my ass, she thought, grabbing a stack of Lean Cuisines from the carry-basket, sliding them over the scanner one at a time. As she reached for the bag of apples, she looked up to see if any of the other checkers were coming. But all she saw was her line of angry customers. Only old Mrs B. smiled at her. Kathryn glanced at lane six, the only other one open. Marianne had just three people waiting in her line, but each had large carts, all very full. As Kathryn continued to scan items, she noted that all three of Marianne's customers were moms with toddlers and/or babies in the front, bulbous legs dangling through the leg holes of the cart, chubby hands idly playing with keys or a pack of gum, while Mom flipped through a gossip rag for a few minutes of escape. Marianne was smiling and chatting with two of the women. The stay-at-home moms were almost always nice. They were rarely in a hurry.

She mechanically but speedily grabbed and scanned items. She knew it made sense for her to be in lane one; she was head clerk, the most experienced and fastest. But she hated the express lane. The endless queue of people with their overbooked calendars invariably blamed her for their lateness and stress, no matter how fast she was. She was beyond tired of their impatience, their lack of even minimal courtesy, and especially their creative math when it came to fifteen items or fewer. 'Oh, sorry. I counted the apples, oranges and pears as one item because they're all fruit.' Or, even worse, the petulant: 'So, I'm a couple of items over. Sue me.'

She passed through a can of frozen orange juice, but it wouldn't scan. She ran it again. Still no ding. She moved her thumb over the bar code, clearing the frost from it. She felt, then saw, a thin line of hardened juice on the bar code: another container had leaked in the freezer case. She used her nametag, with its decade-of-service gold star, to scrape it off. She hated the star; to her, it felt like a tick, latched on up there, sucking the life out of her. She'd been working here since high school. Living here, since high school. Dying here, since high school. She'd imagined so much more for herself.

Her hand closed tightly around the can. She felt the blood surge up from her swollen feet, anger rising through her like a deep-sea diver coming up too fast, knowing it was certain death, but the need for air too great. A young man wearing a too-small business suit stood in the middle of her line, checking his watch, scowling.

Where was Tom? Or Shirley? Or Ting? Or Mr Fucking Knelbrecht? Was this some kind of April Fool joke? But she knew it wasn't. It was business as usual.

Kathryn froze, closed her eyes, orange juice in hand. She wanted so much to hurl the can. She imagined it, spiraling upward, breaking through the narrow horizontal windows above the high shelves of charcoal briquettes, stacked above the bags of de-icer. Barbecuing season still seemed a long way off, but the de-icer hadn't been needed for a while either. It wasn't winter, but it sure as hell wasn't spring yet in northern Iowa. The sun was shining only anemically today. Kathryn knew more snow would come before spring truly arrived. 'Betwixt and between,' her mother would say. 'You're just betwixt and between, honey. Wait a spell. Something'll shove you one way or the other.'

Kathryn tried scanning the juice again, to no avail. She began punching in the numbers from the bar code, but found that her star had scratched through two of them. She pressed the intercom code again. 'Price check on one.' She kept her finger on the button, toying with the idea of announcing, 'Naked woman on one.' That would get Matt and Mr Knelbrecht, and the guys from the back, running up for sure. Tom would emerge from his break only if she said 'Naked guy on one,' and then he'd try to saunter by inconspicuously. She put the juice aside and returned to the basket, picking up item after item, not looking, not counting, not caring that this woman probably had thirty items in her basket.

Betwixt and between. *Ding.* Her mother. *Ding.* Just thinking of her made her blood boil anew. *Ding.* What she'd done was unforgivable. *Ding.* Kathryn was already pissed at her for just planning the trip, let alone actually going on it. *Ding.* *Ding.* Didn't she realize how much Lucy would miss her? She wasn't thinking about anyone but herself. *Ding.* Even when she'd shown that damn picture to those men in the restaurant, she'd been thinking about herself. *Ding.* Another example of C.C. Byrd dealing with that one messy corner left in her life: the embarrassing unmarried daughter situation.

Matt arrived just as she scanned the last item. Finally. Kathryn held up the juice, he nodded, ran to get another. Good kid. She sacked the woman's groceries, then reached under the counter and grabbed the paper towel and Windex.

She angrily scrubbed the scanner while she waited for Matt.

It didn't seem right, her almost-fifty-year-old mom taking off on a road trip, like a college kid. And here *she* was, working overtime at the SavR King. Being the responsible one. One irresponsible moment with that handsome blackjack dealer in Las Vegas had determined a level of responsibility for her that would last her lifetime. She adored Lucy, and would do anything for her. But she battled the persistent feeling that doing anything for herself was at odds with doing something for her daughter. Not to mention what she made her daughter do. Lucy had tearfully begged yet again this morning not to be made to go to school. Pretty tough to take from a second grader.

She leaned on the intercom button again, knowing it would be more productive to try to get a response from deep space. 'Checker needed up front, *please*.' Was Matt squeezing the damn oranges to get the juice?

Standing there at register one, under the sign that, this morning, falsely advertised 'EXPRESS', Kathryn picked up the scratched can of juice. She closed her eyes, felt her fingers clenching around the can.

'Kathy, honey? Are you okay?'

Kathryn opened her eyes. It was Mrs B. Sweet old Mrs Benettucci, standing there, still holding her basket, with maybe five items, but starting to sag under its weight. Kathryn reached over and took her basket. 'Here, Mrs B., let's set that up here.'

She turned to the woman waiting to pay. 'Free juice today,' she said, tossing the scratched can into her bag, smiling, punching the total key. The woman looked only mildly placated as she swiped her credit card. Kathyrn handed her the long receipt, far too long to be under fifteen items. 'Have a good day,' Kathryn told her. The woman silently took her receipt and left.

Mrs B. shuffled to the check-writing platform; it came only to her chest. She placed her knobby hands on top.

'How are you today, Mrs B.?' Kathryn asked, punching the numbers into her keypad so Mrs B. could swipe her SavR King Valued Customer card. As the old woman worked at threading her card into the slot with her trembling hand (Kathryn knew she liked to do it herself, and if anyone was to be indulged, it was Mrs B.), Kathryn smiled, looking at the top of Mrs B.'s head. She knew from long experience that Mrs B. had twenty-two silver bobby pins holding her eleven gray pin curls in place, her head a neat pattern of Xs so she could look nice for someplace other than the grocery store.

'Oh, can't complain,' she said. They smiled at each other, an unspoken acknowledgement that Mrs B. had a lot she could complain about, but rarely did. Kathryn quickly scanned a small box of fiber cereal, two bananas, a small drum of old-fashioned oatmeal, a quart of milk and a tube of arthritis ointment. Mrs B. had pen in hand, poised above her checkbook, waiting to dole out a quarter of her weekly budget for, basically, breakfast. Kathryn wondered if Mrs B. ate cereal for two, if not three meals a day.

She looked at Mrs B., then suddenly was aware that only one very irritated man remained in her line, the guy in the ill-fitting suit. He was watching the remainder of her line following Ting toward register six, like little goslings with grocery baskets over their wings, following the goose. Ting, about as high as she was round, even waddled like a goose.

'Oh, and this please,' said Mrs B., after she'd checked the total on the screen. She handed Kathryn a small tin of mints.

'Sure,' said Kathryn. 'Do you want it in your bag or your purse?'

'Bag, please,' she said to both Kathryn and Matt, who was now standing at the end of her counter.

'Sorry,' said Matt, almost breathless. 'We're, like, completely out of that kind of juice, so I went to the back to check and they spilled, like, a whole box of cabbages back there.' He grinned. 'They're rolling all over the place. Tom's back there imitating Knelbrecht, saying, "Heads will roll for this!"' Kathryn thought Matt had a great laugh.

She smiled at him. 'No problem. But in the future, if the item's not up front, just come tell me right away, please.'

129

He nodded, then tucked the mints into one of Mrs B.'s two canvas bags. Kathryn made a mental note to thank him for remembering to use both of Mrs B.'s bags, even for just the few items. Mrs B. walked and bused everywhere, therefore liked the weight split between two bags. Plus, Kathryn knew, she liked getting double bag credit.

She took Mrs B.'s proffered check, stamped it, opened the register, slipped it under the drawer, and removed a dime. She placed the coin carefully in Mrs B.'s soft, wrinkly palm. 'Here's your bag credit, Mrs B. Don't spend it all in one place.'

Mrs B. chuckled, and Kathryn fed on it like a transfusion. She knew it wouldn't cure her disease, but it might help her survive one more day.

CHAPTER 8

MEG

'Y'all better pull over soon, Shel.'

Meg heard C.C.'s voice, understood her words, but they sounded hollow, as if they were coming from the far end of a tunnel. Lulled by movement and the low and steady drone of the motor, she'd fallen into a deep car-sleep; emerging was like swimming up to an unseeable surface. She wondered how long she'd been asleep.

'There's a lot of traffic right here. I'll pull off at the next exit.' Shelly's voice too sounded distant, boxed in. Meg blinked, started to lift her head, felt a sharp pain in the side of her neck. She licked her dry lips, groggily remembered C.C. announcing several miles ago that M.J. had woken up and might need to pee. But Meg had drifted right back into a sleep that felt deeper than she'd had in weeks. With her head resting against her wadded-up sweater on the window, her neck felt like it had petrified at that angle. She massaged it with one hand, rubbed her eyes with the other, finally coming out of her stupor. A loud, sharp bark made her jump, sending a shooting pain down her neck.

M.J.'s bark was surprisingly deep, given her small

size. Meg gingerly turned around in her seat. M.J. barked again, staring directly at her. There was an unmistakable look of urgency in the dog's eyes. She remembered the same look in Buster's eyes when he would stand by the back door, waiting to be let out. He never barked, though they'd wished he would. Meg had tried to teach him to bark, to *complain*, because too often she would come from another room to find him standing silently by the front door, waiting patiently, looking absolutely pained, and she would have no idea how long the poor dog had been suffering silently. Sometimes she would just get a feeling, maybe noting his absence for a while. She'd often find him leaning on the door, looking like he'd give anything for the power of speech at that moment. Or opposable thumbs. After a while, he learned to come find them, then just her. Grant, whether watching TV or reading a book, would be so absorbed he would rarely notice the dog's urgent stares. So he'd find Meg, home his big brown eyes in on her.

Buster. Meg closed her eyes again, a small moan escaping as she pictured not their old lovable, floppy-eared shepherd mix, but instead his urn. She had initially set it on the mantel, thinking: that's where urns go. But unbeknownst to her, days before the trip, Grant had moved it. Merely moved it. She'd thought he'd taken it.

For three days, Meg had believed Grant's note: that he was going to Lake Louise to sprinkle

Buster's ashes. She had been hurt and angry that he would do such a meaningful and important ritual without her. But she had not suspected more to his unannounced departure. It was only on the third day that she found Buster's urn. It was completely full, tucked behind the curtain on the wide, low windowsill of the living room. It was as if Grant had said his own final goodbye to the dog by placing the urn where Buster had so often sat in life: at the window, watching the squirrels cavort across the hillside and into the woods. Panicked at what her bones already knew, Meg had searched the house, found all the wrong things missing: Grant's camera equipment, his laptop, his box of old manuscript starts from college. His baseball cards. The photos of the kids from his dresser. Left behind were his Fighting Cougars mug from work, the Cougar book ends – a gift on his retirement – many of his clothes, all of his ties, and his briefcase. Their wedding photo remained on his dresser.

Although Meg had tried to rationalize all this – Well, he's just gone off to do some photography, some writing, she thought, even though he'd never actually done that before, just talked about it – after finding the urn, there was a foreboding inside her for the rest of that day, one that grew all night, like a tsunami slowly rolling in from another continent, not knowing when it would crash over her. It had kept her awake all night.

The next morning Meg wandered in her thin,

blue robe, no slippers on her cold feet, through the quiet house, clutching her robe closed with one hand, checking all the spots where the missing items should be. Only hours later, when, sobbing again, she'd picked up Buster's urn, cradling it in her arms, had she seen the other note. He'd anchored it – or hidden it – under the urn. It only confirmed what her heart already knew.

> Meg, I've left. I had to. I'm doing this for both of us. All the bits of glue that were keeping us together are gone. I think we both know that. I have needs I can no longer deny. I've ignored my own dreams and aspirations for too long. Maybe you'll find a dream of your own.
> I'll write when I land somewhere. Take care.
> Grant

His words ate at her like parasites, from the inside out. Who was he to say she didn't have a dream? Hadn't she already *achieved* that dream? Of raising a family, meaningful work, a life-long marriage? It was his note that had ended her dream.

A car honked. Meg blinked, that amorphous pain in her torso again. She couldn't even tell exactly where it was. Maybe that's what a broken heart felt like, when it spilled over inside you. She stared at the traffic zooming along the lanes of interstate.

'I am not kiddin', Shell!' said C.C. 'She's going t'pee on me! She won't even eat a cookie.' Meg looked back and saw C.C. offering the dog a piece of Nilla Wafer, saying, 'Cookie? Cookie, girl?' but M.J. turned her head.

'All right, all right. I'm working on it! Hang on,' said Shelly. She made a hissing sound as she frantically scanned the heavy traffic. She flipped on the turn indicator. 'C'mon, somebody let me in!'

Shelly made her way, at seventy miles an hour, across one of the lanes. The dog was whining in the back seat, punctuated by nervous noises from C.C.

Meg rubbed her face vigorously, sat up, rubbed and stretched her neck till it was moveable again, then helped Shelly watch for holes in the traffic that they might dart into.

'Maybe after this green car, get ready . . . No! Wait! That van is changing lanes.'

'Nice signal, asshole,' Shelly said to the van as it flew by.

Meg felt displaced and disheartened. A passenger in her own little car, far from home in every sense, she was just so much flotsam being carried along this anonymous highway, and her suddenly anonymous life. That tsunami had hit, swept through her life, her home, shot her over the edge, a crushing, noisy waterfall, dropping her here. A passenger, in her car, and in her life.

Another horn blared. Cars of every color and shape whizzed by, passing the slow ones doing the speed limit. Why was everyone in such a hellfire hurry? What, exactly, were they rushing to with such life-threatening speed? Did they even know? Meg wondered. Did she?

'I swear, girls! If we don't get this dog outta this car, and soon, we are gonna have a little sea of dog pee back here!' Meg looked back, saw C.C. trying to carefully ease her coat under M.J., over her lap, just in case.

'*Shit!*' said Shelly, scanning and twisting back, then forward. 'Come on! *Somebody* let me in! Please? *Damn!* Okay, if you want to play hard-ball . . .' She pulled on the emergency flashers. Nervously monitoring traffic both in front and behind, she cried, 'Meg, roll down your window and point! I'm going to have to just go for it!'

Meg stared at her briefly, then, like an automaton, rolled down her window. The wind made her eyes water as it whipped into the car. She waved at the driver coming up, mouthed 'Emergency' and pointed. Amazingly, the driver slowed. Shelly veered into the gap, then kept on going. Meg screamed as they cut off a huge pickup truck, his horn blasting. M.J. started barking in the back seat.

'Coming through! Dog pee-pee emergency! *Sorry!*' yelled Shelly, veering across lanes. The pickup truck driver shot Meg the finger. She pulled herself back into the car, rolled up her window, holding her back tightly against the seat. Finally Shelly got the car to the wide shoulder of the highway, braking slowly at first, then very firmly. Meg felt squeezed by her seat belt.

'Jesus, Mary and Joseph!' cried C.C. Meg clicked her seat belt release and was out of the car before it had come to a complete stop. She pulled open C.C.'s door. She grasped M.J.'s narrow sides, lowered her to the asphalt. She wasn't sure the dog's toenails had even touched down before the relief finally flowed into M.J.'s eyes, and a yellow rivulet twined along the asphalt.

'Thank you, Jesus! In the nick of time!' C.C.'s hands were on her heaving chest as she sat in the car. 'Better tie this on her again.'

She thrust the twine toward Meg. Meg untangled it, made a slipknot, and placed the loop over M.J.'s needle-nose and small head, remembering again that they needed to get her a proper leash and collar. But maybe not. They'd made good time. They'd likely be dropping her off later today. And the dog didn't seem to mind the twine at the moment. Though Meg thought she probably wouldn't mind an inverted spike collar, at the moment.

'Wow. She has a big bladder for such a little dog,' said Shelly, who had appeared by Meg's side. 'Boy. Look at her go.'

M.J.'s eyes were glassy and fixed. Meg tried not to look below, but found herself mesmerized by the pee moving across the asphalt. It was meandering down the slight grade, toward a dry ditch on the side of the road. C.C. was waiting, still sitting on the end of the car seat, door open, her spiky heels hooked on the edge of the car frame, staring at M.J., directly at her feet.

'Girls?' said C.C., her voice small and pained. Meg moved her entranced gaze to C.C., 'I have to go too.'

Shelly carefully stepped to the other side of M.J., and held her hand out to C.C. 'Here honey, just step over. We'll go together.'

C.C. withheld her hand. '*Go where?*' she said, looking on the verge of tears.

Oh, no, thought Meg. She closed her eyes. It was one of the first personal things she'd learned about C.C., way back on the morning that first photo of them had been taken. Toward the end of their hike that day, they'd all had to go to the bathroom. To Shelly and Meg's shock and disbelief, C.C. had never, and she swore *would never*, pee '*au naturel*'. Shelly and Meg had both found private spots in the woods, but they'd then had to hustle back with C.C. so she could use 'proper facilities'. No doubt, Shelly did not remember this important fact about C.C.

'Ohhhhh,' C.C. moaned.

M.J. was finished, but she didn't move. Meg picked her up and held her.

'Into the woods,' said Shelly. 'We'll go far in, so it'll be completely private. C'mon.'

C.C. shook her head. 'I can't. I never . . . I don't—' She looked up at Shelly, then Meg. 'I can't.'

'Oh, come on, C.C.!' said Shelly. 'If ya gotta go, you gotta go.' Shelly snapped her fingers impatiently, still waiting to help C.C. out of the car. 'C'mon, let's go! I'll help you. No options here, babe. This is your path, your destiny.'

Meg smiled, thinking Shelly was brilliant.

'Ohhh,' C.C. moaned again, not looking at her, but finally giving Shelly her hand. M.J. squirmed in Meg's arms to get to C.C., but Meg held her firmly.

Shelly pulled C.C. by the hand and they squeezed past Meg and M.J., then past the rear of the car. C.C. walked along the asphalt in her high heels, keeping her legs so squeezed together that she looked like an upside down bowling pin.

'Um, it's a little steep to cross right here,' said Shelly, stopping.

'How 'bout up there? By that sign,' called Meg. She pointed ahead a dozen yards, to a 'No Littering' sign.

'Ohhh,' moaned C.C., her misery clearly increasing.

Meg watched them walk to the sign. M.J. seemed homed in on C.C. Shelly held C.C.'s hand high, steadying her, down and up the other side. They were still holding hands as they disappeared into the shrubs and trees. But Meg could hear them. Especially C.C.

'OHHHH!' she cried. 'What if there are vagrants and ne'er-do-wells in here?'

'Then pee on 'em.'

Meg couldn't help but laugh, but she heard nothing to indicate that C.C. had found the comment amusing.

'There's a good spot,' said Shelly, just before another semi sped by, his deep horn blasting the air around them, making both Meg and M.J. flinch. C.C.'s startled yelp shot out from the trees.

'Fuck you!' Meg yelled at the tailwind of the semi. Her swearing surprised her almost as much as the horn blast had. But as she rubbed a soothing finger behind M.J.'s ear, she smiled. She wanted to yell it out again, but restrained herself.

'Here,' said Shelly's disembodied voice. 'Step right over here. This spot's just made for a nice pee. Go ahead.'

'How?'

'What do you mean, "how"?'

'I mean, well – *how*?'

'You have to squat, darlin'.' There was a pause, then, 'For crying out loud! Have you *never* peed in the woods?' Pause.

'In your whole life?'

Pause.

'You're *kidding* me!'

Meg bit her lip, trying not to smile. It was uncanny how Shelly didn't remember these kinds of things. But better Shelly in there with Ceece than her. She felt bad for C.C., she really did. But still . . . She could no longer restrain her smile.

Shelly sighed loudly. 'Look, you can hold on to

that branch there. It's perfect. Just pretend it's a towel bar!' There was further discussion that got cut off as another semi roared past, but Meg guessed Shelly was doling out instructions in the art of not peeing on one's clothing bunched around one's ankles.

Should she shout encouragement to C.C., Meg wondered, but the thought was interrupted by Shelly's bellow rocketing through the trees.

'Criminy, C.C.! We're both women!'

Meg thought again to yell encouragement, but then worried that it might make it worse for C.C. that she was out here listening.

'*Okay!* I'll avert my eyes!' said Shelly resignedly.

There was a long pause, then C.C.'s voice, defeated. 'I *can't. Ohhhh!*' she moaned miserably.

M.J.'s ears went back, then up again, and she squirmed in Meg's arms, evidently feeling some responsibility to go save her new mistress from whatever horror was befalling her there in the woods. Meg stroked her small, quivering body.

'You can do it, C.C.!' shouted Meg, deciding a cheer was very much needed after all. 'M.J. says just do like she did!'

Two women's laughter from the woods. Meg smiled as M.J. put her ears up again, her little tail wiggling against Meg's stomach.

'Here, I'm stepping away so you have privacy.' Shelly's voice was robust again and Meg could hear her footsteps crunching through the under-brush. 'Okay. I've stepped out of the bathroom,

141

and now I'm walking out of the bedroom. It's a master bath that you're in there, did you know that?' A small giggle from C.C. 'I'm walking down the hallway now, the nice long hallway! And now I'm into another bedroom, and I'm closing the door – bang! – and now I'm turning on the music.' Shelly started singing a song from the sixties, but had to replace most of the words with lahs. Meg and M.J. could hear C.C. laughing over Shelly's caterwaul. M.J.'s ears first lifted, then lay flat against her neck.

'Baby you, something, something, la, la, la-la lah-lah, la-la, lah-lah lahhhh!'

The singing continued, and as goosebumps of embarrassment pimpled her skin, Meg felt the need to glance over her shoulder, then to inspect M.J.'s toenails.

After a long minute, C.C. shouted out, 'Okay! I did it!' Her voice was ebullient.

Meg laughed, kissed the top of M.J.'s head.

'Excellent!' said Shelly, her voice and crunching sounds indicating she was walking back toward the victorious C.C.

'Wait! Don't come back yet! What do I do for toi— Oh, just a sec! I have tissues in my pocket here somewhere. DON'T LOOK YET!'

'No worries. La, laahh, la, la, lah your beautiful eyes are something, something la la,' sang Shelly, apparently ready to sing an entire lah-lah medley, if need be.

'Okay. You can come back now. I'm proper.'

Crunching sounds again. 'Thank you, Shelly! Okay, let's go.'

'You can't just leave that tissue there.'

'Well, what am I supposed to do with it? Put it back in my *pocket*?'

'It's just got a little pee on it. Put it in the trash bag in the car.'

Meg felt her own eyes widen at that.

'That's just . . . disgusting, Shelly.'

'Well, you can't just leave it. It's litter. It's wrong. Besides, there's a big fine for littering along an interstate. Didn't you see the sign?'

'Yes!' shouted C.C., her voice breaking again. 'I've seen *lots* of signs. Signs that this whole trip was a big, fat mistake!'

Meg's chin touched her chest, a heavy sigh escaping. Poor C.C. Poor *Shelly*.

'Now you want me to make our whole car . . . *smell*, just so I'm not a litterbug. *Well, I can't do that. I can't take anymore!* This is just too hard. It's just bad omens everywhere.'

None of us slept well last night, thought Meg. C.C. sounded like she was at the breaking point. They were all so tired. Not just a-couple-bad-nights'-sleep tired, either. They were life-tired.

'Oh, sweetie, come here.' Shelly's voice was determinedly strong, but kind. 'There, there . . . Do you have another tissue? Good, here we go, dry your tears. Hey . . . wait a sec . . . What luck! Look! I still have my baggie from my sandwich from yesterday in my pocket. Here, see, I'll just

143

turn it inside out, put my hand in – s'cuse me. There! *Voilà!* All sealed up in there. The baggies folks should point out this handy use in their commercials. Now, we'll just put it in the trunk – all sealed up in there – till we get to a gas station and toss it. Okay? Good deal. You did real well, for your first woods-pee, Ceece! I'm proud of you.'

'Thank you,' said C.C., sounding sincerely grateful.

Neither of them said anything else, but Meg could hear them hugging. She gave M.J. another little squeeze, thinking about hearing a hug, not sure what she heard exactly. Forgiveness, maybe. Friendship.

Their footsteps approached through the bush. With M.J. in her arms, Meg repositioned herself in front of the car. She leaned back on the hood, closed her eyes, lifted her face to the thin but warm spring sun, and pulled the smile from her face. She wanted to appear the picture of oblivious relaxation, and not let on that she'd been a well-entertained audience for the two-woman show, Off-Road Peeing.

As they emerged, C.C. called out, 'I did it, Meg!'

'*Brava!*' said Meg, turning languidly to look at her friends, as though just pulled from a distant daydream. But only Shelly was glancing her way, and even that was darting. They each were concentrating on their footing, holding hands and helping each other back down the bank of the ditch. Shelly held the baggie aloft in her other hand, pinched between finger and thumb.

Meg felt such love for the two of them, such trust, that she had a moment of something like vertigo. She'd had a lot of that lately. Like the rug of her life was being pulled out from under her feet, a good hard yank when Grant had left, and little tugs and pulls ever since.

'Huh?' Meg stumbled backward. Before she realized what was happening, Shelly screamed.

'*The car! Meg, the car is rolling!*'

It had started almost imperceptibly, but just as Shelly screamed, it lurched. Meg stumbled backward, trying to catch herself, not fall. Her immediate concern was M.J.

Shelly screamed again, '*The ditch! Stop the car!*' Meg got her feet under her and gently tossed M.J. to the ground, in the general direction of Shelly and C.C. She had just the briefest awareness of M.J.'s impressive speed, then Meg lunged toward the car, which had rolled backwards a foot already, and was picking up speed. Surely being towed twice in two days would be some sort of record, one that Meg did not want her name attached to, but especially wouldn't want Grant knowing. He would make some comment about women drivers.

She ran sideways, her hands palm over palm along the side of the car, casting panicked glances to see how close it was to the edge. Everything seemed to be happening in slow motion. And yet, all too fast. She lunged, got hold of the side mirror, then got her hand on the driver's door handle. She pulled, jerked the door open and almost fell onto the seat, grabbing the steering wheel for balance as she thrust her right foot toward the brake, her left foot dragging across the asphalt. She connected hard with the brake pedal as she simultaneously yanked the emergency brake on. The car jerked to a stop on an angle and the door closed painfully on her left shin. She winced, but did not cry out. The pain, physical pain, was almost a relief. She didn't move though, thinking the car might be perched on the edge, and that any motion might send it into the ditch. She held her breath, waited, her body steeled for a backward plummet.

Finally, she unpeeled her hand from the latched emergency brake, but kept her foot jammed on the foot brake. She carefully pushed the door, opening it just enough to slip her throbbing leg inside. She gingerly let the door close, too soft for it to latch. The car was definitely tilted, the back tires lower than the front, the passenger side lower than the driver's side. It wasn't a terribly deep ditch, but it was still a point of no return without a tow truck. How the hell was she going to drive up this incline, not slip back into the ditch? She carefully shifted into first, only then realizing the car had been left in neutral. The handbrake off. *Shelly*. She took a deep breath, and looked up.

They were both standing up ahead, near the sign. C.C. had her hands completely covering her face; Shelly had her head slightly turned to the side. She was looking at Meg out of the corner of her eye, her face squeezed by the helplessness of watching the near-disaster. Or else full of guilt. The baggie was at her feet. Both women looked like statues, frozen in fear.

Meg closed her eyes. She didn't even want to think about the tricky clutch work that would be required to get the car up and back onto level. There was loose gravel and dirt on the shoulder; if the tires spun out, she wouldn't have a chance. She felt like she couldn't get enough air, no matter how deeply she breathed. Her now-numb right foot was still hard on the brake. She touched her left foot to the clutch, experimentally. A sudden tapping on the glass made her scream.

'*Jesus!* Shelly! You scared the *crap* out of me,' Meg said angrily, her free hand flying to her chest. Shelly, outside her window, lifted her hands to cup her ears, indicating she couldn't hear. Meg lowered the window and repeated herself, annunciating clearly. 'You – scared – the – crap – out – of – me. *And you left the fucking car in neutral! With no brake!*'

Meg turned away from her, embarrassed by her anger, angry at her embarrassment. She stared at C.C., who was now leaning against the sign post, clearly trying to compose herself by doing deep breathing exercises.

'Shit,' said Shelly, looking contrite. 'I'm so sorry, Meg. C.C. was yelling and the dog was barking . . . and the traffic; I was trying to steer and slow down and then that damned truck, and I was worried the dog would—'

Meg held up her hand, nodded tiredly. 'It's okay. We've just got to get it back up on the level, not let it go back any—' She stopped, looked at Shelly, then C.C., then everywhere. 'The dog. Where *is* the dog? *Where is M.J.?*'

'Oh . . . shit!' whispered Shelly. They both looked up the road. Evidently finished with her breathing, C.C. was now holding on to the sign post with one hand, her right leg bent. She appeared to be grasping for her shoe. 'Don't tell C.C. the dog's missing,' Shelly whispered.

Meg faced her with an expression she hoped conveyed the full weight of her incredulity. 'Shell. *Dear.* How are we supposed to *find* the dog, let alone *call* the dog, without C.C. knowing? It loves her best anyway. It'll be more likely to come to her calling it.'

Shelly shrugged, sighed, rolled her eyes. 'Okay, but we're gonna get another round of signs and omens, y'know.' Meg shrugged, then Shelly bellowed, 'Go find the dog, Ceece!'

Meg shook her head. Once Shelly gave in, she really gave in.

'Wha . . . ?' said C.C., shaking something from her shoe, then sticking it back on her foot, looking around her. 'M.J.? *M.J.!*' She stepped away from the sign post and called again. '*M.J.* Come here, luvey!' She made loud kissing sounds while clapping her hands on her thighs. 'Here, littleittybittybabygirl! Here, pookeymookey-bookeypie! M.J.? Here, sweetiewheatygirl!' Suddenly she shouted, 'COOKIE! *Cookie, cookie, cookie!*' She clapped her hands together three times. 'Yummy, yummy! COOKIE!' Suddenly a gray blur shot out from behind a bush, down one side of the ditch and up the other into C.C.'s waiting arms. '*Good* girl!' She yelled toward the car. 'Quick! Someone bring me a cookie from the box! From the back seat!'

C.C. hugged and kissed M.J. on top of her head, then looked at Meg and Shelly, waving and grinning broadly. 'Hurry!' she yelled. 'I taught her what a cookie is, for just this very reason! Hurry! I need to reward her.' Shelly, looking stunned, stared at C.C., then blinked at Meg. Meg reached carefully into the back seat. She groped around till she felt it, then handed the yellow box to Shelly.

Shelly jogged over to C.C., handed her the box. While M.J. and C.C. each enjoyed a reward of Nilla Wafer, Shelly returned, found two large rocks, and placed them behind the back wheels. Meg was too afraid to get out of the car, despite Shelly's assurances that she had 'a couple good inches' before the tire went over the edge. C.C. and M.J. stayed where they were, well out of the way. Shelly stood at the rear and to the side of the car, ready to push.

Meg took another deep breath and started the car. Teeth clenched, she let her left foot slowly depress the clutch. Even more slowly, she lifted her right off the brake, and held it poised over the accelerator. Easing off the brake handle as if it were attached to explosives, every muscle tensed again for the plunge backward into the ditch. A little more gas. A little less clutch. Finally, the gears caught, the tires gripped and the car crept forward and she drove onto level ground. She braked, turned the ignition off, double-checking that the stick was in first. She firmly yanked the handbrake back on and took what felt like her first breath in several minutes.

Through her open window, she could hear their cheers. Meg was suddenly, and unexpectedly, giddy with laughter. She wished Grant had seen that bit of driving! He would be shocked. He nearly always drove when they both were going somewhere. She was a perfectly competent driver, but she rarely drove when it was the two of them in the car. The three most recent times she'd driven with him in the car were to the hospital, when he was having what he was certain was a heart attack and what each time had turned out to be an anxiety attack. He probably had no idea that she was as good a driver as she was. She knew that if someone asked him if his wife could do what she'd just done, he would say with a laugh: 'I certainly doubt it.' He loved the word 'certain'. 'I'm *certain*,' he would say, sometimes even when he had no clue what he was talking about.

Meg shook her head, still smiling, realizing that if someone had asked *her* the same question last

150

year, she probably would have said, 'Well, I'd hope I'd never get myself *into* that kind of predicament in the first place.' A rueful smile crossed her lips: *she* liked the word predicament. Mostly used to describe other people's misfortune, or what she termed 'lack of common sense'. Car trouble. Bankruptcy. Divorce. It could all be avoided with the proper maintenance and care. She avoided predicaments by being judicious in all things. Those kinds of dramas happened to other people.

She laughed again, shaking her head at herself. Look at her now! Not just her car breaking down yesterday, but now this. Not to mention Grant. 'Predicament', indeed. Finally, she lifted her foot off the brake.

'Well done, Meg! Well done!' said Shelly, again appearing at the side window, her thumb up. She reached in, clapped Meg on the shoulder. '*Nice* driving! Shit, woman! I don't think you even needed me or the rocks back there. Where'd you learn how to *do* that?'

Meg gave Shelly a weak smile, and shrugged. Then, her smile stronger, she asked Shelly, 'You okay to drive again?'

Shelly looked at her, her eyes softening. 'Really? You want me to? Even after . . . ?'

'Oh, come on!' said Meg. 'That could have happened to anyone, what with the dog and the semi and all. Here, let me out of here and you hop in.' Meg opened the door as Shelly stepped aside.

It *could* have happened to anyone. *Anything could happen to anyone. At any time.*

As Meg climbed out, Shelly wrapped her arms around her in a tight hug. Meg felt the air squeezed out of her, but an odd euphoria filled her up again. Shelly released her, then put her middle finger and thumb in her mouth. Meg ducked her head, covering her ears as Shelly let loose a shrill whistle, then shouted, 'Let's go, C.C.! On the road again. You and M.J. assume your positions!'

No one spoke as they climbed in. But once the three clicks of their seat belts sounded, Shelly pushed on the turn indicator and slowly pulled forward, watching for a gap in the mirrors. Meg couldn't help herself from looking over her shoulder and checking the traffic too. Thankfully, it seemed significantly less dense than forty minutes ago, but still a challenge, scanning for a place to merge in from a stop, at interstate speeds. Shelly waited, biding her time. Finally, well behind them, a semi flashed his headlights as he changed to the middle lane, leaving the near one vacant for them. Shelly accelerated, then floored it and merged skillfully back out onto the highway and up to speed. The semi roared past in the outer lane.

When it had passed, C.C. said quietly from the back seat, 'Well. That whole stop, back there? That surely was another omen.'

'Aww, for crying out loud, C.C.,' said Shelly, once again putting voice to Meg's feelings. Shelly changed lanes and passed an old couple in a white LeBaron.

152

'No. I mean a *good* omen,' said C.C. 'When M.J. came back, right to me, she looked so happy. And *I* am so happy! I decided right then and there that this trip really was supposed to happen. I mean, *think* about it. We've talked about a trip for years, then Georgie leaves her house to me, right when all three of us are at a point in our lives where we are discombobulated, and . . . I don't know, need each other more than ever, I guess. And I even think we were supposed to break down, and go to Tupper, which wouldn't have happened without *you*, Meg, wanting to do that detour. And I think we were supposed to meet M.J., and help *her*. I mean, doesn't it all just seem a little too *coincidental?*'

Meg thought it sounded *entirely* coincidental, one happenstance event after another, completely unrelated. But she didn't say anything.

'I'm not sure why I was supposed to pee in the woods,' C.C. went on, apparently not needing any response, 'but I did it, and – well, I don't mind telling you, I'm suffering one of the seven deadly sins right now.'

'*You're what?*' asked Shelly, staring back at C.C. in the rear-view mirror.

C.C. shoved her head forward between the seats, M.J., held under her chin. 'Pride!' she said with satisfaction.

Meg laughed again; she felt filled with helium. Happy gas. 'You know what? Me too! Me too.'

'You should both be proud,' said Shelly. 'Hey!

Look. That's the trucker who let us in!' Meg looked, and there it was, the blue semi, back in the right lane again. Shelly tooted the horn and waved as they pulled up even.

'Herr-row, Mister Twukker!' C.C. sang out. Meg watched as she held M.J. up to the window, waving the little dog's paw at the driver. Meg turned forward, slunk down in her seat, feeling the heat of embarrassment coloring her cheeks. Finally, she stole a furtive glance at the trucker. He had a long, thin face, with huge ears sticking out under a well-worn baseball cap. He was alternating looking at them and watching the road, but waving back and grinning. He tipped his hat to them and pointed at Meg. She smiled shyly, put her fingers up to the window, gave a little wave. As they drove by, he flashed the peace sign. She returned it. Peace. Indeed.

CHAPTER 9

SHELLY

Shelly squirmed slightly in the driver's seat, repositioning herself to get blood to the places it hadn't visited in a while. She'd finally stopped listening for any dips or drags in the drone of the motor. Good job, Alternator, she thought, reaching for the dash to pat it, but quickly retracting her hand before she even touched it. At least she hadn't said it out loud. She checked on her companions, breathed a sigh of relief. She was safe from recriminations; all three were still sound asleep. Meg seemed like she was hardly breathing, but M.J. and C.C. were both snoring, the dog, surprisingly loudly.

Nina snoring. The school loudspeaker. The knot of jeering girls.

What was it about driving long distances that made the memories swirl up, like sudden squalls? Something about hours on the highway made time collapse. Past became tangled with the present. Future seemed not to exist.

It was her senior year, so Nina must have been a sophomore, maybe fifteen? Yes, because she couldn't drive yet; Shelly was still driving them both in to school every day. That day, Nina had needed to go to school early for a choir meeting, and Shelly had been made to drive her. She complained to and about Nina the whole way, about having to get up early when she had a test that day, and how Nina's snoring had kept her awake half the night. It wasn't till she'd dropped her off and parked in the Senior Lot that she hatched her plan. It had started innocently enough, as all bad plans do. She sat in the parking lot before first bell, smoking and making her friends laugh with imitations of Nina snoring. 'You can't get me away to college fast enough!' Shelly had moaned. 'I'll get more sleep even if I stay out half the night partying!'

Shelly jerked from her thoughts, braking suddenly as a grocery bag blew onto the highway in front of her. She silently ridiculed herself for the instinct to spare the life of a grocery bag. As the bag blew ahead, she changed lanes and stepped on the gas, aiming for it. But the wind carried it up and away, sparing it.

Shelly tried to think of grocery bags, of grocery stores, of that new, cute young sacker at the SavR King. Anything. But the memories muscled in. She thought maybe it had actually initially been Susan's idea to tape-record Nina snoring, not that that absolved Shelly of anything. She could see the gang of kids, her 'group', practically rolling around the parking lot, laughing at their idea to play yet another practical joke on Shelly's little sister. Whosever idea it was, Shelly hadn't wasted any time. That afternoon she signed up to do morning announcements at the next available slot, the following week. She'd never done them before. It was mostly left to the student council geeks and to the cheerleaders on game days. Or the choir nerds on concert days. Shelly remembered that Nina had done the announcements her sophomore year for the 'Winter Holiday' concert – the name newly and carefully changed to reflect the new *sensitivity* they were all supposed to have, even though the concert still consisted exclusively of Christmas carols. It made their mother absolutely nuts, but amused both Nina and Shelly. It wasn't like their family had been going to temple every week. Or even on high holy days.

On Shelly's assigned announcement day, she'd slipped the cassette tape into the pocket of her coat, and she'd had to stop herself from snickering a couple of times as she drove to school. Nina had looked at her from the passenger seat of their old Buick with a questioning smile, then shrugged, probably figuring her older sister was 'on something'. Shelly knew that Nina thought she was much wilder than she really was. But, thinking back now, Shelly realized she was probably wilder than *she* thought she was, back then. She just thought she was fun-loving. Spontaneous. Daring.

That day, after she'd read the usual announcements into the bulbous black microphone – the lunch menu, the upcoming events, the reminders – Shelly had popped the tape into a player that Susan had left for her under the announcement desk. Just before she pressed play, she'd said, in her best sultry-DJ voice: 'And now, a special musical offering from Nina Kostens,' and played her sister's snores to the entire student body of McClivet High School.

A small moan came out of Shelly before she could stop it. It happened that way. Often. Her personal failings left something like physical smolderings in her, which came out like audible wisps of smoke. Meg stirred. Shelly adjusted her position in the driver's seat, pretending a small physical discomfort had made her moan. It wasn't pretending, really. And it wasn't small. She had to work to not close her eyes with the falling-down feeling she had inside.

The traffic was rapidly increasing. They were coming up on Indianapolis. She checked the gas gauge. Just under half a tank. Good. They could cruise on through. She didn't like getting off the highway at these big cities. She focused on her driving, her memories kept at bay by the tension of navigating a city at noon rush hour.

As they emerged on the other side of Indianapolis, the traffic thinned with each off-ramp they passed. Finally she breathed deeply, wondering just how much her blood pressure and other vitals spiked in heavy traffic. But as long as there wasn't some dog and woman in the back seat howling because they had to pee, driving through traffic was a relief to the monotony of the highway. Not to mention the idle mind that went wandering down that endless black stretch.

But too soon the black stretch returned. Driving was weird. Or at least driving alone, which she wasn't really, but kind of was, given the lifelessness of the others. She wished one would wake up, talk to her, keep her from herself. But there was no one to hold her on this narrow ledge above her past.

Like most practical jokes, the hurt had ended up far outweighing the humor. For weeks after the announcement, the popular choir kids had teased Nina relentlessly, snoring or snorting like pigs whenever they passed her in the hall. Then, that conceited group of girls sang 'Snore, Sister Snore' as Nina walked into the choir room. Nina was as gawky a teen as they came, frizzy red hair, thick glasses, overweight. But she had a sweet, pure voice, and she loved to sing, beyond all else. But after Shelly opened the door, those bitches had it in for Nina. She dropped out of choir shortly after.

Shelly blinked her stinging eyes. She forced herself to look at the scenery flying by. There wasn't much to look at, other than the gathering clouds. It was getting colder too. She clicked on the heater, the fan on low. There was a faint burning smell, and she nervously checked the temperature gauge. Normal. The smell dissipated.

Dust. Just dust burning off. She squinted up at the sky. She hoped it wasn't going to snow. *Nina, in her purple down coat that made her look much fatter than she was, walking to school, not even looking up as Shelly drove by, honking, the window down, the cold air blowing in, Shelly imploring Nina to get in the car.*

Might Nina be thinking of her? Did she have a similar falling-down feeling for what she'd done to Shelly, two years later? Even all these years later, Shelly still didn't know if it was retribution. Or, as Nina had tearfully stated, as Shelly packed, it had 'just happened'. *Damn.* Until this trip, Shelly had perfected avoiding thoughts of her. She just had ceased to exist. She didn't even remember where in Tennessee she was living. It was a long state. She could be hundreds of miles away from where C.C.'s house was. Maybe Nina wasn't even in Tennessee anymore.

They had never been much alike, but after high school, it was like their personalities flipped: Nina got into drugs, lost a lot of weight, got busted. And Shelly was working two jobs, married, toeing the line. She hadn't hesitated to bail Nina out of jail, let her stay with them.

Nina wasn't solely to blame, of course. Vince was there, a willing participant. But for Shelly to come home from her second job, to find her unemployed husband in bed with her jailbird sister, had more than shattered her world. She'd left them both, without a word, ever again. Then she'd turned

160

around and done nearly the same thing to her second husband, sleeping with his best friend, and that had ended her second marriage.

Shelly felt like she couldn't breathe. She opened her window slightly, clicking the heater up a notch to compensate for the cold brought in by her sudden need for air.

'Mmm? Brrr.' Meg lifted her head, blinking like a mole. Shelly couldn't look at her. 'It's cold,' Meg said sleepily. Shelly finally looked at her. Meg's eyes still looked somewhat unfocused. 'What's up with the window?'

'Sorry. I needed some air.' Shelly rolled it up.

Meg stared at her, rubbing one eye sleepily. 'Is something wrong?'

'No.' She looked at her knuckles, white on the steering wheel.

'Shell?'

Shelly held her breath. *Don't let it out. Don't talk about her. You must keep it contained.* 'I keep thinking about Nina, and I sure as hell don't want to.' She couldn't believe the words had come out of her, as if they had a will of their own.

'Nina?' Meg waited.

Shelly almost whispered. 'My sister.'

'Your sister?' Meg repeated. Shelly could tell that she was still emerging from her fog of sleep. As if to confirm it, Meg yawned, stretched her arms down between her legs, then yawned again. Meg looked at her, waiting.

'Yes.'

'What about her?'

They were both speaking in hushed tones. Shelly stared at the dashed white lines flowing by the side of the car, one then the next then the next, separate when she looked at a distance, but merging to one connected line as they flew by. She couldn't find her voice to answer Meg.

Meg finally spoke. 'I know that you don't like to talk about your sister, but I don't actually know why. I just know that you two haven't spoken for a long time.'

Shelly stared determinedly at the road. 'She . . . It's a long story. Never mind.'

'Okay,' said Meg tenderly.

After a long silence, Shelly said, 'I may have to pull over for a minute.' Her voice didn't sound right to her. Something knotted and tied up tight for years was coming undone. She felt like pieces might start falling off of her at any moment.

'Sure, okay. I can drive now,' said Meg.

Shelly drove to the next exit, a fairly deserted area, one of those off-ramps to God-knew-where. As she pulled off, there was nothing in sight in either direction. She drove onto the opposite on-ramp, but pulled over on its wide shoulder, and immediately got out. She took several deep breaths as she walked around the car, swinging her arms. The cold air felt bracing, restorative. Meg looked like she was going to give her a hug as they passed near a taillight, but then thought better of it. Shelly realized she'd turned her shoulder away from Meg.

As Shelly climbed in the passenger side, C.C. shifted position slightly in the back seat, but slept on. M.J. blinked at Shelly, then she tucked her nose back into her folded legs and went back to sleep. She looked like a tiny fawn. In sleep, C.C. gently closed the circle of her arms around the small circle of dog in her lap.

Shelly kept an eye out the rear window as Meg began to merge back onto the interstate. 'Watch that red pickup,' Shelly said. 'He's coming up fast!'

The red truck flew past in the near lane, despite the outer lane being vacant.

Meg swerved. 'Whoa. I saw him but didn't realize he was going so fast. Glad you did. He must be doing eighty or ninety! Thanks.'

Shelly nodded. 'You're welcome.' She paused, smiled. 'Thank you, for thanking me. You know, most men would not only not thank you, they'd get pissed off and tell you to stop back-seat driving. Even if they *were* about to die in a car wreck.'

Meg nodded, unsmiling. She shrugged. 'Yeah, I have to keep my mouth shut in the car with Grant.' She paused, pursed her lips. '*Had* to. Past tense, I guess. I did an awful lot of pretending I was asleep, just so I could close my eyes and not watch him drive. He was a terrible tailgater.' She added quietly, 'Is. I'm sure he still is. Present tense.'

'It must be hard to not talk about him like he's—' Shelly stopped herself.

'Dead.' Meg nodded again. 'Yeah. Although I have

my moments of wanting to kill him.' She gave Shelly a small smile.

Shelly laughed, patted Meg's knee. 'Rightfully so.' She's getting better, she thought. Slowly but surely.

'Hey, look what's coming,' said Shelly excitedly. Then, her fingers dancing in front of her face, she added in an ethereal voice: '*A sign!*' They both laughed quietly. 'We . . . are . . . now . . .' she continued, 'officially – wait for it – in . . . *Kentucky!*' They drove by the slightly rusted sign welcoming them to the Bluegrass State. 'Woohoo!' said Shelly. 'We're in Kentucky!'

'Whh-what?' C.C.'s sleepy voice drifted up from the back.

'Sorry, C.C.,' said Shelly, clapping her hand over her mouth. 'I got a little excited about being in Kentucky for the first time. Why, it makes me feel like a cowboy, just being here,' she said, doing a bad southern accent. 'Makes me feel like *having* a cowboy, if you know what I mean!' She elbowed the air.

'Well, you should probably go to Colorado or Wyoming, or someplace like that, if you want a cowboy,' said Meg. 'But you can probably have your fill of jockeys here.'

Meg. Ever the precise teacher, thought Shelly.

C.C. yawned noisily, stretching. 'Naw. Shelly wouldn't want a jockey,' she said, then added in a squeaky voice: 'They too leetle!' eliciting more laughter.

But Shelly interjected. 'You can't always go by height, or even shoe size, contrary to popular belief. I once dated a guy who was maybe five-eight, tops, feet smaller than mine, but let me tell you, he was . . .' She started to gesture with her hands but Meg swatted her, shrieking gleefully. Then Shelly felt a small sting on the back of her head and realized that C.C. had flicked her. 'You vixen!' she scolded, turning and flicking C.C.'s knee. Shelly felt a joyful release, kibbitzing with the girls again. She should have woken them much earlier.

Suddenly C.C. shouted. 'Look! The sign!'

Shelly's first thought was that C.C. had seen or thought of another omen. But following C.C.'s eager pointing, she saw an actual sign, hand-painted, set back from the road, but large.

FORTUNE-TELLER:
SATISFACTION GUARANTEED.
NEXT EXIT, THEN JUST 1 MILE.

'Oh, please, please, pleeeese?' C.C. begged from the back seat. 'Y'all, please let's do this. It'll be fun!'

Shelly laughed, looked at Meg, who was glancing back at her, a slightly repugnant look on her face. 'Up to you,' Shelly told her. 'You're the driver. But we're almost there. Lexington can't be more than fifty miles from here. And I could do with a leg stretch.' Shelly had never been to a fortune-teller of any kind. She would not admit it to Meg, but she was kind of curious.

Shelly watched Meg staring evenly at the road as they flew past the sign. All was quiet in the car. Shelly saw the exit come into view, held her breath, then knew it was not to be. Meg always signaled any turn well in advance of making it. She was precise in driving as in all things. If she was going to turn, the blinker would be on by now. Shelly understood. They'd already had two unscheduled stops. And poor Meg hated getting off-schedule. Shelly began to stretch her arms down between her ankles, easing her stiffness from driving. They came upon, and then passed the turn lane for the exit.

Suddenly Shelly felt herself flung toward Meg, bruising her forearm on the emergency brake. But what surprised her the most was not the car careening onto the exit ramp at the last possible second, nor the astonishing fact that Meg had not used her turn indicator *at all*. It was Meg's almost maniacal grin as she did it. Shelly clapped her on the shoulder as C.C. let out a loud whoop from the back seat.

CHAPTER 10

MEG

Meg blinked several times, coming from the bright sunlight outside, into the dark room. The sign on the door had told them to knock, then enter. Once her eyes adjusted, she stared, surprised. She'd imagined that a fortune-teller's place would be filled with a thin haze and a thick scent, crystals spinning small rainbows from every window and light source. Maybe even a crystal ball on the table. But this place was more like a sweet cabin getaway. It reminded her of the place near Lake Louise where she and Grant had celebrated their tenth anniversary. That was the last time they'd gone anywhere for their anniversary.

'I'll be right with you,' called out a cheery voice from a back room.

C.C. and Shelly wandered toward a large fish tank, while Meg did a slow, surveying turn. It was really just one big room, this cabin, divided into areas. Small, irregular wooden shelves jutted from random spots along each log wall. In the kitchen on the far side, several copper pots hung from a suspended iron ceiling rack. The thick oak counters were scrubbed clean, with jars of legumes, grains and herbs lining the back wall. The rest of the room was a combination dining/living room. Several mismatched wooden chairs circled a round table in the middle of the room, a silky white cloth covering it, hanging in voluptuous folds on the sides.

Meg joined C.C. and Shelly at the fish tank, opposite the kitchen. It sat atop a sturdy wood table. The tank was brightly lit from within and it looked clean and refreshing. C.C. was holding M.J., and both dog and human were rapt, watching the colorful fish.

'Pretty,' Meg said to C.C., watching a small school of neon blue and green fish dart in and out of a fake coral reef and a tall green castle. Two larger, bright yellow fish trolled about at a more leisurely pace.

'Look at that guy,' said Shelly, pointing to an ugly but fascinating brown thing, its huge, gelatinous lips stuck to the side of the glass, inching along at a glacial pace. He appeared to be eating the bits of algae on the side of the glass. He was probably the reason it looked so clean. Meg wondered if the other fish had 'jobs' within the tank.

'Hi, I'm Janet Cole.'

Meg, startled by the voice right behind her, rose from her fish-gazing and turned toward the woman standing behind her. She was immediately struck by her silver hair, shoulder-length, wavy, gorgeous, held back by a thin blue headband. Meg was secondarily but equally impressed with her height: she was taller than Shelly, and quite thin, with very blue eyes. Not rotund, dark-haired gypsy type to go along with all Meg's stereotyped images. Janet wore clean but faded blue jeans, a pink, plaid flannel shirt over a black turtleneck, both untucked. On her feet were thick gray wool socks and bright turquoise rubber clogs with holes in the top. If they weren't such a pretty color, they would be astonishingly ugly shoes, Meg thought.

They introduced themselves all around.

'Shall we get started?' Janet asked pleasantly, gesturing toward the table.

They each took a seat, C.C. to Janet's right, Meg on her left, Shelly across the table. M.J., as ever, on C.C.'s lap. The little dog seemed fixated on Janet. Meg couldn't tell if it was wariness, or just intense interest.

Janet lifted the table cloth and opened a small drawer, built in under the table. She grabbed something, then closed the drawer and repositioned the cloth. Meg watched carefully, the word charlatan circling her brain, suspecting some sleight of hand, or the surreptitious pushing of a button to make spirits appear in a corner. But Janet held her closed fist near M.J., then slowly opened it, revealing a small handful of Cheerios. M.J. delicately but enthusiastically ate them off her hand. No wonder the dog was excited.

Janet smiled. 'I keep these here for toddlers when

I'm doing readings for moms. Zat good, girl?' she asked M.J. As the dog snacked from her hand, Janet looked up again. 'Okay, first, the preamble.' Her smile was beautiful, Meg had to admit. Her teeth nearly perfect, except for a small gap between her top front two. Meg guessed she was a little older than they were, maybe late fifties, maybe older, but her face seemed to be welcoming its wrinkles, not succumbing to them. There was an openness and ease in her lightly tanned, makeup-less face. 'My fee is thirty-five dollars per person. Your satisfaction is guaranteed or you don't pay. Shall we start with—' She paused, looking at C.C. 'I'm sorry. I'm blanking on your name.' She smiled. 'You just told me a minute ago.'

Meg almost laughed out loud. Right. A fortune-teller who could see into the future, but she was no better than any other middle-aged woman at remembering a name she'd been told sixty seconds earlier.

'C.C.?' asked C.C.

'Of course! C.C.' Janet shuffled the cards. 'Okay, so you're all on some new venture together?' she asked conversationally.

C.C. gasped. Meg wished she wouldn't do that. No sense egging these types on. What middle-aged woman *wasn't* on some new venture? By choice, or by circumstance. C.C. nodded vigorously. Meg grimaced.

'And, Meg? It's Meg, isn't it?' Meg nodded. 'I feel

170

that you are in a particularly big transition.' Janet paused. 'Several, in fact.'

C.C. gasped again.

Meg gave Janet a half-smile, just to be polite. Really, though. Again: what middle-aged woman *wasn't* in some kind of big transition? *Several, in fact.* But what the hell. Meg reached for her purse, thinking this could be entertaining, but at the same time some chord of warning strummed deep within her, low and deep. She laughed and it sounded forced, even to her. She opened her purse. Let's just get on with it, she thought. Get back on the road again as soon as possible. But Janet stopped her.

'We can do that after. If, and only if you're satisfied.'

Meg looked at the other two, C.C. smiling with gleeful anticipation, Shelly seeming somewhat less enthusiastic. But she gave Meg a little sideways glance, then said what Meg had just thought. 'What the hell!'

'Okay. Let's start with you, C.C.,' said Janet. C.C. beamed. 'If you'll just give me your hand.'

'Okay! Which one?' C.C. was grinning like a fool. So enthusiastic, in fact, that Meg thought she might even hand over M.J., if this woman asked her to.

Meg marveled at her friend's pliable belief systems. C.C. was, in her own words, 'a mostly devout Catholic'. But Meg knew she was, in fact, a shining example of a cafeteria Catholic, picking and choosing the parts of the faith that didn't conflict with her more modern mores and sensibilities. Meg couldn't help but wonder what the Pope thought of fortune-telling. But C.C. loved all things mystical and magical, and even managed to pound their squareness into the round holes of her Catholicism.

'Both, but one at a time. Your choice,' said Janet.

'Okay. Uh,' she had both hands wrapped around M.J., but she extended her left hand, the closest to Janet.

'Thank you.' Janet slowly ran her fingers over C.C.'s palm, almost Braille-like, but she studied it with her eyes too.

'Okay, now your right, please.' C.C. withdrew her left, putting it back on M.J., and extended her right across herself. Janet nodded. 'Ahh. Okay. Very interesting.' Meg and Shelly discreetly exchanged smirks. Didn't these types *always* start with 'Very interesting . . .'?

'Your palm is compact, squarish, and your fingers well balanced to that. I'd say you have a curious nature, are open to new things, and particularly like to be entertained, made to laugh, and to make others laugh.' Meg looked at Shelly again, their smirks gone. 'You tend to run late, are not the tidiest of housekeepers, but you like pretty or fanciful things, especially in your home. Hmm. Do you tend to overlook your self-care?'

Shelly mouthed 'wow' to Meg.

Meg's brow furrowed at Shelly, trying to silently

convey: Well, you could probably guess that about C.C. from looking at her. High heels and sweat-suit? And overweight? Come on!

'Okay, let's look at your life line,' Janet continued, still looking down into C.C.'s palm. Janet lifted her head and looked around the table. 'Contrary to popular belief, the life line doesn't say anything about how long a person will live, or her health or anything like that. It is, however, revealing of how you *live* your life.' She looked back at C.C.'s palm. 'C.C., yours is tasseled, you see how it looks almost braided, especially in here?' C.C. nodded, her face almost fearful.

'You are a good friend to others, many others. You are giving and generous, but don't like confrontation. You like to keep the peace, some-times at any cost.'

She paused, as C.C. said shyly, 'That's probably true.'

Janet continued, 'Some may take advantage of that. And here, your fingertips are rounded. This usually indicates a very social individual, and, again, a good friend, but sometimes you might step over the lines, trying to do too much. Inadvertently, of course.' Meg felt her eyes widen. That was certainly on target, given C.C.'s blunder in the mall.

Janet moved on to Shelly. 'You have a deeply etched life line. You live life with gusto, it's an adventure to you.'

'That's true!' C.C. almost shouted, her eyes sparkling with delight.

'And look here, where it starts? Way up here under your index finger? This is a life line of an ambitious person, one who can be, and probably should be, her own boss. You like to be in charge and are a natural leader. You enjoy praise, and sometimes have a hard time acknowledging mistakes.'

'*That's* true!' Meg exclaimed, finally succumbing to the fun, poking Shelly in the arm. Shelly stuck her tongue out at Meg, then turned back to Janet and urged her to continue.

'I'm guessing you are divorced?' Shelly nodded, held up two fingers. 'Do you have a sibling, or family member that—' Meg saw Shelly's panicked look, just before she turned and faced Janet directly. Janet locked eyes with Shelly for a few seconds, looked at her hands again, then smiled softly. Finally, she said, 'I'd guess these two women are like sisters to you.' Meg was astonished to see tears in Shelly's eyes. She withdrew her hand from Janet's and wiped her eyes quickly with the back of her sleeve, laughing lightly. 'Yeah.'

Had Janet seen something in Shelly's hand, or eyes, about her sister, and opted not to speak aloud about it? No. Meg twitched her head, shaking off the thought. Even she was getting caught up in this . . . charade.

'Next?' said Janet.

Meg felt her chest tighten. She withheld her hand, suddenly gripped by fear; if this woman really did have some power of clairvoyance, Meg didn't have the faintest idea what she might see in her. Meg felt like an amoeba, single-celled, a life without structure, definition. She wasn't a mother, she wasn't a wife, she wasn't a teacher. She was like M.J. on the lam from her life. But no one to be delivered to.

'C'mon, Meggles!' cried C.C., grinning. 'It's fun! She's really good!'

Exactly. Meg took a deep breath, then reluctantly stretched her arm out on the table, feeling as if she were about to have blood drawn.

'You have an interesting hand, long slender palm and medium-length fingers. I'd say you have a quick mind, love to discuss things, love to read, to learn. Other hand, please.' Meg obliged. 'Yes. You are definitely a thinker, you have a strong intellect, are precise and demand precision, and may depend on logic to see you through a crisis. You have a strong intuitive side, but you may ignore it, in favor of logic.'

'*That's* true!' C.C. and Shelly said in unison. Meg smiled, but shook her head. Didn't everyone do that, sometimes? Wasn't every woman torn between the 'oulds'? What you thought you *could* do, versus what you thought you *should* do? And didn't all women do too many shoulds, not enough coulds?

'See how your life line starts lower here, but sweeps wide, out to here?' She touched first the webbing near Meg's thumb, then traced the line to the lower outside corner of her palm. 'A life line that stays close to the thumb suggests that you might feel more comfortable in the background. C.C.'s life line stayed close all the way, yours is close up top, but then sweeps open at the end. So again, it's an interesting mix. I'm thinking that maybe you are not comfortable in the spotlight, unless you feel it's a way you can help others. Then you're willing to be up front and in charge.' Meg's mouth opened, then she closed it. She didn't say it, but she couldn't help but think it. *Wow.*

She remembered when she'd first started teaching high school, she wasn't a whole lot older than her students. Her first weeks she'd felt vulnerable and exposed, like a fraud, even. She had more than once come home crying, confided to Grant her insecurities. But his only words of encouragement had been: 'Be tough. Don't expect too much, of yourself and especially not them. And never let 'em see you sweat.'

Wow. This wow was for herself, at a sudden epiphany: that was the difference between how their teaching styles had evolved. Meg maintained high expectations, for herself and her students, whatever 'high' was for each individual. She expected them to reach, fail, reach again, and eventually succeed. She made them read the literature not just that she loved, but what she thought *they'd* love. And she trusted those stories to pull out of them the unique questions, and maybe a few answers, each student needed. She knew it was questions they needed, much more than answers. But Grant, he somehow seemed to regard the kids as the enemy, especially toward the end of his career, growing more and more bitter about the time he had given them, not to himself to become the writer he'd always wanted to be.

Meg tried to think when she too had been put in that same camp by her husband, when he'd grown bitter toward her for the demands she'd made on his time. But she could change, give him more of whatever he needed, stop with the schedules. If he needed space and time, she could give him that. If only he'd give her the chance.

'Here, your head line travels straight and level – that's logic again,' Janet pulled Meg back. 'But this is interesting: see how deep it is?' She tilted Meg's palm around so each of them could see. 'That's intelligence, and optimism. Now, your heart line is also deeply etched, that's the sign of someone who enjoys the arts, and, given your head line, I'm going out on a limb and say you love good literature.'

Meg smiled. Yes . . . but! Didn't every woman love a good book? But deep inside she was proud that something physical about her revealed her love of literature.

'*This* is interesting,' said Janet. 'Your heart line is also rather short.' Meg instantly felt her pride melt away, replaced by naked vulnerability. Did a short heart line mean she wasn't loving enough? Or worse, had this short line, in her hand since birth, foretold the end of her marriage? Her *long* marriage? No. Grant would come back to her. She willed this woman to see that, to look for and find that line in her hand. She couldn't imagine any other future.

'This tells me that you take love and commitment very seriously, that you don't jump into things lightly, but once you do, you commit one hundred percent. The possible downside of that attribute could be that you might sometimes be a bit regimented. On the positive side again, I would guess that you keep both your household and your work organized and efficient.'

Meg was simultaneously aware of two things: the stunned looks from C.C. and Shelly, and feeling tired. So damn tired.

'Now,' said Janet, 'I'd like to do some oracle cards for you three, as a group.' She tapped the deck on the table. 'If you're up for it. You are a fascinating trio and I'd like to see what it says about this journey you're on. No charge. Just curious.' They all three looked at each other, C.C. nodding and smiling. Meg was just grateful for the change of subject. But she had noticed Janet's use of the word trio. She thought maybe C.C. had noticed too, but she was looking at Janet now.

'Fahn by me,' C.C. said, her accent slipping out again.

'Fahn bah me, too,' said Shelly, imitating C.C.

C.C. grinned. 'Just you wait, Shelly Kostens! It'll come in handy that I speak southern!'

Everyone looked at Meg. She shrugged her tacit agreement, her hands clasped tightly in her lap.

Janet fanned the cards on the table. The backs all had bright orange suns. Janet picked them up, clamped them into a neat rectangle again, then fanned them on the table with the opposite side up. They were upside down for Meg, but she could see that on this side were beautiful illustrations of women – fairies? angels? Meg wasn't sure. And it looked like each had some kind of banner with a few words at the bottom.

Janet lifted one end of the line of cards and deftly flipped them back to the sun side. 'When I tell you, I'd like each of you to take your left hand and mix the deck, pull one out, all with your eyes closed and thinking of a question. Maybe it will relate to this journey, or to each other. It's best if it is a personal question that doesn't have a yes or no answer. Or it can be a statement around getting some guidance or direction. "Show me blank." Or, "How might I blank?"'

C.C. lifted M.J. in her arms and gave her a hug, kissing the top of her head again. M.J. twisted around, eagerly returning the affection. Shelly's eyes were closed, her chin on her chest, her hands clasped in her lap, for all the world looking like she was praying. But Meg seriously doubted *that*. More likely, deep concentration in self-restraint not to burst out laughing at this whole idea. But without opening her eyes, Shelly suddenly placed her left hand on the cards. Meg exhaled, closed her eyes, and placed her hand on the cards. But no question formed. There was only one word in her mind: Grant.

Janet said, 'Okay, now swirl!' Eyes still closed, her hand bumped into Shelly's and C.C.'s, swirling the cards.

'Okay, good,' said Janet. 'Now keeping your eyes closed, use one finger to pull a card toward you.'

Meg pulled, and waited for Janet to tell them to open their eyes. It seemed a long time was passing. It occurred to her, with a flutter of alarm, that maybe Janet was cleaning out their purses. Meg opened her eyes. Janet was still just sitting there. Without meaning or wanting to, Meg looked directly into her piercing blue eyes. Janet smiled at her, nodding toward Meg's hand and whispered, 'Look.'

Meg followed Janet's eyes to her own finger, on top of not one but two cards in front of her. She'd pulled two out.

'Oops,' said Meg.

'No oops at all,' said Janet. Shelly had opened her eyes and was looking at Meg's two cards, but C.C. was sitting very upright, obediently still with her eyes squeezed shut, her head tilted, her index finger touching a card in front of her on the table.

'Can we open our eyes yet?' asked C.C.

'Oh, yes! I'm sorry,' said Janet. 'Meg has pulled out two. Doesn't happen very often, that two cards make it all the way back to you. Okay, flip your cards over.'

'Oh, my!' C.C. exclaimed. 'Look!' She held her

card up. It was a beautiful illustration of a naked woman, her arms crossed demurely over her chest, her hips covered with a flowering vine, her head tilted to one side, angel wings stretched out behind her. She seemed to be staring out at them, deeply contented.

'Did you read the banner?' asked Shelly. C.C. looked at the card again, took her thumbs off the bottom, then looked crestfallen. '*That's* not helpful.'

'What does it say?' asked Meg.

C.C.'s lower lip was quivering, her eyes glossy. She turned the card back around so Meg could read it for herself. The yellow banner at the bottom read: 'Be Your Own Best Friend.'

Meg sighed. She guessed that C.C.'s question had been about M.J. Poor C.C. But Meg wished she wouldn't take this stuff so seriously. And she shouldn't have let herself fall in love with someone else's dog, plain and simple. 'I guess we should pay up now and get going,' said Meg, rising.

'No!' said C.C., taking a tissue that Janet was handing her. 'Thank you. I want Janet to tell me what this means, and . . . and I want to see what your cards are.' C.C. sat stiffly upright again. 'I'm okay now.' She dabbed at her eyes, then waved the tissue at Meg to sit back down.

'Okay,' said Meg, sitting again. 'But we really do need to be moving on here pretty soon.'

'Here. Here's my card,' said Shelly curtly, showing it around the table quickly. Meg could barely read the banner, Shelly waved it so fast in front of them. The card was orange and the woman was in some sort of castle library, walls of books, with birds flitting about.

Meg stifled a little laugh. *Well, if there was anything to this at all, I should have gotten that card, with the books and the birds. I love birds; Shelly hates them.*

Shelly read the banner aloud. "'Journey Within.'" She looked at Janet. 'Gotta tell ya, hon, not very helpful for me either. My question was—'

'Wait!' said Janet, holding up her hand. 'Don't tell your question at all, at least not till I give you the reading. Meaning will be clearer if it's only within you, not outside of you.' Meg looked at Shelly and they gave each other the slightest eye roll.

'Okay. Your turn, Meg. Let's get on with this,' Shelly said impatiently. Evidently, the palm reading was one thing, but Shelly didn't like being told to do anything, not by a fortune-teller, not by a card. And especially not to 'Journey Within'. Meg knew Shelly would journey almost anywhere but there. The final frontier.

Meg flipped over her two cards. One was bright green, a wood sprite in a leaf dress in a tree. The banner read: 'Miracle.' The second showed a Rubenesque woman sitting on a flower. The banner read: 'Wealth.' Meg shoved them toward the middle of the table so all could see.

'Op!' squeaked Shelly, but said nothing more.

'Again, very interesting,' said Janet. She looked

at Meg with those intense blue eyes again. 'I suspect this relates to your period of transition.' Again with the transition!

Meg couldn't stop herself, but she managed to say it pleasantly, not with the cynicism she was feeling. 'Well, aren't we all? Especially at this time of our lives?'

'Tell me mine,' said C.C., shoving her card toward Janet, 'because it isn't at all what I was hoping for.'

Janet looked at C.C. 'We are each our own best friend. We must take care of ourselves – our spirits, our minds, our emotional selves and our physical selves.'

Oh, for crying out loud! Meg started to rise again. The only good thing that Janet had said was that C.C. needed to take care of her physical self. Maybe it would help C.C. to hear it from someone other than her two friends.

Janet ignored Meg standing, and addressed Shelly. '"Journey Within" tells us many things. First, that love is not found outside of yourself. Nor are we truly fulfilled by or with material things. Whatever you asked for, the wisdom of the divine feminine says that you need to not look to others for it, but inside.' Janet put her hand over her heart. Shelly made a face, and a sound not unlike a fart came out her pursed lips. Janet laughed, then looked up at Meg.

'Meg. Pulling two cards, thinking you had one, this makes me think that you have one foot in each of two boats in your life now. Wealth is not always about getting money.' Shelly harrumphed. 'But it does suggest prosperity in general. If you have recently made an investment, I would say it is likely a good one. Stay the course. This card can mean abundance in general, so I would say that areas where you felt some lacking will soon feel full and rich. Now, this other card, "Miracle". If your question or statement was asking for some sort of miracle, it looks like it will be granted.'

Despite herself, Meg gasped audibly, placing her hand on the table to steady herself. But Janet continued, 'You are perhaps coming through a dark time, but never as dark as you've imagined. I am seeing resolution here for you. It is important that you keep faith in yourself, speak only the truth, to yourself and others, and walk with gratitude.'

Janet stood. 'Okay. That's it. I know you ladies are in a hurry today, so I kind of breezed through that, but I gave you the impor—' She stopped abruptly, closed her eyes, tilted her head, listening. Meg felt goose bumps rise up on her arms. She knew it was all a ruse, but oh, how she wanted to believe now, believe in it all, believe in her miracle.

'I'm . . .' Janet sat down, staring at M.J. 'I'm not sure, but I think the dog is trying to communicate something.'

Shelly laughed loudly. Meg gave up on her miracle, right then and there.

Janet looked at them, smiling. 'I know. It seems

unlikely. But sometimes I can pick up on animal frequencies. They're not that different than ours, but they tend to be shy about it. But this one . . .' Janet reached out her arms, wordlessly asking C.C. for M.J. Without hesitation, C.C. handed her over. Meg's goose bumps suddenly returned. It was as if *she* had had a premonition! She had just been thinking about C.C. handing M.J. over before they'd begun.

Janet held M.J. in her lap, facing her. She stared into the dog's eyes for a long minute, then bowed her head, closed her eyes again, and sat still for an awkwardly long time. Just when Meg was going to say something, Janet handed M.J. back to C.C. 'Well. Let me think a moment. It was fast and furious. If I could describe it as talking, which I can't, I would say this little dog talks very fast!' Janet smiled and Meg found she couldn't help laughing. They all did. It was easy to imagine that M.J. was a fast talker.

'I think she was trying to express that she doesn't understand the point of something she's been asked to do. Does that make sense?' Meg looked at C.C., then Shelly, all of them pondering that idea. Did M.J. not understand why she was traveling with them? Meg, still standing, suddenly straightened. Janet had gotten them all to buy into this crap! So much so that they were believing she could talk to dogs! Or listen to them, anyway. Meg exhaled, not really caring that it sounded exasperated.

'Oh!' exclaimed C.C. 'I know! That newspaper article! Remember? That Mick had? M.J. was at some sort of competition – gymnastics for dogs, or something. And remember?' She glanced back and forth from Meg to Shelly. 'She didn't do very well. Maybe she doesn't understand the point of that!'

Meg thought that C.C. might actually be right. At least about the dog not liking to compete. But it seemed ludicrous, communicating with a dog! But then she remembered all the times she and Grant would be watching TV in their bedroom and, suddenly thinking about Buster, she'd get up and find him sitting by the front door, needing to go out. Had he somehow communicated with her? Probably just her subconscious registering his footsteps near the front door. But two floors and a closed door between them? And then she remembered the times she'd be grading papers and think about maybe taking a break, going for a walk, and Buster would suddenly appear at her side, tail wagging.

No. It was too far-fetched.

As soon as she'd thought the words, Meg laughed out loud at her inadvertent pun. Suddenly the insanity of the whole situation seemed to cave in on her and she began to giggle uncontrollably. Pure, unchecked emotion flowed out of her.

What in the hell was happening to her? Meg Bartholomew. If her students could only see no-nonsense Mrs Bartholomew, teacher of Honors

English, now. Mrs Bartholomew on a road trip with friends. Mrs Bartholomew going to do construction work she had no idea how to do. Mrs Bartholomew *getting her fortune told*! Her students would be rolling in the aisles.

Meg got control of herself, held up her hand. 'I'm sorry. I just . . .' No, never mind, she decided. It wasn't worth it. Just play along and get out of here. She said primly, 'I do think it's quite possible M.J. doesn't understand the point of doing doggie gymnastics.' Shelly burst out laughing. Meg tried not to look at her, but couldn't stop herself, and she too dissolved again. She saw that Shelly was shaking in silent, throbbing laughter.

Janet looked mildly amused, but C.C. looked embarrassed. Maybe even angry.

'I'm sorry, I'm sorry,' gasped Meg. 'We're just tired, all the driving. We're punchy.' She slowly pulled herself together, but Shelly was still shaking, her head down, one hand over her mouth, the other on her stomach.

'I know it's hard for people to accept that dogs can communicate like this with us,' said Janet, still smiling pleasantly, seeming not at all offended. 'And I'm no expert here. I just say what I feel. And what feels like the thoughts given to me. And I have just one bit more, then you ladies can pay or not, as you choose. But this may be important. I *think* M.J. said that she might have a physical difficulty of some sort, possibly some sort of health problem, or—' C.C. gasped, hugging M.J. Janet put her hand on C.C.'s arm, quickly adding, 'But this might be about whatever she doesn't understand the point of. You know, that it's physically hard for her to do, whatever it is. I'm sorry I can't be more clear. She's very excited and agitated about a lot of things. It's been a while since an animal has been so eager to communicate with me. But this is like a ball of twine; I just can't sort it all out.'

Shelly was now holding her nose, trying to nod soberly, but turning red with the effort.

Meg opened her purse. Bogus or not, this whole thing, the roller coaster ride of giving in to it, and then not, seeing herself here through her students' eyes, at a fortune-teller's, of all things: she'd had a good laugh. And *that* had felt good. It had somehow broken through some of the numbness. She dug into her purse and pulled out a twenty, slid it across the table toward Janet. Then she looked at her cards, still on the table. Wealth and Miracle. She thought a minute, then reached back into her purse and pulled out another twenty, and handed it directly to Janet.

CHAPTER 11

C.C.

C. was trying not to think about M.J. at all, but especially not about handing her over to Candy Suddle. But each was an impossible task. M.J. was sitting on her lap, like a small loaf of bread, just from the oven, warm, with an unmistakable scent of goodness. C.C. felt she could almost hear the odometer, like a clock, ticking down the miles and the minutes she had left with M.J.

After they'd left the fortune-teller's, C.C. had tried experimenting, placing M.J. first on the seat next to her, then on her knees, rather than against her stomach, hoping that a little separation now would help ease the transition later. But each time, M.J. would worm her way back, nestling against C.C.'s stomach. She would sit for a while, then curl up in her bony little circle, wrapping her tail around herself like a ribbon round a package, tuck her needle nose into the crook of C.C.'s arm, and fall happily asleep. C.C. decided to enjoy the closeness while she still could.

She gently stroked M.J.'s tiny ears between her thumb and forefinger, one then the other, smiling at her little snoring sounds, marveling at her lightness, like a bird, and admiring her every feature, from her neatly dipped white paws, to the white tip at the end of her tail. C.C. felt the grip of fear and sadness tighten. What had been excitement at reaching Fleurville and Dogs' Wood, had become dread at reaching M.J.'s departure. Whether M.J. was on the seat, on her knees or on her lap, it didn't matter, in the end. In love or not, she had to give this darling little dog back to her rightful owner. Soon.

'How's our gas?' she asked Meg, who was driving.

'Eee!' gasped Meg. 'Not even a quarter tank! Glad you reminded me.'

They all began looking ahead for a gas station, C.C. feeling just the tiniest reprieve. The time it would take to pull off, fill the tank, use the restroom, maybe get a beverage or snack, would make for more minutes with M.J. There had been nothing for miles, but as they crested a hill, they all saw the gas station with the hundred-foot-tall sign that screamed: 'Pruitt Bros., Gas, Food, Coffee.'

'Right there,' said Shelly, pointing. 'See the truck stop sign?'

'Yeah,' said Meg, flipping on the turn indicator, but saying nothing more.

Their chatting had been minimal since they'd left the fortune-teller's house. C.C. thought the visit had been fun, mostly. Even though she could tell that both Meg and Shelly thought it was a lot of hooey. Or were trying to talk themselves into that notion. But Janet had been so right, about so many things. Then again, Meg was kind of right too. Most everything Janet had said could have applied to any of them. The only two comments that Meg had made in the car about the experience, and sounding very Meg-ish about it, was that it 'was relatively good entertainment value', and that the few things that Janet had said that didn't relate to all three of them, she could have 'surmised' by things like how they each dressed, wore their hair, spoke, things like that. C.C. guessed that was true, but she also just had a feeling about Janet, that she had – what? C.C. supposed it was some sort of openness, open to the vibrations and energy that was around everyone all the time, just some folks were more receptive than others. Like human antennas. C.C. felt she was more receptive than either Meg or Shelly. The gas, for example! What had made her think about the gas right then, when the tank was low? And then right after she says something – *right* after! – a gas station comes into view. Things like that.

C.C. thought probably some women were more antenna-ish than other women, but that most women were more antenna-ish than most men. Men had different antennas altogether. But, she had seen a man on TV who claimed to speak to the dead and whatnot. And maybe he did. But once, when she had sweet-talked Meg into watching one of those shows with her (she'd lured her really, with some home-made pralines), Meg had pointed out how the fellow's eyes darted around as he asked the person (almost always a woman, Meg also pointed out), 'Does her name begin with K? Or maybe C? Or E?' and the woman would shake her head, no, every time, looking worried. And his eyes would get all shifty and he'd keep on guessing, 'Is there someone named Ann, or with the middle name of Ann, or a nickname that sounds like Ann?' And the woman would get all excited and nearly pop out of her seat and say, 'Yes! Her nickname was Sam, short for Samantha!' Where C.C. herself had been sort of impressed, Meg had cringed and shouted at the TV Give me a break! He guessed three of the most common letters for female names of that woman's mother's generation, *still* got it wrong, so he went to a very common name and middle name, and *still* nothing. So his last-gasp attempt was a "sounds like", and that poor woman is so desperate to talk to her dead mother that she was looking for any possible hint that he could be on the right track so she gave it to him!' Then she had added with disdain, 'The guy's a slick purveyor of false hope. Like re—' C.C. knew that she'd been about to say 'religion', and had caught herself. Meg called herself a . . . what was it? One of those 'a' words, not an atheist but the other one. C.C. couldn't remember the name for the people who, as Meg had explained it to her, 'were more comfortable with the questions than with any particular answers about spirituality'.

C.C. blinked her eyes and looked outside, stunned. They were at the gas station! Meg was already filling the tank. *Boy howdy. There was something about driving in a car that puts babies to sound-sleep and grown adults to hard-thinkin'!* She unbuckled her seat belt and opened her door, and there was Shelly, holding her arms out to take M.J. Bless her heart. She handed M.J. over. She was so stiff and numb from sitting for so long she didn't know if she could get just *herself* out. She did, with much effort. Standing next to the car, she patted her arms and legs to get blood moving. She smiled at Shelly, who was hugging and kissing M.J. making little 'hmm' sounds. Every once in a while Shelly forgot to be Shelly.

They each took a step toward the building, but C.C. nearly fell. She felt pinprickles up and down her right leg; it wouldn't support her weight. 'Jesus, Mary and Joseph!' she cried, grabbing on to Shelly's shoulder. 'I don't think I can walk in there! My leg's asleep.' She lowered her voice to a whisper, 'But I've got to pee like a racehorse.'

Shelly extended her elbow to C.C. 'Here, hook your arm through mine and lean on me.'

'Can you carry M.J. and help me, both?' asked C.C., hesitantly lacing her arm through Shelly's.

'Sure! M.J. doesn't weigh a thing.' C.C. watched Shelly's face blanch as soon as she'd said it. 'Oh. I'm sorry, Ceece. I didn't mean—'

'Pshaww, Shel,' said C.C., smiling. 'I know I weigh a tad more than M.J.!' They both were laughing as they walked toward the little store, arm in arm. Shelly was so much taller than she was, and C.C.'s right leg was so numb that she was nearly being dragged along. As they entered the store, a harsh buzzer sounded. Lord, thought C.C., a person in the back *county*, let alone the back room, would hear that thing!

'Y'all caint bring that dawg in here!' said the pimply-faced young man who popped up from behind the counter before the door had even closed behind them. He was short, had a high-pitched nasally voice, greasy black hair. And he was scowling. C.C. got a bad feeling about him: he was one of those kinds of young men that has been given more responsibility than he has ability. Like a guard dog on a short chain. She started to turn around, but Shelly tugged her forward, making her stumble badly on her near-useless leg.

Shelly caught C.C.'s weight on her hooked arm, steadied her, then seemed to fix her in her sights. Uh-oh, C.C. thought. Shelly had that look in her eyes. Shelly quickly turned to the clerk, pointing at C.C. 'But she's got Kosten's Palsy. Did you see her just then? Almost fall down? That was a mini-seizure right there. This dog is a Seizure Dog. She's trained to tremble when she senses that her owner is going to have a big seizure. It has to be with her at all times.'

C.C. felt her eyes growing as big as supper plates.

M.J., perhaps sensing C.C.'s nervousness, was fairly vibrating.

'See, now,' Shelly continued as she dragged C.C. and her limp leg up toward the counter, 'if you look carefully, you can see the dog shaking. See that? And look at her.' Shelly directed the boy's attention to C.C. again. 'See how her eyes are all wide and fearful? She could be about to have a big seizure, what they call a grand mal, sometimes brought on by a full bladder.'

C.C. felt like she might have an actual seizure, brought on by embarrassment.

'Okay, okay!' said the boy frantically. He turned his body but not his head, keeping his eyes on C.C. He clawed blindly at the wall behind him, felt for and found the handle of a tall closet, opened it and, still with his eyes fixed in near-panic on the two women, grabbed something off the inside of the door. 'Here's the key; go right around the corner. *Here!'*

He shoved a key at Shelly, attached to what looked like a small boat oar. C.C. stared at it. Then she had to work very hard not to smile, thinking about what a serious problem this place must have with folks running off with their bath-room key for them to attach it to, basically, a paddle. 'Raht there!' The kid pointed to his left, jabbing his finger in the air toward the restrooms, clearly wanting them to move along before C.C. began thrashing around right in front of the hot dog rotisserie.

Arm in arm, they made their way to the rest-room, C.C. still needing to lean on Shelly, dragging her asleep leg behind her. At the door to the ladies' room, Shelly was shaking so hard herself from barely restrained laughter that M.J. was bouncing up and down in her arms. She had to hand the key over to C.C. C.C. unlocked the door as fast as she could and they burst inside together, their hands over their mouths.

'Oh! I declare! I'd better pee or I sincerely *will* have a serious accident!' After a minute, C.C. called out from the stall, 'Whatever in the world possessed you to say that, darlin'?'

'I don't know,' said Shelly, from outside. C.C. leaned to the left and could see her through the rather startlingly wide space between the door and the frame. Shelly had her back to C.C., staring at herself and M.J. in the mirror above the sinks. 'I really don't know,' she repeated. 'I guess I just didn't like that kid's tone, telling us we couldn't bring M.J. in, seeing as she was in my arms and there was no chance she was going to wee on his floor or anything.' She looked down, made a face. 'Not that the floors are any too clean in here to begin with. It just came to me, with you limping and all, so I just blurted it out and—'

There was a knock on the door. 'Shelly? C.C.? It's me, Meg. I gotta go!'

Shelly let her in, just as C.C. emerged from the stall. 'Here,' she said reaching for the dog. 'Let me take M.J. so you two can avail yourselves of

196

the facilities.' As her friends went into two stalls, C.C. turned, faced herself and M.J. in the mirror. They looked good together, she thought. She set M.J. on the counter, the little dog trembling more as her feet touched the hard, tractionless surface. M.J. didn't move, clearly aware that any effort to that end would be risky at best, life threatening at worst. She just stood in front of the mirror, staring at C.C., waiting, shaking. C.C. quickly washed then dried her hands, then cradled M.J. in her arms again, and the dog relaxed, completely.

'Hey, Shell?' C.C. called.

'Yeah?' Shelly answered back from the stall.

'M.J.'s stopped trembling . . . Guess I'm not going t'have a seizure, after all.' They both laughed.

'*What*?' asked Meg, from her stall.

C.C. told her the story, eliciting shrieks of laughter from Meg.

As both Meg and Shelly stepped to the sinks, C.C. asked Shelly, 'Where in heaven's name did you ever come up with a fool idea like a Seizure Dog?'

'I didn't make that part up!' exclaimed Shelly. 'There really is such a thing.'

'You are pulling my leg so hard I'm gonna be a foot taller when I walk out of this ladies' room!'

'No,' said Meg. 'She's not kidding. I've read about dogs who can alert for all kinds of things: epilepsy, heart attacks. I think they smell a chemical change in the body or something.'

'And I also saw a thing on Nova,' said Shelly, 'about dogs being used in doctors' offices to smell melanoma.'

'Cancer? No kidding?' asked Meg, looking impressed. 'I read in a magazine about a woman who swore her Labrador retriever knew she had breast cancer because it kept jumping on her, right on that spot. That's what made her go get checked out.'

'Yeah, I read about that too,' said Shelly, drying her hands with evident irritation at the tiny piece of paper towel the dispenser had allowed.

C.C. looked from Meg to Shelly, then down at M.J. 'Well, if dogs can do all that, why can't Janet sense a few things about us? And M.J.?'

Meg looked at Shelly; Shelly looked at Meg. Then Meg put her finger under M.J.'s chin, gave her a little rub. 'Y'know, Ceece? You may have a point there. Maybe she can. Maybe she can.' She turned, pulled her lipstick out of her purse and reapplied it. As she poked it back into her purse she said, 'This may surprise you, but I'm choosing to believe that Janet foretold Grant coming back to me. That's my miracle.'

C.C. didn't dare look at Shelly. Instead she used her damp paper towels still in her hand to wipe up water splashes around the sink. Then she gave a thorough wipe where M.J. had briefly stood. The silence hung in the air between them. They were saved by a tentative knock on the door. 'Y'all okay in there?' It was the poor clerk. C.C. had gone from feeling wary of him, to feeling sorry for him.

Shelly grinned at C.C., again offering her arm to her. C.C. poked one hand through the triangle of space, holding M.J. to her chest with her other arm. Then C.C. gestured for Meg to grab on too, and together they worked their way toward the door, C.C. calling out loudly, 'Crisis averted! Thanks to my wonderful Seizure Dog.'

Even though they were less than an hour away from saying goodbye to her, they stopped in the pet aisle and bought M.J. a leash and harness set, red, with little white hearts. C.C. fastened it on as Meg paid for it and the gas. The red against M.J.'s gray coat was charming, and even the finally smiling clerk reached across his counter and gave her a gentle pat on the head.

CHAPTER 12

LUCY

Lucy watched the red, needle-like second hand on the big clock above the chalkboard. She knew she shouldn't be watching the clock; she was supposed to be finishing her reading test. Or at least *starting* her reading test. But before she could take the test, she had to read the story, and it was too hard. The sentences on the page always looked like ants marching across a big white desert. And rivers of white space twisted down the page, flowing around the words, through the sentences and paragraphs. The rivers didn't want her to read the words. But the clock didn't mind being watched; in fact, it seemed to want it, with its thin red arm twitching mesmerizingly from one red dot to the next, all the way around, and then the long black arm would slowly bump to the next black dot. Lucy wished she could take a comprehension test about the clock.

Her butt felt like it was going to sleep. She squirmed in her chair; it was getting harder and more uncomfortable by the minute. She stared across the table at Jeremy. He was picking at the threads around the big hole over the knee of his jeans. She wrinkled her nose; she was always getting put at a table with Jeremy Bach. He smelled. But she and Jeremy and Angela Wobleski and Kyle Johnsen were all blue-level readers, and Mrs Diamont always put blues with blues and greens with greens and reds with reds. Stupid with stupid, medium with medium and smart with smart. Lucy stared at Carmen Gonzales, at the table at the front of the room. Carmen was already finished, her test turned over and her pencil on top. She was busying herself with peeling her pink nail polish off a fingernail. Carmen was a red. She was smart. But she was also nice. She was the only red who would sometimes play with Lucy at recess. But lately, Carmen played with Kendra. Kendra was mean.

Lucy sighed, stared at the clock again. A second went so fast if you were at recess, or even in gym, but a second of reading was not the same amount of time. It just wasn't. It couldn't be. And the longest seconds of all were the ones when you had a test on the table in front of you and everyone else was on the second page and you only had your name on the first page and two flowers in the margin. She looked at her drawings, then looked at the clock again, then remembered what Meemaw always told her, 'A watched pot never boils, Lovebucket.' Thinking of her Meemaw made her throat sting, especially remembering saying goodbye to her, and to Aunt Meg and Shelly. But she thought about Meemaw filling her up with brave, and about her funny names for her, like Lovebucket, or Sweet Potato Pie, or Miss Sweets, or Lucylovee. She drew a heart on her test, wrote 'Meemaw' in the middle of it.

'Time's up!' said Mrs Diamont crisply. Lucy turned her test over, squared it neatly in front of her, put her pencil on top, just like they were supposed to. She breathed a sigh of relief. At least this way, it looked like everyone else's test.

'Let's see . . . Which table is ready for recess?' Mrs Diamont walked through the aisles between the tables, looking left, then right. Lucy put her hands together and squeezed them between her knees. She wondered if her hair was all sticky-uppy again, and if that would count against them. She could hardly wait to start recess, even though her bare legs were already cold, just sitting in the classroom. And it was sort of snowing outside – what Meemaw called 'spittin' snow – even though the weather guy said it would be *warm* today. Stupid guy. Those weather people were never right! It was never warm in Wisataukee. At least not in March. Oh. That's right, thought Lucy. She looked to the wooden calendar up front. It had changed to April. This morning, Jennie Shendecki changed the month block from March to April and the day block from 31 to 1. Last fall, Lucy had gotten to change the day block from Wednesday to Thursday and the number from 7 to 8. Rosemary Pettibone, another red, was lucky. She had gotten to change the year, month *and* day block when they came back from winter break.

There was a grunting noise. Lucy almost didn't even have to look up to know what it was. Sure enough, over at Green One, Taz had gotten his foot stuck in the V of the table leg again. What a stupid-head! His name was Charles Tazelaar but everyone called him Taz. Or Taz the Spaz. Lucy didn't call him that. But she did wonder why he kept sticking his foot in there. Maybe he should be a blue, she thought. He must be stupid. But Taz was smart in some ways. Like, he drew good exploding things. Lucy felt smart in *some* ways too. Especially in art, especially when they got to do Squiggle Stories. Ms Martin, the art teacher, would give everyone a big piece of construction paper, and then she'd walk around the room and put a different kind of squiggle on everyone's paper, and then you had to make a picture using that squiggle. *That* was fun! And three times now Ms Martin had held Lucy's picture up to show the rest of the class how creatively she had used the squiggle to inspire her artwork. Ms Martin called all their drawings 'artwork', and she called them 'artists'. Lucy liked that about her; it made her feel smart. And her mom was always telling her that she had a 'creative' mind. So she knew there was some part of her that was smart, but she guessed it didn't like to come out very much at school.

'Number Two Blues, you're looking good now.

Thank you. You may go.' Mrs Diamont, standing right next to her, surprised Lucy. Wow, she thought. We never get to go first! She blinked, looked up, and realized that they weren't first. They were second to last. Again. Only Green One was still in the room. Because of Taz. He had pulled his foot out of his shoe (he had a big hole in the heel of his sock; in fact, there was no heel at all to his sock), and now he was working to free his shoe from the table leg.

But, she had been so daydreamy that she hadn't even heard the others being dismissed. As Taz was trying to unknot his shoelaces to get his shoe back on, Lucy scooted her chair out, quietly, like they were supposed to. And she walked quietly out the door, into the sea of loud voices, even though they were supposed to be quiet in the hall too. Lucy was always quiet. No one talked to her much, so it was easy. She joined the last of the class as they pulled their coats off the rack in the hall. Lucy zipped hers as she headed down the hall to the big doors at the end. Several kids were running, but you weren't supposed to do that either. She pulled her hood up and tied it, walking through the hallway. She pushed the door open and headed outside, onto the cold playground.

There were only islands of snow left, a long thin one in the shade of the slide, a big mound at the end of the four-square area where it had been dumped after shoveling. Lucy stared at her shoes, crunching over the frozen playground pebbles.

She kicked at a small mound of snow that was almost in the middle of the playground, not near anything. She wondered why it was here. A small stick that was the shape of a V caught her eye. It was frozen into the top of the mound. Oh. She remembered now. This was Kevin and those guys' leftover snowman. Lucy bent and scraped the stick out of the snow with her bare fingers. The stick looked like a wishbone. It must have broken off the snowman's hand. She picked it up and looked at it on her wet, cold palm. She scanned the playground, looking for Carmen. She would ask Carmen if she wanted to pull it with her and make a wish. But Carmen was on the swings again, with Kendra.

Lucy looked at her stick, feeling sad, then, suddenly, very happy. She held one side of the stick in each hand. All she had to do was pretend she was two people so she could make two wishes, and then one of her would for sure get her wish! And probably she would have to wish two different wishes, because otherwise it would be like telling someone your wish and then it wouldn't come true. And she should wish with her eyes closed. She closed her eyes. She would be Left Lucy and Right Lucy. She opened her eyes and looked at her hands. She could never remember which was her left hand and which was her right. She always had to look. Her mom had given her a thin silver band to wear on her right ring finger – ring-right-ring-right they had practiced. She saw the ring, rubbed her thumb against it, feeling which hand was right so she wouldn't forget, then she closed her eyes again. Right Lucy wished as hard as she could that she could have gone on the trip with Meemaw. Then Left Lucy told Right Lucy that she didn't think she should wish about something that had already happened, that you couldn't change the past. Instructively, Left Lucy demonstrated how to wish: *I wish I never, ever had to go to school again.* Then Lucy scrunched up her face, and the perfect wish for Right Lucy came to her. She felt it in her brain, then it raced down to her heart, then back to her brain again. It was almost the same as Meemaw's prayer that she had said the other night when they had that fun picnic on the floor in her empty house. Meemaw had said, 'Blessed Mother, blessed Father, please look over Kathryn and Lucy here in Wisataukee, and help Meg and Shelly and me get to Dogs' Wood safely. Amen.' Lucy only had to change it a little bit to make it just right. *Blessed Everyone, please look after Meemaw and Aunt Meg and Shelly and Mom, and help me get to Dogs' Wood.* Then Right Lucy and Left Lucy pulled the two sides.

There was a happy snap of a small piece of brittle wood breaking in the cold winter air. Lucy smiled before she even looked. Either way, she was going to get her wish.

CHAPTER 13

SHELLY

'Check the map again,' said Shelly, changing lanes. 'We keep coming past here.'

They'd driven past the Circle C convenience store three times now, looking for Dahlia Lane. Shelly was surprised that she wasn't feeling frustrated. But it was just like work, and she missed it. She had spent many hours driving people around looking at properties, and that was more or less what she was doing here.

Lexington had some beautiful country and this was a tony neighborhood. The lots were expansive, most looked to be a half-dozen acres or more, with large homes, all set back a quarter-mile from the road or more. Each property was bordered by white fences, all looking improbably freshly painted. Within nearly every fenced area were several glossy-coated thoroughbreds, grazing or snoozing, standing in the late afternoon light. The grass was already green and lush here. Did it stay green all winter? Shelly wondered. Most of the trees had visible plump buds and many had broken out in blossom already. In another week, this whole area would be an explosion of leaves and flowers, perfect for showing a home.

It occurred to her that spring was on a road trip too, but traveling south to north. Right here in Lexington, Kentucky, they seemed to meet.

The other reason she wasn't feeling frustrated at not finding Candy Suddle's house, although she would never admit it, was that she too was dreading saying goodbye to M.J. But C.C. had fallen so in love with the darn dog, *she* was a wreck.

'Okay, wait a minute,' said Meg, snapping the map, folding it in half, then quarters. 'I see where we went wrong. We're on Dahlia Road. We need to be on Dahlia Lane, which, believe it or not, is right off West Dahlia Boulevard.'

'Oh, for crying out loud!' said Shelly, suddenly feeling some frustration. 'Do these developers just sit in their offices rubbing their hands together and cackling, coming up with street names that are virtually identical? Bunch of sadists, is what they are.'

'Go left up here, I think. This should be Acadia Road,' said Meg, staring alternately at the map through her reading glasses, then lowering her chin to look out the windshield over the tops of them. 'Yes, it is. Turn here.' Shelly navigated the turn as Meg kept talking. 'Then up here on the right should be . . .'

'. . . Dahlia Lane,' came C.C.'s morose voice from the back. Shelly had also seen the large sign ahead, but said nothing, merely flipped on the turn indicator, a heaviness in her hands as she turned the wheel, steering them all toward a place they didn't want to be.

Shelly distracted herself by appraising the houses. This neighborhood was far less affluent than the previous, more of a standard subdivision, but a nice one, with large, half-acre lots. There were no fences in the front, but every house seemed to have a large, fenced backyard, most with several dogs romping or lounging in the late sun. Shelly chuckled. 'Apparently Dahlia Road is the horse neighborhood and Dahlia Lane is dog territory.' She wished she could stuff the words back in her big mouth. In the mirror, Shelly saw that C.C.'s eyes were closed, her cheek pressed into the top of M.J.'s head.

'We need fifty-two eighty,' said Meg. She'd pulled off her reading glasses, now squinting into the setting sun to read the house numbers as they trolled by. 'There's forty-eight hundred, so even numbers are on the right.' They slowly rolled past several nice homes, large, but rather homogenous, Shelly thought.

'Fifty-two hundred . . . fifty-two . . . forty . . .' said Meg.

A sorrowful moan came from the back seat.

Meg stopped counting. But seconds later she said softly, 'Right up here, Shell. It must be the blue one.'

Shelly pulled into the driveway and parked.

No one moved or spoke. Finally, Meg said, 'Well, let's get this over with.' She twisted around, said to C.C.: 'Do you want to just stay out here, honey?' But the sound of a slamming screen door pulled their attention to the house. A petite woman, about their age, with very short, spiky black hair, was trotting down the steps to the driveway. She wore a pale orange top and black stretch pants; Shelly noticed with some distaste that the legs of her pants were covered with dog hair.

'You're here!' she said, smiling broadly, approaching the car, bobbing and squinting, peering inside.

Barely audibly, C.C. said, 'I guess that's Candy.'

Shelly rolled down her window, drawing Candy to her side.

Candy nearly stuck her head through Shelly's window, her face brightening with recognition as she looked into the back. 'There's my little devil-dog!' She jogged over to C.C.'s door.

As C.C. opened the door, Candy reached in and lifted M.J. from her arms. Shelly and Meg quickly exited the car, both offering C.C. a hand out of the car. But C.C. refused help getting out.

'I'm fine,' she said, laboriously pulling herself from the car.

Candy rubbed her knuckles on the top of M.J.'s head, then held her up, her hands under M.J.'s armpits, the little dog's scrawny legs hanging in the air. 'Hello there, you little Houdini!' Candy tsked, then, in one swift, practiced movement, tucked M.J. under her arm. M.J. stared at C.C., then looked at the other two. Shelly opened her mouth to speak, but, for once, had no idea what to say.

Candy looked at each of the three women, one at a time. 'Y'all, I can't thank you enough. Was she any trouble on the way down?' Shelly wanted to stop looking at M.J., but couldn't. The dog was again staring at C.C.

'No trouble,' said C.C., her voice cracking slightly.

'Whyn't y'all come in, have a glass of lemonade while I get you your reward check? I already sent the other to the fellers up north.'

The three looked at each other. Meg checked her watch. 'That's very kind, thank you, but I don't think we have time for lemonade. We'd like to get to our destination tonight. So we'll have to get back out on the road pretty quick.'

'Well, let me go scrounge up my checkbook then. C'mon in!' She hustled into the house, not bothering to wait for them. The three of them stood, paralyzed, in the driveway.

Shelly and Meg each took one of C.C.'s hands. 'You okay?' asked Shelly, trying to make her face look brighter than she felt.

C.C. pulled back. 'I just don't think I can go in there. I'll wait in the car.' She turned, headed for the car. Her voice caught as she said, 'In fact, I think I'll . . . just . . . walk . . . a bit.' She passed

211

the car, continued down the driveway, her high heels clicking on the concrete. She choked out, 'I'll just head up the street, the way we came. Y'all can pick me up on your way out.'

'Here, I'll walk with you, honey,' said Meg, turning to head toward her. Shelly caught Meg's arm, gently pulling her close, speaking quietly. 'I want to try to buy M.J. with the reward money. Or more, if necessary. Offer her the airline part of the reward too. Buy the damn dog for C.C.'

Meg bit her lip, stared at C.C.'s retreating figure, then looked up at the house, then back to Shelly. 'Yeah. Do it. We'll figure the money out later.' Shelly nodded. As Meg took off toward C.C., Shelly reached through the passenger window and grabbed her purse. She opened it and walked her fingers through the bills inside, then looked up the street. C.C. was walking very fast; Meg ran to catch up. She watched as Meg slipped her hand into C.C.'s. Each adjusted her pace to match, walking in step. Suddenly C.C. stopped, her free hand going to her face. Meg stopped too, and C.C. let her head fall onto Meg's shoulder. Meg wrapped her arms around her. Shelly walked up the few steps into Candy's house, the sense of mission surging in her.

She stepped through the door, up three steps to the living room. She had to clamber over a baby gate, and was immediately surrounded by swirling dogs of various colors, but all of them one of two breeds: Italian Greyhound or Whippet. Shelly tried to count them, but they moved too fast, tumbling over and around one another, barking and yelping. One or two would dart in to sniff Shelly's shoes or legs, then dash off. The dogs were careening into each other, running around the room, then three or four others would run over, bang into each other, and her, and zoom off again. She guessed there were over a dozen, maybe twenty.

Shelly realized that her mouth was hanging open, and closed it. Who could live with this many dogs? She couldn't help but laugh at the sight of them, but was also slightly appalled.

'C'mon now, you mongrels!' yelled Candy jovially. She pulled open a huge sliding glass door, which led to her second-story deck. She launched M.J. out from her arms into a rushing current of other dogs. A few were more recalcitrant. 'Out with you all! C'mon, Curly, Elvira!' She whistled through her teeth. Several more headed out. 'Rufus! Get out from under that table! *RUFUS!* No, Jazzy, Kermit! Stay out! *RUFUS!*' she bellowed. *'Get over here!'*

Shelly couldn't help but clap her hands over her ears at the cacophony of Candy yelling and dogs yelping and barking. Finally, all the dogs except for Rufus, who was still huddled under the table, exited on their own. Candy closed the door behind the last one. Outside, the dogs continued to swirl over and under and around each other, first across the big wood deck, then down a flight of stairs, and out across the huge yard. Shelly stepped over to the sliding glass door to watch them. They looked like one throbbing organism, a giant canine mass. As they raced around the perimeter, their noise level increased. Shelly shook her head again. The neighbors must love this canine choir. Not.

Candy fished the reluctant Rufus from under the table. Shelly stepped aside as she deftly set him on the deck with a little scoot from her foot, and slid the glass door shut again. Rufus immediately sat next to the glass, quivering away, looking forlorn and miserable. Suddenly M.J. was next to him, as were five or six other dogs. Then all but Rufus and M.J. did a pretty good imitation of a whirlpool on the deck, then flowed down the stairs again. M.J. and Rufus sat trembling outside the door together, balefully asking with their soft eyes to come back inside.

'Okay, now, lessee, where'd I set my danged checkbook?' said Candy, drumming her nails on her counter, scanning the kitchen. 'Ah! There it is!'

'Wait,' Shelly said.

'Yes?' Candy turned, checkbook now in hand.

Shelly straightened to her full height. 'We are perhaps interested in buying M.J. from you. We're prepared to forgo the reward money for her, and maybe sweeten the pot a bit.' Shelly knew how to negotiate: remain very cool, expressionless, start low to leave some raising room. Above all, keep emotion out of it. It was the emotion that tipped your hand, weakened your position. Shelly had always excelled in the dispassionate negotiation.

Candy smiled, leaning one elbow on the counter. 'Well, now. *This* is a sir-prahhz.'

The doorbell rang at the same moment the front door burst open. Shelly and Candy both stepped around to the living room to see Meg helping a breathless and flustered C.C. over the baby gate.

'I forgot! The fortune-teller! Did you tell her about the fortune-teller? What she said about M.J.?' C.C. was gasping, holding on to the wall. Meg was right behind her, still holding on.

Oh, no. Shelly's eyes fell shut, her chin dropping. The fortune-teller nonsense was going to weaken their negotiating power *considerably*. If not rule them out altogether as sane owners. Why hadn't Meg just kept her away? Shelly glared at her, shaking her head. Meg shrugged helplessly behind C.C.

C.C. must have thought Shelly's disheartened head-shake meant that, no, she hadn't yet told Candy about the fortune-teller. With supreme effort, and a big lift from Meg, C.C. made it fully over the gate. Meg followed.

'Well,' said C.C. 'Oh, forgive me.' She stuck out her hand. 'I'm C.C. Byrd.' Candy looked bewildered, but shook C.C.'s hand, letting her own be pumped up and down. 'You see,' said C.C., putting her other hand on Candy's, holding it tight and speaking rapid-fire, 'I didn't want to come in, because I was afraid I'd get all emotional, and I did, out there, but then I remembered something very important that I must tell you. You see, we stopped at a fortune-teller's house, along the way, and she was very good, really very good, knew all about each of us and all like that. Well, anyway, she said – oh, her name was Janet, Janet Cole – anyways, she said, near to the end, after she'd done us humans, that M.J. was communicating with her and telling her something was wrong. She said, that is to say, Janet said, that she didn't understand the point of something – I mean little M.J. didn't.' C.C. took a gulping breath. Shelly put her forehead in her palm. C.C. plunged on. 'Janet said little *M.J.* didn't understand the point of something and she said she couldn't be sure what that meant but *I* thought it might be the doggie gymnastics you've got her doing. And *then* she said – Janet, I mean – she said that she thought M.J. might also be saying that there could be something *wrong* with her! Her, M.J., not her, Janet. Maybe a health problem. Now, mind, she said she wasn't sure about this either, but she said she could get M.J.'s vibrations pretty strong.' C.C. stopped, fanned herself, took another deep breath. 'So please, promise us you'll take her to the vet, straight away? Because this fortune-teller was right about so much! *Please?*' C.C. was still holding Candy's hand in both of hers, gave them a slight, imploring shake. Candy continued to stare at C.C. Shelly looked at Meg, but Meg's chin was down, her head shaking dismally.

'Heh, heh,' Shelly laughed. 'Yes, well . . . maybe we can take M.J. to a vet ourselves, C.C. I've just told Candy that we'll forgo the reward to buy M.J.'

C.C. and Candy both looked at her, but with opposite expressions. C.C. looked ecstatic; Candy looked stunned.

'Now, hold on,' said Candy. 'I didn't say M.J. was for sale. She's not.' C.C. looked crestfallen.

Shelly reached into her purse and pulled out her checkbook. 'Come on, now. Everyone has their price. C.C. has fallen for that little dog in a big way, and she's lost enough in her life, and I'd be grateful if you'd let us buy M.J. for her. I know this is all a bit sudden, but please consider it.' She paused, then leaned toward Candy and said out of the corner of her mouth, 'You do have a few dogs to spare.'

No one spoke for a minute. Candy looked from one to the other, then outside. M.J. and Rufus still sat together on the other side of the glass, slightly bumping each other with their trembles. Then C.C. saw M.J. She took a step toward her, then stopped, her clasped hands over her heart.

'Look, I'm sorry, but I can't,' said Candy. 'I've invested a lot of time and energy in training M.J. Most dogs love doing agility, and she's the smartest of the bunch, so I think she'll come 'round to it eventually.'

'But she doesn't understand the *point* of it,' moaned C.C.

Candy looked at Shelly, then Meg, clearly asking for a reality check.

'What if we tripled the total reward money? Offered you eighteen hundred dollars?' asked Shelly.

C.C. and Meg both gasped.

'No, now hold on,' said C.C. Meg looked relieved that she didn't have to be the one to object. 'We can't afford that, Shelly.' She sighed, then looked back at Meg, pleadingly. 'Can we?'

'No,' said Meg, quietly. 'We really can't.'

'But—' said Shelly.

'Look, it doesn't matter!' Candy interrupted, looking slightly irritated. 'M.J.'s not for sale. At any price. Period. I'm sorry.'

They all four stood there. Two sharp barks came from outside. Shelly didn't know if it was M.J. or Rufus. Candy leaned on the counter and wrote out the reward check. 'Here,' she said, handing the check to Shelly, 'I've left the name part blank. You fill it in however you decide.' She walked through them, across the living room. She unfastened the baby gate and held it open. 'I sincerely thank y'all again for bringing her down. I really do. Now, y'all have a safe trip to Tennessee.'

'Let's go,' Shelly said, touching C.C.'s shoulder. Meg headed toward the door, but C.C. looked across to M.J. She sucked in a sharp breath, blew a kiss toward the sliding glass door, held her hand outstretched in the air. Tears streaming down both cheeks, she turned, walked across Candy's living room, down the steps and out the door. Shelly followed. As she passed Candy, Shelly handed her her old Wisataukee Realty business card, whispering, 'If you change your mind, please call my cellphone number. Please.' Candy reluctantly took the card.

Outside, the sounds and sights didn't match Shelly's anger and frustration. The sun was setting and the dusky light made the green grass look like velvet, the blossoms on the trees looked lit from within. There were soft neighborhood sounds drifting on the evening air, kids' voices, the soft regular smacking of a basketball on a driveway, a screen door banging shut, a dog barking. Sounds of summer, thought Shelly, and it was only March. No, she reminded herself, it's April now. They'd left home in March, and would arrive in Tennessee in April, and only two days had transpired. But a season had changed, and a still-healing heart had broken anew.

They all climbed into the car, Meg taking the driver's seat for the final leg. She slowly backed the car out of the driveway, shifted into first gear. Shelly had a sudden and somber thought: Candy had never even said she loved the dog. As they drove away, the only sound was C.C.'s soft crying in the back seat. Without turning, Shelly slid her hand back through the gap between her seat and the car. Meg was shifting into second as Shelly felt C.C. grasp her hand. They made their way out of the neighborhood, then out of Lexington, finally back onto I-65 South.

Shelly's hand and arm were numb when they crossed the border into Tennessee, but she kept a tight hold on C.C. anyway.

PART II

ARRIVING

CHAPTER 14

MEG

Meg peered over the steering wheel, amazed at how dark the night had become. She slowed as they came upon a thin, tilted street sign. 'Is that it? CR-Twenty?'

'Yup!' said C.C. 'County Road Twenty! We're gettin' close!'

Meg turned the car, her hands feeling heavy and tired as they worked their way around the steering wheel. CR-20 was paved, but narrow, and with each mile they drove, the buildings grew fewer and farther apart, the vegetation more dense, the late night darker. Meg felt very, very far away from home.

She asked, 'Are we close to Dogs' Wood yet? I didn't realize it was going to be in –' it took her a few seconds to think of another way of describing their environs without using terms like 'the boonies' or 'the sticks' – 'such a remote area.'

'Well, we're getting close!' C.C. repeated. She was leaning forward excitedly. Driving into Tennessee had seemed to buoy her a bit. But Shelly, conversely, had seemed to shut down at about that time. She had been holding on to C.C.

for so long, Meg wondered if the mood could have physically passed from one to the other. Maybe there was such a thing as emotional contagion. She'd recognized a pattern of trading moods in her marriage; she didn't know why it happened.

'Look!' C.C. exclaimed. 'There's Hickory Pete's Café! I can't believe it's still here!' The small café was a converted house, sitting back from a circular dirt parking lot. The only light came from a forlorn-looking streetlight on the edge of the parking area, and a neon sign in the window that read 'CLOSED', the E flickering on and off. 'Almost home!' said C.C., as they drove past.

'I know I've asked you this, but how long has it been since you've been to Dogs' Wood?' Meg asked, trying not to sound as tired, old and forgetful as she felt.

'I think about fifteen years. Kathryn was a teenager, last we were here. Then Georgie moved to Paris for nearly twelve years. She only came back because she was ill.' C.C. sighed. 'But, of course, I didn't know she was ill. She never told me. Just kept writing me happy letters, telling me what was in bloom, or about the ice storm, or a new neighbor, or some new book. Never a word about being sick. I wanted to come down, but she kept saying it wasn't a good time. I'm sure she just wanted to protect me, especially after Lenny died.'

'So was Dogs' Wood vacant for all those years she was in France?' asked Shelly. Meg was glad to see her finally joining the conversation.

'Not all,' said C.C. 'But she had some trouble with renters, so it was vacant for the last few.'

'Wow,' Shelly said quietly. 'I didn't realize that. So, bad renters, then vacant, then she was ill; she probably wasn't able to maintain it.' She paused. 'A lot could have changed since you've seen it.'

'I suppose so,' said C.C.

Meg leaned into the steering wheel, stretching her back. No one spoke. The silence settled. While Meg couldn't see the clouds that made for the dark sky, she could feel the weight of the atmosphere, heavy, full of portent.

She glanced at the dashboard clock. Almost eleven thirty. They had dawdled too long over dinner, out of sheer relief to be out of the car. Shelly had suggested that, when in Kentucky, one should eat Kentucky Fried Chicken. Meg felt queasy, just remembering. She had merely picked at some coleslaw. The chicken had looked heavy and fatal.

The mere memory made her smell chicken. Then she heard paper rattling in the back seat, C.C. snacking on the leftovers. 'Amazing,' she murmured.

'Hmm. What?' said Shelly, emerging from her silent reverie.

'I was *just* thinking about that KFC, and then C.C. pulls out the chicken.'

'See? I was reading your mind again!' C.C. laughed. 'Y'all want a snack?' Meg and Shelly both politely declined, and both cracked their windows.

Meg wondered what the difference was between them that sadness and grief made C.C. eat, sometimes compulsively, but Meg couldn't seem to find her appetite anywhere since Grant had left. And the smell of the chicken wafting up from the back brought his memory close again. His favorite dinner. *Her* fried chicken. The recipe was from an old cookbook she'd gotten at a yard sale, but she had tweaked it over the years. The first few attempts had been unmitigated disasters. Greasy, naked pieces of chicken with most of the breading floating in the pan of oil. But she had persevered and finally was able to consistently produce what Grant called 'damn good chicken'. Meg loved to cook, but she never enjoyed frying chicken. It was the whole production: all that handling of raw meat, the dipping, the breading, the frying. Then the air becoming laden with the heavy odor of oil and meat, the counters and stove spattered. The smell lingered in her hair and clothing till she showered and changed. Grant refused to eat any fried chicken but hers. She'd initially been flattered by his loyalty. Less so, as the years wore on. It began to feel like a test: 'If you love me, you'll make fried chicken.'

Tonight, when her meal had been set in front of her, the years of dead chickens had rushed through her like a butcher's bad dream. Sitting there at that KFC, Meg had suddenly felt as if she'd eaten fried chicken every day for the past thirty-three years. She'd thought she might be sick. But tears had come instead. At least she hadn't run off to the restroom. Just sat there, tears and all. She'd just gotten through it. That's what Grant had always said to her and the kids if they were upset. 'Do what you have to do to just get through it.'

Is that what he'd done in their marriage? Just gotten through it? Till it was at some preconceived end? Or till he just couldn't stand to 'get through it' any longer?

'Is it just me,' asked Shelly, 'or is it getting darker?'

Meg and C.C. both murmured agreement, Meg grateful for the interruption of yet more thoughts of Grant.

'Meg?' asked Shelly. 'Who is it who said: "Life is like driving a car on a dark road; you can't see anything beyond your headlights, but you can make the whole journey that way"?'

'E. L. Doctorow,' said Meg. She sighed, shook her head, deciding not to speak her thoughts. *If only it were true. Sometimes what's ahead is a cliff, leading you into a giant black abyss, and no set of headlights is strong enough to see it coming.*

'Wait!' C.C.'s ill-timed shout scared Meg half to death, making her brake sharply. 'There's the little chapel!' Quietly, she added, 'I used to go there . . . sometimes. I've never much cared for the name, Crown of Thorns Chapel. It's such a lovely little church, the grounds especially. I wonder if the same old gardener is there?

'Anyway,' she went on, a renewed energy in her voice, 'given that the chapel is here, Raven Road should be just up ahead a piece. And then we go down there a mile or so, and we'll be home! Dogs' Wood!' She made a throaty, giggling sound. 'I am so jibberty right now you'd think all my dearly departed family was going to be there to welcome me home!'

Raven Road. Edgar Allan Poe images flashed through Meg's mind. *Nevermore.* That, plus C.C.'s comment made Meg almost shudder.

'Look! There it is!' shouted C.C. 'On the right, up ahead. There's my dear Raven Road.' A small sigh floated up from the back seat.

The street sign was slightly twisted, but once the headlights caught it fully, Meg could make out the letters on the old metal sign. A glow of distant lightning sketched across the far horizon. She flipped on the turn indicator, glad they were almost there. Finally. She turned onto the unpaved and slightly washboarded road.

'Dear Raven Road,' said C.C. again, sounding more southern than ever.

'You say that as if you're saying Little Lambie Road or something. Not spooky, old Raven Road,' said Shelly. She and Meg both laughed.

'What's spooky about Raven?' asked C.C.

'You know, "Nevermore"! The Poe poem?' said Shelly. She cawed once for effect.

'I was just thinking the same thing!' said Meg.

As they passed the first house, a sprawling

Victorian on a huge lot, C.C. cried out, 'Look! That's the old Rabinowitz place, there on the right! I think. But it looks different. The whole road looks different. Smaller. It's just . . . I've been away so long, and you know how things kind of shrink when you're away?'

They drove past an empty lot, then another house, equally large on an even larger lot. Then another. 'The houses aren't as big as I remembered them either.'

'Are you kidding me?' asked Shelly, the excitement fairly ringing in her voice now. 'They must be, like, three to four thousand square feet each! Or more! And incredible lots. A couple acres each.' Meg smiled at her. Nothing like a little real estate to shake Shelly out of a funk.

'Maybe,' said C.C., distractedly. 'Oh!' Her fingernail tapped on the window. 'This house here used to be the Kunkels'.' They rolled past a large house with a full wrap-around porch.

'Nice!' said Shelly. '*Very nice.* Does your house have a porch like that?'

'It's got a nice big veranda in front, but it doesn't go all the way round.'

Meg glanced again at the other side of the road. There hadn't been a single house on that side the entire length of the road. Just wild-looking land.

'Who owns the other side of this road, Ceece?'

'Uh, I believe that's all county land. It's not tended over this side. It's open to the public, though, and it's a lot of land. There's a marshy clearing just past Dogs' Wood, and a Civil War cemetery, way on the other side. It has a big ol' parking lot where they set off fireworks every Fourth of July. We get a great view from the house, without all the noise.'

They drove on in silence, passing more large houses and empty lots. Meg figured they'd driven well over a mile already. 'I didn't expect Raven Road to be so long.'

'We're nearly there. We're the last house. Oh! This house here was the Spodeckers', our next-door neighbors. They were a nice family, and well-to-do? Yes, ma'am!'

'Wow,' said Shelly reverently. 'It looks like the whole thing was redone recently. It's gorgeous.'

'Georgie wrote that the Spodeckers sold it a while back. The new owner's supposedly some kind of bigwig.' She squinted, trying to see in the dark. 'Georgie wrote that the guy is hardly ever there. He travels a lot, I guess. It looks pretty dark in there.'

'Ceece, it's after *midnight*. It's pretty dark in *all* these houses.' Shelly sounded tired again.

'Well, *excuse me*,' said C.C., sounding hurt, 'but most of the others have their porch lights on.'

The fatigue was setting in on all of them, but Meg kept the speed very slow as the road had become ever bumpier. The woods to the left had grown increasingly dense, and dark. Lightning flashed again in the distance. She reflexively checked the gas gauge: half a tank.

'There's Dogs' Wood! On the right!' yelled C.C. 'Look! Oh Lord! See the three trees?' C.C.'s voice was breaking. 'They're full . . . of flowers . . . already!' She was silent a minute, then added softly, 'I wish M.J. was with us. She'd love it here.'

Meg marveled at the white blossoms in the head-lights. It was as if those pearl-white petals captured every bit of light, and reflected it back out. She turned, followed the long gravel driveway that ran along the side of the property. It wound back behind the house, to a large square parking area, also gravel. The headlights landed on a detached two-car garage, with a lovely carriage house on top. It had an open staircase on one side, two large windows in front, with garden boxes under each.

'Oh! That's new!' said C.C.

'The garage?' asked Shelly.

'No, the little thingy up top. Probably Georgie's artist's studio. She had it built just before she got back from France. When I lived with her, she used the formal dining room as her studio.'

'Really?' said Meg. 'She used the—'

'It's fabulous!' said Shelly. 'Turn on the brights, Meg.' Meg obliged, despite feeling miffed at being interrupted, especially followed by the order from Shelly. 'Cedar shake siding, great windows. *Nice!*' said Shelly. 'Carriage houses are very popular. They add a lot of value. You can rent them out, use them as an artist or writer's garret, mother-in-law or nanny quarters.' She lightly clapped her hands together. 'Big plus!

Depending on the interior quality and floor plan, it could add—'

'C.C.? Should I just leave the car here?' Meg asked, cutting short the real-estate lesson. She was glad Shelly was out of her funk, but they'd been idling a while, and Meg knew Shelly could go through the remaining half-tank of gas assessing the property.

Shelly pointed in front of Meg's face. 'Circle around, then back in to that door there. Make it easier to unload right into the house.'

Meg's jaw tightened. She hadn't asked *her*. Shelly turned in her seat, toward C.C. 'Ceece, what's the straightest shot to get our luggage to the bedrooms? Back or front?'

'Uh, lessee,' said C.C. 'This'n here goes into the mudroom, which leads to the kitchen. Then there's a hallway, and another, then past the dining room, living room and library, till you get to the stairs. So, I guess the front door probably. Because the front door opens right to the foyer and the stairs. Oh! Wait a minute! We could use the dumbwaiter! Meg, back up to that door there, like Shelly said. Please.'

Grateful for C.C.'s manners, afterthought though it was, Meg backed the car around, still feeling a bit like a hired driver as the other two chattered away.

'You have a dumbwaiter? How cool!' said Shelly, almost cackling with delight. 'And it's big enough for a suitcase?'

'It's huge! Theresa and I used to play in it all the time when we visited Aunt Georgie when we were just mites. We used it as an elevator, one riding, one pulling. 'Less we could get an adult to pull us both. It was also a dungeon, a castle, a cave, a spaceship, an undersea hideaway.' C.C. chuckled.

Meg parked, pulled the brake on, hard, removed the keys with a twist and jerk. She climbed out, into the dark night. She almost immediately calmed, struck by the tactile quality to the air, almost voluptuous. But there was an electric quality, too. She could feel it on the hairs on her arms. Meg scanned the horizon, watching for another glowing rip in the fabric of the night sky. But the blackness was complete, with no beginning or end. As the other two climbed out and stretched, the only sound was the settling and clicking of the engine cooling.

'Ladies, we have arrived,' Shelly said reverently. 'Man. The air is like velvet. *Dark* velvet, but velvet.'

Meg rummaged in her car till she found the old emergency flashlight she kept under the driver's seat. She clicked it on. A very weak beam barely shone to the ground. 'Damn,' she said. 'Flashlight's almost gone. I should have gotten new batteries. Didn't think of it. Either of you bring a flashlight?' *No,* she knew before they answered.

'No.'

'Nope. But we might find one inside,' said C.C.

'D'y'all want to see what's what in there, before we haul everything out?' She held something up. 'I've got the *key*!' She squealed the last word, her feet tapping a little dance on the gravel, which made her wobble on her high heels, almost tipping over. Both C.C. and Shelly started to laugh, but the sky suddenly cracked open with light, a loud boom, making all three shriek.

'Better hurry!' yelled C.C., grabbing Shelly's hand and steadying herself. She tottered across the stones, holding on to Shelly, with only the weak flashlight to guide them. 'Meg, we'll just go flip on some lights. Just be a minute.'

Meg watched C.C. walk up the narrow, wooden steps, holding on to the plank handrail, the paltry beam ahead of her. Shelly waited at the bottom. C.C. pulled the screen door open, and screamed again, quickly covering her head with her arms as the door toppled half onto her, then over the side of the landing, and onto the bushes.

Meg ran to her, calling up, 'You okay?' C.C. nodded uncertainly.

Shelly climbed the steps, took the flashlight and inspected the doorframe where the hinges had been. 'The screws stripped right out of the frame. This wood is all rotted.'

'Ya think?' asked Meg. She checked herself. 'You sure you're okay, Ceece?'

'Yes. But – Lord have mercy! Bought near t'killed myself before we even got inside the blessed house!' She grabbed the wobbly handrail. 'But I'm okay. A fine welcome home, huh?'

No one spoke; they all just stared at the screen door, prostrate on the bushes. Another burst of lightning brightly illuminated them, the house, the screen corpse, as if they were being X-rayed from above. The thunder clapped nearly simultaneously, making them all duck.

'Whew!' said C.C., covering her ears, the flashlight still in one hand. 'We could be in for a toad choker.' She pushed the key into the lock of the wooden door. 'I reckon we ought to put "screen door" at the top of our fix-it list. And one of these panes is cracked in the door. That's number two.' She turned the key and pushed the complaining door open.

Meg and Shelly followed C.C. and the feeble light into what Meg guessed was the mudroom.

'Uh-oh,' said C.C. 'I think the flashlight just got weaker.'

'Try shaking it,' said Shelly. 'Here. Give it to me.'

Meg couldn't see, but she could feel Shelly push past her, then heard the batteries being shaken violently inside the casing. The weak beam stopped altogether. Good one, Shelly, Meg thought, stepping forward, feeling for C.C.

'Now what?' said C.C. 'I can't see my hand in front of my face!'

'Well, we can *feel* the back of your head just fine in front of our faces. Move *forward*!' said Shelly. 'C.C., find a light switch!'

'Quit ordering everyone around, Shelly!' said Meg, her anger surging.

'Girls. Now, c'mon,' said C.C. 'We're all tuckered out. Let's just hang on. I mean it! Grab hold!' The three of them shuffled into the mudroom, each holding on to another, a short, blind, crabby parade.

'This is ridiculous,' said Meg, letting go suddenly. She turned, walked toward the door, feeling her way. 'I'm going to check my emergency kit. I think there's a mini-flashlight in there.' She found her way back out, down the steps and toward the car. As she walked across the gravel, she stopped abruptly. There was a loud rustling in the bushes behind the garage.

'C.C.?' she shouted.

'What, hon?' came C.C.'s voice from inside.

'Are there . . . animals, wild animals, around here?'

'Well, sure. Skunks and raccoons and the like. Maybe a possum. Why?'

'Something's in the bushes.' It sounded bigger than a raccoon to Meg. Maybe a bobcat. Or a bear! She strode quickly to the car, jumped inside, slammed the door shut. She opened the window an inch to hear. The breeze was kicking up with the approaching storm. *It was the breeze. Just the breeze.*

She pulled the kit from the glove box, rummaged through it, finally finding the small flashlight. She clicked it on. Nothing. 'Shit!' She looked out her window, half-expecting to see a bear's face staring at her.

'Another dead battery?' Shelly shouted to her from the small landing of the steps, making Meg jump.

'Apparently,' Meg called back through the inch of open window. 'Look, I'm going to turn the car around, shine the brights in there while you guys find some lights.'

'I'll go tell C.C.'

Meg did a quick three-point turn, aiming the car toward the open door, then flipped on the brights. She opened the window more, shouted, 'Can you see in there now?'

'Here's a light switch!' C.C. called, her voice muffled from inside. But Meg could see no light go on in the house. 'Tarnation!' Even C.C. was getting angry now.

'Well, shit and a half,' said Shelly, stepping back out onto the porch, shielding her eyes. Meg dimmed the headlights.

C.C. appeared next to Shelly. Between the screen door falling on her and the wind now blowing as if it meant it, C.C.'s hair hung in chunks, most with several pins hanging from the ends. Meg was glad C.C. couldn't see herself. Knowing her, she'd want to come into the car to fix it. Meg unrolled her window fully as the other two approached the car. 'Has anyone been paying the electric bill?'

C.C. nodded. 'I think so. The estate attorney

was supposed to be paying all the bills, till we got down here.' She evidently felt some of her hair blowing around her face. She patted her head, felt for what was amiss, and pulled a bobby pin out, pulled it apart in her teeth, and expertly wound up a piece of hair, pinning it in place.

'Well, looks like he didn't,' snipped Shelly.

'Should we . . . go back into town and get some batteries? And more flashlights?' asked C.C., sounding like that was the last thing she wanted to do.

'Oy!' said Shelly. 'I'm so damn sick of being in that car! And it's a long way back into town. *And,* I doubt we'd find a store open at this hour. I say we just use the headlights as best we can, get our overnight stuff inside. Maybe we can find some candles or flashlights in there, and then just get to bed. I don't know about you girls, but I'm beat.'

Meg felt like she could sleep right there in the car, but the thought of a bed rallied her. She put the car in park but kept the headlights on. She climbed out and opened the trunk. 'Everyone come get your bag and we'll call it a day.'

With the wind whipping around them, they all three hauled C.C.'s big suitcase out, then Shelly and Meg each got theirs. It wasn't nearly the size of C.C.'s, but still it took all Meg's strength to lift it from the deep well of the trunk. She let it drop heavily to the ground by her feet, stared at it. The emblem of transition.

As she slammed the trunk closed, Meg said, 'At least we're—'

She let out a small, ironic laugh. She'd been about to say 'home'. But it wasn't. Not by a long shot. She pictured the darkened rooms of her house in Wisataukee, all the things that were familiar, the things that made it home. Then she thought about what wasn't there.

Home. Her whole notion of the concept seemed to be unraveling.

'Here,' she said finally. 'At least we're here.'

CHAPTER 15

C.C.

C. walked through the mudroom, still holding the useless flashlight in one hand, the other pulling her big rolling suitcase behind her. This felt all wrong, arriving in the middle of the night, with no electricity. Suddenly her toe bumped into something. A boot. *A man's boot!* She pawed the darkness. A coat. *A man's coat!* She shrieked, stepped backward, accidentally stepping on Meg, but continued backing up furiously.

'Ow! Ow! Stop! *What!*' yelped Meg. 'What's wrong?'

'What did you say?' asked Shelly, farther back. 'Meg?'

'Shhh!' said Meg.

'*What?*' asked Shelly.

'There's someone up there,' whispered C.C., hastily crossing herself.

'Who?' Meg, also whispering now, backed up with her.

'*I don't know who!*' C.C. wormed her way behind Meg, abandoning her suitcase. Her grip on the flashlight tightened. She mentally practiced whacking an intruder on the head as hard as she could. But she doubted she'd even be able to move if attacked. She'd be frozen in fear, just like in her nightmares. All he'd have to do would be to lift the worthless flashlight from her frozen fingers and whack *her* over the head into un-consciousness. She should just save him the trouble and pass out now.

'Are you sure?'

C.C. couldn't speak.

'I mean, are you sure it's a person, not just a coat hanging there, over some boots? I mean, there's a coat here. Feel.' Meg grabbed one of her hands and thrust it into a coat. Fleece. Georgie's. Coat hooks. The memories were flooding back.

'What's going on?' asked Shelly again, finally catching up to them.

'Ceece, do you remember coat hooks along here?' C.C. felt Meg's hand on her shoulder.

'Y-yes, now I remember coat hooks in here. But would you go first? Please?'

Meg sighed, sounding exasperated. C.C. knew she should lead; it was her house. But not really. And it didn't even feel familiar. Not anymore, and not in the dark. Plus, Meg and Shelly were the brave ones, not C.C. Any time she heard a sound at night, she'd wake Lenny up and he'd go investigate. She was spineless; Lenny even dealt – charmingly – with it when she was overcharged at the store, or if the dry-cleaning was lost. As Shelly said, C.C. didn't *do* conflict.

'Oh, Ceece,' said Meg, pushing past her. 'It's *coats*. A row of them. Boots, too.'

C.C. put the useless flashlight on the shelf above the hooks. She let her free hand drift over the different coats as she followed Meg, but now they were like old friends. There was Georgie's flannel-lined duck canvas that she wore 'hunting' with her camera; another fleece, maybe a vest? Corduroy. C.C. smiled. That was for Georgie's 'stewing' walks around the property or up and down Raven Road when she was stuck on a painting. The coats were comforting, but also melancholy; as if they were waiting for Georgie to return and replace them with summer-wear – sweatshirts and jean jackets. C.C. pressed her face into the corduroy. The smell of Georgie was still surprisingly strong, evocative, a combination of powder and paints. And cinnamon, from the toothpicks she'd been addicted to ever since she'd quit smoking years ago.

They continued on through the long mudroom, pulling their suitcases, shuffling into the dark kitchen. Meg slowed and C.C. let go of her coat. She felt safer in the kitchen. When she lived here, this was where she'd spent most of her time with Georgie. Eating, talking, washing up, playing Yahtzee at the little table. The waves of memories crashed over her, her mind's eye seeing more than if she could take it in visually.

She sighed again. There probably wasn't a soul alive who didn't wish, like she did now, that she'd known it was going to be the last time when she'd visited her old aunt. But that was probably part of the plan, C.C. decided. That, apart from the rare exception, we never know. That's the challenge, she thought. To live the moments of life so fully, so present, that when your time comes, you can say, 'Yes. That's done. That's how I wanted it.' Come to think of it, just how Georgie did with a painting.

Another burst of lightning flashed in through the window above the sink, accompanied by a booming clap of thunder. Then all at once, a loud, pelting rain hit the house.

C.C. reached across the counter, her hand probing tentatively. The tins were there, all lined up. God only knew how old the ingredients were. C.C. knew that the only tins Georgie opened with any regularity were the coffee and the sugar.

'I know it's dark, but can we move a little faster? Please?' asked Shelly.

'Sorry, Shelly,' said C.C., moving on and calling out, 'Hold up when you get into the hall, Meg.' When she felt the back of a chair, she knew she'd reached the breakfast nook at the end of the kitchen. She felt along the wall, into the hall, then to the doors to the pantry.

'Hold up, Meg. It is o-dark-thirty in this hallway.'

'I'm right here.'

C.C. felt her touch her arm. 'I've been waiting, as instructed,' said Meg.

'Shel?' C.C. called over her shoulder. 'You coming?'

'Right here. My suitcase wheel got stuck coming around the corner.' Her voice was close enough that C.C. pressed on, her hands again moving along the wall.

'The dumbwaiter should be right – *here!*' C.C. said, her hands bumping into the thick metal handle that lifted the sliding door. She parked her suitcase and grabbed the dumbwaiter handle in both hands. She pulled upward, then pushed from below, to no avail. 'It's stuck, dang it all!' She was unprepared for how perilously close to tears she suddenly felt again. She began to cross herself but screamed shrilly as someone grabbed her arms.

'Calm down! It's just me!' She felt Meg's hands moving along her own arms, joining her hands on the handle. 'Here, let's push together. On three. Ready? One—'

A loud clatter came from behind them. They both froze, barely breathing. But the only sound now was the rain and wind outside.

'*Shelly?*' Meg asked, her fear audible. 'Please tell me that was you.'

'No!' Shelly whispered, suddenly next to them. 'What the hell *was* that?' They merged into one. C.C. closed her eyes, began silently praying. They waited, standing as one trembling unit. Slowly, C.C. opened her eyes. There seemed to be some light coming from the kitchen.

As one, they shuffled toward it. C.C. wasn't sure who had initiated their movement; she hadn't. They took silent, mincing steps, C.C. feeling involuntarily pulled along, sandwiched between the other two. They crept forward. Finally, reaching the corner, they leaned, peered into the kitchen, keeping their feet and bodies behind the wall.

'Oh!' said C.C., noticing the strong beam of light low and flat along the floor, angled into the cabinet. A flashlight. On the floor. Their flashlight. Not only working, but now shining brightly.

'Hail Mary, full of grace,' began C.C.

'Hello?' Meg called out toward the beam.

'Don't worry, girls!' said Shelly, her voice unnaturally deep and loud. 'I've got my gun right here. Cocked and loaded.'

'Your wh—' said Meg before being elbowed by Shelly.

'Yep. Got my gun, aimed right down this kitchen.' She sounded like she'd swallowed a beaker of testosterone. 'Come on, sucker, make my day!'

Meg whispered: '*You* are cocked and load— Ow!'

'Sure glad you brought your guns,' C.C. yelled, catching on.

There was a muffled click from the mudroom.

'*What the hell was that?*' Shelly whispered, her volume and testosterone suddenly gone from her voice. *En masse*, they reversed back into the hallway. C.C. flinched as she was pressed up against the handle of the dumbwaiter, but fear kept her silent.

'Was that sound a . . . a gun?' whispered Shelly.

'I don't know,' Meg said, equally softly. 'Sounded more like the door closing to me. Maybe the wind pulled at it.'

They waited in the roaring silence.

Finally, Meg broke away, stepped forward slowly, to the kitchen. 'Hello?' she called.

C.C. could hear her steps, one, then another, into the kitchen. C.C. knew she should go with her. At least follow. But she stayed put, clinging to Shelly.

Why was Meg so brave, C.C. wondered. Shelly was the bold one. But Shelly was still there, her arms around C.C. Then it dawned on her why Meg was particularly brave now. Grief. C.C. knew from experience that when grief has its teeth in you, there's hardly anything that will scare you; with all that pain, there's no room for fear.

'*Who's here?*' demanded Meg, sounding more angry than C.C. had ever heard her. 'If you know what's good for you, you'll get the hell out of our house *right now*, or you're going to be carried out in a body bag, with a bullet hole in your head.'

'You get 'im, Meg,' C.C. made herself say aloud, trying for gusto, but her voice cracked. She suddenly felt her forearm held aloft, gripped in both of Shelly's hands.

'I'm right behind you with my rifle, Meg!' Shelly said, walking down the hall. Apparently Shelly thought she could make her act more convincing with a prop, so C.C. followed, letting herself be towed by her arm. They rounded the corner and

246

C.C. saw Meg's feet illuminated by a bright beam from the floor. Meg bent, picked up the flashlight, then slowly turned, staring at the two of them. She put her hands on her narrow hips; shook her head at Shelly. Shelly squared her shoulders, took a deep breath, but then dropped C.C.'s arm. Meg turned, took a few steps; Shelly followed. C.C. felt paralyzed.

Meg and Shelly slowly stepped across the kitchen together. C.C. closed her eyes again, crossed her fingers and arms and kissed the back of her wrists three times each, as she and Theresa used to do before making their most fervent wishes or prayers. Then she watched her friends head into the mudroom.

'How did our flashlight get over there?' Meg asked. C.C. could see her looking at the distance between the shelf and where she'd picked it up.

'At least it's working,' said Shelly.

'C.C.? Did you set it down in the kitchen?' asked Meg.

'No, I set it on the shelf, above the coats. In the mudroom,' said C.C.

'Well, how did it get from here,' she shone the light on the shelf, 'to here?' She moved the beam to the middle of the kitchen floor, then toward C.C.

C.C. held up her hands. 'Wow, that's bright!'

'Sorry,' said Meg, lowering the beam to the floor. 'It *is* bright,' she said, as if just realizing it.

'Uh, girls?' said Shelly. 'Isn't that a long way for

a flashlight to roll? From the shelf back there in the mudroom, all the way to here?'

'Wait! The floor!' said C.C. 'Feel the floor with your feet. It's slanted! It's always been slanted there.' She watched Meg and Shelly run their feet along the floor as Meg painted it with the light, both of them nodding.

'It's slanted all right,' said Shelly.

'Whew!' said C.C. 'I thought I was about to have a heart attack! I sure don't want to be working on a house that has spirits hucking resurrected flashlights around at night!'

The other two looked at each other. 'Well, that explains it. I guess,' said Meg. 'The slanted floor, I mean.' She sounded dubious. 'Maybe the fall knocked some rust off the battery contacts. Or something.' She moved the light around the kitchen, staring at the bright beam.

C.C. breathed a sigh of relief, and looked at the old kitchen as the light moved around. On the far wall, it caught a small still life Georgie had painted decades ago. Apples and oranges in a colorful ceramic bowl. C.C. knew that painting well. At least *something* felt welcoming.

The other two rejoined her and they all made their way back to the dumbwaiter, this time with the aid of the flashlight.

'Let's see if we can get this door up,' said Meg. 'If not, we'll just have to carry our suitcases up.' She used the butt of the flashlight to tap all the way around the bottom of the door, then the handle.

Then all three pushed. It gave way, sliding upward surprisingly easily, once it came unstuck. C.C. took the flashlight from Meg, found the hook, and latched it in place. She then directed the beam into the cavernous dumbwaiter itself. C.C. directed the light up the shaft, showing her friends the mechanism of pulleys.

'Lift your suitcases up here, girls,' she said, patting the base of the cabinet. Meg and Shelly lifted all three bags in as C.C. held the flashlight and the door. Then she touched the near ropes with the flashlight. 'Pull on these,' she said, grinning. 'It shouldn't take both of you. Try it.' Shelly put her hands on the ropes, began to pull, hand over hand. The shelf containing their suitcases rose up and out of sight.

'Wow! It's easy. And those suitcases aren't light,' said Shelly.

The system of counterweights and pulleys made for a magic trick of sorts. C.C. had always loved showing it to friends. 'Let Meg try it!' she said. 'But don't let go!' she added quickly. Shelly held on till Meg took hold and resumed the pulling.

'Wow, it really is like almost no weight is on there!' said Meg.

'You'll feel it get kinda tight, where you have to pull a little harder, but stop there. That'll be the second floor. There are three bedrooms there. We'll sleep there.'

When Meg told her it had gotten harder to pull,

C.C. secured the dumbwaiter by sliding a lever over the ropes, clamping down on them.

'That's it!'

'Uhh,' said Meg. 'I've got to go turn the headlights off.' She didn't move.

They looked at each other a minute, then C.C. said, 'Let's all go.' She didn't even want to go back into the kitchen, much less the mudroom or outside. But they had to stick together. Now more than ever. They clasped hands and walked together, Meg leading with the flashlight. When she pulled the back door open, she let out a small gasp. 'What the hell . . . ?'

'What?' asked Shelly.

C.C. grabbed on to the back of Meg's jacket.

'My car. The headlights are off.'

'They probably turned off automatically. You know, after five minutes or whatever,' said Shelly.

'No. It's an old model, made before they did that.'

'Are you sure?' asked Shelly.

'I think I know my own car after driving it for twenty years, Shelly.'

'Are the keys in it?' she asked. 'Maybe they drained the battery?'

'Yes, I had to leave the keys in to keep the lights on. But the battery is new. Mick just replaced it. The battery couldn't be drained in that short a time.' C.C. grabbed even tighter to Meg's jacket. Someone out there wanted them in complete darkness.

Meg started to walk outside, but stopped abruptly. She turned her head. 'Ceece, honey, you've got to let go of me.'

'Oh! Sorry.' C.C. released her grip and Meg headed down the steps, her head down as she ran toward her car, the beam of the flashlight bouncing ahead of her. C.C. held her breath, till she realized she was. Soon Meg was running back, then joining them in the mudroom, breathless and wet, the keys in one hand, the flashlight in the other. 'Seems okay, but,' Meg took a deep breath, 'the headlight switch was turned to off.'

'Jesus, Mary and Joseph,' said C.C. It was spirits, she just knew it. Her mother, likely. She was always going around after them as children, switching off lights, admonishing them for wasting electricity. In fact, maybe it was her mother who had turned off the power to the whole house. That would save a lot.

Meg handed the flashlight to Shelly, then slid the deadbolt closed on the door, then the chain lock. Shelly led them through the mudroom, picking up a coat that had fallen off its hook. C.C. watched her look at it, then at the hook, then at the shelf. She knew what she was thinking: was it possible the flashlight had rolled all that way? And why was the coat on the floor? Shelly unceremoniously shoved the flashlight back at Meg, who took over the lead again, C.C. grateful to be sandwiched between them.

'Straight down here,' she directed as they walked

along the hall, past the dumbwaiter. She pointed. 'That was the formal dining room that Georgie used as her studio.' They continued on, turning into another larger hallway. C.C., too tired to be tour guide, simply murmured, 'Front door directly ahead. Library on the right. Living room across. Stairs up ahead to the left.' They got to the front foyer and to the grand staircase. Meg shone the beam up the wide, dark wood stairs. C.C. could picture herself and Theresa sitting on the large, square landing, halfway up, playing with small metal cars, or tiny wooden animals. Barbies, if C.C. could talk Theresa into it. From the landing, the stairs turned, continued up to the second floor.

They climbed up slowly, C.C. wondering how she had ever run up and down these stairs. Meg and Shelly were waiting on the landing for her to catch up, and then waited more for her to catch her breath. On the second floor finally, they made their way to the dumbwaiter, and pulled out their suitcases. C.C. stepped down and opened a bedroom door, shining the flashlight inside.

'Meg, why don't you take this room? It was mine and Theresa's. Then, just mine, but it's still got the twin beds.' She walked to the other end of the hallway and opened another door. 'Shell, this one's got a queen bed. It gets nice light. I'll take Georgie's room, there.' She pointed with the flashlight toward the front of the house. 'Bathroom's right here, between you two,' she said, pointing the light back again. 'Each of you has a door connecting, so make sure you lock both doors if you want privacy. Georgie has her own – I mean, I have my own bath. Oh. You'll need towels. They're—' She stopped. Something was working its way through her tired mind. 'Wait a minute . . . Georgie's bathroom deodorizers!' She stepped to a built-in cupboard next to the stairs, and pulled open one of two small drawers below. She rummaged through small bars of soaps, bobby pins, old dried-out compacts of rouge, and odds and ends. She pulled the other drawer open, again shining the light on the contents. 'Ah-ha!' said C.C. She smiled, handing first a ceramic holder, then two candles and a box of matches to Meg. 'Georgie called these her bathroom deodorizers. Two of us can use these for light, the other one can use the flashlight.'

'You keep the flashlight, C.C.,' said Shelly, reaching for the other holder and more candles.

C.C. bit her lip. 'Thank you.' She knew she should argue, offer it to them, her 'guests'. But she needed the light. She didn't want to go into Georgie's room at all, let alone by herself. Let alone sleep in the bed that dear Aunt Georgie had passed in. C.C. looked toward the room.

'Hey,' said Meg. 'There are twin beds in here, right?' She pointed to the room C.C. had just assigned her.

C.C. nodded. Meg returned the candles and holder to the drawer, handed the matches to Shelly. Then she took the flashlight from C.C. in one hand, and C.C.'s hand in her other, pulling her toward the bedroom.

'Sleep in here with me then. I'd be grateful for your company,' said Meg. C.C. nodded, swallowing the lump of gratitude in her throat. Shelly was already in her room.

Even with just the flashlight, C.C. could see that nothing had changed in the room. There were the twin beds, one against each wall, their blue and white log cabin quilts smooth and neatly tucked under the pillows. The long dresser under the south window still held pictures of her mother and father and Theresa. One of Georgie with C.C. at high-school graduation. One of Lenny, C.C. and Kathryn, just after Kathryn's graduation from high school. Next to that, a tiny frame, containing Lucy's birth picture from the hospital.

'Let's get our p.j.s and get to bed,' said Meg, rubbing C.C.'s back lightly.

Meg held the light as C.C. opened her suitcase on the floor, pulled out her nightgown and toiletries kit. She then returned the favor as Meg kneeled and unzipped her suitcase. C.C. gingerly sat on the edge of her old bed, where she hadn't slept in years.

She held the beam steady as Meg carefully sifted through the neat stacks of her clothing, then flipped the top closed and dug for something in a side pocket. C.C. stared at the circle of light on top of Meg's cherry-red suitcase. She could see images in the patterns made by the bulb and filament, maybe dust on the lens. Like cloud shapes. She saw a pair of jumping dolphins. A hot-air balloon. Other smudges and shapes that her tired brain couldn't imagine into anything. But as she twisted the light slightly, there on the side, a skinny triangular shape that was nothing more than that. No one else in the world would have seen anything at all in it. But C.C. did. The narrow head, with laidback ears, a small, cool nose that liked to nuzzle into her side.

What she wouldn't give to have M.J. now, to curl up under the covers with her, tuck her hand between M.J.'s spindly front legs, petting the swirl of hair just below her throat, tucking M.J.'s small head under her own chin, keeping each other wrapped in love, safe in sleep. It was as if all the unanchored wisps of love for all those missing in her life had somehow attached themselves to that little dog. C.C. touched her fingers to her lips and blew two kisses northward, hoping they would travel far enough to reach her girls in Wisataukee. Then she twisted slightly on the bed, and aimed a third kiss toward Kentucky.

CHAPTER 16

PURDY

'Mick, did they put an address on their bill?' Purdy asked, leaning on the counter of Mick's shop. 'The ladies, I mean?'

'Dang, Dad! You're really a goner for that woman,' said Mick, at first grinning, then not, as he noted his father's determined expression. 'Hang on, lemme get the invoice.'

Purdy drummed his fingers on the counter, noticed his fingernails. Clean, short, square. He lifted his fingers slightly, imagining her hand, her fingers laced through his. He slapped his hand back on the counter. It was beyond ridiculous. It was also beyond an ache. Seeing her leave had been like watching a train pull away from the station. The train home.

He hoped Mick wouldn't ask him any questions, wouldn't demand that he explain why her, why now? He didn't know himself. But he did know that since he'd met her, he'd hardly stopped thinking of her. And something else. The anxiety and panic attacks that had returned after Keppie's death had seemed to quiet. He'd even phoned up Dr Fitzmarin, his shrink in Chicago.

Again. But Purdy didn't want to write in a journal. He wanted to write letters. Again. Thankfully, Fitz had said he thought that would be just as good, if not better.

Never in all his years had he felt like this. Never. Was it love at first sight? No. He wasn't so foolish as to think that he loved her. But there was something. There was some sort of connection between them. He leaned his elbows on the counter, chin in hand, turning his head away from Mick's rear end, bent over as he dug through his 'files'.

Mick need someone in *his* life, Purdy thought. An assistant or secretary. Or an archeologist, maybe. His filing system was a big cardboard box on a table, stuffed with receipts, invoices, shipment slips. The works. Every so often he would dump everything out, throw away the things he didn't think he needed to hang on to anymore, and put the rest back in, in his 'special layering system'.

'You need help there, son?' Purdy asked, trying not to sound as impatient as he felt.

'Unh-uh. Thanks, Dad. It's right down here . . . somewhere. Couldn't be past level two. But maybe it's still in level one. I think I might've dug too low.'

Purdy shifted his weight from foot to foot.

'Got it!' Mick turned, triumphant, holding a slightly rumpled yellow carbon. 'Top of level two, like I thought. It's just I thought level two was lower than it turned out to be.' He set the invoice on the desk.

Purdy grabbed it. 'Thanks, son!' He spun toward the door and was pushing it open after just two long strides.

'Hey! I'll need that back! For my records!'

Purdy waved the yellow slip over his shoulder without looking back, then broke into a jog across the dirt street. He passed a small clump of daffodils that Keppie had planted outside the restaurant years ago. It was amazing to him, that they kept coming up, year after year, no matter what happened. Small yellow trumpets proclaiming infinite newness, hope. He gave them a small salute as he ran past.

He wouldn't let himself even look at the address till he got into his room. With the key in the lock, he noticed, as if for the first time, the very solitary-looking number affixed to his room door. Room 1 at Purdy's Motel. Not much of an address.

He'd moved into the room after Keppie had died, not wanting to stay in the house. It had helped. A little. But mostly he felt like he'd just given up. But now, there was something pulling him along. It was almost too much, like a swift current.

In the room, he decided to write the letter before he looked at her address. He folded the yellow carbon twice, then set it at the top of the desk blotter, like a small gift waiting to be opened. It was where she lived. Where she was, right this minute. Maybe still sleeping. Maybe just waking up. He sat carefully in the old upholstered chair. He leaned back, getting his belly out of the way, and pulled open the thin desk drawer. The pens and pencils rolled slightly from the movement. He surveyed his choices. This was important. Finally, he selected a pen that Mick had found for him, made with gelatin or something, Mick had said. What would they think of next? But it was supposed to be quick-drying, which was good. Being a leftie, it was hard not to drag his hand across the page as he wrote, and he often smeared the ink. He pulled out a few sheets of the motel stationery that Keppie had purchased – how long ago? – he couldn't even recall. It had a parchment look to it, but he thought it had originally been white. He wouldn't be surprised if near about every piece was still in the desk drawers in each of the rooms. No one wrote letters anymore, hadn't for a long time. And if they took a mind to, who'd want to write a letter on stationery shouting: *Stay at Purdy's Motel, in beautiful Tupper, Illinois!*

Keppie. Bless her heart. She'd loved this little place so much – loved the work of it, the work that kept her from herself, and him. She couldn't see that everyone wouldn't love what she loved about the place: the town that kept to itself, didn't bother anyone, the peace and quiet, the home cooking. She had faith beyond faith that word would spread as people sent letters all over the world about the splendors of Tupper, Illinois.

On this stationery. But word hadn't spread. The motel was really only a destination for the odd folk that liked to find out-of-the-way spots. But most of their guests over the years had been families on road trips, not planning at all to stay in Tupper. Road-weary parents that, once they saw the little sign out on the highway, were happy to make Purdy's Motel & Restaurant their *new* destination. These were Purdy's favorite guests; they were always so grateful to have someone take care of things for a bit. He would get the parents a cup of tea, or something stronger. He would set the kids up with some old blocks from his little trunk, all sizes of pure oak, polished to a smooth finish by years of little hands. Most kids had no experience with plain old blocks, but they would fall into playing with those like they were the world's best toy, which, Purdy knew, they were. *Thank God for tired parents and automobile breakdowns.* Those were what kept the motel going. That, and the honey business, especially once they set up a website. If not for the honey, they simply would not have made it.

Well, they would have made it. Purdy rubbed his thumb across the embossed letters at the top of the page. They always would have gotten by. They always did. By grace and by gumption, Keppie used to say, they would get by.

But he couldn't help but wonder now, what was beyond getting by? In business. In love. Maybe, it depended on what you risked.

He held the pen, poised above the paper. It didn't feel right. Too light. For this letter, he needed a pen of consequence. He opened the drawer, looked over his choices again. There was a red felt-tip pen. That wouldn't do. A couple of ballpoints, and another like the one in his hand. He put it back in the drawer, rubbed his chin thoughtfully, staring at the meager selection. 'Oh!' he cried out loud, remembering. He opened the drawer as far as he could, till it bumped into his protruding stomach. He leaned to the side and reached all the way to the back, scraping the inside of his elbow a little on the desk edge. Finally his fingers bumped into the rectangular case. He pulled out the velvet box, set it on the desk, and lifted the top off. Inside, was a blue fountain pen, fat, shiny, almost iridescent. He ran his finger over the gold trim, and his gold initials on the side, MLP. A gift from Keppie for his sixtieth. She'd ordered a special ink – his favorite color, turquoise – called 'Peacock Blue'.

Purdy put one finger on the fountain pen. Likely it was dried up from lack of use. He picked it up, pulled at the top, remembered it was threaded, and carefully unscrewed it. The gold point looked clean and elegant. He knew he'd written Keppie a thank you note with it, but couldn't remember if he'd used it past that. He held it in his hand, cradled it. Yes, this felt right. He felt sure Keppie would want him to use this pen to write to C.C. To maybe begin again.

He put the point on the desk blotter, drew a line. Nothing. He gave the pen a couple of shakes, put the tip on the blotter paper, and drew it across again, making a sharp scraping sound, but no line. He repeated it several times. Then it occurred to him, scratching away, that maybe Keppie *didn't* want him to use this pen for this purpose after all. And then, like a miracle, yet another small miracle, a bright turquoise line. A little tumble of breath fell out of him, and he laughed. He put the pen on the stationery, then lifted it. How should he begin? What should he say? What *shouldn't* he say? He took a deep breath to calm his trembling hand, then began again. The Peacock Blue words flowed, and he found that, like riding a bicycle, one did not forget how to write a letter.

CHAPTER 17

SHELLY

Shelly opened her eyes, blinking in the bright sunlight streaming through the east window. Unlike at the motel, where she had awoken disoriented, she knew immediately where she was, remembering their dark arrival at Dogs' Wood. Dark was no longer the issue. Last night, C.C. had touted the natural light in this room as if that were a good thing. But Shelly hadn't said anything. They'd all been too tired. C.C. especially. Shelly yawned, but it came out more like a sigh. Poor C.C. She'd heard the soft sounds of her crying, and Meg's comforting, last night. Between saying goodbye to that little dog, and their tense arrival, it had been rough on her. But they'd get right to work today, figure out their supply list, go shopping, maybe even start to paint a room today. Nothing like paint for some instant, uplifting change.

Shelly's heart beat faster just thinking about it all. Now, finally, they were getting into her area of expertise. And it would necessarily include sanctioned shopping! Even if it was just for paint and tools and the like. She rubbed her face with her hands, stretched luxuriously, then rose and walked to the window. The sun was well up. She glanced around the room, looking for a clock. On the small bedside table was an ancient-looking rotary phone, an ugly, pond-scum-green color, a phone book underneath, but no clock. Across the room, atop a mahogany dresser she found one, also ancient-looking. It was a round, brass-looking thing, little domed metal ringers on top. It read ten minutes after three o'clock. Even in her newly awake state Shelly knew that it was neither three a.m nor three p.m. She guessed it was close to eight a.m.

She surveyed the rest of the room. It wasn't huge, but not cramped either, almost square, two large windows. She walked to the near one. North, she thought. The other one was east. From both she could see the driveway turnaround, the garage and carriage house, and the woods in the back. But from the east window she could see the neighbor's house, separated by a thick row of shrubs and trees, many blooming, or with fat buds. But a large overgrown bush by the carriage house had giant round balls of flowers. And they were moving.

She took a step back. The popcorn balls moved again. She stepped to the side of the window, shielding herself, and peered out. Was that a face? There was nothing now, but the flower balls continued moving, as if something was inside the bush. Then the shrubs behind it wiggled and shifted, like a thick, slow breeze moving through them. Then, all was still. Shelly looked at the leaves on the trees: no breeze. Had she seen someone? She couldn't be sure. After last night . . . Then the leaves did riffle, the treetops swayed gently, the grasses leaned their heads the same direction, rocked back. Just the breeze.

She turned away from the window, distracting herself by letting her realtor's eye again appraise and assess. The queen-size bed had a large bird's-eye maple headboard. Beautiful! It nearly touched the bottom edge of a large painting on the wall above. Oils, she thought, a sensuously shaped slender white vase – maybe Grecian? – filled with a colorful array of delicate wildflowers, a dusky gray background. She saw a narrow, precise signature in the corner: Georgie Tucker. Shelly gazed at the painting again. The colors, the play of light on the edges of the petals, the graceful arc of stems. 'Nice,' she said quietly. 'The woman was talented.'

Shelly walked across the room to the closet, opened it, half-expecting it to be empty. It was far from that. Almost oozing forth was an astonishing variety of vintage dresses, coats and other items. Stacks of unusual hats were piled haphazardly on the long shelf above. A costume collection? Shelly wondered. Or just generations of family collections? She fingered a pale blue satin dress that looked like it had been purloined from Little Bo-Peep.

Coffee. It was as if her brain had said it aloud.

She opened the door and stepped quietly into the hallway, listening for sounds from the other two. But all was quiet behind their closed door. She headed downstairs, nodding approvingly at the natural light from the large south-facing windows at the end of the hall. She'd have to research the local market, do some comparisons, but she was already getting a feel for the house's potential.

At the bottom of the stairs, she peeked into the long narrow living room. It appeared to have been decorated, if one could call it that, into two areas: the far end a sort of conservatory, with bookcases and a piano, the near end a sitting area with two ratty couches, one facing the fireplace, the other under the south window that looked out onto the front porch. But the most immediately striking thing was the rug. A huge oriental carpet ran nearly the length of the long room atop the dark hardwood floor. It was one of the biggest oriental rugs Shelly had ever seen. And, amazingly, it seemed to be in good condition, its multicolored floral and geometric patterns relatively unworn and vibrant. She would advise C.C. to include the rug with the house, to the right buyer. It was one of a kind, and fit the room perfectly.

Still standing in the entryway, she assessed the rest of the room, making tsking sounds. The rug was by far the best thing in it. The walls were stained from age and there were several holes and cracks in the plaster. The fireplace mantel and surrounding stonework were chipped and broken.

Shelly looked up. The ceiling plaster looked okay, and the texturing was a beautiful pattern of swirls, and there was a gorgeous medallion around the light fixture . . . Oh dear. Shelly shook her head. Staring upward, she tried to come up with a word for the chandelier. *Hideous.* It looked like the base was an old wagon wheel, painted black. From it were suspended little box-shaped copper lanterns. Each lantern looked like it was wearing a small, red, pointed Chinese peasant hat. Various sizes of gray feathers hung off each lantern.

'That's the ugliest damn fixture I've ever seen,' she muttered. She sighed again. This room *alone* would need paint, plaster work, new windows, or at very least new panes. The fireplace tile and mantel would have to be redone. And, as soon as humanly possible, a new lighting fixture.

She walked down the hall toward the kitchen, retracing their steps from last night. She peeked briefly in through the panes of the library's closed French doors, noting walls of books, two handsome brown leather chairs, and a bay window with a built-in seat, complete with fitted yellow floral cushion, an assortment of gold and pale blue satin throw pillows on top. What a perfect nook for curling up with a book! She imagined prospective buyers picturing themselves there, as she was now. She continued down the hall, her need for coffee now pressing her past more house inspection. She hoped there was coffee in the house.

Otherwise she might have to slip into their bedroom and nab the car keys from Meg's purse.

She came around the corner and stopped dead. Seeing the kitchen in the light of day was, to say the least, startling. Not that it was all that light in the dim, narrow room. She shook her head. For a house of this size and stature, it was surprising to have little more than a gloomy galley kitchen. It had only one, small, north-facing window, above the sink. The old tiles on the counter were cracked and missing in places. There was a hole in the plaster on the wall next to the refrigerator. The linoleum floor was worn through to the subfloor in several spots. On the back wall, the faded blue-flowered wallpaper was stained and peeling. But between the fridge and the sink, she spotted something that made her smile: a row of silver tins along the back wall of the counter. 'Yes!' she said, grabbing the one marked 'COFFEE'. She opened it, delighted to find it was half-filled with beans. She stuck her nose in, cautiously sniffed. The dark, rich smell she knew and loved didn't exactly jump out at her, but it still smelled like coffee. *Hallelujah!*

Now, if she could only find a grinder. She looked around and quickly found one on the windowsill behind the sink. This was going very well! She unwound the cord from itself, plugged it into an outlet next to the sink, poured in some beans, screwed on the top. But she stopped herself from pushing the button. As strong as her need was, she didn't want to wake her friends. Trotting into the mudroom, she grabbed a coat, returned, draped it over the grinder. Then, reaching her hand underneath, she felt for the button. Gritting her teeth in anticipation of the noise, she gently pressed the button. But no sound came. Not a click, much less a grind. She squeezed again. Nothing. She lifted the coat, checked the top to make sure it was on properly, squeezed again.

Then she remembered. No electricity. '*Shit*!' She glanced around, looking for evidence that something was plugged in and working. Anything. But it was as if she'd stepped back in time. There was no microwave. No toaster. Not even a clock on the ancient stove. She opened the short, bulbous refrigerator. She immediately slammed the door shut, clapping her hand over her nose and mouth as an odious stench filled the kitchen. 'Ugh!' she said, backing away. 'I don't even want to know what's in there.' She unlatched the small window above the sink, pushed it open.

She paced up and down the kitchen, opening cupboards, closing them quietly, not sure what she was looking for. She really, really wanted a cup of coffee. No, she *needed* a cup of coffee. As she pulled the last cupboard open, the door came off and she barely caught it with her other hand, the fingers of her left hand twisting painfully in the handle.

'Ow! *Shit, shit, double-shit!*' She set the door on the counter, trying not to let her mind go to calculations about how much everything was going to cost to repair or replace. She stared into the now-doorless cupboard, crammed with jars of spices, their labels old and yellowed. She rummaged around with both hands. 'Aha!' She pulled a mortar and pestle from the cabinet, set them on the counter. She would grind the coffee herself! She was about to grab the silver tin when a terrible thought occurred to her. Heating the water. No electricity. She glanced at the stove. It was old, but she could tell by the open-pronged grates that it was gas. 'Yes!' she said softly. She rummaged through some lower cupboards till she found a saucepan. 'Heh, heh, hee,' she said, stepping to the sink. She shoved the pan under the faucet and turned on the tap. A startling, rasping sound came out. A feeble squeak came out of Shelly. Her hand still on the handle, her head collapsed on her arm as she loudly moaned, 'Noooo!'

'What's wrong?'

She jumped. Meg stood behind her, dressed in her bathrobe, but otherwise looking annoyingly bright-eyed.

Shelly showed her the empty saucepan. '*No coffee!*' she moaned. 'Well, there's coffee – beans, anyway – but no electricity to make the grinder work. But that's moot *because there's no water*!' She wailed the last part. She realized she was sounding like a junkie who'd lost her stash. But she needed her coffee in the morning. Everyone knew that about her! Shelly reached into the tin of coffee beans, popped one in her mouth. It was hard and bitter, but she still sighed at the flavor of it on her tongue.

Meg's eyebrows furrowed. 'Man. We need to send you to Caffeine Anonymous.' She removed a small red, square packet from her robe pocket. 'But, I must admit, I was really looking forward to a cup of tea.' She idly tossed the wrapped tea bag onto the counter.

Shelly shook her head, impressed, but not surprised that Meg had not only packed her own tea in her suitcase, but remembered to bring it down with her. Knowing Meg, she'd probably tucked several of the packaged tea bags into the pocket of her bathrobe before putting it in her suitcase. Shelly realized that she hadn't even thought to pack *her* bathrobe for this trip. She sucked harder on the coffee bean.

But Meg had clearly moved on from thoughts of tea. She was eyeing the kitchen. 'Gad. Some work needed here, eh?'

Shelly nodded. 'Here and everywhere, I think.' She didn't want to talk about the house, so great was her need. She put her clasped hands under her chin. 'Meg? Meggles? Darling? Sweetest friend on earth?'

Meg turned, looked at her with narrowed eyes. 'What do you want?'

'Need, my friend. I *need* coffee. Please can we go get some? Please-oh-please? I'll buy! My treat!'

'Aww, Shel. I'm sure we need a lot of things. But I don't want to drive all the way into town before C.C.'s up, and before we've made at least a beginning list of supplies.' She was walking through the kitchen. 'Boy, this is a relic!' she said, staring at the refrigerator. She grabbed the silver handle.

'NO!' yelled Shelly. But it was too late. Meg had pulled the door open and the stench wafted out again.

'Yaahhgh!' said Meg, wincing and slamming the door closed. She pinched her nose, striding away from the refrigerator. 'What is *ind* dere?'

'I don't know. I got it open about as far as you did and slammed it shut just as fast.'

The sound of a toilet flushing came from upstairs. 'Well, C.C.'s up now,' said Meg.

'Good! Maybe we can all go into—' Shelly tipped her head to the side, looked up. 'Wait . . . a . . . minute! Wait just a doggone minute!' She strode to the sink, turned the tap on full. Still just a hoarse, rasping sound. She shut it off. 'I completely forgot that I used the water upstairs last night. So there *is* water in the house.' She squatted down, opened the sink cabinet. 'Maybe there's just a valve— Uh!' Shelly gazed at a long-dead mouse in a trap. She stood, stepped backward. 'You're not going to like this,' she said to Meg.

'Oh, shit,' said Meg. 'A mouse!' She skittered to the other end of the kitchen. 'Oh, please. I can face a lot. But not mice.'

'It's dead, hon.' Meg's fear of mice was equal to

her own fear of birds. Shelly wasn't too squeamish about *live* mice, but something about a mouse in a trap . . . Ugh.

'What's going on?' C.C. stood with her hand on the back of a chair at the breakfast nook. Shelly stared, amazed that C.C.'s bouffant hairdo, that last night had looked like something had been detonated from within, was poofed and primped and pinned into place once again.

'Uh, some unpleasantries in this kitchen,' said Shelly. 'The fridge is a giant science experiment – don't open it, whatever you do! There is a dead mouse under the sink. Oh, and the sink doesn't work. But the good news is, I can grind coffee with this mortar and pestle, and we can get water upstairs, if not here. Then we can boil the water because the stove is ga—' Shelly abruptly stopped speaking. She stepped over to the stove. 'Assuming the gas hasn't been shut off.' She reached for the knob. 'Hopefully it works and we can heat water and—'

'Wait!' yelled Meg. 'You might blow us all up, given the state of disrepair around here.'

Shelly looked at her beseechingly, her hand still on the knob, then sighed. 'Damn. You're probably right. Then *please* can we all get dressed and go into town for a nice breakfast and some coffee?'

'I really don't think we should,' said Meg, looking from Shelly to C.C. 'We need to start pinching our pennies. We knew this would be work, and that we wouldn't be staying at the

Hilton.' Shelly could tell she was trying to get C.C. to back her up. But Shelly had seen C.C.'s expression brighten at the mention of breakfast out. Apparently Meg noticed also. 'Remember last night at dinner?' Meg said, like an admonishing parent. 'We all agreed we weren't going to go out for any more meals. Too expensive.' She stared, then put her hand on her hip. 'We *shook* on it.'

C.C. looked at Shelly, then back at Meg. Shelly sighed when C.C. nodded reluctantly. 'We did.'

Shelly walked over to the breakfast nook, glaring first at Meg, then at C.C., who took a step back. But Shelly merely slumped into a chair, defeated.

C.C. came over and patted her shoulder. 'But if it's any consolation,' she told her, 'I think we have some coffee left in the Thermos in the car. It'll be cold, but—'

Shelly sat up, shrugged. 'It's better than nothing.' She looked at Meg. 'Will you get the keys. *Please?*' she asked, frostily.

'I'm on my way,' said Meg. 'But I have to get dressed before I go out there.' She marched across the kitchen. 'So I will go upstairs and get dressed and go out to the car to get the cold coffee for the addict.' She stopped, turned. 'But will you please deal with that mouse?'

Shelly jumped up from the table. *Leverage.* 'Yes! Yes, dear Meg, I will deal with that disgusting, awful, revolting mouse for you. *After* a cup of *hot* coffee. And breakfast.' She held up her middle three fingers in a Girl Scout salute. 'Promise!'

Meg looked at C.C. C.C. shrugged. 'Y'know, we made that deal thinking the kitchen would work.'

'That's TRUE!' shouted Shelly, almost dancing.

C.C. laughed. 'So I guess one more breakfast isn't going to make all that much difference. I could go for a stack of flapjacks.'

Meg sighed, letting her arms fall to her sides with a slap. 'I give up. But once we get this kitchen up and running, we eat in.' She poked her finger at the floor emphatically.

'Absolutely!' said Shelly. She did a little jig in the middle of the kitchen. As Meg headed upstairs, Shelly ran to C.C. and threw her arms around her. 'Thank you!'

But Shelly stopped smiling. C.C. looked shell-shocked as she gazed around the kitchen. 'It's in really bad shape, isn't it? The whole house.'

Shelly hesitated, keeping her arm around C.C. Finally she said, 'Well, it's a little worse than we expected.'

C.C. stood clutching a tissue she'd pulled from her robe pocket. 'What are we going to do?' she asked, her voice weak.

Shelly looked at the wreck of the kitchen. Then, with a forced brightness, she asked, 'You know what we're going to do?'

C.C. slowly shook her head again. Her lip wasn't quite quivering, but it was close.

Shelly steered her out of the kitchen and into the hall. 'We're going to go upstairs and get dressed.

Then we're going to go out to breakfast, get us some *hot* coffee and some good ole southern flap-jacks. *That's* what we're going to do! Then we'll figure out how to deal with this house.'

CHAPTER 18

THE GUY IN THE TENT

He stayed crouched behind the dense vegetation, waiting till their car was at the end of the long driveway. Through the branches, he watched it turn, then listened till the sound of the engine disappeared up Raven Road. He waited till he was sure they weren't going to turn around, come back right away. Women were always forgetting things. All three of his wives had been like that. When they were driving down the road, he'd hear: 'Oh, wait! I forgot my coat!' or, '*Stop!* I forgot my lipstick!' or, 'Oh dear. Turn around. I forgot the grocery list.' Women's brains must be in their asses because it was as if they had to sit on them for a while before they realized they'd forgotten something.

Satisfied they were gone, he stood, stepped out of the bushes, scratched himself. He realized his hand was on his underwear. Jesus! He'd forgotten his pants.

He did a quick reverse, zigzagging through the bushes on what was getting to be his well-worn path. He ran all the way back to his tent and darted inside. He came out, still pulling on his

277

old sweatpants. He'd lost weight, plus the elastic was shot, so he had gathered up a bunch of extra material on one side and wound a rubber band around it a couple of times, which held them up, but perhaps wasn't the most attractive solution. But it wasn't like he ever saw anyone anymore. That was the whole point. Not seeing anyone. Till these damn women showed up.

He stood in their driveway, looked at the house. He'd gathered that one of the women was old Georgie's niece. Probably here to pick over her possessions, then put the house up for sale. He looked at the door, still lying on the bushes, then at where their car had been. He scratched his chin through his shaggy beard. These gals weren't getting any points from him for intelligence, arriving in the dark, shrieking at thunder. They had woken him out of a dead sleep. He'd grabbed his baseball bat and flashlight, thinking it was those kids, back to throw rocks at the windows again. He'd stumbled barefoot across bramble and stone ready to give those boys what for.

But it wasn't the boys. Just those three dim bulbs, stumbling over each other in the dark. He shook his head, looked up the road, snorted. *Literal dim bulbs!* He'd had to take the batteries from his own flashlight, put them in theirs, and roll it in after them, then take off. But he was *not* helping them. No, indeed. He was helping *himself*. He just wanted them to see the shape the place was in, thinking then they'd surely go to a motel. But no. They had spent the night.

He felt like he'd only just gotten to sleep, when he woke up again with the sun. He thought he ought to find out a bit more about who was in there. In fact, he felt entitled to eavesdrop. Camping out back there for as long as he had, chasing off the hoodlums, he'd come to feel proprietary about this whole end of the road. But he'd had to sit under the forsythia by the carriage house for nearly an hour till one of them got up. Just one. He couldn't see through the little window into the kitchen. But then she had opened it, and he'd snuck under, to listen. Shortly after, another came down, then the third. He shook his head, almost laughing, remembering their conversation: do we go to breakfast, do we not go to breakfast, we should, we shouldn't. The first one, he guessed it was the taller one, she had a coffee habit as bad as his own. Worse. And the mouse! Standing in the driveway, he laughed out loud now. They were terrified of a dead mouse. What in the hell was a dead *anything* going to do to a person?

Women. He didn't miss them one bit. He didn't miss people, period, but women had always seemed especially to complicate his life. Now he had three of them to deal with.

He stared at the empty house, thinking, plotting. He would pull the boogeyman routine with them. Like he'd done with those boys. The women would scare even easier than those teenagers.

Then again, those boys had been a bunch of weenies. He hadn't had to do much more than rustle a bush, let them see him through the branches, and they had run like the wind. He grinned, looked down at his torn, dirty T-shirt, the flannel shirt over it, also beyond shabby. His old black sweatpants were not only missing the elastic in the waist, but also in one ankle. He ran his hand through his long hair. He couldn't remember the last time he'd had a haircut. He'd taken scissors to it himself six months ago or so. But last month, when he'd found that great spot between the two houses, he'd pitched his tent, and let it all go. Decided the hell with it. All of it. What did it matter? What did any of it matter anymore?

In the end, last night, he had decided not to scare them, afraid one of them might have a heart attack or something. Although that redheaded one looked and sounded sturdy. Maybe he could give her a little fright, if they came back. Judging from their conversation, they were planning on it. Going to fix up the old place. He laughed as he turned and walked back into the woods, the first time he'd laughed in . . . he couldn't even remember how long. He gave them three days, tops. But just in case, he might find a way to let the redhead see him. He'd get her good. Then they'd all go. And good riddance.

He realized he'd been mumbling out loud. He wondered how much he did that, talked to himself. More and more, he knew. More and more. Like

Doctorow said, his profession was a socially acceptable form of schizophrenia.

He didn't care. He turned, headed back toward his tent.

He just wanted them the hell out of here. He didn't want *them* here, or anyone else.

Why couldn't the world just leave him the hell alone?

CHAPTER 19

MEG

They'd left so late that Meg was thinking they'd be more in time for lunch, rather than breakfast. But she'd been thinking they'd have to drive all the way into Fleurville. She'd forgotten about Hickory Pete's. Even so, *en route* they had barely spoken or noticed the scenery. C.C. had taken too long to get ready, standing in front of the big bathroom mirror, carefully holding first one sparkly clip, then another, up against her hair, trying to decide which to wear. Meg had first had to restrain Shelly from throttling her, then take C.C.'s hair accessories away from her.

They had spoken fewer than a dozen words to each other by the time they pulled into the dirt parking lot of Hickory Pete's. As they stepped inside, Meg felt like she'd been transported back in time. The 1950s-themed diners of today have it all wrong, she thought, gazing around. This was the real deal. The floor was ancient-looking black and white checkerboard, faded and worn, but still had the look that it could withstand a nuclear attack. The tables in the center were small and rickety-looking, but the booths along the wall looked like they'd been made from 1950s muscle cars – thick table tops, edged in ribbed chrome, big silver pedestal, bolted to the floor. The booth cushions were mostly green, but had been patched here and there with black tape. Already, in April, several flies were buzzing along the large sill of the window. Meg watched their up and down flight along the glass, wondering what their fly brains made of the invisible barrier that imprisoned them.

She turned away, checked out the human clientele. There were mostly large men, most of them bulging out of plaid shirts and suspenders. Smoke filled the room; there was only one small, half-wall separating a tiny section in the back, only three booths, one filled. A woman and a boy of about five sat opposite each other, the woman reading a menu, the boy coloring his paper placemat.

'Y'all want smokin', or non?' enquired the elderly woman who had greeted them at the door. 'Non? Please?' said Meg, questioningly, wondering what part of the restaurant was supposedly protected from smoke. Shelly was waving her hand through the air. As Meg suspected, the woman gestured toward the small area behind the half-wall. 'Just head in yonder. Any them tables.' The woman pointed, and handed Meg three menus. Then she stepped back behind the register counter to a toddler who was sitting placidly on a stool, holding a small, worn yellow rabbit. Meg had to take C.C.'s elbow to keep her from walking over and picking the child up. She pulled her along to the back area.

'Could you have someone bring us coffee? Right away, please?' called Shelly, over her shoulder.

They settled in at a table and silently read their paper menus. Shelly glanced over her shoulder every few seconds. 'Wish they'd bring coffee,' she muttered.

'Shucks,' said C.C., glancing at her watch. 'No flapjacks for me. We've missed the shut-off time for breakfast. Guess I'll have to settle for meat plus two.'

A youngish teenaged boy with buzz cut hair arrived with a tray of steaming coffee mugs, which he shakily placed one at a time in front of the women. 'Bless you, my boy,' said Shelly. She lifted the mug to her mouth, sipped, said, 'Ahhh!' She closed her eyes, sipped again. 'Ahhh.' Then again. 'Ahhh.' The boy was rapt. Meg almost burst out laughing: the kid looked like he was watching porn, some tiny part of him knowing it was wrong to stare, but too fascinated to pull his eyes away.

'Uh, could I have hot tea, please?' Meg asked. The boy came out of his trance, nodded, set the Thermos pitcher of coffee on the table, and left.

Meg stared at the menu, then looked at C.C. 'What is this "meat plus one, meat plus two"?'

'You just pick one or two vegetables and a meat and they all come on your plate. Or you can pick meat plus three, or four.'

Meg read the listings. First were the five daily meat offerings: meat loaf, fried chicken, chicken fried steak, breaded pork chop, and fried catfish. Under that was the heading: 'Vegetables'. 'This is unbelievable!' she said, half chuckling, half stunned. '*These* are considered *vegetables*?'

Shelly stopped making love to her coffee long enough to read it aloud. '"Macaroni and cheese, potato salad, buttered apples, mashed potatoes." Oh, here's an actual vegetable. Sort of. Fried okra. And look at the last one. What the hell are chow-chow pickles?'

'It's a kind of relish, made with all different types of vegetables,' explained C.C.

'*Vegetables* . . . as in macaroni and cheese?' asked Meg, smirking.

'No,' said C.C. 'Like cucumbers, onion, beans and the like.'

Meg read the meat choices again. Not a single one appealed to her. She'd never been a big meat-eater, but now, inexplicably, she saw a face with every one. And the 'vegetables' weren't much better; each seemed to be fried or made with mayonnaise, butter or gravy.

The boy arrived with Meg's tea and set it in front of her, but kept his eye on Shelly. She winked at him and that sent him trotting away, scarlet-faced.

'Ohhh! Glory be!' cried Shelly, looking at her menu again. 'I'm gonna get me a fried bologna sandwich!'

'Land! I haven't had one of those in . . .' said C.C., drifting off. 'Georgie and I used to make fried bologna sandwiches all the time.'

When they'd walked in, Meg had felt as hungry as she'd felt in weeks. But given these choices, her appetite was fading. She hopefully flipped her menu over. 'Glory be!' she mimicked. 'They have green salad!'

Their rotund waitress took their orders – Luncheon Salad Bowl for Meg, meat loaf plus two (macaroni and cheese and chow-chow pickles) for C.C., and, indeed, a fried bologna sandwich for Shelly. All ordered iced tea, despite C.C.'s warning that it would be southern sweet tea, 'unless you ask different'.

Meg shrugged at Shelly. 'When in Rome . . .'

Their food arrived promptly and they all three ate hungrily and silently for several minutes. 'This is actually really good!' said Shelly finally, nodding at what remained of her bologna sandwich. She took a sip of tea, and grimaced. 'Yoww. That is *sweet*! Too sweet for me.' She poured more coffee into her mug from the pitcher.

'So, the first order of business is cleaning, then repair, then painting,' said Shelly officiously, holding her coffee mug in both hands now. 'But we've also got to get the electricity and phone fixed, pronto.'

Who died and made you Queen? Meg thought, but then silently castigated herself. She stabbed her fork into a large chunk of iceberg lettuce.

As she chewed thoughtfully, she had to admit, Shelly was the businesswoman among them, though not without a few dings in her résumé. And if this flip scheme was going to work, it would largely be because of her knowledge and expertise. And, Meg knew, the disastrous mall investment had not been entirely Shelly's fault. Just bad choices in business partners – all men – who had been a little too creative with their financial practices. Shelly was lucky to avoid prosecution, though Meg knew that her huge financial loss could hardly be deemed 'lucky'.

Still, Meg didn't relish the idea of being Shelly's employee for several weeks. She glanced at C.C., who had said nothing, and was now distractedly moving a few remaining pieces of macaroni around her plate with her fork, not looking up.

'Well, if it was up to me,' Meg said, 'I'd just as soon we didn't hook the phone up. And while I don't think we can do without electricity, I must say, I like living by candlelight. And I *love* not having a TV in the house!'

C.C. looked up, brightening. 'Me too! I mean, about the candles. Like *Little House on the Prairie*. Since Kathryn has Shelly's cell number for emergencies, I'm all for not hooking up the phone.'

Shelly continued, as if neither had spoken. 'So, given what I just mentioned, we don't have enough money. And the kitchen! It needs a complete overhaul. New floor, new cabinets, new appliances. And we should really consider expanding it. Maybe knocking out the wall with the dining room. That could be great! So, I think we're each going to have to dip a little deeper into our savings.'

Both Meg and C.C. objected together, but Shelly cut them off.

'Look, it costs money to make money. But I'm telling you, the house is even better than I expected. Not in terms of repair; that's actually worse than I'd thought. But it's a gem, underneath the wreckage. She's a stately old dame, well worth the investment of money and labor. I'll have to research the local market, but I bet we can make a pretty penny on this.'

As Shelly explained to C.C. the finer points of maximizing investment returns, Meg fumed for a minute, thinking that dipping into their savings meant hers and C.C.'s, since Shelly essentially had no savings left. And should they trust her with their money? Trust. Her ability to trust had walked out the door with Grant.

Meg looked out the window. The table conversation faded, dimmed by the volume control of her wandering mind. And eye. Outside, a man was walking a little dog. It looked a lot like the dog she'd given to Grant, years ago. Shit. Everything seemed to come back to Grant, no matter how much she didn't want it to. The dog outside jumped up on the man's shins, wagging its fluffy tail, and he picked it up, making Meg smile, in spite of herself. It really did remind her of that dog . . . What was its name? It was on the tip of her tongue. It was a female . . . Chelsea, Chessie. Something like that. They'd had her all of an hour before Grant had taken her back to the shelter.

He'd wanted a dog for much of their marriage, but she'd insisted on waiting till the youngest was seven. Finally, the day before Grant's birthday, she and the kids had gone down to the shelter and adopted an adorable little female terrier mix. The morning of his birthday they surprised him, the oldest standing on tiptoe, covering Grant's eyes, the youngest setting the dog in his lap. *Giselle.* That was it. 'Oh my,' was all he'd said, as the kids laughed and squealed with delight. Grant looked at Meg, then the dog. He'd given a mordant laugh, which Meg had correctly construed as, 'Right concept, totally wrong dog.' That same day he had taken the poor thing back to the shelter, exchanged her for Buster. Buster was sweet, but way more dog than Meg was prepared for. But Buster had become a beloved member of their family, all the more so when the last child flew the nest.

Buster. She pictured herself sprinkling his ashes. She imagined Grant beside her, there on the hillside. Which, of course, he hadn't been.

'Yoo-hoo! Meg?'

Meg blinked as Shelly waved in front of her face.

'We're all paid up!' Shelly said with too much enthusiasm, and ill-masked concern. C.C. was also looking at her with worried eyes.

Something tickled her cheek and she scratched it. Wet. Tears. *Christ.* She'd gotten to the point where she didn't even realize she was crying. She shook her head miserably. The thought exhausted her. She wiped her cheeks with her napkin, then slowly slid out of the booth. Shelly and C.C. stepped to either side of her, each taking an arm. They walked her out of the restaurant, just as they might a newly blind person.

Behind the wheel again, all the windows down, fresh spring air blowing over them, Meg felt more in control. She drove a touristy five miles an hour down Raven Road so they could admire the stately homes and gardens they'd not seen during their nighttime arrival, and been too intent on breakfast to pay attention to earlier. Like Dogs' Wood, a few homes had not been given the care over the years that they deserved. But others were in perfect condition, architectural and botanical gems.

One house in particular was spectacular. Meg braked to a stop as they all three took in its splendor. Along one side of the lot, a long line of white, pink and three shades of purple lilacs formed a living fence. The result was a bulging, almost oozing barrier of blooms. Along the painted white brick front of the house were soldierly rows of red tulips, brilliant in the sun. To the side, growing in the shade of a large and welcoming veranda, was a hyacinth garden, filled with fat, conical blooms of deep purple, bright white, soft pink. Meg thought she could almost smell their sweet fragrance through the closed car windows. She rolled her window down, stuck her head out, deeply inhaled. The others followed her lead.

'Just glorious, isn't it?' said C.C., as vibrant as the spring blooms. 'Don't you just love it? Fleurville must be a full month or more ahead of Wisataukee in pulling on the spring outfits.'

Meg looked back at her. She was grinning ear to ear. Nothing like the light of day and abundant blooms to welcome a person home.

'It is gorgeous here,' agreed Shelly. 'It is sort of like we've traveled through a time tunnel.'

Meg nodded. Somehow their mere arrival here, in full-bore spring, without ever having quite walked out the back door of winter, felt miraculous. Even she, in this moment, felt hopeful.

Once back at the house, they took stock of the cleaning supplies. Shelly squatted in front of the sink, wearing rubber gloves she'd found, handing the bottles and cans backward to C.C. and Meg, holding a plastic trash bag. 'Not much usable,' said Meg. She held the last bottle, its label long gone and the contents a suspicious, viscous yellow. Glad for the thick leather work gloves she was wearing, she dropped it into the bag and it clattered against the others.

'Stand clear! Mouse removal! Gimme the bag,' barked Shelly. Meg dropped the bag and walked to the other end of the kitchen, turning her back. She shuddered as she heard it drop into the bag.

She didn't turn around till she heard Shelly step outside with it.

Meg squatted at the sink again, found the valve, then stood and turned on the sink. There was an explosive whoosh, and water came out of the faucet.

'Yay!' C.C. clapped her hands. 'One task down, one thousand to go!'

Meg smiled at her. What a trouper.

'We've got to arrange for garbage pickup,' said Shelly, returning. 'There's a full can in the garage. By the way, the side door is unlocked, Ceece. Does the house key fit that?'

C.C. shrugged. 'Well, make that one thousand and one more things to check.'

'Hey,' said Meg, 'how would you two feel about me going to town to get some cleaning supplies while you both keep taking inventory here? C.C., you know the house, and Shelly knows the most about remodeling. I figure my talents are best used behind the wheel.'

They quickly agreed, and ten minutes later Meg was jogging back out to the car. As she drove away, she thought they were probably as relieved to be rid of her unpredictable moods for a few hours as she was to get away. She'd left them cleaning up broken glass, talking about window replacement possibilities. She didn't care about windows or anything else at the moment. She was as desperate for a fix as Shelly had been earlier. But Meg didn't need caffeine; she needed mail, a letter. From Grant.

C.C. had given fine directions to get her into town, and to the grocery store, even though she reminded Meg that it had been several years since she'd been in Fleurville, and that things probably had changed. But as she pulled into town, Meg found that the grocery store was still on the corner of Main and the first stoplight, just like C.C. had said. (Although C.C. hadn't been able to recall the name of the cross street, which, ironically, turned out to be Memorial Avenue.) Meg smiled as she drove past. She'd stop at the store after.

She'd asked C.C., discreetly, away from Shelly, for directions to the post office. C.C. hadn't questioned her. Meg was sure Shelly would have, lecturing her about not expecting anything from Grant. But Meg *knew* there would be a letter from her husband. Surely, having had some time alone now, Grant would have come to his senses. They needed to save their marriage. The world didn't make sense, otherwise. Meg smiled, pulling into the parking lot of the post office. She thought it quite likely that he'd even returned home already, and probably wanted her to do the same.

It was an old brick building, a bronze plaque near the door identifying it as an official historic landmark of Fleurville. As she stepped inside, Meg could, in fact, smell the history. What that smell was, she couldn't put her finger on. But if someone had led her in here blindfolded, she would have known by the smell that she was in an old building.

Maybe some combination of old stone and metal, dust and mildew.

At the end of the long corridor was the service desk. As she approached the elderly man sitting behind the counter, reading a newspaper, she said hello. The man jumped a little on his stool, then quickly closed his paper. He put his finger to his ear, made a twisting motion. A hearing aid, Meg realized.

'Sorry, miss,' said the old man, smiling now. 'I didn't hear you come up. You must be a visitor. Everyone round here knows to clap their hands, give me a little warning. What can I do you for?' His face crinkled into a stunning number of wrinkles when he smiled. That, and his long thin neck made him resemble a turtle.

She smiled at him. 'I'm sorry I startled you. I'm here to pick up mail for seven thirteen Raven Road.'

'Ahh! Georgie's old place. You her niece?'

'No, that's C.C. I'm her friend, Meg.'

The man stuck out his wrinkled hand. 'Please t'meet you. Warren, Postmaster of Fleurville. I had a last name but it fell off, due to lack a' use! Ever'body calls me Warren.' He straightened up on his stool as he said the last bit.

She took his hand in hers. 'Nice to meet you, Warren.'

'B'right back.' He slapped the counter lightly as he winked at her, then hopped spryly off the stool and disappeared behind a wall.

In a moment, he re-emerged, holding a white

plastic crate marked 'U.S. MAIL', over half full. Meg's heart quickened at the sight of it. 'Here ya go,' he said, heaving it onto the counter. 'Bet it's a tree or two of junk mail, mostly.'

Meg nodded, knowing that was likely true, but also knowing that a letter from her husband was in there too. She could *feel* it. C.C. was right about gut feelings: there were some things a person just knew before they happened.

'You can just take that crate home, hon. Bring it on back next time you're in town.'

'Thank you, Warren,' she said. He offered (half-heartedly, she thought) to carry the crate out to her car for her. She politely declined, saying that he should not leave his post. He smiled, nodded and she turned to leave.

'Say,' said Warren, 'you want me to start delivery out to y'all again? Or are you only here for a short time?'

Meg hesitated. Define 'short time', she thought. She was already feeling eager to get back home, back to Wisataukee, back to Grant, back to *normal*. And, more and more, she thought the work needed was beyond them. But she imagined walking across the lawn of Dogs' Wood, to the mailbox, pulling out a letter from Grant. She smiled. 'Well, we may end up putting it back on hold again soon, but, yes, please start delivery.' She thanked him again, then walked away, holding the crate in front of her. Despite its weight, she was almost jogging by the time she got to her car.

She settled into the back seat with the crate, feeling giddy. She pulled a clump of mail out, began sorting through. She tossed the fliers and advertisements quickly to her feet, set the letters on the seat next to the crate. As the stack at her feet grew, there were only four or five bills, or at least non-ad-looking letters on the seat, along with a few other indeterminate envelopes. Another from an attorney's office, which Meg assumed was the estate guy. She found two hand-written letters for C.C. in square, blue envelopes. From Lucy, who must have sent these even before they'd left town. Meg smiled, patting the letters as if the little girl herself was keeping her company there in the car.

She began sifting faster, abandoning the sorting, and tossing everything that wasn't a letter from Grant onto the floor. When only a bright green card announcing a special on yard work remained in the crate, Meg's shoulders slumped, and she began to cry.

'Stop it! Stop it!' she told herself sternly, wiping the tears away. 'It's only been two weeks since he wrote.' So what if she had written him *five* letters since he'd left. She'd left four on the kitchen table for him, written in the days and weeks after his departure. She'd mailed one from Tupper, certain he'd return home after she had left. But she knew now he wasn't there. She began picking up all the mail, putting it back into the crate. As she put the last piece in, she closed her eyes, said quietly, 'Please Grant, wherever you are, please, just write.'

She moved to the front seat, started the car and followed the one-way exit signs out of the parking lot. But they directed her to the back of the post office, not the front, the way she'd come in. She glanced around. It was the only exit, and only allowed for a right turn onto a one-way street. She knew she needed to be headed the other way. But she didn't have a choice. She took a deep breath and made the turn. She'd just have to make two more right turns, then she'd be back on track. But the next intersection was also one-way, the wrong way. 'Dammit!' she shouted, driving on. The road began to snake around, winding past modest homes, then a neighborhood park. She took the next available right, but it too curved, and all the side streets in both directions were into neighborhoods.

She felt caught in a current again. 'Dammit!' she repeated, this time hitting the steering wheel with her hand. She slowed, checking the street names of each cross street, hoping to see Main or Memorial, or even something that looked like it might be a through street. Buchanan. Carter. Delano. Eisenhower. Grant. She slammed on the brakes, turning the car abruptly onto Grant. C.C. would say it was a sign, wouldn't she? (Shelly would say a bad one, no doubt.)

Grant was wider, suggesting a through street, but through to where, she didn't know. It meandered first past houses, then past an area of open fields, then into an industrial and warehouse park. After a little over a mile, she decided she was going nowhere fast and looked for a good place to turn around. She turned into the first drive she came to, feeding into a large parking lot. Only after she'd made the turn did she see the small sign: Fleurville County Animal Shelter. She jammed on the brakes. She sat in the idling car for a few seconds, till a car horn sounded behind her. She quickly pulled into a parking spot.

She was trembling. From being lost, she told herself, not because Grant Street had led her to an animal shelter. Just after she'd been thinking at the restaurant . . . She stared at the goose bumps on her arms, shaken.

She'd go in and ask for directions. That's all. She was not even going to *look* at those animals. She repeated the admonition to herself as she walked toward the entrance. Her hands pressed the air down on either side of her, reinforcing her resolve as she strolled toward the glass doors. Directions, directions, she muttered. *Can you please tell me how to get to Main and Memorial?* Simple.

She pulled open the heavy door, and stepped into the cool lobby of the building. A cheerful blonde, college-age girl greeted her from behind the reception counter. 'Welcome! Can I help you?'

Meg stared at her. 'Dogs?' she asked weakly.

'Thattaway,' said the girl, pointing to her right.

Meg nodded, went through two more sets of heavy glass doors, finally into a barking cacophony. She smiled at their faces, but at the same time felt her broken heart break again. There were about a dozen kennels, all with cement floors, each about six feet long by four feet wide, with a small arched entrance where the dogs could go inside a little den area. The place looked relatively new, and in good condition. But still. Nearly every kennel held two dogs, or several puppies. About a third of the dogs were standing at the front of the cage, tails wagging, eyes shining and pleading, trying to be their own best advertisement. Another third cowered in the back of their cells or hid in the den area. The last third walked fretful or excited circles or figure eights, desperate to move. Meg walked by a couple of black labs, then past several mixed breeds. She stopped briefly at a beagle's cage, smiling as she read the name on his blue information card: 'Sammie. Age: 5. Surrendered. Reason: Allergic.' Meg sighed. She stuck a finger through the cage and Sammie licked it.

She wished she could take them all home.

But she felt nearly as homeless as these dogs were. She walked to the very end, where an empty cage greeted her. Unlike the blue name cards on the front of the rest of the cages, this one had a red one. 'I'm out for a walk!' it read. Meg peered out the tall skinny window next to her, a view of the parking lot. A young boy with a blue smock

was just passing out of view, walking a small dog
– *an Italian Greyhound*!

Meg rushed down the aisle, through the doors,
the lobby and burst out the front doors. She raced
around the side, just in time to see the boy disappear around the back of the building, a tiny,
fawn-colored dog right behind him. She jogged
down the length of the parking lot, her loafers
clapping against the asphalt. Despite her weight
loss, she felt more out of shape than ever. And old.

'Excuse me,' she said, nearly breathless. The boy
stopped. He turned and looked at her, seeming a
little alarmed. The dog had disappeared into a
bush, the leash taut.

Her hand on her chest, she caught her breath.
'Sorry! Didn't mean to startle you. I wanted to
ask about the dog.' She smiled, admiring his
freckles, guessing he was about ten.

The boy smiled back, straightening importantly.
'Yes, ma'am. He's mah favorite!' His thick drawl
made him even more adorable. 'He just came in
yesterday. He's a Chihuahua.' He scooped him up,
handed him to her. She gathered the tiny dog into
her arms, gazed into his small, milk-chocolate
eyes, barely able to keep listening to the boy.
'Y'know how t'spell that? Ah do! It's spelled like
chee-who-ah-who-ah. That's how I remember it!'
Meg tore her eyes away from the dog, to the boy.
He grinned. 'He's a surrender, not a stray. His
family couldn't keep him 'cause the daddy lost
his job and they had t'move away. I hate it when

that happens. I feel so bad for the people. And the dog.' He pronounced it 'dawwg'. 'Anyway, his name is Dollop, which means like a little spoonful, or somethin'. I had to look it up. Isn't that the best name ever for him?'

Meg smiled, nodded, but she couldn't speak. She felt like she needed to sit down, but there was nowhere to sit. She could feel tears in her eyes again, but these were different. Could there be tears of amazement? It took every bit of self-restraint not to hug this boy, tell him that no matter how lost he might feel at some point in his life, to remember that sometimes you never knew where the road might take you. That sometimes, maybe, being lost could lead to something good. Instead, she nodded again. When she found her voice, she answered him. 'Yes. Yes, Dollop is the best name ever.'

She parked the car in a shady spot in the grocery store parking lot. Dollop had laid quietly on the seat next to her the whole drive, which, armed with directions from the blonde girl who'd helped her with the adoption, had taken less than ten minutes. Meg had been worried that the boy would be sad that she was taking Dollop away from him, but he had seemed genuinely happy, proud, even, for finding Dollop a new home.

Meg eyed the Super Seconds discount store next to the grocery store. She told Dollop, 'You wait here, sweetie. I'll be *right* back.' She grabbed her small purse from the back seat and ran into the store. The clerk at the counter stared at her as she burst in the door. 'Purses?' she asked. He pointed. She took less than thirty seconds to select one. It was bright floral canvas, a simple leather loop latch at the top, with a braided fabric shoulder strap. It was just $15.99. But more importantly, it was big. She paid for it and ran back to her car.

'In you go, punkin!' she said, slipping the little dog into the canvas well of her new purse. 'Imagine! Having a dog you can carry in your purse!' She carefully tucked her wallet in next to Dollop. Meg chortled, looking at him. He was already curled up in a little circle, looking very much like this was not his first time riding in a purse.

CHAPTER 20

C.C.

C. whistled happily as she spritzed some vinegar and water onto the window, rubbing at it with a wad of crumpled newspaper. She looked up to see Shelly entering the living room, pushing an old Hoover.

'Look what I found in the— *What in God's name are you doing?*' asked Shelly.

'Um, washing the windows?'

'Why in the world are you washing the windows? We're just going to replace them.'

'Well, we're not going to do that *today*,' said C.C. softly. 'Are we?' She hated when Shelly blustered.

'Well, no, but there's plenty of more important work to be done. We need to clean up the plaster around the fireplace, roll up the rugs, take down that hideous light fixture.'

C.C. looked up. She and Theresa and Georgie had made that light fixture. Not that she'd want it hanging in her home either, but did Shelly have to be so . . . abusive toward it? But C.C. said nothing, her hand still pressing the sodden ball of newspaper to the glass. She stared through a half-cleaned pane, outside. 'I guess I just thought it'd

303

be nice if we got to look out at the dogwoods through clean windows.'

'Well, it seems like a waste of time to me,' said Shelly. 'Here, you vacuum this rug, then we'll store it away till we're done with the construction. It's a nice rug, you know.'

C.C. didn't move. She wanted to say something, but couldn't. She set the spritzer and newspaper on the floor. She walked past Shelly, out of the living room, up the stairs and into the bedroom she shared with Meg. She shut the door carefully, quietly.

'C.C.! *C.C.!*' Shelly yelled from downstairs. C.C. sat unmoving and silent on the bed. Then she heard stomping and banging around, then the front door slamming. C.C. fell sideways onto the bed. She tried to cry, just for the release, but could not. She sat up, pulled open the drawer of her bedside table. She pulled out the yellow box of stationery with the butterflies. Leaning back against two pillows, she began a letter.

Forty minutes later, C.C. was back in the living room, sweeping up plaster, when she heard the car crunching on the gravel driveway. Minutes after, Meg came into the room. C.C. did a double-take at her big grin. 'Well, don't you look like a bee in a bouquet! What's up?' She was pretty sure she knew: Meg had received a letter from Grant. The thought filled her with a certain amount of dread.

'I bought a new purse,' Meg said unexpectedly, and in almost a sing-song voice. C.C. was stunned. She stared at her old friend. She didn't look like herself, she didn't sound like herself. C.C. looked at the purse. It was the complete opposite of the small, black leather one Meg had had some version of for as long as C.C. had known her. Meg's new purse was large, colorful. She wore it over her shoulder, and made no move to take it off as C.C. walked over to inspect it. It was cute, young-looking. Floral, which C.C. knew that Meg did not like. It was almost more of a tote. And it had only a simple loop latch. Now that was just plain odd! Meg practically padlocked her purse! She thought anything less than a full zipper was an invitation to pickpockets. C.C. scratched her head. Perhaps Meg *hadn't* heard from Grant, and had gone on a drinking binge. But no matter how despondent Meg might be (and she looked far from it, at the moment) Meg would never drink and drive.

'Did you hear from Grant?' she asked warily.

'Nope. Not a word,' said Meg, still smiling.

'Okay, what's up? You look like you have a secret just bustin' to get out of you! It's something about the purse, isn't it? It's . . . not one I would expect you to buy.' C.C. reached out to touch it, but Meg backed away, still grinning.

'Yes, sort of. It's what's inside. That's what's really special about this purse.'

Several things ticked through C.C.'s mind: a

compact mirror? A cosmetics bag? Sunglasses? 'What?' she said with mock impatience. She was thrilled that Meg was feeling playful, whatever the reason.

Meg lifted the fastener, slowly slid her hand into the big bag, and even more slowly withdrew it.

C.C. gasped. 'A *dog*! Why, she's just a speck of a thing! Even smaller than M.J.!'

'It's a boy,' said Meg, bringing the dog to her chest and kissing the top of his head. She gazed at him for a minute, then extended her dog-filled hands toward C.C. The little dog looked nervously over its shoulder, back at Meg. 'I got him for you,' said Meg. 'Not to replace M.J., exactly . . .' She was still smiling, but there was a definite dimming of the wattage. Meg blinked, one too many times. 'His name's Dollop.'

'Oh, my stars! You are a sweetheart, honey,' C.C. told the wide-eyed dog, taking him into her arms. She kissed him, felt his warmth, breathed him in. Then she handed him back. 'But you keep him. I'll enjoy him and love him up, but I think this fella is a goner for you.' Meg bit her lip slightly. C.C. gave her a reassuring smile. Meg took Dollop back, held him close to her, tucking his little head under her chin again, relief and bliss easing over both their faces.

'I can tell already that you two belong together,' said C.C., feeling true happiness for her friend. Meg had on a Christmas morning smile, big and unharnessed, a pink of thrill coloring her cheeks.

Finally, thought C.C. Finally a face not washed out by grief. Reaching over Meg's elbow, she stroked Dollop's tiny chin with one finger. 'You're already in love for life, aren't you, hon?'

Meg's smile remained, but C.C. saw it twitch. She blanched, realizing too late that her words had been a bit insensitive. Meg was hanging on like a bug on a branch in a breeze to the hope that Grant would come back to her. And who knew? Maybe he would. But C.C.'s gut told her that it was over between them. Had been for a long time. Grant was gone, and M.J. was gone.

Meg took her arm and steered her toward the couch, still holding Dollop. 'Where's Shel?' she asked. She sat delicately on the sofa, Dollop on her lap.

'I guess she went for a walk,' C.C. said flatly, sitting heavily next to Meg. She looked out the window.

'Uh-oh,' said Meg. 'Did something happen between you two?'

C.C. looked at Meg. She didn't want to spoil Meg's happiness. Nor did she want to talk behind Shelly's back. They'd all three long ago vowed to not do that, agreeing it was the surest death of a friendship of three.

C.C. looked at the window, then chuckled softly, shaking her head. *Let it go*. 'Oh, nothin' more than two hens and one nest, I guess. We fussed a bit about whether we should clean the windows. I wanted to, she didn't, saying we're just going to replace them. But it was making me gloomy to be looking at the dogwoods through the grime.'

Meg set Dollop on the oak floor. 'Okay, little guy, go explore!' Dollop stood, blinking, looking up at Meg. Then he put his nose to the ground and did as told. Meg rose from the couch, stepped to the window, and picked up the spray bottle. 'Let's clean the windows. Even if we replace them tomorrow, we'll enjoy them clean today.'

They set to it, C.C. humming rather than whistling this time. After a minute, Meg stopped, seemed to look at nothing for a minute, then faced her. 'You know, Ceece. I've always admired that about you. How you can enjoy the view, from wherever you are, for whatever moment you're there. You know?' C.C. smiled. Meg turned back to the window. 'I guess there's a view of something everywhere, right? You just have to look for it.'

'I think so, honey. I think so,' said C.C. quietly. 'Maybe even a good view.'

'Besides,' Meg said. 'I *seriously* doubt we'll be replacing these windows tomorrow. Or the next day. Or the next.'

They both laughed and kept on spritzing and rubbing, improving the view, one pane at a time.

CHAPTER 21

PURDY

Purdy stepped outside, one hand holding the door open, waiting for Jess, the mail carrier, as she walked toward the restaurant. Or rather, he was waiting for what he hoped she had for him. As she eyed him warily, he realized his standing outside to intercept her might be somewhat alarming.

Jess had been the first person on the scene when Keppie had collapsed. Just on her regular route, delivering the mail, and the poor thing had opened the door, the little bell ringing, and Purdy, not knowing who it was, started hollering for help. She'd found him behind the bar, giving Keppie mouth-to-mouth. She'd pulled out her cellphone, called 911, then dropped down next to him, checked for a pulse, and began giving Keppie chest compressions. Then the little bell again, and Doc Butterfield took over. Then the sheriff, Mick, EMTs, the bell ringing with each entrance. Jess stood crying, and Doc's hand on Purdy's shoulder and grim expression said it all as the ambulance took Keppie away, lights and siren blaring. That's when Purdy heard what wasn't there: the chopper blades, screams, gunfire. Ever since, the little bell ringing, a siren or flashing light, even poor Jess herself, set his brain on the endless loop of traumatic memories. But he had refused to take the bell down; he couldn't get away from bells and sirens and lights for the rest of his life, so he did what he'd learned to do once his PTSD had finally been diagnosed initially: he learned ways to control his brain, rather than letting it control him. And it was working. Again.

But Purdy figured it stood to reason that Jess was now a mite jibbery around him. He gave her an extra big smile and a small wave as she continued toward him. She looked relieved, returned the greeting, then looked down, sorting through the mail in her bag. Purdy, his hand still on the open restaurant door, inhaled. It was a beautiful day, sunny, clear, with just a hint of crisp in the air. Spring had truly arrived. He inhaled again, imagining the still-hidden summer flowers, their heads bent, tucked in on themselves, wrapped up in their own protective layer, heads down under their roof of dirt. Soon they'd push through, lift themselves up into the world, buds slowly exploding into colorful flowers, beckoning his bees. Then summer would become, as he used to joke to Keppie, s-hummm-er.

'Hiya, Purdy. What a day, huh?'

'Hello, Jess. Indeed it is,' he replied politely. But his gaze was locked on the stack of letters in Jess's hand, all thoughts of sun and plants and bees instantly gone from his head. He'd refused to let himself even have hope till ten days from the date he'd mailed his letter to C.C. Marked them off on the calendar, even. But yesterday had only been day six, and he'd practically lunged at poor Jess.

He looked at the clump of letters in her hand now. He wanted just to snatch them from her, sort through them himself. Instead, he took another breath, ran a finger under his collar, loosening the neck of both his undershirt and his old, but clean white button-down.

'Here you go,' Jess said, finally handing him a small batch of letters and a magazine. 'Expecting something special?'

Purdy blushed, silently cursed it. Her asking prevented him from looking through the letters in his hand right away. 'Well, hoping for a letter. Always hoping. Don't get many nowadays.'

'No, not a lot,' said Jess. 'But I think some people'd be surprised how many folks still take the time to write a letter. And not just at Christmas, although that's when most of them come through. Now, personally, I think it's one of the real pleasures in this world to brew up a pot of tea, prop my feet up and open a newsy letter from a friend, especially handwritten. There's just nothing like it.'

Purdy stared at her, till he realized he was. He was surprised, is all. One might guess a letter carrier would have a less-than-romantic notion about them, having to haul them around all day.

311

Plus, Jess was young, into tech stuff. Maybe she even had one of them Blueberries, where she could send a message any old time she wanted, instantly. And, though it maybe was just small-town gossip, she had a reputation of being a little wild, going off to big cities to meet men. It was hard to picture her cozied up in her living room, sipping tea and reading a letter.

Purdy nodded, trying not to be rude, but at the same time trying to surreptitiously peek at the mail in his hand, check at least for a postmark from Tennessee. 'Hmm,' he said absently. 'Yes, I guess there's a special kind of thoughtfulness to a hand-written letter.' He figured she would move on; she did have her route to finish. But she evidently didn't see the need for moving on just yet.

'I had a boyfriend once who used to write me love letters,' she said, almost dreamily. Purdy felt his cheeks warm again. What was compelling her to tell him this? Was it the spring day? 'He lived in Chicago. We met at the aquarium, when I took my nieces down there. It was a long-distance love affair.' She sighed deeply. Purdy shifted his weight from foot to foot. He wanted to go inside, take a good look at his mail, see if maybe, possibly, *he* might have hope of just such a letter. If there was, he surely would grab a cup of coffee and sit down in the back, take his time. First he'd hold it, look at the handwriting, the stamp, maybe even smell it. Then he'd open it up carefully, pull out the paper, then read her words as slowly as he could, breathing them in like rationed oxygen. His heart thrummed at the thought.

'Those letters were amazing,' she said, milky-eyed.

'Uh-huh. Well, I'd best get back in there,' Purdy said, hitching his thumb over his shoulder. 'If . . . there's nothing else?'

He was sure she was just making a show of it, but she dug around in her bag once more. 'Nope. That's it. But I think there might be something in that stack you're holding that might be hand-written. Think I remember seeing that.' She looked at him, waiting.

'Well, I'll take a look, inside. Soup's on. Thanks, Jess.'

Jess turned finally, and started walking up the road. Over her shoulder she added, 'Well, hope it's what you've been waiting for.' She held up her hand, fingers crossed.

She's a good girl, he thought, as he nearly leaped through the door of the restaurant.

He slipped behind the bar. He took one letter at a time off the stack, setting them on the counter next to the sink. Bill. Bill. Bill. Ad. Postcard! Spring flowers! He flipped it over. Sighed. It was another advertisement, this one for an oil change, of all things. He had only three letters left in his hand, and he could see the top one was another bill. Slowly, he lifted it, but simultaneously raised his head to look at the emptiness of the restaurant, the dark red floor.

Finally, he lowered his head, allowed himself to look at the second-to-last letter in the stack. Church newsletter. To a church he hadn't been to in over two years. Baptist. My, but they were persistent. He left the newsletter on top of the last letter.

One letter left. He brought his hand to his chin and mouth, massaging the skin, the softening stubble of graying beard, feeling his breath on his hand, smelling his own skin under it. He had to believe in the possibility. If he didn't believe in at least that, then why *should* she be interested in him? Suddenly, as so often happened now, Keppie appeared to him, standing in the middle of the red floor, her toe tapping, her hand on her hip, her head tilted to one side, that mildly impatient look on her face. She didn't speak, but she didn't have to. How many times had Keppie told him over the years, when he'd asked her if she'd seen whatever it was he was looking for high and low, 'Look for it like you're *expecting* to find it.'

Still, he didn't want to lift the Baptists off the last letter. As long as the Baptists were there, there was a chance that a letter from C.C. was underneath. He closed his eyes, pulled the envelope out from under the church newsletter. He hefted it, his eyes still closed, trying to feel if the weight and thickness felt like that of a handwritten letter.

Letters had always carried weight, ever since Nam. More than meals or the occasional beer, it was mail call that soldiers hungered and thirsted for. Letters from home nourished them, sustained them, reassured them of a life without blood and death, without a fear so thick you could smell it. A life happening without them. Letters opened the curtain on that life. He wondered if soldiers still felt that way about mail, real tangible letters that you could grasp and smell and hold close to you and read, over and over, the penmanship like the familiar face of whoever wrote it. In this age of cellphones and computers he guessed that they preferred that real-time exchange. Heck, he knew that they were even doing video phone talks. Any contact was contact, he supposed, but soldiers today probably had never really experienced letters the way the soldiers in Nam had. Letters were typically their *only* communication, so much more was left to the imagination. That's where love grew best, in the imagination. Purdy leaned back against the counter, thinking about a video phone call versus a letter. It was sweeter somehow, he thought, to read about the little bits of news from home, like a story. A soldier sitting on his bunk, reading about his girl in her new job, working as a car hop, the description of the little skirt she had to wear, well, chance was he might not even hear the choppers off in the distance. Or the memory of yesterday's march through jungle, feeling the eyes on you, could be kept at bay by his mom's description of his dad cursing at the lawn mower, then finally figuring out how to fix it; or his dad telling about his mom, thanking the neighbor for the brownies she handed over the fence, both women crying.

Purdy thought that the soldiers today missed out on those small stories, their images more varied and vivid than any video conference or phone call could offer. But letters . . . He remembered nearly crawling into those letters, wrapping himself up in the words – his mother's, Keppie's, a couple of friends from high school, the rare one from his father. Letters made a familiar road home that soldiers could stroll down, walk away on. And when they had to come back to their awful reality, more than a few of them would carefully fold a letter from their girl or mom, or both, and tuck it away on them somewhere, usually close to the heart, maybe with a picture. Those letters went into battle with them, made one more layer, thin but stronger than armor, against the violence. Even the Dear John letters that made grown men cry got carried into the fields with some, the pain giving them a fearlessness that sometimes got them killed, but sometimes saved them.

Purdy sighed. He slipped the unseen letter in his hand back under the newsletter. He wasn't ready. He stared out the window, nervously drumming two fingers lightly on the Baptists, deliberating. He saw Mrs D'Blatt, hobbling up the road, coming for her noontime bowl of soup. She didn't care what kind, as long as it was hot. Even in summer. Joe Spurn, coming from across the street, jogged ahead of her to get the door.

Joe pulled it open with care, but still, the little bell rang. Purdy glanced down, quickly lifted the Baptists. Then he looked up at the little bell. He went to help Mrs D'Blatt to her usual table, his breath and step light, giddy, as he tucked the handwritten letter with the Tennessee postmark into his apron pocket.

CHAPTER 22

THE GUY IN THE TENT

Those women had been here almost a month and they'd been quiet enough, he'd grant them that. They left him alone. And, for whatever reason, they didn't seem too concerned about not having electricity, or a phone. He'd seen them hauling that old generator out of the garage, knew they'd hooked up the old fridge. But he was shocked that they were content to live like that. It had occurred to him that he could do worse if someone else bought the place, much worse, so he'd decided against scaring them. But that skinny one – the one with that little dog; he didn't know quite what to make of her. She often brought out an old blanket and sat completely still in the backyard (was she praying? meditating?); either way, it gave him the creeps. She had spotted him once or twice, had even waved to him a week or so back. It had startled him, and he'd ducked back into his tent.

Then there was that especially disconcerting discovery he'd made about two of the women: he often saw both the skinny one and the fat one writing. *Writing*. The first time he'd seen them, both at once, he'd gone back to his tent, fuming. He'd seen them several times since. Each had her favorite spot outside where she'd plop down and write away. He was pretty sure the fat one was writing letters; he'd seen her pull sheets of stationery out of that yellow box she toted around. But the skinny one wrote in one of those black and white college exam books. He thought she must have gone through a couple by now. She just wrote and wrote and wrote. As if it was just pouring out of her. Like her hand couldn't move fast enough to keep up. Watching her write so effortlessly irritated the hell out of him.

That's what had made him change his mind again, deciding that giving the ladies a scare was a good idea after all. Maybe he'd get Richter to help him. But he didn't want to give them too big a scare. And Richter had no clue how scary he was.

But he felt an overwhelming need to protect his privacy.

You're scared.

That damn little voice again. For months he'd quieted it by simply giving up, checking out of his normal existence. But then he had started watching the thin one, writing away. She would be so absorbed that she had no idea he was there, lurking. Yesterday he'd gone back to his tent, dug the old pad out from under the heap of clothes, found his pen. But still, nothing came.

He had seen her again, just minutes ago, writing,

writing. He suddenly remembered a quote from the great sportswriter, Red Smith. 'There's nothing to writing. All you do is sit down at a typewriter and open a vein.' Something like a moan had come out of him and she had gathered up her things, calling the little dog, and hustled inside. He had darted back to the tent. He threw his own pad and pen across the tent, then dug through dirty clothes, looking for something else. When he found it, he picked it up, slowly. Even more slowly, he unfolded the blade. Numbly, he scraped it broadside across his palm, feeling the sharpness. *Open a vein.*

A muffled shout in the distance. Another in response. A loud clatter. The voices again, harsher. Those women. What were they arguing about *now*? He closed the knife, threw it into the cardboard box with the canned goods. More shouts. Those damn women! Couldn't they just keep quiet? Clearly they were getting on each other's nerves. And his. And yet . . . He stared at the box. And yet, there was a part of him that was glad they were there, disturbing the aching silence that was threatening to consume him.

CHAPTER 23

SHELLY

Shelly had to stop stomping; it was hurting her knees. She'd left the house fuming. Again. This was the third or fourth time she'd stormed out of the house, mad at someone. The first was with C.C. over the windows. Was that three weeks ago already? So much had changed, yet little about the house had. She shook her head. She pulled her cellphone out of her pocket, stared at its blank screen. Non-payment had finally caught up with her, yet here she was, still carrying it around, like some animal that can't let go of its expired young. Nothing was turning out like she'd imagined. Like it was supposed to.

Even the gentle southern clime had pulled a Jekyll and Hyde. As she marched down Raven Road, the air seemed determined to wrap her in sponge-like humidity, and the heat determined to squeeze it back out of her. She kept walking. Not toward anything. Just away. Away from C.C. From Meg.

This morning's argument was once again about working. Or rather, *not* working. Shelly had lost count of how many squabbles they'd had since they'd been here. And she seemed to be losing them all. Even that first one, about the windows. She'd returned to find Meg on the outside (with a little spit of a dog she'd adopted, not checking with anyone!) and C.C. inside, cleaning every damn pane of every damn window in the living room. It had made that ratty old couch look even rattier, as Shelly had known it would. Then that letter from the estate attorney had informed C.C. of various accounts due, additional bequests, and other financial entanglements. That had derailed the whole project. They'd been working on those for weeks, and still didn't know what their financial situation was. For all this, she could have just stayed in Iowa and sorted out her own mess.

But C.C. and Meg both took it as some sort of windfall – of time! They'd suddenly decided they were on vacation, or living in the 1800s or something. Shelly picked up a long stick on the side of the road and whapped leaves off the bushes as she walked.

Remodeling? Nooo. The two of them had scrubbed out that kitchen, even that disgusting, *non-working* fridge. Meg worked up the nerve to try the gas stove, and, though it had to be lit with a match, it worked fine. Then C.C. had to go and find hurricane lamps, and that stupid generator in the garage. Over Shelly's strong objections, they hooked the fridge up to that, deciding that not reconnecting the house electrical would save money and the environment. The two of them giggled like schoolgirls together at night. 'Having only lamplight at night is fun!' said C.C., trying to cajole Shelly. 'Yeah!' said Meg. 'Like *Little House on the Prairie*, or *Little Women*.' Shelly whapped the leaves off another unsuspecting shrub.

Shelly had been somewhat mollified when C.C. also found an old coffee percolator in Georgie's studio; it actually made decent coffee on the stove. And goofing off was okay for a few days; pulling each other up and down in the old dumbwaiter was a hoot. For a couple of times. But those two were forever giving that little dog rides in there, sending bedtime snacks up to each other, plates down in the morning. Meg and C.C. rejoiced in going back in time, had all the modern conveniences they wanted in the fridge and the stove. Meg didn't even want the phone hooked up! And C.C. *had agreed*! Shelly couldn't believe it. What if Kathryn called with some emergency, Shelly had asked her. C.C. had just taken a deep breath and determinedly stated that 'back in the day' not everyone could be reached at every moment. If there was a true emergency, she said, they could contact the Fleurville police. 'Besides,' C.C. had said, 'Kathryn probably needs to be truly on her own, for once. Maybe that's the only way she can become ready to be with someone.'

Exasperated, Shelly had tried another tack: 'What about Grant? What if he's trying to reach you?' 'He has the address,' Meg had calmly replied. 'He can write. He wanted some distance from me, and, who knows? Maybe it's good for both of us to have some time alone. Maybe it's meant to be.'

Shelly whapped the heads off some tall grass at the side of the road.

When she'd stormed out today, C.C. was inside sipping sweet tea and writing letters to Lucy, and that Purdy fellow. She wrote to Kathryn too, apparently. But unlike the other two, her daughter never wrote back. And Meg was cooking, as always. She must have bought a half-dozen vegetarian cookbooks, some new cookware, and every kind of bean grown on God's green earth from that stupid food co-op she'd discovered in town. *Could she afford materials to work on the house? No. Could she afford cookware? Of course!*

It was ridiculous! She'd gone along with them for a while, knowing both were grieving some pretty big losses. But since Meg had gotten that little dog, she seemed suddenly not to care one whit about Grant. She'd stopped writing him letters, stopped checking the mailbox (C.C. more than had that covered anyway). But when Meg wasn't cooking or reading some treatise on how to save the planet by eating kale or algae or some fool thing, she was constantly jotting in one of those little blank books, recipes, notes on recipes, and who knew what else.

And C.C.! Well, she was acting like a teenager in love with her pen pal! Trotting out to the mailbox every day, finding a letter there, nearly every day. Holding them to her chest like valentines. She'd scurry up to her room, or out to the back under the tree to read her letters, over and over. Then she'd pull out her box of stationery and write them back.

Shelly looked around. She could be eaten by wolves out here and those two probably wouldn't notice for days, so enraptured were they with this 'simplicity' kick they were on. Meanwhile, *she* was going stir-crazy. She took at least two walks a day. She'd read nearly half Georgie's collection of paperbacks. Georgie had what appeared to be the entire collection of one author, and Shelly had actually really enjoyed those books, but now she'd read them all. She'd even read a couple of Georgie's romances, though she'd never admit that to Meg or C.C. But the romances just made . . . *things* . . . worse.

She slapped her stick through another bush. *Whack!* C.C. was essentially dating Purdy by mail, and Meg seemed not to need anything more than kisses from that little dog. Apparently neither of them missed the physical part of a relationship with a man. Cuddling and kissing. *Whack!* Nookie. *Whack!* Lively, aerobic, acrobatic S-E-X. *Whackwhackwhack!* Shelly hit the bush over and over, back and forth, back and forth, till it was nearly denuded.

She couldn't remember ever being so restless and . . . alone. But she had nothing and no one to return to in Wisataukee. And it wasn't like she could find a man around here. The only men she'd seen were wrinkly old postmasters, or derelict hobos camping out in their neighbor's back woods.

And what about that guy? They really ought to call the cops on him. He still gave her the creeps. He had pretty much steered clear of them, but she kept her eye on him. She could just make out his tent from her bedroom window. She had often seen him pacing in front of it. Once, she'd thought she'd seen a bear snuffling around near the tent. She'd actually worried about the guy, and had run to find C.C. and Meg. They'd laughed! At her. She took off the tops of more of the long grass.

C.C. and Meg didn't seem concerned about *anything*. Shelly knew they just flat out didn't believe her about the bear, and they'd both said they thought the homeless guy was harmless. But Shelly thought they should at least try to contact the owner of the house, let him know he had a squatter. 'We like the solitude of Dogs' Wood, and maybe he just wants to be left alone too,' Meg had said. 'He's not hurting anyone.'

'Arrghh!' Shelly threw her stick as hard as she could into the thicket. They were both in some kind of southern coma! This house, this town – they were C.C.'s. And Meg had her dog, *and* the only car. It was she, Shelly, who was trapped. No work, no money, no man.

'No thanks,' she said angrily to the bushes. 'I'm out of here.'

She started running, out of pure frustration, as

she so often did here. She'd *never* been a runner. But it worked. As it was working now. She got into a rhythm, and something about the physical strain on her body forced her brain down to a single pure strand of consciousness. It was always a relief. But this time, as her anger seeped out, a tremulous awareness seeped in.

There was something running alongside her in the thicket.

She veered away, to the middle of the road, stopped. The rustling stopped. Her heart rate was faster than the running warranted. She had seen that creepy guy this morning, picking some kind of berries at the end of the road. She was going to be raped and murdered by that vagrant! Right here! He would drag her lifeless body into the woods, and little frigging Laura Ingalls and Jo March in there wouldn't know she was gone till the mouse trap went off again and she wasn't there to dispose of the carcass for them!

There was more rustling, louder this time. Shelly backed all the way across the road, picturing him: his raggedy clothes, his scraggly beard that had gotten noticeably longer in the weeks since they'd arrived. She stopped and listened. All was quiet. She looked around, wishing she hadn't thrown her stick. She found another one, a little larger than a pencil. But it was all she had. Holding her stick high, she took a few tentative steps toward the side of the road. *More rustling.* She jumped back again, holding the stick out in front of her. She realized that with the thin stick, she probably looked like a paranoid conductor.

Listening hard, she heard only a few skittering noises, soft enough to satisfy her that it was neither a person nor a large animal. But it could be birds.

She wished she hadn't thought about birds. She looked at the dense growth all around, vines and shrubs and trees. This place, which had seemed so vibrant and lovely and full of life when they'd arrived, now, only just into May, was hot and humid and overgrown, and threatening to close in on her. But all she had to do was think about how mad she'd been, and the fear shriveled. She walked right up to the edge of the road, bent down, and peered into the underbrush. The relief was only minor. In the green labyrinth, she saw various small, gray birds, hopping along the ground, flitting on and off the low branches. She walked quickly on in the enveloping heat. 'Pink elephants, root beer floats, George Clooney,' she said aloud, trying to think of anything besides birds or the homeless guy.

A loud cracking, breaking-wood sound sent her sidestepping across the road again. Those were *branches*, not twigs, breaking. Maybe even the size of branch a human foot could step on and break.

Like, if he was getting a club with which to beat her senseless.

She looked at the paltry stick in her hand and tossed it. If she didn't have a weapon, she should look like she didn't need one. She assumed what she hoped would look like a karate position. But having never taken karate, she took up what was, in fact, the best her inflexible body had ever been able to do: a yoga pose called 'The Warrior', standing in a semi-squat, feet aligned as if on a tightrope, one arm stretched out in front and the other behind. Every muscle was held taut, her attention focused on the bushes. The sound had stopped, which made her listen harder. She felt her quads burn as she held the long-unpracticed position.

She held it for thirty seconds, then a minute. She kept on much longer than she ever had in yoga class. Vance would be proud. She smiled, then grimaced. She'd had a less than exciting fling with her yoga instructor; it turned out his body was indeed flexible, but, perhaps not coincidentally, his personality also resembled an overcooked noodle. Thinking about William, she momentarily forgot to be afraid. Until the sounds crunched closer through the bushes. Her heart banged against her sternum. She had to concentrate, knowing that all she could hope for at this point was that she *looked* poised to fight. She felt the heat of the sun on her skin, the weight and texture of the humidity; she breathed in the metallic smell of the dirt and chlorophyll and the odor from her own body. She saw every leaf, every rock. She heard every sound. She'd never had a focus like this. But just as suddenly as it had started, the sound stopped again.

The silence was almost worse than the noise. She didn't know whether to run, or stay in the pose. Did everything ultimately come down to fight or flight? She took a deep breath, then another. She realized that between the breathing and the yoga pose, she'd calmed down. 'This shit really works!' she said, looking at her legs, amazed. She felt centered, balanced. Strong. Maybe it was the anger, but she checked her position, intrigued. Then she started to laugh. Standing there in that pose, she realized she looked like a fencer without a sword. Hardly a threatening or even potentially defensive position. Still smiling, she stood up finally, shook her legs out. Then there was another rustling in the bushes.

'Dammit!' she said, putting her hands on her hips. It suddenly occurred to her that someone was toying with her. There was nothing that Shelly Kostens hated more than being toyed with. 'Come on out, fucker!' So much for centered.

Her heart was racing again, but now she couldn't tell what was fear, what was anger. 'Hey, *asshole*,' she demanded of the bushes again, deciding she had a choice; she would go with anger.

Crunch, snap!

She quickly assumed her yoga pose again, and just as quickly dropped it. It was absurd. She raised her fists, then let them drop too. She was tired. Tired of fearing whatever might be in the bushes at the side of this road. Tired of fearing what was in the bushes at the edges of her life.

She could make out a dark mass, moving closer. The sounds of breaking wood, louder. Whatever it was, it was big. And not human; it was lumbering along on four legs.

Bear! 'Ohhhh, shiiiiit,' she whispered. This would show C.C. and Meg: she'd been right all along about the bear! They'd find her mauled body on the road as they drove to town for more tofu and stamps.

She decided, this one time, she'd just as soon not be proved right. Adrenalin shot through her, giving rise to panic. Her thoughts raced. Somewhere she'd heard: 'Don't run from wildlife.' She glanced around for a big rock or stick, or even the smaller stick she'd had moments ago. But just as she did, the thing burst from the bushes.

She screamed. It stopped, its eyes locked on her.

Breathless, Shelly stared at the thing. *What in the hell . . . ?*

She continued backing as it ambled toward her. *Oh. My. God.*

Was that a dog? It was. An incredibly big, very dirty dog.

Jesus! Was it on steroids? It was *freakin' huge!* It stood regarding her as she regarded it. It was so dirty that it was hard to tell, but it looked like it might be tan with brownish markings. It did not seem threatening. Its tongue was lolling out the side of its mouth, its big lips jiggling as it turned its head first to one side, then the other, for all the world looking like it was checking for traffic before it crossed the road. But it just stood there.

She thought it was a Rottweiler, maybe. But no. It was not the right color. And too big. And, more importantly, its face was somehow friendlier-looking than a Rottweiler. She hoped that the last observation was not just wishful thinking. She'd never seen anything quite like it. Wait. Yes she had. In a movie. That one with the gorilla in the end; she didn't remember the name of it. But the guy had a big dog that looked like this. A mastiff! That was it. But that movie dog, though huge, wasn't *this* big!

Somewhere in her unconscious mind came the thought that a friendly greeting on her part might be a good idea. 'Hey, buddy! Good dog. Here . . .' *Boy? Girl?* She held out one flat hand, trying to seem friendly and at the same time bend forward low enough that she could peer under . . .

Oh my God. Definitely male. It had the hugest . . .

Suddenly the dog came galumphing toward her, his catcher's-mitt paws slapping down, puppy-like on the road. Globs of dried mud jiggled from his stomach and legs, even from his jowly chin. Only his ears were relatively free from mud. His ears were actually small, considering the rest of him. He lumbered up to her, a long strand of white drool hanging off one side of his mouth. Shelly couldn't help but laugh at his enormous and comical face – his colossal lips, hanging like two cow's livers off either side of his nose, the skin wrinkling in its excess; his big nose, also almost like a cow's, pinkish-black and pushed up slightly. His lips alone could make up a Dollop-sized dog. One of this guy's legs would make two, maybe three M.J.s. But he had the softest, sweetest brown eyes.

He pushed his big head – something between a bowling ball and a beach ball – against her hip in greeting, and nearly knocked her over. 'Hello, big fella,' she said, scratching his ear. He leaned into the scratch, and into her, and she had to move her feet quickly not to fall. She inspected his coat, suddenly worried about mange as she patted him. But as far as she could tell, he looked healthy, just dirty. He had what appeared to be a pale blue collar, but it too was very dirty. But there were no tags at all.

'You look like you've been on your own for a while, buddy.' He licked her hand. He didn't look painfully thin, but he wasn't fat. Just huge. And with a lot of extra skin. Where M.J. and Dollop's skin and fur seemed shrink-wrapped onto their bony bodies, it was as if this fella had been issued a coat several sizes too big.

'Sit, boy,' she said. 'Sit.' She pointed her finger at him, repeated her command. He licked her finger. Shelly laughed. 'Okay, not so much on the training, I see. Do you have a name?' She backed away from him a couple of steps. 'Here, King!' He sprang forward. 'No, never mind. King is a stupid name, even if it is your name.' She backed up a few more steps, but before she could try out another name, he trotted over to her. She started walking back toward the house, just to see, and he followed. Smiling, she started jogging. He followed, trotting, his ears up. Her heart, which had been racing in fear a few moments ago, now swelled with affection. Clearly, he needed a home. And she needed a friend.

She jogged backwards, up the middle of the road, watching and encouraging him as he trotted after her, his big lips waggling to and fro, the skin on his huge torso quivering with his movement. She turned, zigzagging across the road. He followed. She stopped abruptly, and the dog stopped too, as if waiting to see what new direction this game would take. She laughed.

'Well you're like my little shadow! Okay, not so little. Hey! *That's* a good name! Shadow! You want to be *my* dog, Shadow?' He wagged his big tail.

'Let's go home, boy,' she said, striding purposefully toward the house, her enormous Shadow following her every move.

CHAPTER 24

MEG

The three of them sat on the dilapidated couch in the decaying living room, under the ugly chandelier, in front of the cracked – but clean – panes of glass, silent and staring. Dollop was perched alertly on Meg's lap, also staring. 'Shadow' was lying on the rug, on his stomach, looking like The Sphinx, and damn near as big, Meg thought. He was looking at each of them, but only one at a time, and briefly. Meg thought he wasn't appraising them so much as aware he was being appraised. He reminded her of the dogs in the shelter who were clearly trying to make a good impression, somehow knowing that a loving home might be hanging in the balance. But how could they keep this dog? They couldn't afford to feed him!

Meg had been outside, weeding her vegetable garden when she had first spotted the two of them. They were practically prancing down the road together. Meg stood, open-mouthed, not sure *what* was following Shelly. Then she'd dashed inside for her camera, shouting for C.C. She'd snapped away as they came across the lawn, then during

Shadow's protracted bath, which had been hysterical. If ever there was a perfect dog for tall, brash, comin'atcha Shelly Kostens, this dog was it.

But now Meg cupped her hands protectively around Dollop. Shadow *seemed* friendly enough, but if he ever took a notion to go after Dollop . . . Meg scooted back on the couch, hugging tiny Dollop to her. Finally, she tore her eyes away from Shadow and looked at C.C. She had her hands on either side of her head, elbows on her knees, as if this turn of events made it impossible for her to hold her head up without the extra support. Pushing her face left, then right, C.C. looked at one dog, then the other. The dismay on her face matched how Meg felt.

But Shelly was beside herself with excitement, pointing out Shadow's myriad splendid features. She'd already commented on his 'big ole liver-lips', his 'gorgeous square head' and his 'hysterically big feet'. Now she said: 'Isn't he pretty?' She let out something close to a squeal. 'I just think this is amazing! Freakin' amazing! *Two* dogs!'

C.C. flinched. Only slightly, but Meg saw it. Apparently Shelly did too. 'Well, three, counting M.J. But now we have two dogs, here in the house. I mean, talk about your signs!'

Meg had rarely seen Shelly so excited, certainly not in the past few weeks. She knew Shelly had been going a little stir-crazy, but Meg thought she, more than any of them, needed to learn to relax, let things *be* sometimes. Now, Shelly didn't even sound like herself. She sounds like C.C., thought Meg. It was a little disturbing. Meg eyed her.

'Think about it,' Shelly explained. 'Here we are, in this house, called . . .' She gestured with her hands, looking first at C.C., then at Meg, waiting for them to fill in the blank. Meg dutifully said, 'Dogs' Wood,' but she didn't smile.

'Right! And now we *have* dogs. Plural!'

Meg sighed. She would never give up Dollop. So how could she tell Shelly that she couldn't keep the dog *she'd* brought home? He was a . . . monster. True, an apparently friendly one, but still. Suddenly Meg smiled. The perfect argument to use with Shelly. *Size matters!* Another of Shelly's mantras, though, certainly never used in this context. But it was true: she, Meg, could afford to feed Dollop. Shelly could not say the same. Besides, Dollop wouldn't cause bodily harm to one of them if he were to run through the house.

Meg stared in awe. He *was* kind of beautiful. And just looking at him made her smile. Shadow, evidently tired of nothing happening other than everyone staring at him, rolled onto his side with a loud groan, and shut his eyes.

Meg gasped.

'Jesus, Mary and Joseph,' whispered C.C.

Meg looked at her, feeling every bit as astonished as C.C. looked. C.C. turned her head away from Shadow's underside and looked at Meg. Then they were both irresistibly drawn back to look again.

'I *know*!' said Shelly, grinning. 'It's *enormous*, isn't it!'

'Leave it to our dear Shelly to bring home a dog with a you-know-what the size of Florida!' dead-panned C.C.

Shelly exploded in laughter and C.C. succumbed, leaning on Meg, hooting. Meg was so convulsed that Dollop climbed onto the arm of the couch, and stared at her. Shadow opened one eye at the commotion, but closed it again, and went back to sleep.

'Oh my,' said C.C., wiping a tear from her eye.

'Whew,' said Shelly, catching her breath. They collected themselves. Meg looked at Shelly. She was beaming. At Shadow.

Meg shook her head. She and C.C. had essentially pulled Shelly's cord from her sole energy source: work. And Meg knew their inaction had been only partly due to financial matters. Mostly they'd slipped into the slow pace of just *being* here. She also knew that neither she nor C.C. entirely trusted their leader on this project. When push had come to shove, they'd both taken a big step back.

It was time to get to work. They'd lollygagged enough. And they could give to Shelly what she needed most: their vote of confidence. But what about the dog? Meg guessed he could stay for now, till they could persuade Shelly to find him a more suitable home.

'So, Shelly?' said Meg. 'Fearless leader! You have been most indulgent as we have . . . settled in. But

338

I think we're ready to work, and we await your direction. Right?' She looked at C.C. C.C. stared back at her a minute, inhaled deeply, then said, 'Right!'

'Seriously? We're going to get to work?' asked Shelly, jumping up from the couch. 'You . . . you trust me?' They both nodded, grinning.

'What's first?' Meg asked.

'Oh! Demolition! Get the big, messy stuff out of the way, work our way down to the detail stuff like windows, painting, et cetera. That is, if it's okay with C.C. to knock out the wall between the dining room and the kitchen, make a sort of great room?'

C.C. nodded, smiling. 'It'll be lovely. I bet Georgie would say "full steam ahead!" if she were here.'

'I have a feeling she's watching over us,' said Shelly, surprising Meg and, judging from her expression, C.C. too.

'So be it!' said Meg. 'First thing tomorrow, that wall is history. We'll go buy tools today.' She stood, Dollop in her arms. 'Ceece, we're going to have to dip into the funds again.'

'Wellll,' said C.C., her drawl in full swing, 'I 'spect we'll have to dig a little deeper into those funds.' She pointed to Shadow. 'I reckon we ought to buy some dog food for Mr Humongous here while we're at it.'

Shelly threw her head back, thrust her fists toward the ceiling. 'Yes!'

★　　★　　★

The next morning, Meg awoke just before sunrise. Listening to the silent house, she wasn't sure what had woken her. As usual, Dollop had slept with her, curled up by her pillow, his head resting on the corner. Lying there, watching him sleep, she now knew what C.C. had felt about M.J. Maybe there was a chemistry between people and dogs, just as there was between people. Either you had it or you didn't. She had liked M.J. well enough, but something remarkable had clicked between M.J. and C.C. Almost instantly. And so had something with her and Dollop.

She couldn't help but wonder if she'd ever truly had chemistry with Grant. Many things had felt right about marrying him, but in a calculated, analytical way. He was the right height, the right look, the right background, the right interests, the right aspirations. But a resonating, unconditional love? Thirty-three years ago, she might have said yes. But thirty-two years ago, she would have said no. Infatuation was as thin as the peel on an apple, yet, if you'd never seen an apple before, you'd think the whole thing was red. But try telling a young person that. Yet, C.C. and Lenny had seemed to have it till the end, that sparkle in the eye for each other. She knew she and Grant had lost that long ago.

Being at Dogs' Wood, spending so much time by herself, writing, cooking, walking, Meg had had a stark realization: she wasn't actually missing her husband. She wondered now if she ever had. She'd just been desperately clinging to her *marriage*. To the word. The concept.

Dollop nuzzled her arm, then stretched luxuriously, his tiny toenails pointed, his spindly legs trembling as they pushed out. She rose quietly, carrying him out to the backyard, dressed only in her T-shirt and pajama shorts. While Dollop took care of business and explored the yard, Meg yawned and stretched, appreciating the glories of the morning. She wiggled her toes in wet grass, then gazed around the yard at her shadow. It reminded her of Dollop earlier, reaching out, stretching.

Dollop's sudden growl made her instantly alert. She scanned the lawn, saw him in front of the overgrown hedge. He stiffened, the short hair on his back rising. He let out another low growl.

Meg stepped over, picked him up, searching, and backing away. 'What's up, Dollop? What's wrong, boy?' She hustled into the house.

She met C.C. in the kitchen, drinking a cup of tea, leaning against the counter. She set down her mug. 'What's wrong?' she asked Meg. 'You look like you've seen a ghost?'

'*Not* seen a ghost might be more accurate. Dollop suddenly started growling. I got the distinct impression someone was watching us again, but I couldn't see anyone. Look, I have goose bumps.' She extended her arm toward C.C., lifting her sleeve.

C.C. turned and looked out the kitchen window.

'This is getting a mite creepy. D'ya think it's Georgie?'

Meg gave C.C. a look. 'No. I think it's probably that homeless guy again. He seems to be spying on us more and more, getting closer and closer. Maybe he's not so harmless after all. Can we find out the name of the next-door neighbor, try to track them down? And maybe we should call the police.'

'Why are we calling the police?' asked a sleepy voice. 'And can I have a cup of coffee before we do?' Shelly shuffled across the kitchen to the percolator, Shadow right behind her. She pulled the top off, but it slipped out of her grasp, clattering to the floor.

'Here, let me help.' Without thinking, Meg set Dollop on the floor. Shadow immediately turned. The two dogs stared at each other, each frozen in place. Meg gasped, bending toward Dollop.

'Wait, let's give them a minute,' said Shelly. Shadow cocked his head, ears up, then back, then up again. He wouldn't look directly at Dollop. Shadow backed up. Dollop barked again. Shadow lay down, still only casting darting glances his way.

'Oh, my stars,' whispered C.C. 'Would you look at that.'

Dollop moved slightly closer to Shadow, sniffing, then stopping. Shadow turned his head, looked away. He pawed the air once, then lay quietly. Dollop bowed down, barked again, then took off at a run, his tiny toenails skittering across the vinyl floor past Shadow. The big dog took off after him as Dollop careened around the corner, disappearing into the hallway.

'*Dollop!*' screamed Meg.

'*Shadow!*' screamed Shelly.

'*Jesus, Mary and Joseph!*' screamed C.C.

The three women ran after the dogs, Meg right behind Shadow, certain her beloved little dog was moments away from becoming a canine canapé. She followed them to the living room, grabbing the door frame as she rounded the corner. She hung on, feeling more breathless than she actually was.

Dollop jumped up onto the couch, then higher, onto the armrest, his little tail wagging exuberantly. Shelly and C.C. joined Meg at the door. Silently, they watched. Shadow sat at the base of the couch, woofed once, then turned a tight circle, dropping to the floor, his mighty tail thumping against the carpet.

'I think they're making friends,' whispered Meg, mostly to C.C., who was clutching her the same way Meg was gripping the door frame. Shelly stood in the center of the doorway, one foot into the room, looking ready to hurl herself between them should Dollop need protection. But Dollop jumped down to the floor. Slowly, but confidently, he walked a wide circle all the way around Shadow, then jumped onto the couch again. Shadow stood, approached slowly, and they nearly touched noses, then Dollop barked again and Shadow sat, waiting.

C.C. shook her head, relaxing her grip on Meg. 'Well. Who'd a thunk it?! The flea gets to be boss of the elephant.'

But just to be safe, they locked Dollop in the bedroom and left Shadow in the kitchen as they headed out to buy tools. Meg drove, feeling lighter and happier than she had in months. Like some wall somewhere had already come down.

CHAPTER 25

C.C.

'Go, Meg!' C.C. cheered, impressed with Meg's focused, determined eye on the wall.

'Ay-yi-yi!' yipped Shelly. Both dogs barked from their respective rooms upstairs.

'Okay, here goes!' said Meg. She flexed the bicep of one arm, then in one fluid motion she raised her sledgehammer and smashed into the wall. Plaster chips flew. When she yanked it out again, splinters of wooden lath came too.

'Hurray!' shouted C.C., even more impressed. Meg looked like a pro!

'Thatta *girl*!' yelled Shelly.

'C'mon, Ceece!' shouted Meg. 'Your turn!'

C.C. looked at them both. Shelly had already put a nice sized hole in the wall in front of her too. Both were using sledgehammers. C.C. had thought, given her small stature, she'd need something sharp to break through, so she had selected a pickax. But now it felt heavy and unwieldy. She looked at the other two; they encouraged her again.

'C'mon, babe! There's nothing like demolition

to make you feel like you can conquer the world!' said Shelly. At the moment, the only thing C.C. wanted to conquer was the wedgie from her too-small coveralls. Georgie was quite a bit taller than she, but thin as a willow stick; but the coveralls and C.C.'s safety glasses, her too-big work boots, everything was already covered with a fine layer of white dust, like flour, so C.C. was grateful for them. She put her hand on the material over her rear, and tugged. Then she took a deep breath, lifted her pick over her shoulder. She stepped close, and banged the sharp end against the wall. Debris did not fly. The pick went into the wall, but just the tip. She tried again, swinging with more conviction, aiming for the same hole. This time the head broke through, disappearing behind the wall and she couldn't free it. 'I'm stuck!' C.C. tugged, to no avail. 'Maybe I should take one of y'all's hammer-thingys, trade you this pick. I can get it in there all right, but then I can't get the darn thing out!'

'Now where have I heard that before?' said Shelly, tapping her dust mask with one gloved finger.

Meg laughed, then C.C. started laughing so hard that she had to drop her pick handle, leaving it hanging from the wall, grab her crotch, and run clomping across the kitchen in her big boots, straight for the bathroom.

When she returned, Meg and Shelly had each enlarged their holes, but were taking a break, waiting for the dust to settle, and waiting for her. They all took their spots again, and C.C. tugged on the pick handle, but still couldn't free the head from the wall. She gave it another determined pull. 'Ugh!' The wall seemed determined not to return her pick.

'Pull hard, Ceece! Put your foot up there and just yank it out!' yelled Shelly. She was working closest to the mudroom, but still only a few yards away, so C.C. thought she really needn't yell at all. But she figured Shelly was in full demolition mode now, and would yell regardless.

'Here, I'll help you,' said Meg. 'Stand back.' C.C. stepped aside. Meg skillfully raised her sledgehammer and let it fly, landing near the hole, widening it. C.C. pulled her pick free.

She gazed admiringly at Meg. 'I declare! You are *good* with that thing!'

'We, Grant and I, have – had – whatever, that wood stove in our living room, so I've chopped a lot of wood. Plus, it helps to be a little pissed off. Hey . . .' She was looking at the wall, seeming to size it up. 'Is there a marker around?'

C.C. noted the gleam in her eye, but didn't question it. She clomped across the kitchen, pulled open the junk drawer. She had to try three markers before she found one that wasn't dried out. A red one. She clomped back, handed it to Meg.

'Good! A blood-red one,' said Meg, uncapping it. She walked to the wall and placed the marker as high as she could reach. Then she drew a circle, followed by a line straight down. Then she drew in legs and arms, completing the stick figure. Meg was grinning as she added a baseball cap on the top of the figure's head. Then, with a flourish, she added the overlapping NY Yankees logo.

'Now who could that be!?' yelled Shelly. C.C. couldn't help but smile, looking at Shelly's big grin.

'Go ahead and write his name too, honey,' C.C. told Meg. 'Get right to the point of the matter.'

Meg hesitated only briefly, then in large capital letters wrote 'GRANT' across the figure, dropped the marker, which clattered to the floor.

'On your mark . . .' Shelly began and C.C. joined in, both standing together, out of Meg's way. 'Get set . . . *GO!*'

All at once, Meg expertly swung the sledge-hammer up over her shoulder and brought it forward, sliding her hand down the long wooden handle as she did. The heavy head slammed through the middle of the stick figure. She repeated the motion several more times, knocking out the A, and most of the figure from the waist down. Meg bent, peering at her handiwork. 'Hey! I can see through, into the dining room!'

'*Brava!*' yelled Shelly, clapping her gloved hands.

C.C. stepped forward, peeked at the hole. She saw daylight.

'Breakthrough, indeed!' said Shelly, almost reverently. She clapped Meg on the back.

Meg let the head of her sledgehammer drop to

the floor, one hand resting on the butt of the handle. She wiped some dust from her glasses with one leather finger, stared at the hole. Suddenly her head dropped, her chin almost on her chest. C.C. stepped over to her, placed a hand on her shoulder. 'You okay, Meg?' Shelly echoed her: 'Meg?'

Meg turned toward them, her head still hung, her shoulders slumped forward. She raised her free hand to her face, slowly raised her glasses, pulled her mask down, then lifted her head. Meg was grinning.

'Whew! Look at that smile, girl!' said Shelly. 'It's about damn time!'

'Anyone else want to take a whack at him?' Meg asked.

'No, thank kew. I got mah own i-deah.' C.C. could hear her accent kicking in again. She picked the marker up off the floor. She put the tip on the wall close to Shelly's section and wrote a big C. Then A. Then L. Then O. Followed by R, I, E. Her last letter, an S, was written over the end of the stick figure's pointy arm. She stuck the capped marker in the breast pocket of her coveralls.

C.C. lifted her pick and did her best to imitate Meg with her swing. But her arms were tired already, and the pick slipped sideways, and slid ineffectually down the wall.

'Put your weight into it,' said Meg. C.C. looked at her sharply. 'Er. No. I mean, you've got to follow through with your body. Like this. Put your legs in a stride, hip forward.' She demonstrated. 'Then as you swing it up over your shoulder, lean back just a little, then rock forward as you bring it over. Like this.' C.C. watched as Meg again expertly swung up and over, the chunky metal head of her sledgehammer sinking into the plaster, splintering lath below. One stick arm was bisected.

C.C. raised her pick again, put her left foot forward, as Meg had. She swung for all she was worth, sliding her hand along the handle, up and over, imitating Meg, and throwing her weight into it. The pick smashed into and through the L. 'Oh!' she said, almost falling forward. 'Oh, my stars! That really works!'

'Yup!' said Meg. Even behind her goggles and mask, C.C. could see she was smiling. Meg helped her pull on the pick handle, and a chunk of plaster and lath tumbled to the floor as they freed it.

'Okay! My turn! My turn!' yelled Shelly. C.C. handed the marker to Shelly. 'Mine's a long word,' said Shelly, 'so I'm going to start clear over here.' She stood near the mudroom, drew a huge B, and continued writing all the way across her section of wall. She had to make the Y small and squished so as not to run into the C of C.C.'s CALORIES.

'Boo! Hissssss! *Bad* bankruptcy!' said C.C., elbowing Meg. Meg laughed, and joined in the jeering.

Shelly capped the marker, handed it to C.C. She pulled off her denim shirt, threw it to the floor, never taking her eyes off the wall. 'Stand back, girls!' She picked up her sledgehammer and side-stepped away from them, almost into the mudroom. Still, C.C. grabbed Meg and the two of them quickly backed up into the kitchen together.

'Now don't hurt yourself, Shell!' said C.C. She didn't like the look in her eyes. Shelly didn't respond, merely backed away from the wall, her fierce gaze locked on her target. She readied her sledgehammer, gave a mighty swing up and over as she charged toward the wall yelling: 'FINAN-CIAL INDEPENDENCE, HERE I COME!' The head slammed into the plaster, just above the B. C.C. and Meg's cheers blended with the familiar sound of cracking plaster and lath. Shelly quickly lined up again. 'DEBT NEVERMORE, NEVER-MORE!' Shelly screamed in a cawing voice. Meg burst out laughing and cawed back at her. C.C.'s gloved hands did a loud drum riff on the cabinet across the kitchen till Shelly's mallet head sailed into the wall again. But this time the cracking plaster sound was immediately followed by a jarring, metallic thunk. Shelly cried out in pain, her sledgehammer falling to the floor. C.C. and Meg rushed to her side.

'What happened?' C.C. asked, afraid to touch her. 'You okay?'

Meg looked at the wall, stepped closer to inspect it. 'Uh-oh,' she murmured.

'Oh. Please don't say uh-oh,' said C.C. 'We don't

need any more uh-ohs. We've had our fill of uh-ohs.' Shelly moved her arm in slow, testing circles. 'You okay?' C.C. asked her again, looking from Meg back to Shelly. Shelly nodded, but still held her shoulder.

'What'd I hit?' she asked, wincing again.

'C.C.?' asked Meg. 'Did there, by any chance, used to be, oh, like, say, a washer and dryer in the mudroom?'

'Yes,' said C.C. quietly. 'But years ago. Georgie moved them downstairs 'cause she didn't like looking at all the dirty laundry. She thought about moving them back up the last—'

'*Oh shit*,' said Meg and Shelly in unison, interrupting C.C.

'What?' C.C. stepped forward and saw a dark, wet circle growing around the hole. Peering in, she saw the damaged pipe, a tiny spray of water spurting out of a bent, soldered seam. 'Oh Lord. What do we do now?' she asked. But as she spoke, the seam bent outward as the water pressure began to enlarge the crack in the weak joint. The tiny spray became an insistent squirt.

'Hurry! Where's the shut-off valve?' asked Shelly. 'We don't want that pipe to—'

But it was too late. As the water tore through the seam, a huge spray fanned out from the wall, and onto the three screaming women.

CHAPTER 26

THE GUY IN THE TENT

He burst in the back door, ran through the mudroom, his bat held high. He was steeled for blood, expecting to come upon a rape or murder scene. He had seen many, most of them in his imagination, a few in real life, when he'd gone on ridealongs with the cops.

But it took a few seconds for his brain to take in the peculiar violence of the actual scene: the holes in the plaster. Lath exposed and sticking out like broken ribs. Fragments of words scrawled across the wall. Water spraying out of the wall.

When he saw no bodies, no blood, merely three, wet, hysterical women, not one of whom even noticed him, he couldn't help but stare at the wall. Especially what he now recognized as a stick figure, missing most of its body. A well-drawn baseball cap with a Yankees logo on a half a head remained. Jesus. What in the hell were these three up to over here? Some kind of wall-busting voodoo? Regardless, they were doing the wrong things now to remedy the situation. The tall one was screaming as she was trying to grab the pipe with her gloved hands, her head turned to the

353

side, the spray hitting her cheek. Her cheeks puffed out, she appeared to be spitting back at it. The skinny one was kneeling beneath the kitchen sink, most of her in the cabinet, screaming about a shut-off valve as she madly threw out bottles and boxes. Shut-off valve. He smiled. *Yeah, you'll find one there, darlin', but wrong side of the kitchen*. The third, the chubby one, was on her hands and knees, pushing two soaked dishtowels around the wet floor, screaming, 'Jesus, Mary and Joseph!' over and over.

'Quiet!' he said. He'd thought he'd yelled it, but he was so unused to speaking that he couldn't be sure. Plus, he couldn't even hear *himself* in the din, and not a one of them paid him the least bit of attention. Even though it had been a while since he'd walked into a room, he was used to deafening applause, or at very least, heads turning. Jack Hatch was not used to people not noticing him.

He cleared his throat, gave it another try. 'QUIET!' he shouted. The screaming continued, unabated.

'SHUT THE FUCK UP!'

That got them. They froze like statues. Then, slowly, each woman moved. The tall redhead was soaked, but she turned slowly toward him, blinking from the water, her hands maintaining an ineffectual chokehold on the cracked pipe. The thin one slowly reversed out of the cabinet on her hands and knees. And the fat one stared up at

354

him, gape-mouthed, from the floor, clutching the dishtowels. They stared at him from behind their wet glasses and masks, as if he was an apparition. He snickered. They should get a look at *themselves*. The silence, the looks, it was priceless! But just as suddenly as they had stopped, as if led by an invisible conductor somewhere, the lunatics all resumed their shrieking. He would have laughed again had the sound not been so piercing. But now he could see pure fear behind their too-big safety glasses.

All those thoughts of wanting to scare them and now that was the last thing he'd intended. If only they knew who he was. But thank God they didn't. That was the whole point of living out here. Of cutting the power and phone lines. Of cutting himself off from the world. Not that it had worked. In fact, quite the opposite. True, he'd quite recently contemplated removing *himself* from the world. But he would never hurt anyone else. But they clearly were of a different notion, what with all their screaming.

He went to cover his ears and only then did he realize that he still had his bat gripped in both hands. Oops. That couldn't have helped. He felt bad. He really did. He also had a headache. He dropped the bat to the floor and covered his ears, also clutching his head.

'*I'm here to help you!*' he yelled. He shoved the tall one out of the way, trying to peer into the hole. He deflected the water long enough to see where the shut-off valve to the old washer hook-up was behind the wall. Out of reach. 'Shit!' Georgie must have done that when she moved the washer-dryer to the basement. At least they'd stopped screaming. The skinny one was out of the cabinet and standing, helping the fat one to her feet. Basement! He'd have to locate the main shut-off to the house. His mind was working fast now; it was a sensation he hadn't had in a long time. He was moving across the narrow kitchen toward the basement, his feet already soaked from the growing puddles, when he saw the skinny one eyeing a sledgehammer. '*I'm going for the shut-off valve!*' he yelled at her. 'In the basement! Move! Outta my way!' There wasn't room enough for *two* people in this ridiculous kitchen, let alone four. Hey . . . That's probably what they were doing, enlarging the kitchen. Well good idea, ladies, but way wrong way to go about it. Why didn't they hire a professional? He yanked open the door to the basement, his wet sneakers slapping on the steps as he hobbled down into the darkness. He held tight to the handrail, his arthritic right knee zinging with pain with every other step. 'Oww, oww, oww, oww, oww, oww!' Finally at the bottom, he clawed at the dark air above his head for the pull chain to the light. He'd carried big paintings up or down these stairs for Georgie several times in the last few months of her life. Before her illness, she had done it herself. Georgie Tucker had been one of the few truly competent and self-sufficient women he'd ever known. His hand hit the chain finally and he pulled, felt the resounding click, but no light came on. 'Shit!' he said again. He closed his eyes in painful realization. *Of course!* Kenny had told him that it would be far easier if he disconnected the dual trunk, which would cut power to Georgie's house as well as his own. He'd told Kenny to go ahead, that no one was living in the house anymore anyway. He'd thought he was so smart, paying his old friend who'd been unfairly fired from the power company to take him 'off grid'. But there had been times, especially now, as he stood in the dark basement with water starting to trickle down the stairs, that there were certain inconveniences to his plan of going completely incommunicado.

'Someone toss me a flashlight!' he yelled up the stairs. 'I need to find the main shut-off valve down here!' His urgent order was met with continued silence. 'NOW, you idiot broads! Unless you want to drown up there!' There was a sudden flurry of thumping footsteps, shouts of 'Where'd you leave it?' and 'There!' and '*You* give it to him.' Then he thought he heard one urgently whisper, '*Get the trollop's shadow!*' Were these gals smoking weed or something?

'I've got it.' One of them was standing at the top of the stairs, yelling to him. But she was standing back, and to the side; he couldn't see her well. 'And by the way, it might help if you stopped calling us "idiot broads", you arrogant, unkempt prick.' Ah. It was the tall one. She stepped forward as she raised the flashlight. 'Should I just throw it?'

'Yeah. But not too—' The flashlight was sailing down the staircase before he could even raise his hands to protect himself. He could only turn slightly before it cracked into the side of his head, then clattered to the floor. His hand went to his head, the pain immediate and intense.

'OWW! *Christ!* You trying to fucking kill me, lady?' He looked up at the woman, standing in the door frame at the top of the stairs. She was oddly illuminated from behind. Almost like an angel or something. A demonic angel.

'Well, I'm *sorry!*' she said, sounding sorry not one bit. 'You *told* me to throw it. It's not like I *meant* to hit you!' She put her hands on her hips, which irritated him even more. 'And, oh, *thank* you. "Lady" is a big improvement over "idiot broad".'

Well. *That* tone was downright snarky. He stared up at her, speechless, as she folded her arms over her chest, one hip and knee thrust out defiantly. It was the redhead. Not that he could see the color of her hair in the meager light. It was her voice, her manner. If you could call it that. As his eyes adjusted to the dark, he could make out small details about her: she had her dust mask around her neck now, goggles on the top of her head, a tight white T-shirt, jeans. It looked like she was wearing Georgie's old cowboy boots. Helluva outfit. But . . . oddly sexy.

Jesus. He touched his head again. He'd gotten whacked in the head harder than he thought! Or he'd been alone too long. She was *so not* his type. His last three girlfriends were under forty, for one thing. One, under thirty. All of them small, petite. Feminine. He looked at the woman at the top of the stairs again, blinking. For a minute, he had to stop and think where he was, what he was doing. He felt a little queasy. What *was* he doing? He shook his head, trying to clear his thoughts, which was a mistake. The pain surged.

'Umm, sir? There's kind of . . . getting to be . . . sort of a lot of water up here.'

It was a gentle voice from the back of the kitchen. The fat one.

He bent, and that made the pain surge again in his head. Groaning, he picked up the flashlight, clicked it on. It still worked, amazingly. He raised the beam, shone it in the woman's eyes briefly, intentionally. Yup. One very wet, very angry redhead. She squinted, raising her hand to shield her eyes. He turned and found his way to the main shut-off valve, and quickly cranked it off.

There was a brief pause, then shouts from upstairs. 'You did it!' 'It's off!' 'Yay!' As if he needed to be told. But he smiled as he walked back to the bottom of the stairs. The redhead was still at the top, looking down at him imperiously. He shone the beam in her face again, this time holding it there. She squinted, held up both hands to block the light.

'Hey! Could you maybe not shine it right in my eyes, asshole?'

'You're damn lucky this flashlight still works at all, the way you chucked it down here, lady. In fact, you damn near killed me with it.' He moved the beam to her chest, grinning. 'There. That better?'

'Yes, er – well, I didn't *mean* to hurt you,' she said. 'I said I was sorry. What more do you want? And get your jollies by shining your little light on someone else's boobs, you perv.'

'Now wait just a goddamned minute!' He began trudging up the stairs. 'I come running over to help you broads, not for the first time, I might add, and all of you scream at me like I'm some serial killer. Then you try to take me out with a flashlight to the head – *my* flashlight, I might add. And then when *I* solve *your* problem, you get your shorts in a bunch and get all attitudy with me.' Between his tirade and coming up the stairs, he was nearly gasping for breath. 'Nice . . . to . . . meet you . . . too, neighbor.'

The redhead had been backing away with his every step up. Maybe she mistook his breathlessness for more threatening behavior, rather than merely the difficulties of hauling his sixty-year-old ass up these stairs on his bum knee. When he finally got to the top, she was in the middle of the kitchen, the other two behind her, each holding sledgehammers upright, their big, wild-horse eyes locked on him. Then he noticed the dogs: the tiny one, wet and shivering in the thin woman's arms. But the redhead had her hand clutching the collar of . . .

'Don't come any closer,' she instructed him. 'Stay right there, or I'll sick my dog on you.'

'*And*, we've got tools and we're not afraid to use them,' chimed in the fat one, completely unconvincingly.

He almost laughed. The redhead rolled her eyes, looked like she wished the other hadn't said that. She jerked her thumb over her shoulder toward the skinny one, who held the teeny dog in the crook of one arm, the neck of a sledgehammer in her other hand. '*She* actually does know how to use that thing, so watch it.'

He shook his head slowly, barely able to contain his amusement. He assumed an expression of mock confusion, pointing at the skinny one. 'Uh, do you mean she knows how to use the sledge-hammer . . .' he almost couldn't get the words out, '. . . Or the *Chihuahua*?'

This was too much, just too good. He couldn't keep the quizzical expression on his face any longer, nor could he hold back the laughter. It washed over him, pulled him under its current. He laughed loud and long, his stomach aching, tears wetting his cheeks. He wasn't completely sure he wasn't, in some way, crying. But it was an unbelievable release. He felt a nearly complete loss of control of his emotions. It took all he had to rein himself in.

He sighed. He thought maybe it was time for help. Professional help. He looked at the wall. A shrink for him. A contractor for them.

He looked up. The women had backed up even farther, the redhead nearly choking the poor dog, who was lunging to get to him. He stepped toward them, about to speak, try to explain himself, as impossible as that might be. He opened his mouth, but was immediately cut off.

'Stay there!' barked the redhead. 'Look, you can see the dog is ready to attack. I'm doing all I can to hold him off, so just don't come one step closer!'

Oh man. This was *funny*. But he restrained even his smile. This was even better than his Chihuahua joke. Okay. He would get them good. Her, especially. This was unmitigated truth he could lob over there. A little grenade of irony.

'Umm, lady?' he said, pointing with the flashlight in one hand, massaging a smile with his other. 'That's *my* dog.'

CHAPTER 27

SHELLY

'What the hell do you mean, "your dog"?' Shelly demanded. It was hard to keep her eyes locked on him, not let them drift down to the phallic protuberance on his right pelvic area. He had apparently gathered up the extra material from his ratty sweatpants, and wrapped it in a rubber band in order to keep them up. It seemed to be pointing at her. She angrily forced herself to look at his face.

'Come, boy!' said the man in response. 'Here, Richter!'

Shadow tore free of her grasp and ran to him. Shelly watched, stunned, as the guy bent and received slobbery kisses on his neck. 'Hello, big guy!' He ran his hands over Shadow's shoulders and torso, wiggling the dog's copious skin side to side over his body. 'Have these women been treating you okay, boy?'

Shelly harrumphed. '*Prove* he's yours.'

The man looked up, gave her a malevolent grin. 'Happy to.' He unsnapped the dog's collar, removing it. He held the inside open and shoved it toward Shelly. She kept her eyes on him, but took a half-step forward, reached out and snatched it out of his hands. Written in black marker across the length of the inside of the collar was: 'Richter. Belongs to Jack Hatch. 503 Raven Road.'

'I just got him a little while ago. I'm having his tags made and it takes a couple weeks, so I wrote it in there for now.'

The pale blue collar hanging limply from her hand, Shelly looked at the other two. C.C. still held the sledgehammer on her shoulder, nervously glancing at the guy. But Meg's eyes were narrowed, and she turned slightly, staring at him out of the corner of her eye, deliberate, judging. Shelly took a double-take at *her*. There was something in Meg's expression. Something like incredulous awe. Shelly glanced at the guy again. *Jack Hatch . . . Jack Hatch.*

That name was familiar. She looked at Meg again, who was now staring back at her. Her look of incredulity had evolved; now she looked utterly stunned. She silently and questioningly mouthed the name to Shelly. *Jack Hatch.* Shelly furrowed her eyebrows. Meg carefully leaned her sledge-hammer against the cabinet, turned her back to the man, and, still holding Dollop tucked under her arm, made little writing movements with one hand into the palm of the other. Then she put her palms together, opening and closing them like a book. She made small, backward jerking motions with her head.

Oh my God! thought Shelly. *Oh. My. God. The*

writer. Of those books she'd been reading here. They were all personally autographed to Georgie . . .

No. It couldn't be.

Meg turned to look at the man again, and Shelly followed with her own gaze, staring at his knowing, triumphant grin, those familiar eyes. She recalled the photo on the back cover. Take off the beard, the scraggly long hair . . .

'Hello. Pleased to meet you,' he said, and then chortled.

She closed her mouth, fuming. She didn't want to give this guy any more satisfaction than they already had.

Matter-of-factly, she said, 'Mr . . . Hatch, is it? I'm Shelly Kostens. This is C.C. Byrd, the owner of this house, and that's Meg Bartholomew.'

He smiled at Shelly, a big, I'm-holding-all-the-cards smile. Her fist tightened by her side.

'Again, nice to meet you, ladies.'

'So you are Jack Hatch the—' Meg began.

'– the official owner of this dog?' Shelly cut in. He nodded, again grinning like a Cheshire cat. She knew he knew that she didn't want to acknowledge his celebrity. She didn't care if he was the goddamn President of the United States, he hadn't taken care of his dog, not like she had, and he wasn't going to waltz in here and take him from her.

'Well, Mr Hatch, I think you are a neglectful, if not abusive, dog-owner. Come here, Shadow!' The big dog trotted over to her, tail wagging. The smile immediately dropped from Hatch's face, anger replacing it. But Shelly, spurred on by what she took to be Shadow's loyalty, smiled. '*I* found Shadow, covered in mud, in the—'

'Richter! Come!' The dog trotted back across the kitchen, tail wagging again, looking up at Hatch.

Sternly, Shelly pressed on. 'Look, buddy. I found this dog days ago, a real mess, traipsing around that jungle across the road, looking like he hadn't been cared for in weeks. If he's yours, why did you let him run loose? And why didn't you come looking for him?' She stood with her hand on hip, her chin jutted toward him. She was aware of warning glances from Meg, but Shelly refused to look at her.

'As a matter of fact, I *did* know where my dog was. And, in case you haven't noticed, we're not exactly in New York City around here. Nobody much comes down to this end of the road. It's the whole reason I bought the place. I knew he was having fun chasing frogs over in the marshy area. And, I knew he was with you gals. I thought he'd offer you a bit of reassurance. He's got a good bark, though I doubt he'd hurt a flea. Besides, I didn't exactly intend on introducing myself to you ladies. I figured Richter would wander back and forth, at his pleasure. And, I'm assuming you won't be staying long. After all, I bought the place next door for the *privacy*. And when I did, this place was vacant, and the owner was an elderly artist who was living abroad, and even when she came back, she kept to herself and didn't smash up walls and plumbing and scream bloody murder. Look, I need *quiet* and *privacy*. For obvious reasons.'

God, he was smug! What a little speech! 'What would those *obvious* reasons be?' asked Shelly, not waiting for an answer. 'That you're an *obvious* nutcase? That you *obviously* don't know how to properly care for a dog? Or yourself, for that matter.'

Shelly wasn't sure what had come over her. This was beyond even *her* usual lack of tact and social decorum. He just irked her! Besides, she loved Shadow. Already. The big, dumb dog was great company. And there just wasn't anything like hugging him; that was the best. Beyond anything Shelly could have imagined. He was so big and solid and . . . and there. For the first time in her life, she understood the whole dog thing. The connection, the happiness, the unconditional acceptance, whether you were crying or laughing, sitting, walking, running. How they were always, *always*, no matter what, glad to see you. Shadow was her friend. She needed him.

She couldn't believe this asshole was going to take him from her. It was just too much. First C.C. lost M.J. Now . . . Her throat was tightening at the mere thought. What next? Would the shelter come and reclaim Dollop from Meg? Were the three of them just somehow destined to lose *every-thing* they loved?

'Come here, Shadow!' barked Shelly. She heard

the harshness, repeated herself in a more soothing tone, patting her knees. 'Come here, sweet boy.' The dog came galumphing through the puddles, back over to her, tail wagging. Ah-ha! thought Shelly. Take that, Hatch! 'I think you'd better just go, and leave the dog here. For now, anyway.' Evidently tired of the Red Rover game, Shadow slumped to the wet floor. He licked at the puddle he was lying in with his giant tongue. After a few slurps, he rested his head on Shelly's foot. She gave Hatch one of his own smarmy smiles. 'You can see he prefers us anyway.'

'I can see no such thing, lady. I think you've got real balls coming in here and telling me that I can't take my own dog.'

'Wha—!' said Shelly. '*Us* "coming in here"! YOU came in here, mister! And "here" happens to be *our* house,' C.C. cleared her throat but Shelly ignored her, 'not yours! You were uninvited and you remain unwelcome!'

'*Fine!* That's the way you wanna play this.' Hatch turned, headed toward the stairs again. Shelly could see his briefs through a significant hole in the back seam of his dirty sweatpants. Tidy whities? She would have pegged the author of some of her favorite books as more of a boxer kind of guy. But she also wouldn't have guessed this vagrant, this Sasquatch, this nutcase, was *the* Jack Hatch. She couldn't help but wonder what had caused such an apparent mental decline in this once-famous author.

'Let's just see,' he muttered. Hatch clicked on the flashlight in his hand. He put his other on the railing and headed down the steps to the basement, a muffled grunt of pain with every step he took.

'Hey!' Shelly yelled as he disappeared down the stairs. 'What the hell are you doing?' She strode across the kitchen. She headed down the first step, but suddenly the flashlight clicked off below.

'C'mon down, Red. I dare you.'

Shelly backed up. She was not going to go down there, in the pitch dark, with that madman. 'Wait a minute. Listen, mister! Don't you dare turn—'

But it was too late. First came the cranking sound again, and the water almost immediately began spurting from the broken pipe, a small stream at first, then a big fan of water across the kitchen. All three women started screaming again, and both dogs started barking.

'Shelly!' cried Meg. 'Let the man have his dog!' But Shelly walked back across the kitchen, folded her arms over her chest, the spray hitting her back, the water soaking into her, head to toe. She'd be damned if she was going to cave in to this guy.

Meg stepped over to her, ducking under a large chute of water coming over Shelly's shoulder. She looked angry. In a way that startled Shelly. But she didn't care. She was not going to budge. Meg grabbed her by both arms. Shelly tried to twist away, but Meg held her, gave her a firm shake as she spoke through gritted teeth. 'Do you *know* who that is? That is *Jack Hatch*. THE Jack Hatch! He's sold millions, maybe *billions* of books. He writes those thrillers. You know, with people getting *hacked up*, or being *pushed off cliffs*. Are you out of your mind? Are you trying to give him reason to do some research on us?'

They were both wet now, but Shelly, her back to the pipe, was taking the brunt of it. She could feel her clothing sticking to her, the chill setting in, but she didn't care. The vibrating, the shaking, it wasn't the water. It was a cold anger pumping through her.

Meg held her grip, yelling toward the basement, 'Enough! We concede; he's your dog! Please shut the water off!'

Again a cranking sound came from the basement, a few seconds passed, and the spray slowly stopped. Shelly watched as the flashlight beam appeared, then Hatch behind, coming upstairs, unsmiling, grimacing with each step. She felt the knots of anger and fear, and – *dammit!* – chagrin, tightening inside her. She broke free of Meg's grip. 'Fine!' she said, wishing she hadn't sounded exactly like Hatch had a moment ago. She stomped out of the kitchen, or intended to. But Hatch was in front of her. He stepped to the side, trying to get out of her way, but did so just as she stepped the same direction. Hatch let out an exasperated grunt, stepped the other way. But again, just as she did. Shelly put her hand on his arm, desperate to get past him. The third time they moved in fuming unison, Shelly let out a deep, growling, '*Arrgghh!* Get outta my way!'

She reached out with both hands to shove him aside, but he grabbed her arms, in nearly the same places Meg had. But unlike Meg's hands on her, his stopped her cold. Shelly shot him a fiery look. He was inches from her face. His eyes, too, were glaring, livid lights, trained on hers, their watery blue now looking like icy steel. She dropped her gaze, unable to maintain it. But she could still smell his skin, his deep musky odor. She could feel the heat from his anger, his body. His grip on her was horrible, the feeling of being held, seized, of being *attached* to him. She felt her eyes being drawn toward his again. His softened slightly, and she couldn't stop herself from staring. Somehow they'd muted; now it was like staring at her own faded, blue denim shirt. His fingers, still tight on her arm, loosened slightly, but kept pulling, pulling. She tried to breathe, she needed oxygen, but she seemed to have forgotten how. His face was close now, inches from hers. Her eyes fell closed involuntarily. She thought she might be passing out.

Suddenly she was on the floor. But she knew she hadn't fainted; she'd been pushed. By some force against her thighs. Shadow. He was hovering over her. He had wormed his way between them, and now was playfully upon her, his huge tongue coming at her.

'Richter! Off!' Hatch yelled, pushing the huge

dog off her. Shelly scrambled to her feet, ignoring his outstretched hand, refusing to look at him. Gasping, she ran down the hall to the stairs, pulled herself up by the banister, hand over hand, taking two stairs at a time. She ran headlong into the bedroom, breathing hard, and slammed the door. She stood in the middle of the room. *The* bedroom. She couldn't even call this *room* hers. Nothing was hers. She had nothing. And no one. She tried to catch her breath, but couldn't. She knew she was hyperventilating. She cupped her hands around her mouth, breathed in and out methodically.

How had she gotten to this point in her life? After so much work, so much determination, so much calculated planning? She'd had such solid independence – how could she end up here, with . . . nothing? No work, no money, no house, no room. No husband, no children. No family at all. Not even enough air to breathe. She had her friends, thank God for that, but at the moment she feared she didn't even have them. She knew they were furious with her.

Damn the tears! She wiped them angrily from her eyes, pulled Georgie's maroon terry robe off the hook of the closet door, wiped her wet face, ran it over her dripping hair, then her arms. She took another deep breath, calming finally. She walked to the bed, sank onto the edge, sitting with her back curved, the damp robe balled in her lap.

Family. She almost said it out loud. It was one

of those kinds of words kids say over and over, convulsing in laughter when it was reduced to just sounds. What is a family, anyway? People who generally have little in common with each other forced to pretend otherwise. You can't choose your relatives, went the old saw. Maybe not. But you could choose your family. She had. C.C. and Meg were her family.

She stared at the old phone by her bed. Slowly, she leaned forward, then bent down. She put just her fingertips on the receiver, her heart racing, then lifted her fingers off. Probably so old it wouldn't work even if the phone line was connected. And it wasn't. They were utterly cut off from the world. So no harm in looking. Slowly, she heaved the phone book from the bottom shelf. She flipped through the *Greater Nashville Area Yellow Pages*. What would it be under? Convents? Churches, she decided. She found the page. They were listed by denomination. She ran her finger down the column, coming to rest on Catholic. She remembered that it was *Sisters of* something. Hard to forget that bit of irony. But if there was more than one *Sisters of* listing, she wasn't sure she'd recognize which it was. She moved it slowly down the list. Then her finger stopped. *Sisters of Jude Abbey*.

She knew right away that was it. If someone had asked her, she wouldn't have been able to come up with the name. But somehow, seeing it written, even so many years later, the words found a match in some ancient, buried file in her brain. She moved her finger across to the number, picked up the handset of the old, green rotary phone, its short, coiled cord stretched taut. She listened to the nothingness of the dead line, less than a seashell held to the ear.

'Nina,' she whispered. She sat with the phone to her ear. 'Nina,' she said again, barely audible, to nothing and no one. 'It's me. Your sister.'

Finally, she replaced the handset to its base, her arm leaden. She could feel the wet sitzmark already on the bed, but she fell back across the mattress anyway, the phone book falling to the floor. She brought the mass of soft, wet terry cloth to her face, and began to sob.

CHAPTER 28

KATHRYN

A thin layer of white powder seemed to be everywhere, as if a small atom bomb had gone off on Register 1. The flour dust was still drifting down, over the scanner, the belt, her register, her. My own personal nuclear winter, thought Kathryn, unmoving, staring at the ghostly whiteness of her hands and arms. The customer whose flour it was had been able to back away in time, out of the fallout. She smiled, said pleasantly, 'Yowzer! Didn't see that cut on the top! I'll go get another one.' She jogged off toward the baking aisle.

Kathryn inspected the clean knife-slice at the top of the five-pound bag. It started at the top, curved down, across the front. So thin and clean a cut that it was invisible. Till she had tipped it over the scanner and it had belched flour out all over the place. Damn stockers! It didn't matter how often they were told to be careful with those box cutters, they regularly sliced right through the outer box, putting sharp cuts into cereal boxes, paper towels, you name it. But the sugar and the flour were the worst. Rather than take responsibility for it by putting it in the damaged stock bin, as they were supposed to, they just put it on the shelf for an unsuspecting customer, and checker.

As Matt headed to get a mop and bucket, Kathryn cleaned up with Windex and paper towel. The woman returned, smiling, holding a new bag of flour. 'Here we go.'

But Kathryn sensed another, more ominous presence. Mr Knelbrecht stood at the end of her counter, holding the two points of his manager's vest in each hand, his tight fists matching his shiny pale pate. Tom had had the whole break room laughing when he announced, shortly after the new manager's arrival months ago, that he had seen Knelbrecht shining his head with the polish the janitors used in the floor buffer. But Tom would say almost anything to get a laugh, so Kathryn didn't necessarily believe him. But she found herself staring at his head now, the reflection of the big ceiling lights on his skull almost too bright to look at.

'A little accident, Ms Prentiss?'

She smiled at him. 'It appears the stockers got a little wild opening the boxes. Again.' She showed him the three-inch slit in the bag.

'Well, if you exercise just a bit of care when you handle the items, you won't make a mess to inconvenience our customers, now will you?' He smiled and nodded at the woman at the check stand.

Kathryn stood, dumbfounded. The customer

stepped toward them, her mouth hanging open, her eyes so wide that Kathryn was amazed at how big her whites were. Kathryn was about to apologize when the woman moved her incredulous gaze to Mr Knelbrecht.

'Chee-zus! It's not *her* fault!' said the woman. Her eyes narrowed and her eyebrows bent in like an angry jack-o'-lantern. 'The bag was slit open, for Christ's sake. And not by her.'

Wow, thought Kathryn. The woman obviously sensed Knelbrecht for what he was, an insecure prick who thought that being manager of a grocery store was tantamount to being dictator of a small country. Kathryn stole a quick look at him; he glared at the woman, then with great effort, replaced the expression with his manager smile.

Maybe it was this stranger coming to her defense, or maybe she'd just had it, reached her limit with Knelbrecht, the store, her life. He'd had it in for her from the moment he'd gotten transferred to this store, simply because she was smart and competent. And she'd worked here over ten years, unlike his ten months. Standing there, in the sea of tension between her boss and a woman that neither of them had ever met, Kathryn felt some vital part of herself just lift up, and float away. Was this what they called an out-of-body experience?

'It wasn't like she was practicing her *juggling* or something,' said the woman heatedly. She'd thumped the new bag of flour on the counter, still eyeing Knelbrecht, her hands on her hips. She took a step closer to him and he backed up a step. Kathryn came hard back into her body. Who *was* this woman? Kathryn smiled weakly, made a silent plea for her to stop, not make matters worse.

But the woman went on. 'Give her a fucking break. And a raise, while you're at it. She deserves one, working for you.'

Kathryn and Mr Knelbrecht both stared at the woman, stunned. Kathryn glanced very briefly at Mr Knelbrecht, then at her register. She didn't know whether to laugh or cry. *Who the hell was this woman?*

Mr Knelbrecht glared at Kathryn, tipped his shiny head toward the woman. 'She a friend of yours?'

Kathryn opened her mouth, but nothing came out. She was convinced she'd never set eyes on her before, but she had to be careful how she responded. She didn't want to seem rude. 'I— We've never—'

'I don't know her from Eve!' barked the woman, still staring at Knelbrecht. 'But I know a jackass when I see one. And I'm looking at one.'

Oh . . . dear. Kathryn stared at her hands, pulled at a cuticle. Then she stared at the tiny drop of blood that sprang out of where she'd torn the skin off.

'Well, as a valued customer of SavR King,' said Mr Knelbrecht, 'we thank you for your suggestions and will take them under advisement. Good day.' He gave an extra tug on his vest points, pivoted, and made his way down the front end, his large ears protruding from the sides of his head like side mirrors on an old lorry. He marched up the stairs to the manager's office where he would no doubt look through the mirrored one-way window and monitor his store from a safe distance.

Kathryn handed the woman her receipt, saying a shy, 'Thanks.' She then urgently waved Marianne over from the service desk, telling her she had a 'fifteen-nineteen' – code for female issue – and needed to take her break *now*. In the break room, she bummed a cigarette from Matt, although she'd quit smoking years ago. She headed outside, not even bothering to grab a jacket. She walked to the end of the building, to the large brick flower planter on the corner where the smokers sat. It still held nothing more colorful than a few candy bar wrappers and cigarette butts lying on the dirt. Their old manager, Doug, would have had some bulbs put in by now. She doubted Knelbrecht had even noticed the empty planters.

The May sun was warm, but not hot. And when the breeze blew, it was chilly. Kathryn stared at the unlit cigarette in her fingers, realizing she didn't have a lighter. She sighed. She didn't really want to smoke anyway. Well, she did, but she had quit for Lucy, and would not succumb. The poor kid had enough to deal with as it was. She set the cigarette in the smooth groove between two bricks next to her, and pulled her peanut butter and banana sandwich from the pocket of her jacket.

It was too early for lunch, but she didn't care. She needed something. Some kind of fortification that she knew wasn't going to come from nicotine, caffeine, or even calories. Still, she pulled the slightly smashed sandwich from its plastic bag, her hands shaking from tension and cold. The breeze had kicked up. Kathryn hunched into herself for warmth, took a small bite of her sandwich. It took effort to move her jaw to chew. Even the smallest things seemed to take such effort lately. Getting up. Brushing her teeth. Getting Lucy off to school. Getting herself to work. Not like any of those things had ever been easy, but since Jordan . . .

She still didn't understand it. She'd wanted to break up with *him* for weeks before her mom left, but hadn't, just to spite her for meddling. She knew it was stupid, but she'd been so angry at her mother. For so many things. Half of them not having a thing to do with her mother. In fact, she'd really hoped, every time the phone rang, that it would be one of the two men her mother had given her number to in the mall. But neither one had ever called.

Then, Jordan breaks up with *her. He* breaks up with *her*! She'd grown to really dislike the guy, yet couldn't summon the strength to end it. Still, she had screamed and thrown things at him when he told her he'd been 'hooking up' with someone else. She hated that term, as if he was a tractor latching on to a trailer. Or, more accurately, the other way around. He was a complete mooch; he'd look for someone to haul him along.

So now what? It was the story of her life: she just waited till something shoved her 'one way or t'other'. Even her piece-of-shit car had broken down before she could trade it in on a newer used car. Kathryn picked up the cigarette, held it to her lips, just to feel it there. She didn't have the energy to go car shopping. Hell, it was easier to take the bus anyway. Better for the environment. She put the cigarette down between the bricks again, where the wind rolled it back and forth, but wasn't quite strong enough to blow it out of the groove altogether. She watched it for a minute, then found herself willing it to hop from that groove and let the wind blow it away.

CHAPTER 29

LUCY

Lucy had been waiting to play foursquare all recess long. The four girls playing weren't rotating out like they were supposed to. But the bricks were nice and warm from the morning sun, and the wall here was out of the chilly wind, so Lucy didn't really mind just standing there, watching, slowly moving her back along the wall, soaking up the warmth. In fact, it would be fine to stay here all day, waiting for a turn, or even just watching. If only she didn't have to go back into the classroom. Because when they did, they were going to have their weekly reading test.

Lucy faced the wall, traced her finger along the smooth cement lines between the bricks, imagining her finger was a car, driving along gray highways that always turned at right angles. Then she imagined that the wall was a magic wall. All she had to do was find the special brick, the one that had been enchanted by the fairies. Then, all she would have to do was push it, or maybe place her hand on it in a special way, and a wiggly, silvery-black, puddle-like thing would appear and she could step into it, and through it, and then she'd be in a magic land where they didn't even know what a reading test was.

Lucy looked for a special brick. She found one that was darker than the others. She pushed it. Nothing happened. She twisted around so she could place her palm inside the rectangle. She held it there, holding her breath. But no puddle appeared. When she turned around, Carmen, Kendra, Holly and Jessica were still playing foursquare. And laughing.

Lucy, embarrassed, squatted, picked up a small rock near her foot. She pretended that she was only over here to look at rocks. Suddenly a whistle blew. At first she thought it was just because recess was over and the bell was broken again. But the whistle blew in fast, loud, short bursts, over and over.

Lucy stood up. Carmen and the other girls were running across the playground. Everyone was running. It was like there was a giant magnet pulling everyone over to the grassy field where the boys played football. The two playground supervisors were running too, still blowing their whistles. They were both older, tubby women, like Meemaw, and they were slow. One of them stopped running, but kept blowing her whistle. Some boys were yelling, 'Fight! Fight!' as they ran past the playground ladies. Lucy stood, looked all the way across the field. She saw them. It did not look like the usual kind of playground fight where one boy pushes another and he pushes back and then they grab on to each other like they're in love or something. It looked like one of the boys might have a bloody nose and he had hold of the other boy's jacket in one hand and was punching him in the stomach with the other. Another boy was trying to pull him off and a fourth boy was starting to slug *him*. Then a bunch of boys jumped in and Lucy couldn't tell who was on whose side, everyone seemed to be hitting everyone.

Lucy glanced around. She was alone. Really alone. She looked at her classroom door. She pictured Mrs Diamont inside, placing a reading test on every desk. Lucy started walking, slowly at first, kind of inching her way along the wall. Then the wall ended. When she walked away from the building, the wind blew her hair and dress. She grabbed the hem in her fists by her sides and kept walking. She was headed toward the teachers' parking lot. It was the nearest gate. She didn't look back. She just kept walking till she got to the gate. It was tall, with lots of bars sticking out, like they had at the stadium, to let only one person through at a time. She put her bare hands on the cold metal and pushed. She still didn't look back, but waited for a teacher's hand to clamp down on her shoulder, or for a whistle to blow, or to hear her name screamed out by a playground lady. But no hand came, no whistle, no shout. The gate was heavy. Lucy lowered her head and pushed harder. She thought about the magic puddle. The gate moved, squeaking as it rotated, the big metal bars passing through the other bars. They reminded Lucy of when Meemaw and Papaw had taken her to the Ice Capades when she was little, how the ice skaters got in big lines and passed through other lines of skaters. A space opened up that she could step into, and she stopped pushing. The gate only turned one way. So strangers couldn't get in. She would be able to get out, but not back in. She took a big breath, then stepped into the triangle space and kept pushing, walking within the bars, till she stepped out into the parking lot.

Lucy walked quickly, pulling her cold hands up into the sleeves of her purple fleece. She passed through the rows of cars in the teachers' lot, mostly small ones, but there was a big, black SUV with a bunch of basketballs in the back that she figured probably belonged to Mr C., the gym teacher. At the far end of the parking lot, she saw a little path through a big weedy area, then it disappeared into the trees. She knew some older kids who walked home this way. It must be safe. She ran onto the path, and into the trees. It was darker and colder in the trees. She ran till she was out of breath, then slowed to a walk. She walked for a long time. Sometimes she felt like someone was walking behind her, but she was too scared to turn around and look.

Finally, she came to a little wooden bridge over a ditch. She remembered the story of the troll under the bridge. She thought about running back to school. Even a reading test is better than a troll. But she thought of Meemaw, how much she missed her, and nothing else seemed important. She closed her eyes, imagined the pitcher of brave. Meemaw had filled her up. 'Ready, set . . . go!' she whispered. She ran across the bridge as fast as she could, on her toes, trying to keep her footsteps quiet, the whole time expecting to hear: 'Who is crossing over my bridge?' She reached the other side, out of breath and with a pain in her side. But no troll had yelled at her.

Lucy continued walking, still listening for footsteps and trolls, but she didn't turn around. She walked and walked, till suddenly the path disappeared. She didn't know what to do. Finally, she looked over her shoulder. She couldn't see the school anymore. She couldn't even hear any playground noises. Probably everyone was inside now. Her class was taking the test. She took a deep breath. She headed back up the path a little way, and saw where it had turned off. Then that path forked. She followed the one she thought might be going south. She didn't know which way south was, but Meemaw had written her how warm it was there, so she took the one that headed toward the sun. She knew she couldn't walk all the way to Tennessee. Maybe someone would give her a ride. But someone she knew, or that looked friendly, otherwise it would be stranger danger. As she walked, the growing clouds sometimes covered the sun, darkening the woods. The aloneness was all around her, almost like it was whispering to her: *Go back. Go back.* 'I'm going to see Meemaw,' Lucy said aloud, her voice quavering only a little as she kept on walking.

CHAPTER 30

KATHRYN

Kathryn checked her watch, pushed her sandwich back into the bag, shoved it in her pocket and stood up. She'd taken her break out of turn; Ting was supposed to be off now. She thought Ting would understand, but still. 'I have to find another job,' Kathryn said out loud. How many times had she said that? She gazed at the entrance to the store, feeling utterly hollow. She had no marketable skills, no college degree. If it was just her, she'd risk it. But with Lucy . . . She had to stay for Lucy. She had a fair amount of savings, but it was for college, for Lucy. If she quit and couldn't find another job, she'd have to dip into that, and she couldn't mortgage her daughter's future like that. Kathryn wrapped her arms around herself in the cold wind, stared at the toes of her black sneakers on the sidewalk for a long minute. She sat back down on the planter, unable to go back inside.

She watched the people walking briskly into the store, unburdened, the others walking out slowly, pushing full carts. One woman looked like a young Shelly, which made her think of her mom. She loved getting her letters, mostly to Lucy, but also to her, yet she couldn't bring herself to write back. Only through Lucy. She wasn't even sure *why* she couldn't write to her mother. And now that Shelly's phone was dead, there was no way to call either. Not that she would. She was twenty-nine, but around her mother she always felt like she was fifteen. It wasn't entirely her mother's fault. Kathryn knew that *she* regressed somehow around her mother, grew easily impatient with her. She wanted love from her mother, but didn't want to be beholden. She felt judged by her mother. And she judged her right back. Judged her tacky velour sweatsuits, her stupid, expensive shoes, and especially, her old-fashioned, bouffant hair style that took ages to fix, and yet aged her. Not to mention the weight she'd put on.

So she just helped Lucy write her letters, sat as patiently as she could as Lucy tried so damn hard to figure out which way a b went and which way a d went. She just couldn't get it. She wrote entire words backwards, sometimes upside down. Kathryn tried to help her, but didn't know how. The reading specialist at the school had been laid off two years earlier, in the budget cuts. Worrying about Lucy, that somewhere there was a key to her special brain but that Kathryn would never find it, was nearly consuming.

She knew her mother worried about her, too. Both of them, her and Lucy. But she wished she would stop trying to *mother* her. Kathryn had vowed that she would stop mothering Lucy the moment she grew up. She, unlike her mother, would know when that was. Lucy would know. Wouldn't she? Twenty-nine was certainly grown up.

Shivering, but still not recovered enough to go back inside, Kathryn watched people and cars mill around the parking lot like confused cows. The lot seemed unusually full this morning, with drivers going round and round, looking for closer parking spaces. She pushed hair off her face that the wind immediately blew back again. It had really kicked up. It was probably because of the cold wind that everyone wanted a close parking space. But she idly wondered how many of those people who didn't want to walk ten or twenty extra yards, would then fill their carts with diet soda, fat-free muffins, and low-cal meals?

Flashing lights caught her eye. A police cruiser had pulled in, lights on but no siren. Must be in a hurry for a doughnut, she thought, smiling finally. Her smile faded as she watched the cruiser park up on the sidewalk, by the main entrance. Two uniformed cops exited together, seemingly choreographed. They quickly disappeared into the store. Something between interest and alarm piqued inside her, then fluttered down like a tired flag. Probably Mr Knelbrecht caught another five-year-old filching a caramel from the candy bins again. He lived for catching kids doing that; he even admitted it. Said it was his opportunity to set the child on the right path, keep them to the straight and narrow. He called the cops to 'make an impression on the youngsters'. Scare the shit out of them, was more like it. But the cops knew Knelbrecht's penchant for nailing sub-juvenile candy thieves, and either didn't respond, or took their time. Usually not a lights-flashing kind of response, anyway. Maybe that wacky woman with the flour had come back with a rifle, just to scare Knelbrecht. Kathryn smiled again.

Ting came trotting out of the store, hugging herself in the cold, a piece of paper clenched in one fist. She glanced around, till her eyes locked on Kathryn. She jogged toward her.

'Cat-wren. Meestah Ner-beck say I bring this ri' away. Say to say not his fault you not get. Yeah, right.' Ting rolled her eyes and handed Kathryn a piece of folded, stapled pink message paper. Then she tucked both her hands under her arms against the chill. 'You see cops? Donn know why. Prory big crim-na, canny-steering, rittle boy, eh? Hee hee. Brrr! It freezing-ass code out here! You okay?'

Kathryn nodded, realizing the clouds had gathered, darkened since she'd been out here. She stared at the message paper. 'Thanks, Ting. And I'll switch breaks with you for this afternoon. I just—'

Ting waved. 'No probrem! Brrr! Bye now.' She jogged inside.

Kathryn pulled the paper apart at the staple. It was probably Mrs Diamont calling again, informing her of another F. Kathryn knew Lucy had another reading test today; she'd begged again this morning to stay home. Even said she was sick and made Kathryn put her hand on her forehead, which was hot, again. But Kathryn had heard her filling the hot-water bottle in the bathroom just before. Still, she felt terrible making her daughter go to school, so miserable and lonely. But what could she do? The school kept saying Lucy was smart and sweet, just unmotivated. Kathryn had tried – doing the special games and books they sent home, buying the stationery, writing the letters – everything and anything the teacher suggested. Except the private tutor, which she couldn't afford.

Sighing, she unfolded the paper with its pre-printed lines, saw Mr Knelbrecht's unmistakable tiny, tight, all-caps block printing.

Message received at: *10.20 A.M.*

Caller: MRS VORD

The principal. Kathryn's eyes closed involuntarily as she sighed. Not Mrs Diamont. It had escalated to the principal. With dread, she read on.

Message: PLEASE CALL THE SCHOOL IMMEDIATELY. URGENT.

She froze. No test news would be marked urgent. Her body surged with adrenalin, then panic. Her fist closed tightly around the paper, a stabbing pain in her chest as she leaped up, and ran toward the door.

She almost ran into the two police officers coming out, led by Mr Knelbrecht.

'This is her,' said Knelbrecht, pointing at her. 'I'll leave you officers to conduct your business.' He spun around and walked briskly into the store.

'What? Is Lucy okay?' Kathryn asked breathlessly.

'Well, she seems to have walked off school property,' began the taller officer.

Kathryn struggled to catch her breath. 'What do you mean, "walked off"?' Her eyes darted from one cop to the other.

'Calm down. We don't believe it was an abduction.'

'ABDUCTION! Don't tell me to calm down!'

'Ma'am, one of the boys on the playground says he saw her walking off. Uh,' he pulled a flip notebook from his pocket and read. 'During recess. Boy's name is Charles Tazelaar. He said he thought she was just heading home. But he said he didn't speak to her.'

'Taz? You're going by what Taz the – by what that kid has to say? That's the kid that gets his foot stuck in a table practically every fucking day! *Jesus.*' She seemed only to be able to take tiny, quick breaths; she could feel the hulking panic taking up all the room in her chest. 'Didn't anyone else see her? One of the playground supervisors? Why didn't anyone else see her leave? We live *four miles* from the school! She wouldn't just walk home for the hell of it! Take me to go look for her, I, I—' Kathryn felt the tears coming, silently cursed herself. 'I don't have a car! I take the bus! *I can't look for my child by bus!*'

'Now calm down, ma'am. We've got the area flooded with patrol cars, and several officers and teachers are on foot. We want to keep track of you so we can take you to her when we find her.'

'What if you don't find her? What if someone else . . . Have you put out an Amber Alert?' Kathryn was shifting her weight from one foot to the other, desperate to run to her daughter, but not knowing which way to run.

'An Amber Alert is if we have reason to believe there's been an abduction. We don't believe that is the situation here. Apparently your daughter left the school grounds just before a test. Her teacher thought she might have been nervous about that.'

Kathryn glanced at her watch: 11.15. 'Jesus! That asshole Knelbrecht didn't give me this message for almost an hour! He had it when he was giving me a hard time about the fucking flour!' Kathryn was screaming now. Her mind, heart, breathing out of control.

'Look, ma'am. If we don't find her in the next hour, we'll issue an Amber Alert, just to get help from the community. But we also don't want to send out the word to the wrong sorts to go looking for a little girl.'

'Wrong sorts?' She looked from one to the other, her eyes filling. 'You mean, like, pedophiles?' She didn't wait for an answer. 'Which way did Taz say she went?'

The officer opened his notebook again. 'Uh, she went through the gate to the teachers' parking lot. But we'd like you to stay—'

Kathryn didn't wait to hear more. She just started running, the tears blinding her as she ran a slalom course in and out of the slow-moving cars across the parking lot.

CHAPTER 31

LUCY

Lucy came to a big clearing, a series of small hills with paths all over. Was this where they rode dirt bikes? She looked around. There were the backs of a bunch of big buildings on the other side, down below. There were dumpsters and big wooden planky things lying all over the asphalt behind the buildings. Lucy's heart skipped a little; she knew where she was! She was behind the ShopKo. Sometimes they came here with Jordan and watched him ride his motorcycle around. She'd never been over on this side, but she was pretty sure that's where she was. And that meant that the SavR King was across the big street on the other side of ShopKo! Lucy started running.

She ran across the field, up and down the steep hills. She was out of breath when she got to where all the wooden planky things were, so she sat on one to rest. She was warmer now from all the running, and it was out of the wind here, but it was getting very cloudy. And cold. Catching her breath, she rubbed the dust off the toes of her sneakers with her fleece-covered wrists. Suddenly there were loud noises. She looked up. Dirt bikers. They were riding up and down the steep hills. Where did they come from, she wondered. At the top of a big hill, they stopped. She saw one pointing her way. Lucy felt the salty taste of fear in her mouth. She swallowed hard. The bikers roared down the hill. They were coming toward her!

Voices! A door opened at the other end of the building. Men. Three of them. The bikers were coming, and now men. Lucy looked around quickly, then jumped up, and ran and hid behind the dumpster. The men stood outside the door, lit cigarettes, and talked and laughed about things Lucy didn't want to hear. She couldn't see the bikers anymore, but they sounded like they were coming closer. She had to run. She counted to three in her head, then ran along the back of the building, across the side parking lot, up a grassy hill. She slipped and her knee dragged painfully down the grass. But she didn't cry. She stood up and kept going, till she got to the top of the hill and came out on a sidewalk. She ran and ran down the long sidewalk till her side ached again. Finally she got to the intersection. She pushed the heel of her hand against the walk button, pressing again and again, glancing over her shoulder. No bikers. No smoking men.

She looked up, holding the stitch in her side, trying to catch her breath. The clouds had completely covered up the sun. Meemaw would say they were 'turning mean', getting all thick and dark. The wind blew right through her fleece as she waited for the white walker guy in the sign.

Waiting, Lucy got scared about something else. Her mom. Was she just going to walk into the SavR King and say, 'Hi, Mom!'? She would be really mad at her for leaving school. Lucy almost started crying again, but pressed her wrists against her eyes. Maybe she could tell her mom how sad she was at school. Maybe her mom would understand because she had been so sad lately too. Because of her job. And because of Jordan. Lucy was glad Jordan wasn't around anymore; he smoked cigarettes and called her Loosey-goosey and talked with his mouth full of food. But she especially didn't like how he talked to her mom. And one time he hit her mom. They didn't know that she knew. But she had seen it. He shoved her shoulder, then he slapped her. Lucy had been behind the couch, trying to get two marbles that were lost from her hippo game. Her mom and Jordan didn't know she was there and she didn't know how to come out once they came in, arguing. Then Jordan cursed at her mom and she yelled at him, then he slapped her. The sound made Lucy's cheek hurt. She was going to climb out from the couch, come help her mom, but Jordan left, slamming the front door, and her mom ran to her bedroom, crying.

Lucy hoped her mom didn't like Jordan anymore. She knew for *sure* her mom didn't like her *job*, especially since Mr Icky Breath started being her boss. So maybe she wouldn't be mad at Lucy for leaving school. Maybe Lucy should tell her mom about her wishbone stick. How one side of her had wished that she could go to Dogs' Wood, and that side of her had got the bigger piece of the wishbone stick, and if they fixed their car maybe now they could both go!

It was raining. Lucy looked up, saw the blinking orange hand, and realized she had missed the walk light. She felt the ache in her throat and the sting in her eyes again, but instead of crying, she pushed the button about twenty times. Then she pretended she had a little pitcher, and poured it over her head. Her legs felt so cold now that she wasn't sure they would work by the time the little walky guy came back on. She jumped up and down. She stopped, because she had to pee. She watched the cars zooming by, both directions. She wondered if anyone was going to Tennessee. She held her nose to keep out the stink from the cars. The rain came harder and colder. Lucy pushed the button again. She was wet and cold, but she was getting more and more excited that her mom would think it was a good idea to go to Tennessee. Finally, the walky guy blinked on and Lucy ran across the street.

She ran down the sidewalk, to the top of the big hill above the edge of the SavR King parking lot. She stopped at the top of the steps; she could see the whole side, and part of the front of the SavR

King. Then she saw a police car with its lights on. She'd heard of people coming into stores and robbing them. With *guns*. Sometimes they shot people. *Mom*. Lucy's heart felt like it was in her ears, pounding there. She couldn't move. Then she saw them, the policemen. *Was that her mom?* Her mom was okay! But why were the police talking to her mom? Her mom was running away!

'Run, Mom, run!' Lucy yelled. She didn't know why the police were trying to arrest her mom, but she was pretty sure whatever it was, it wasn't her mom's fault. But her mom couldn't hear. She was too far away and the wind and rain were making too much sound. Her mom was running through cars, like she told Lucy to *never, ever* do! Lucy felt frozen, from the wet cold, from being so afraid for so long. The policemen were getting in their car. Her mom didn't have a car! She couldn't run from the police by waiting for the bus! Lucy cringed as she watched her mom put her hands on the hood of a car as it screeched to a stop, nearly hitting her.

Her mom was talking to the person in the car. Now she was opening the passenger door to that person's car. Lucy didn't recognize the car. 'Mom!' she screamed again. Then, as loud as she possibly could: 'MOM! STRANGER DANGER!' But it was too late. Her mom was in the car and the car was driving out of the parking lot. The police car drove out of the parking lot, too. But they turned the other way. Lucy didn't know what to do or feel. She didn't want her mom to get arrested, but she kind of wanted the police to be following her mom in that stranger's car. Because if her mom got arrested she could get a lawyer but if she was with a stranger she could get murdered!

Lucy lost sight of both the stranger's car and the police car. She turned around to see if the dirt bikers were following her. She didn't see them, but she was scared they could see her. She felt very alone on top of that big hill, and all out of brave. She walked to a big tree and curled up under it in a tight little ball. This time, she couldn't stop herself from crying.

CHAPTER 32

KATHRYN

Kathryn was almost overcome by the picture in her mind: Lucy lost, crying for her. Then, much worse, the picture of her being grabbed by a pedophile. Everything that Kathryn had known as suffering prior to this point paled, disappeared entirely. It felt like every one of her internal organs was missing.

Lucy, hang on.

The need to get to her was beyond physical, and it propelled her through the parking lot, running pell mell, the rain pelting her, half blinding her. A car honked and she jumped back, realized she had run right in front of it. She began to move away but the driver was waving at her. Beckoning. The window rolled down. It was that woman. That crazy woman with the flour.

'Hey, you okay?'

'No. My daughter. She's missing. From school. I need . . . to . . .' Kathryn caught her breath, trying not to cry. 'I don't have a car.'

'Get in!'

Kathryn stared at her. The woman said again, 'Get in. I'll take you wherever you need to go.'

The woman drove fast but carefully through the pouring rain, the only talking between them a quick exchange of names – Anna, Kathryn – and directions to the school. Then, for twenty agonizing minutes of traffic and rain and red lights, Kathryn tried to scan the sidewalks on both sides of every street, looking for a purple fleece. The only sound was the fast, tense beat of the windshield wipers. Kathryn was out of the car before it had fully stopped in the school parking lot. She ran past another police cruiser, parked right in front, by the flagpole.

No. PleasedearGodno.

Kathryn ran inside, hearing Anna's footsteps behind her.

She saw Taz, sitting on the tiled bench, near the windows, his hands tucked between his legs, looking small and lost. She almost ran to him, but then she saw the cops. There were four, their backs to her, huddled in the front hall, near the principal's office. Kathryn stopped dead. The dark, brooding fear inside her broke open, filling her. She raised her trembling clenched fists to her lips. The only thing keeping her standing was Anna's strong arm, suddenly around her. The cops turned toward her, first one, then another, their gritty expressions landing on her just as Mrs Vord emerged from her office.

Mrs Vord saw the cops, turned, saw her. Kathryn looked from her to the cops and back again, to the principal. Mrs Vord was walking toward her,

her arms open, extended . . . *sympathetic*. Kathryn started sobbing. She couldn't hear Mrs Vord's words. Her head was full of her own silent screaming, that she only vaguely realized was not silent at all.

'*No! No! No!*' Kathryn screamed. She couldn't breathe. She was drowning. She wanted to drown.

Slowly, other words rolled in. They swam down through the depths of fear to find her. Mrs Vord's words, and Anna's, repeating, like echoes: '*She's okay. She's safe. Lucy's okay.*' Anna was still holding her, her eyes locked on Kathryn's, making her hear, until she did.

Kathryn collapsed. Anna went to the floor with her, supporting her. This stranger, this *strange* stranger, this unknown woman, was holding her together. Mrs Vord squatted next to them, holding Kathryn's shoulder firmly. *Lucy is safe. She's at the store. They said to tell you Ting is with her.* The words wrapped around Kathryn like a rope, pulling her up to the surface. 'When you ran off, the police officers at the store circled around, thinking she might try to come find you at work. Sure enough, they found her under a tree on Gaman Hill,' explained Mrs Vord. 'She's cold and wet and scared, but fine.'

For the first time in years, Kathryn closed her eyes and gave a prayer of thanks. To God. To the Universe. To everything in the Universe, that, at that moment, felt connected, each and every one, to her, to Lucy, to Mrs Vord, to Anna, to Ting, to the cops, to the clouds in the sky, to the whole round spinning earth, to the small beetle crawling across the floor in front of her, across the speckled green tile floor of the elementary school, lost perhaps, but crawling determinedly. *Taz*. She looked over at him. He was sucking his thumb, nervously watching her.

'Taz, honey.' Kathryn opened her arms and Taz ran to her and Mrs Vord stood and stepped away. The boy fell into Kathryn's arms, crying. 'It's okay, honey,' she told him. 'You helped so much. Thank you. You saw her, didn't you?' Taz nodded. 'And you told a grown-up and now Lucy is found.' He nodded again. Kathryn held him, close, as if he were her child. At that moment, he was, the way every child in need is every mother's child. She felt him relax into her, as he would into his mother, and Kathryn felt transported by the connection, by the sudden awareness that everything connects to everything else, forms a net. And the net had caught Lucy. She looked at Anna, kneeling beside her, smiling. And the net had caught her. Kathryn had never known relief like this. She had never known gratitude like this.

As Mrs Vord walked away, Taz's hand in hers, to get him some lunch, both Anna and the cops offered to drive Kathryn back to the store. She thanked them all, looked at Anna, said she'd be grateful.

'Thank you. Thank you for this,' repeated Kathryn as they climbed back into the car.

'My pleasure,' Anna replied. She reached into the back seat, unearthed a slightly crushed box of tissues from the mounds of fabric and other detritus on the back seat, took a couple herself, then handed it to Kathryn. She wiped the rain from her face, then gave Kathryn a reassuring smile. 'You okay?' Kathryn wasn't sure she was, but she nodded. She used several tissues to dry herself, blow her nose. She thanked Anna again, said it was incredibly generous to do this for a stranger. 'Are you kidding?' said Anna. 'We women gotta be here for each other. We just do.' She said it with such conviction, yet there was some vulnerability there somehow.

Kathryn looked at her as Anna started the car and backed out of the parking space. 'Anna, can I ask a sort of personal question?'

'Fire away,' she said, carefully checking right and left before turning onto the street. The rain was still steady, but not the driving force it had been. Anna clicked the wipers down a notch from their frenzied pace.

'Back at the store, with the flour. And Knelbrecht – my boss?'

Anna laughed, breathy, embarrassed. 'Yahhh! Well. Sorry. Not normally like that.' She had a pleasant, ringing sort of laugh. 'I just recently went through a whole . . . thing.' She waved her hand. 'See, my boss – I was a secretary – he had propositioned me a bunch of times. Jesus! I said no to that man every way possible over the years.'

She glanced at Kathryn. 'Anyway, I doubt you want to hear that whole story!' Anna gave that ringing laugh again.

'You know, I think I do. Take my mind off things.'

Anna nodded. 'Well, mostly I just tried to ignore the schmuck, and sometimes he'd back off, but then eventually he'd start again. It was so damn tiring, just, you know, that I had to keep dealing with it. But then something snapped in him; I think his wife left him. He told me I'd be fired if I didn't sleep with him, that he knew just how to frame me to do it. Well, the funny thing is, I was going to quit anyway, y'know? Been thinking about it forever. I hated that fucking job, and especially him. I just didn't have the guts to really do it. I had been through a tough divorce before I got that job and I was just kind of empty, y'know?' Kathryn nodded. 'Anyway, it was a job, a decent paycheck, benefits, and I was scared to lose that. And I've been trying to put myself through college for, like, more than a decade. And that ain't cheap. So it was hard to just quit. But I was going to. Even had the date circled on my calendar, as soon as my bonus came through.' Kathryn watched Anna's hands on the steering wheel, one going over the other as she turned onto Grape Street. Kathryn said nothing, just listened to the wipers, their beat, slow, methodical.

'But, for better or worse,' Anna continued, 'a co-worker had overheard him threatening me. So, with her support, I filed harassment charges

407

against him. It was awful, the trial. Exhausting, embarrassing – you name it. It was more like me on trial. But, *but!*' she held her finger up, glanced briefly at Kathryn, then back to the road. 'The bastard got fired. And after? It was like every female in the whole office came forward and told me what a dick he'd been to them too. So we'd all just been there, like, suffering in silence! If only someone had . . . Anyway, they were all really grateful, asked me to stay on. But I quit. I still hated the job. But, it's better for them now. Way better. And I'm proud of that. Hard to know why some things happen; I do feel kinda scarred by the whole thing. But I also kinda feel like I can get through anything now, y'know?' She laughed again. 'And I guess I feel a little too free to lay into asshole bosses when I see them, huh? Have to work on that one.'

'Oh, I dunno,' said Kathryn. 'That might actually be a useful skill. Just don't put it on your résumé.' She smiled as Anna laughed again. 'So . . . what are you doing now? If I may ask. Do you have another job?'

'Yeah. I'm helping a fabric artist over at the U in Cedar Rapids. That's where I live now. I was just over here at the fabric store that's going out of business, just down from the SavR King. The pay's not great at the new job, but she, the artist, has this tiny little apartment attached to her house, and she gives it to me dirt cheap. It's in a cool neighborhood, close to campus. I'm taking some classes, and working for her. I've always loved sewing and that, and she makes this awesome art, so . . .' Anna shrugged as she flipped on the indicator, then turned into the SavR King parking lot. 'It's perfect, really. I feel like I'm young again.' She laughed. 'You know what they say, thirty-four is the new twenty-four!' Kathryn was amazed at how Anna's laugh just kept bubbling out of her, like it was overflowing in her. 'Anyway, it's all good. I never would have believed it, in the middle of it all, but it worked out. It's like, once I got out of the wrong place, y'know, where I was doing the wrong thing for the wrong person for the wrong reasons? Well, like, right away a lot of good things happened.' She kept her eyes forward as she drove through the big parking lot, but Kathryn noted her sudden crooked smile. 'And I met a guy. Super nice. The son of the artist's best friend. I wasn't even looking! It just feels like I stopped bucking my own current or something.'

She pulled up in almost the exact spot where the police cruiser had been, and braked. She turned, shot Kathryn a grin. 'So, go get your kid, Mom.'

Kathryn smiled, her hand already pushing her door open. 'Thank you,' she said, stepping out into the rain. She turned, bending in, her hand on the open door. 'God. Really. Thank you so much, Anna.'

'Hey, no problem. I hope it all goes okay for you, y'know?' She held out her hand, and Kathryn

409

reached in and grabbed it and they shook the way women do when one has just thrown the other a life line. Anna winked, then nodded her head toward the store. 'Give her a hug from me.'

Kathryn stopped just outside the open doorway to the break room. The old radio on the counter was on, tuned to the Disney radio channel. Kathryn recognized the squeaky, almost chipmunk-voiced woman DJ. Lucy and Ting were at the far end of the long line of end-to-end tables. They were sitting close, both drawing in a big coloring book on the table, between them, talking softly. Ting's red sweater was over Lucy's shoulders. A half-eaten cupcake – white frosting, colored sprinkles, Lucy's favorite – sat on a napkin in front of her. Her wet fleece hung on the back of an empty chair. As much as she wanted to run to her, scoop her up, Kathryn waited, breathing.

She'd thought about it on the drive over. While listening to Anna, even being profoundly struck by her words, Kathryn's thoughts had still circled around Lucy. She had decided that she shouldn't run, or grab her, or cry. She had to avoid anything that might scare Lucy more than she probably already was. She should just act natural, normal, 'Hey, Kiddo . . .', that kind of thing. Let Lucy tell her what had happened, in her own time. But as soon as she saw her there, Kathryn had no plan, no thought in her head, other than drinking her daughter in with her eyes, her hand tightly gripping the door frame. She was amazed at how all the little details of Lucy both cracked and filled her heart. Her dark blonde hair spraying out of her red headband, as if it was electrified. The chunky crayon in her hand, her favorite color, a watery blue. Her dress bunched indecorously at her thighs, her bare legs with the dry skin bumps because she hated lotion. Her little pink sneakered feet swinging under the table, her ankles crossed, her lace-topped socks that her meemaw had given her and that she loved so much she wore them nearly every day, washed them out at night in the sink herself, and were now all tumbled down into little wrinkled lacy doughnuts around her ankles. Kathryn took all this in, separately, yet all at once. Her *plan* became simply to hold her daughter. She burst across the room and Lucy looked up, sprang from her chair. They met midway, Kathryn bent as Lucy leaped, wrapping her thin arms around Kathryn's neck, her legs around her waist. Kathryn clung tight too, burying her face in Lucy's neck, the smell of rain and cupcake and fear and gratitude, all right there.

CHAPTER 33

SHELLY

Still in her nightshirt, Shelly pulled open the blinds, just to let the morning sun in, as she had every morning since the fiasco with the pipe. She was not looking for him. She had merely acquired a new appreciation for the morning light. She made a mental note to herself to thank C.C. for putting her in this room. For the light. Besides, even if she *had* been curious about him, he had been nowhere to be seen for days.

She pulled the blind up to the top, looked out, and immediately flung herself back against the wall, out of view. She yanked the cord sideways, quickly lowering the blind again. Still with her back against the wall, she lifted up the side, just a crack. *It was him!* He was standing near their carriage house, Richter by his side. He looked so . . . different. Her hand went to her chest. Oy. What a transformation. His hair was cut, his beard gone. He was wearing jeans and a flannel shirt. Tucked in. *That* was unfortunate. But he looked ten, maybe fifteen years younger.

Suddenly he looked up, toward her. She dropped

the blind. She leaned back against the wall again, closed her eyes, her heart pounding. After a minute, she lifted the edge again. He was gone. She scanned around, found him. He was back on his property, heading toward his tent. She watched his retreating back, his slumped shoulders. When he got to the tent, he started trudging back and forth on that path of his. When he turned, facing her direction, she still couldn't see his face; he stared at the ground as he walked, his hands in front of him, working over each other. He walked twenty paces, turned, walked the other way. She watched his heavy footfalls for several long minutes as he trudged back and forth, back and forth in front of his collapsing tent. She knew from Meg that he wasn't living in it anymore; he'd moved back into his house. But still, he left the tent there, trod in front of it as though it were some kind of shrine. Was he merely very odd, eccentric, she wondered. Or . . . worse?

Shelly stepped away from the window, and dug the novel out of the desk drawer where she'd shoved it. She flipped open the back cover. He looked maybe early forties in his author photo. Decades younger than he had looked in their kitchen that day. But only a little younger than the man pacing out there, though surely Hatch was well past fifty by now. She thumbed through the front pages, looked at the publication date, his list of titles. She'd read nearly all of them in the past weeks. She'd devoured his complex plots, intertwined storylines. His characters were typically outsiders, flawed, but so relatable. Really ordinary people getting caught in extraordinary circumstances, like organized crime, or corporate corruption, international spying. His books were exciting. Satisfying. She looked at the book in her hands. His last. There hadn't been a Jack Hatch book released in years. Maybe the well had run dry. Or, she thought, glancing toward the closed blind, maybe the brilliant mind had short-circuited.

She tossed the book on the desk, sat down, and pulled from the thin top drawer the notebook in which she had made a makeshift calendar. She also used it to jot notes on the house. And other things. Venting her frustration with Meg and C.C., among them. Shelly checked the calendar; the plumber was due today. After the fiasco with the pipe, Shelly had breezily told Meg and C.C. (ignoring their tentative attempts to ask her about her own short-circuiting with Hatch) that their next course of action should be to leave the water off and go ahead and remove the rest of the wall, then the plumber could come cap and remove the old piping. Then they'd be ready to start construction. They'd decided on a large, arched passageway between the two rooms. It hadn't taken long to take out the remaining center portion of the wall. They'd cleaned up the plaster and lath and dust, then gone to town to schedule a plumber. Shelly couldn't help her smirk: even Meg and C.C., lovers of simplicity, had grown tired of hauling water in from the hose outside.

She stood, peered out the window again. He was back! Hatch was standing by the carriage house, talking to Meg. Again. Shelly thought she should remind Meg that she was still married. Technically. Shelly dropped the blind and carefully sat in the chair again, which, like so many things, felt too fragile for her.

Last week, Hatch had promised Meg that he'd have the phone and power restored to both houses, and had. Hatch had kind of poured his heart out to Meg. Turned out that he had been fed up with calls from his editor and agent, and lawyers, hounding him for another book that he'd signed a contract on, and had received an advance for, *three years ago*. He'd told Meg he didn't think he had another book in him. So, after Georgie died and the house ultimately went black from no one paying the bills, he'd evidently thought it was a good idea and he took it farther. Too far. Then he moved out to the tent.

Why hadn't the fool just stopped answering his phone? Or unplugged it? More evidence of mental illness, Shelly pointed out to Meg and C.C., who seemed to understand completely the notion of wanting to cut oneself off from the world. And both women seemed naively star-struck by living next door to *the* Jack Hatch. In fact, Shelly had told Meg that she had become way too buddy-buddy with Hatch. That given his instability, they should all keep their distance. But Meg persisted in whatever salvation mission she was on. The day after Hatch had burst into their kitchen with that bat of his, Meg had seen him pulling one of his fancy cars out of the proverbial mothballs from his big garage, ready to fulfill his promise to drive to the phone and power company and ask for resumption of services to both houses. Meg had actually said she'd thought it was a miracle that she'd been passing by on a walk and had stopped him just in time. She'd suggested, in her tactful way, that he might be more persuasive if he shaved, cleaned up a bit, before he headed out.

Shelly shook her head. Did the man not realize his mere appearance scared the wits out of people? Meg had offered to give him a haircut; having cut Grant's hair for years, she was pretty experienced. Shelly told her, again, that she thought that was an inappropriately intimate thing to do. Not to mention the potential hazard of wielding sharp implements around him. But Meg had shot back that Shelly should ease up on Hatch, *and* that cutting his hair had gotten her inside his beautiful – albeit a bit dusty and neglected – house.

A jealous flare had rippled through Shelly, and Meg evidently saw it, smiling wryly at her, asking, 'Do I sense a little attraction between you and Mr Hatch?'

'Are you *kidding*? Absolutely not. No. Not in a million years. I would like to see inside his *house*, is all,' Shelly had replied tersely.

Shelly stepped back to the window, lifted the blind the tiniest crack. Meg was gone, but Hatch was sitting with his back against the wall of their garage, his eyes closed, soaking up the sun. Why didn't he sunbathe on his own damn property? Since he had his eyes closed, Shelly lifted the blind a bit more.

She had to admit, Meg had done a good job. The short cut showed off the distinguished gray brushes at his temples, and really brought out his eyes. He had nice ears too. Not too big, a small silver cuff on one, glinting in the sun. He had a strong jaw too, previously hidden under that awful beard. He did have rather thin lips, but good skin and— 'Stop!' Shelly loudly admonished herself. She let go of the blind.

But not a minute went by before she heard a car on the driveway, and lifted the blind again. Hatch jumped up to meet a white van, 'Fleurville Plumbing and Heating' across its side. He walked to the driver's window, his back to Shelly. They spoke for a minute, Hatch gesturing over his shoulder with his thumb, toward the kitchen.

'Oh no you don't, *Mister* Hatch!' Shelly yelled. 'This is our house!' She had no idea what he might be talking to the plumber about, but she didn't want him involved at all. She quickly dressed and ran downstairs.

The plumber was just walking in the door, carrying a big tool box, when Shelly burst into the kitchen. Meg and C.C. were already there, but ignored her as the plumber looked at the wall, and gave a low, hissing whistle. He set his tool box down and walked to and through the hole between the kitchen and dining room, touching the exposed, broken plumbing, staring into the cavities on either side and above.

'Man. He was right. You ladies took out part of a weight-bearing wall. Your neighbor told me he'd bring over some lumber, left over from his remodel. I'll help you shore it up, temporarily, get the pipes taken care of. But you're going to have to get a construction guy out here who knows what he's doing to rebuild the support. You've compromised the integrity of the whole structure here.' No one spoke. 'You got a building permit?'

Damn! Shelly wished he hadn't asked that.

Meg shook her head no. The plumber cocked his head, whistled low and soft. 'Better hope the county don't send someone by. They'll slap you with a stop-work order, maybe a big fine.' Meg and C.C. both looked at Shelly.

Shit. She thought they could bypass the permit, and the big fees that usually came with them. Before she could speak, though, Hatch came walking through the mudroom, carrying some long two-by-fours, maneuvering them through the narrow space, and finally into the kitchen. As soon as Shelly saw him, she ran back upstairs, feeling like she was fifteen, but unable to bear being in the same room with him. She hated – *hated* – being rescued, especially by a man, especially by an arrogant man. And maybe most of all, by Jack Hatch. Twice, now.

She went back into her bedroom. *Her* bedroom. She was making herself say it, needing to claim something of her own. She sat on the bed, looking at nothing, but then found herself staring at the phone. She had been sure the ancient phone wouldn't work, even after the line was repaired. But she had been wrong about that too. Now the ugly green phone felt like a dark presence in the bedroom. She'd thought about getting rid of it, or maybe putting it in the closet. Or better, out in the garage or carriage house with all the other ancient crap out there. But she hadn't.

She watched as her hand, seemingly of its own volition, reached out to the old receiver, her fingers resting there. She looked down, to the phone book on the shelf below. She closed her eyes, took a deep breath, filling up, pouring out. Energy. Calm. She lifted the handset from its cradle, but didn't bring it to her ear. She held it in her hand, in her lap. She could hear the loud dial tone, even from there. Like a loud, insistent insect. She replaced it in its cradle. She sat staring vacantly for a minute, then rose and walked to the little desk again. She gingerly sat in the spindly chair. She pulled open the drawer and lifted out the notebook, thumbing through it, past the calendar, past the notes on the house, past a couple of pictures from home magazines she'd put in for inspiration, should they ever get to some actual remodeling. Her rants, seven pages' worth. She kept turning pages, looking for a blank one, for another rant.

She stopped. She'd almost forgotten about these. She'd written down a couple of peculiar dreams she'd had. One of them, about her sister. It had amused her in the morning, when she'd first remembered it: the grown-up two of them playing a game that they had played when they were young. House Vet, they called it. When they were little, Nina always wanted to play house, Shelly, vet. They'd figured out a compromise, with Shelly being a pediatrician-vet who made house-calls to Nina's myriad dolls and stuffed animals. But in her dream, she could see Nina through the window of her beautiful mansion, dressed in black, tending to real babies and puppies. That was when dream Shelly realized that she didn't have her medical bag, or any supplies at all. She was, in fact, naked.

Shelly read through her journal entry now, shaking her head. Nina, who as a little girl had insisted on playing the little wife and mother, had grown up to be childless and married to Jesus, of all things. And the ironies didn't stop there. As a girl, Shelly had kept a diary with plans and dreams for her Bar Mitzvah. But she never had one; her parents had stopped going to temple after they divorced. Neither parent had any interest in sending her to Hebrew school, let alone paying for a big party. And she had pledged to that same diary, repeatedly, that she would become a doctor and get rich. But she had hated science as passionately as she had liked boys, so pursued the latter, and not the former. But the Bar Mitzvah thing she always regretted. True, it was the party and the attention she had wanted, but as much as not having one herself, Shelly had equally regretted that Nina had not had one either. That maybe if she had . . .

Shelly listened to the hammering starting downstairs. She turned to a blank sheet in the notebook. She fished a pen from the drawer, pulled the cap off, placed the point at the top of the page. 'Bar Mitzvah,' she wrote. Underneath, she made a little arrow and wrote: 'Lox and bagels, lots of fruit, margaritas, coconut cream pie'. Under that, another arrow, and 'Dancing'. She stared at the page, then slowly put large Xs through everything, and flipped to another blank page. She stared at it for a long minute, then wrote: 'Dear Nina'. She stopped, the trembling pen point poised above the page. Then she carefully placed the pen under the words, and scratched across each till they were one inky black box. She flipped back to notes on the house, with guesstimates of costs. She wrote in 'Building permit' and under that, 'Plumbing repairs' and two question marks next to them.

Abruptly, she slammed the notebook shut. It was no use. They had to face it, they all did: they were done here. The house was too old, needed too much. *They* were too old, and had too little. And she sure as hell wasn't going to stick around and let Jack Hatch dole out his financial supremacy.

Coming to Tennessee, far from empowering them,

as she had hoped, had ended up enfeebling them. They'd come off looking like weak, stupid women. At least as far as Hatch was concerned. As far as she was concerned. This whole trip had somehow just ended up stirring up all her insecurities, every one. She knew she had tried one too many times, in one too many places, to pretend to know more than she did, to bluff her way through larger and more complicated contracts and transactions – and remodeling – knowing for a fact how often the men she worked with over the years had done the same thing. First you promise, *then* you figure out how to deliver. But it had caught up with her, as it had caught up with them, she now realized. Sooner or later. Andy, in her old firm, had cautioned her against shooting too high, too fast. Enroning, he'd called it, flying on one wing. No matter how good the initial updraft is, when it stops, you're going to spiral down, fast.

She looked around the bedroom. She'd gotten used to this little room. She'd imagined putting up some wainscoting, painting, maybe even building in a window seat. She sighed. The only thing left to do was throw in the towel. Give up. Raise the white flag. On everything. The trip, the house, the money, the dog. Go home, call her attorney, and start negotiating with the creditors.

CHAPTER 34

MEG

Standing at the sink, Meg put her hand deep into the big bowl of water, swirling the red lentils. Mis-named, she thought. If it were up to her, she'd name legumes like they named cosmetics. Red lentils – these, not red at all – would be Soft Tangerine Sunrise. Or maybe Sunset, since this was to be their dinner tonight. Their final dinner at Dogs' Wood. Meg lifted a small handful, then let them fall again, landing in little plops and splashes. She plunged her hand back in, swirling them with her fist, mixed emotions swirling in her.

Her hand went still in the water, her eyes rising to the window above the sink. The rosebushes outside had fat buds – deep blood red, canary yellow, pale orange, creamy white; they would bloom in a matter of days, maybe even tomorrow. And they were going to miss it.

They'd miss everything that would bloom throughout the summer, flowers and blossoms that they didn't even know about. And so much else. They'd already gotten a flier about the Fourth of July parade and fireworks, still nearly two months away. Meg had pictured them sitting on the front porch, sipping a cool drink, watching the Fleurville version of pyrotechnics light the night sky.

They'd already stayed longer than Meg initially had thought they would. Not nearly long enough, for either the house or for her, as it turned out. She stared out the window again, wondering where the hidden blooms might be under the weeds. She had cleared only a small portion of Georgie's old perennial gardens. Leaving the overgrown beds was like walking away from Christmas morning, packages left unwrapped.

She was going to miss so much about being here. Maybe most of all, the evening show. The fireflies had only just begun their seasonal appearance. She loved sitting on the front porch steps in the evening, a glass of wine in hand, watching the darkness slowly descend. She'd wait, smiling, as if she were seated in a theater, awaiting the Royal Ballet. The orchestra of crickets, cicadas and frogs from the marsh across the street was the first act. Then, slowly, miraculously, a lone blinking light would appear in the grass, then another, and another, and she'd watch them floating slowly upward.

Meg sighed, her hands and wrists in the lentil water. Still, she used her shoulder to wipe perspiration from her forehead. She wouldn't miss the heat. That might be the only compensation of heading back north. But it would be hot up there too, soon enough. And she would take all the heat the south could dish out, to stay. She loved it here. She loved the pace and the warmth – of the air, the people, even the funky hardware store in town that looked like it had been beamed into this century from the last. And she wished she had discovered the food co-op sooner. She had fulfilled a long-time goal. Years ago, C.C. had given her the *Legumes Are for Lovers* cookbook for her birthday, knowing her interest. But it contained too few descriptions of the exotic-sounding ingredients, and thus, was intimidating. And, the title had turned out to be a real misnomer. The first and only meal she'd cooked from it – a colorful vegetable and chick pea curry – had actually driven Grant away. He'd tasted the smallest possible bite, then gone out for a burger. Meg didn't want to cook two meals every night, so she'd let go of the whole vegetarian thing. She had let go of a lot.

She'd begun to wonder if, by letting so much go, she and Grant had actually let go of themselves, and therefore each other. His leaving had only outlined both their absences from the marriage. But she honestly didn't know what she could have done differently. She had tried many times over the years to find common ground with him. But they simply flew in different orbits around the same sun: their kids. And when the kids were gone, there was nothing to prevent the force of their separateness from hurling them out into space. Literally, in their case.

'A piece of meat never looked like this,' she said to Dollop, admiring the lentils again, desperate not to think about Grant anymore. Dollop lifted his sleepy head. 'But you'd probably take meat over lentils, wouldn't you, boy?' He tipped his tail, then curled back up on the old gold floral couch pillow. Meg had grabbed both of the throw pillows for beds for Dollop after Shelly had bought C.C. (with funds borrowed and full support from Meg) a new couch cover and two new pillows. 'If you can't afford to redecorate,' she said, 'reaccessorize!' It was a lovely teal color, but it had a two-tiered frilly skirt, which neither Shelly nor Meg cared for. But Shelly had selected the cover because she knew C.C. would love that skirt. Meg was stunned by her deed. Not only buying a gift for C.C. to make amends, but going out of her way to get something that she, Shelly, didn't particularly like, but knew C.C. would. And getting it exactly right! And that plus some new paint had made the living room the only updated room in the house. Though not exactly market-ready. Especially with the big hole in the wall.

C.C. still hadn't made up her mind about when to sell Dogs' Wood. She'd tentatively decided to put it on the market sometime next spring, maybe over the winter hire someone to spruce it up a little, or at least fix the hole they'd made. She was clearly torn about it, and Meg had urged her to take her time, not to rush into selling it. While Meg genuinely had C.C.'s interests at heart, she also hoped and dreamed about coming back to Dogs' Wood herself, at least once before it was sold.

Meg checked her watch, lying on the counter. Almost noon. Shelly was on one of her long walks with Richter again. C.C. was in her room, writing a last letter to Purdy, even though they planned to stop in Tupper on their way home, and they would surely beat the letter there. They'd discussed stopping in to visit M.J., but C.C. said it would be too hard to say goodbye to her again.

Meg glanced at her watch again. She hoped Shelly was moments from walking in the door. 'I'm starving!' she told Dollop. She stepped down the length of the counter to the old Crockpot. She wondered if the ancient appliance might not be one of the originals, from the first year or two they'd come on the market. It was small – tiny, by today's ever-increasing standards – but again, quite serviceable. She lifted the thick glass lid, inhaled the steam rising from the vegetable stock inside. She stirred the broth, bringing up chunks of vege-tables – the leftover zucchini, green and red peppers and onions she'd roasted on the grill a couple days ago, and some halves of small red potatoes. Various herbs and spices swirled on the top. She stirred them in, then carefully sipped, testing. She tipped some dark brown liquid from a squat bottle into the mix. She looked at the bottle. This would have been one of those intimidating ingredients she would not have bought before. Liquid amino acids.

It sounded like something you had to be a licensed chemist to purchase. But it was right there on the co-op shelf, and had become a favorite flavoring. She dumped the drained lentils into the Crockpot, pushed the stragglers off the sides of the bowl with her fingers, put the lid back in place.

As she dried her hands on a dishtowel, she leaned back against the counter, one ankle over the other. She smiled at the sleeping Dollop. Odd, that they had made the trip down with one small dog, and they would be making the trip back with another. She wondered how Grant, if he was even there, would react to Dollop. She also wondered how it would go with C.C. and Purdy. Time would tell with that one, but C.C. was clearly excited about their stop in Tupper. But no matter what, they would all be returning home to holes in their lives. Meg folded her arms, almost hugging herself. Going back felt like a bear crawling back into her dark cave, just when spring has arrived.

She gazed at the tiny kitchen that she had come to love as it was, but for which they had dreamed many things: new appliances, new cabinets, more counter space. If only they had the wherewithal – finances, skills, strength, fortitude – to do the work on this lovely old house. But they'd discussed it at length, agreed they did not. That they should go back. Their lunch in town today would be their farewell outing, the lentil soup their last supper in Dogs' Wood.

★   ★   ★

Meg held the door of the co-op for Shelly and C.C. The grocery was to the left, and by far the larger portion of the space. The café was to the right, a short, narrow room, parallel to the street outside. There were only five small tables, each up against the window. The kitchen was open, diner-style, with a large eat-on counter separating it from the tables. Four stools at that counter provided additional seating. A small archway separated the co-op from the café, with corkboard covering the entire wall space around the arch. It was festooned with colorful fliers advertising for roommates, concerts, classes, and more.

Meg pointed to the nearest of the two unoccupied tables and they sat, just as a young man pushed through the swinging half-door from the kitchen area.

'Hey, Meg! Great to see you!'

'Hey, Kevin. These are my friends, C.C. and Shelly. This is Kevin.' Meg smiled as both women took in Kevin's long dreadlocks, held back in a fat ponytail, his various piercings, his loose pink and orange balloon pants extending below his muslin apron.

C.C. flashed a smile and held out her fingers. 'Hello.' Kevin set the paper menus on the table and took her hand. Shelly immediately began perusing the menu, then, apparently remembering her manners, looked up briefly, smiled, said nice to meet you and dropped her head again. 'I'm starving,' she said. 'What can we get quick? Like, right away?'

'I can bring you a bowl of our barley-mushroom-kelp soup,' said Kevin. 'Soup of the day!'

Shelly made a face, and Meg laughed. She'd mentioned to Kevin during her various shopping trips that the women she lived with were not quite as adventurous as she when it came to eating.

'I'll try it. Thanks,' said Shelly.

'Three, then?' asked Kevin. Meg and C.C. nodded. 'Great! I'm so glad to see you here for lunch finally, Meg. And friends. We're big fans of hers, y'know,' he said, pointing to Meg, making her blush a little. 'Glad t'have y'all. First of many lunch visits, we hope.'

Meg tried not to look as crestfallen as she felt. 'Sadly, this is our farewell luncheon. We're heading back north tomorrow.'

Kevin's face and posture fell. 'No way! Why? I thought y'all were redoing that house, going to be here a while.'

'Long story,' said Meg. 'But the house needs more than three middle-aged women – at least *these* three middle-aged women – can give it.'

'Oh, very bumming indeed,' Kevin said sincerely.

Shelly let out a little laugh. 'Yeah, we're way bummed too. But, um, soup? Please?'

'Right! Well, the soup'll be on the house. A farewell gift.' He hurried off.

'Oh! *This* actually sounds good,' said Shelly, reading from the menu. 'Grilled Portobello mushroom on toasted wholewheat bread with sun-dried

430

tomatoes, goat cheese and – oops! There we are again. The damned, ubiquitous bean sprouts.'

Meg laughed. 'I'm sure they'll leave them off if you request it.'

Kevin returned with their soups and took their sandwich orders, the Portobello all around, with sprouts. Shelly dipped her spoon into her soup and gave it a tentative taste. Her face brightened. 'Not bad. Not bad.' She continued to spoon it up with gusto. Meg savored every mouthful.

The steaming sandwiches arrived moments later. Shelly took an enormous bite. Her eyes grew huge and she opened her mouth and let the bite fall on her plate. 'It's good, but *hot!*' She noisily sipped her water.

Embarrassed, Meg looked out the big window, watched a bicyclist dismount, then prop his bike against a street sign pole. Shelly could be so . . . Shelly. Meg smiled. But thank God for that. She turned back toward the table, finished off her soup. Just as she took a small bite of her own sandwich, the door to the co-op opened. In the way of very small restaurants, all eyes turned toward him.

Aware of the attention, the man flushed, stood awkwardly. After a few seconds he looked at Kevin behind the counter, and pointed to the corkboard. 'Okay if I post a sign on your board?' he asked, barely audible. He pulled a sheet of pale green paper from a roll in his belt. The paper had small, cut tabs fringing the bottom.

'Be my guest,' said Kevin.

Meg couldn't take her eyes off the man, in part because their table was the closest to him, and she was on the far side of the table, facing him. But also because he was strikingly handsome, though he looked very underweight. He was tall, olive-skinned, and his brown eyes made Meg think of tiger's-eye stone. But most remarkable was his mane of black hair, a mass of soft curls making a dark frame around his head. He had several days' growth on his beard, but otherwise looked clean and neat. As Shelly and C.C. returned to their meal, Meg couldn't quite return her attention to the table. She watched as he surveyed the bulletin board, carefully rearranging postings. She felt her lips ease into a smile; she could tell that he was making sure not to cover anyone else's current sign, looking at each one, carefully removing those that were out of date. Meg guessed he was a few years older than her oldest son, so maybe in his early thirties. His worn but clean yellow T-shirt was emblazoned with an orange sun and something about solar energy. The T-shirt was tucked into khaki shorts, looking a size too big. They were cinched tightly with a cracked leather belt. A corner tear in the back of one leg looked carefully but inexpertly mended. They looked like hiking shorts, with lots of pockets and thick belt loops. That, combined with his sturdy hiking boots and thick socks struck Meg as a curious choice for bike riding, especially on this hot day. She looked again at the old, red ten-speed outside.

Meg took another small bite of her sandwich as she watched him push two tacks into his sign. 'Thanks,' he said to Kevin as he threaded his arms back into his backpack straps.

'No worries,' said Kevin.

The bicyclist, his hand on the door, paused. He was staring hungrily at the food on the tables. Then he saw Meg watching him, flushed again, and hurried outside. Meg quickly looked down at her plate, but surreptitiously watched as he swung his leg up and over the seat, and pedaled off. She leaned closer and closer to the window, till she couldn't see him anymore. When she turned back to the table, C.C. and Shelly were staring at her, both grinning.

'Well! *This* is a development!' said Shelly. 'Look who is checking out the testosteronic landscape! I thought you had a crush on *Hatch*.'

Meg felt her face warm as her mouth opened in protest. 'No, I wasn't checking that guy out. It wasn't that. And no! God, no! I in *no way* have a crush on Hatch. I just don't think he's evil incarnate, like you do. You know, Shel, the man was in a pretty serious depression. He's on medication now, changing his diet. He's really trying. Maybe you could cut him some slack. Anyway,' she said, gesturing out the window, 'I was just wondering what that kid's story is. That's all. He's so thin, and his clothes . . . He looked hungry.' Shelly's eyebrows raised lasciviously. 'Not hungry *that* way. For God's sake, Shel! He's about my son's age!'

'Riii-ght,' said Shelly, taking a big bite of her now cooled sandwich. Meg and C.C. both laughed at the alfalfa sprouts hanging out the sides of her mouth.

CHAPTER 35

C.C.

C. couldn't believe it when Meg stopped to read the green flier on the corkboard .as they were leaving. 'You fixin' to get his phone number?!' she asked, teasing.

They had paid up, Meg had hugged Kevin goodbye, and Shelly had even complimented him on the meal, though C.C. thought Shelly was mostly flirting. But C.C. had been delighted to see *Meg* man-gazing, even if the guy who posted the sign was substantially younger than she was.

'Yes. Yes, I am,' said Meg, tearing off one of the tabs. C.C. glanced worriedly at Shelly, waiting outside on the sidewalk. But Shelly was looking longingly toward the window of the little boutique next door.

'You are? Really, Meg? I was just pulling your leg! Are you really going to call him?' Meg had apparently rebounded even farther than C.C. thought, if she was contemplating an anonymous, one-night fling before they headed out of town. C.C. briefly imagined herself sleeping alone tonight in the bedroom she and Meg had been sharing. She guessed it would be okay if Meg and the skinny stranger . . . used . . . Georgie's room. The image made her shudder. It was just so un-Meg. 'Are you sure that's wise, darlin'?'

'Look! Read it!' Meg demanded, jabbing her finger at the green paper. She pulled off her reading glasses, handed them to C.C.

Perplexed, and a little alarmed by the ferocity in Meg's voice, C.C. stared at her, then slowly took the glasses. She slid them on, put her finger on the green paper, and read.

> Room or apt. needed immediately. Due to circumstances beyond my control, I am in urgent need of housing. Can't pay rent, but I'm a licensed G.C. and will trade that or other labor. Responsible, hard-working, non-drinker, non-smoker, non-drug user. Vegetarian. References. Please take a tab and call number printed below if you have a room or any possible lead for me to follow up on. *Namasté*.

Then a signature that C.C. couldn't read. But on each tab at the bottom was typed: 'Azaad Dubois' and a phone number. The door chimes rang. Meg was already out the door. C.C. hurried after her.

'Shell, hand me your phone, quick,' said Meg. She snapped her fingers repeatedly. 'Hurry! Hurry!'

C.C. stared at Meg, wondering what had come over her. Shelly's phone had been out of commission for a long time now; Meg knew that! Shelly spoke C.C.'s very thoughts. 'Hell-ohhh? Earth to Meg. I have no phone. The company got a little picky about the whole money thing. Remember?'

'Shit!' said Meg. She dashed back into the co-op. They watched her through the window, talking to Kevin. He pulled something from his pocket, handed it to her. She emerged seconds later, holding a cellphone, staring at the small tab of green paper. 'Give me my reading glasses, C.C.! I can't see the damn numbers!' C.C. patted her head, pulled off the glasses she'd forgotten she'd put there. Meg snatched them from her hand.

'Man! What is going *on* with you?' demanded Shelly. C.C. stared at Meg, as confused as Shelly was.

'That guy!' said Meg. 'That *guy*! I need to call him before someone else – *gets* him!' C.C. had never seen Meg like this; she'd almost lost the ability to speak coherently.

'Man!' Shelly repeated. 'Are you hot for this guy or what? I'm all for rocking the cradle, hon, but . . .'

C.C. tapped Shelly as Meg punched numbers into the phone. 'Shelly, what's a G.C.? A "licensed G.C."?'

'What? What are you talking about?'

'Well, that sign in there said he was a licensed G.C. and would trade labor for room and b—'

'Oh my God!' yelled Shelly. 'Are you kidding me?!' She started bobbing up and down, reminding C.C. of Lucy.

'What? What?' cried C.C.

Shelly grabbed C.C.'s wrists tightly, looked her in the eye. 'A licensed general contractor. A builder! Somebody who knows how to remodel a house!'

'Oh my stars,' said C.C. flatly. Then she and Shelly bobbed up and down together. C.C. couldn't believe it. She began a silent prayer that what appeared to be happening was really happening, that staying in Fleurville, at least for a little while longer, was meant to be.

'Hi, is this, uh . . .' Meg glanced at the tab in her hand again, '. . . Azaad? Hi. Hello.' Meg laughed giddily. So unlike her, thought C.C.

Shelly was standing motionless, her clasped hands in front of her mouth, her eyes locked on Meg.

'My name is Meg Bartholomew,' Meg continued, more evenly now. 'We were just eating lunch at the co-op and happened to see you posting your sign and—'

Meg abruptly stopped speaking, astonished amusement on her face. She mouthed the word 'sign' to C.C. and Shelly, grinning. C.C. began a happy dance on the sidewalk.

'*Un-fricking-believable*,' muttered Shelly.

'Anyway, we would like to talk to you, right away, if you could ride back over to the co-op. I think we could maybe help each other out.'

Back at the house they showed the very shy Azaad around, and then sat together at the dining-room table with glasses of iced tea. They'd seen his résumé, called a reference, and then offered him either of the two bedrooms on the third floor, as well as all of Meg's vegetarian meals he could eat, in exchange for his expertise, labor, and instruction to three 'willing and maybe only moderately able women', as Shelly had put it.

'So we have a deal?' asked Shelly. Azaad nodded. 'Then the only thing we need to do,' Shelly looked from C.C. to Meg, 'is earn some money to buy supplies. I've been thinking, and I believe I can get work doing house staging around town. What about you two?'

'I can do some tutoring,' said Meg. 'I'll put a sign up at the co-op. Signs seem to work miracles.' She grinned. Azaad smiled, but C.C. laughed, knowing he didn't know the half of it.

But suddenly her mood changed. 'I can . . . maybe I could . . .' C.C. stammered. She felt like she was going to cry. What could *she* do? The damn menopause, or peri-menopause, as Meg insisted she call it, was making her bloat like a puffer fish, and her back ached all the time. She was short and fat and weak, which limited what she could do on the house. And she had no marketable skills to go out and find a job. 'What can I do?' she asked weakly.

Shelly was smiling, her eyes shining. 'Well, Ceece? I've been thinking about that and I have an idea. Y'know all those antiques and cra— uh, things, out in the carriage house? And in the

439

basement? And in the attic?' C.C. nodded. 'I thought maybe you could go through all that, and whatever you don't want, you could sell on eBay.'

C.C. brightened. 'I could do that! I think. I've never sold anything on eBay before. But I hear it's easy.'

'And who knows?' said Shelly. 'Maybe you'll come upon some treasured antique like on that TV show, and it'll be worth thousands! And then we can really do this old girl up right!' Shelly glanced around the room, no doubt imagining how she'd like to see it done. But then she looked at C.C. 'And besides, you'll be busy making decisions, lots of decisions. Colors, types of tile, wood, flooring. You'll be plenty busy!'

Meg was first to thrust her hand toward the center of the table. C.C. grabbed hold, then Shelly reached out, took hold. They all three looked at Azaad. He seemed to turn four shades of red, hardly able to look up from the table. But he reached in too, and all the women grabbed on to him, and together they raised and lowered the mound of hands in a sort of shake. C.C. was surprised that Shelly hadn't pulled out a piece of paper, spelled out the terms each party would agree to, asked for signatures all around. But maybe living in the south was rubbing off on her. C.C. knew that here, the handshake was as good as a contract. Besides, the deal was simple: they were going to help each other out, in every way they could.

CHAPTER 36

SHELLY

*T*he grass was growing under their feet.

Shelly chuckled, looking at the mangy lawn, grown long and wild already again, after her last attempt at mowing. She was sitting on the porch swing, in shorts and an orange tank top, sipping iced tea in the welcome shade, a respite from sawdust and noise. She watched a pale yellow butterfly in its dipping, circuitous path across the yard. She wasn't sure she had ever felt so . . . she wasn't even sure what the word was for what she was feeling.

In the weeks since Azaad had arrived, they'd gotten a good deal of work done on the house, but much of it had been pulling things apart, and finding just how bad it was – mold, decomposing wood, dated plumbing and electrical. And pulling nails from boards and boards from walls and floors – all of which was easier than pulling words from Azaad. At first, Shelly had felt tiny little flares of jealousy that he'd warmed up only to Meg; the man was handsome enough to turn any woman's knees to jelly, after all. But it made sense, since he and Meg spent the most time together, driving back and forth from the hardware and lumber stores in town. Shelly had learned not even to try to have a conversation with the man. She didn't think she'd ever met anyone so shy.

Shelly looked out to the yard again, and laughed again. C.C. was inching down the front walk, barefoot. The grass had grown long and prickly again between the flagstones. C.C. was carefully placing her bare feet on the warm, red stones as she walked out to the mailbox. Good thing the mail was delivered in the morning; by noon on these June days the stones would be burning hot.

Shelly pushed her bare toe on the wood floor of the front porch, set the swing in motion, and leaned back. She loved the porch swing. It was an impulse buy that Meg and Azaad had made on one of their supply trips into town. The only bad thing about the swing was sharing it at night. They all liked to sit out on the veranda with glasses of wine or beer, and watch the fireflies.

Shelly glanced at her watch; Meg and Azaad were on yet another run for lumber, and she couldn't help but wonder if they'd gotten delayed by another impulse buy. She hoped another porch swing. They could afford it. Or rather, C.C. and Dogs' Wood could. C.C. had done well on eBay and Craigslist both, surprisingly well. She'd been selling clothing, antiques (though Shelly had asked to keep the old green phone in her bedroom) and some first edition books from Georgie's collection. But C.C.'s most surprising sale was a painting of

442

Georgie's. She'd found the artist Georgie Tucker had some renown, especially locally. C.C. hadn't been able to bring herself to sell any more of her aunt's art, but she wasn't ruling it out.

Meg had gotten a few tutoring gigs, but not many, as school was ending and no one wanted tutoring over summer vacation. So Meg had become Azaad's main assistant. Shelly was pleased with the money she'd brought in by working as a buyer's consultant and house-stager. She was sort of stunned by how much she enjoyed it. It was a lot less stressful than being the actual agent. It was fun spending other people's money, rearranging their houses, coming up with small but impressive design touches that made the sellers almost want to reconsider selling their home.

Shelly had had quite a run of clients for several weeks, and C.C. was taking it easy, her back bothering her more and more, till she finally agreed to go to the doctor just last week.

'Middle age!' she'd reported, flapping a piece of paper with back exercises when she and Meg returned. Meg had driven C.C., but had run errands while she was at her appointment. In perfect Meg style, she'd bought a box of ice-cream sandwiches to celebrate C.C. finally getting herself to the doctor. As they had all sat around the table, C.C. swallowed her last bite, licked her fingers, then said, 'That was so good, I don't even care that I have to go back next week for all those stupid tests to check for cholesterol and whatnot.'

'Wait till you're fifty and get to do the colonoscopy!' said Meg.

'Oh, yeah. *That's* fun,' said Shelly. And they'd all helped themselves to a second ice-cream sandwich.

C.C. was not alone in her discomforts. Shelly's shoulders hurt regularly, but not from injury so much as holding her tension there. Meg gave her almost nightly shoulder rubs. In exchange, Shelly rubbed Meg's tired feet. But despite their various infirmities, Shelly thought, swinging there on the porch, they'd done okay. Oh, sure, they'd had to work out some kinks. They'd had a couple more disagreements. But they'd been muddling along, enjoying the work, each other, the slower pace. Shelly's only real complaint about living at Dogs' Wood was their neighbor, that damn Hatch. He was over here too often to visit with Meg and C.C. But when Shelly bumped into him, either she would disappear, or he would. Their rancor was mutual, and avoiding each other suited Shelly just fine. She would endure the neighbor-from-hell as long as they had to, in order to finish the work on the house. And for Richter. When Hatch visited the other two, Shelly would usually disappear with Richter. She had been working with him on some basic obedience, and either he was a very quick study, or Hatch had been doing the same. So maybe there was that one tiny redeeming quality about Hatch. But otherwise, she found him arrogant, and still a little unbalanced. But she'd

444

get the last laugh; when Dogs' Wood went on the market she'd make sure buyers knew that the famous Jack Hatch lived next door, as if it were a selling point. The poor souls would never suspect that he was a bigger liability than black mold.

She looked at her watch. A little after one. She'd expected Azaad and Meg back well before now. They must have stopped for lunch. At the co-op, no doubt.

She tipped her glass side to side, marveling at the bar of sunlight in the deep ruby tea. It was some new thing Meg had discovered at the co-op, full of antioxidants or some such. They kept a pitcher in the fridge. Shelly had grown rather fond of it, but C.C. kept to her sweet tea.

Shelly held her drink on the flat arm rest of the swing, looking out at the lawn. She groaned: she was going to have to mow it again. She'd already mowed it once with that ancient push mower, but the blades were impossibly dull and it had pulled out about as much grass as it had cut. That damn Hatch had watched her, smirking, though she never gave him the satisfaction of knowing she'd seen him, her eyes hidden behind her sunglasses. He'd disappeared after a few minutes of staring and she'd thought she was rid of him. But moments later, a roar startled her, and there he was, riding across his big lawn on a John Deere tractor mower. That damn smirk back on his face.

He'd parked the mower on the boundary of their

properties, dismounted with a flourish, and yelled toward her, 'Shelly Kostens? Meet my alias! He's rather handy for just the task you're doing. I thought you'd like to get acquainted.' Then he bowed deeply, sweeping his arm across his waist like a Shakespearean actor. He left the key on the seat and walked away. What an idiot. What did he mean, his alias? She didn't care. The man often made no sense. She ignored him and determinedly, ferociously, finished mangling their weedy lawn with the push mower, leaving clumps of grass littered like small corpses across a sod battlefield. The following morning, the knobs of uprooted lawn were already turning brown, and the John Deere was still where he'd left it, as if it had been standing sentry over the grim scene all night.

Shelly squirmed in the porch swing at the memory. She looked out to the mailbox. It looked like C.C. had already torn into one letter, now clamped under her arm as she sorted through the mail, grinning like the fool in love she already was. Shelly sighed again. She was hoping beyond hope that this thing with Purdy wouldn't end up hurting C.C. But what were the chances of that? The epistolary romance was worse than a fling, in Shelly's opinion. C.C. had given her heart and soul over to that man, word by word. Far more dangerous than bumping bodies with a stranger for a couple of hours, in Shelly's opinion. Providing one took the proper precautions, of course.

At least Meg had long since stopped writing to Grant, and seemed much the happier for it. But C.C. was a goner, and Shelly knew that it was deceptively easy to create what you wanted in letters, let a fantasy grow. She remembered writing to a soldier in Vietnam when she was ten or so. She and Nina had both signed up for the 'You're Not Forgotten' campaign started by Susie Kablonski, whose dad and brother were both over there. Shelly had wanted the metal bracelet with a soldier's name on it, initially because it was a fad, the thing to do. But she'd grown genuinely to care about the faceless soldier on her wrist. She'd worn her bracelet twenty-four hours a day, despite receiving only one letter from her soldier in return for the dozen or so she'd written him before she graduated. But the lack of reciprocity had not kept Shelly from building a fantasy about him. Bryan Coffey.

'Wow,' she whispered. She was stunned that she still remembered his name; hadn't even thought of him in years. But it was a memorable name; Nina had teased her about it, singing, 'Shelly loves Coffey, she doesn't love tea!' after Shelly had made the mistake of confiding in her that she'd thought about maybe meeting him one day. In fact, she had spent hours daydreaming while painting her toenails Flame Red over old newspaper on top of the orange shag carpeting in their living room, the tiny brush poised over her toes, the polish drying on the bristles as her mind wandered through her fantasies. She would meet his plane when he came home. He would know her on sight, from the pictures she had sent. He would spot her in the crowd, run toward her. She would run toward him. They would fly into each other's arms and he would lift her, swinging her legs, bare and tanned under her yellow miniskirt, the one with the daisies, the sunlight breaking apart and showering down on them like confetti.

'Ha!' she said, and pushed the swing hard into motion again. That had not been the first of her romantic fantasies to bite the dust. And it sure as hell wasn't going to be the last. She took a sip of her ruby-colored tea, wondering if Private First Class Bryan Coffey had made it home alive. And if so, had someone been there to meet him?

She watched C.C. strolling back up the walk, a wad of letters in her hand, two under her arm, another in her other hand. But she was not smiling. 'What's wrong?' Shelly asked, her hand tightening around the glass. Had Purdy cut her loose already?

C.C. flapped an unopened envelope in front of her. 'For Meg. *From Grant.*' She pinched it. 'It's thin, one page. This can't be good.'

Shelly groaned. C.C. was right: either way, it couldn't be good. If he wanted a divorce, it would be a blow to Meg, even though Shelly thought it would be for the best. And if that bastard wanted to try to mend things now, after all poor Meg had been through, not just over the past few months, but after *years* of putting up with him . . . God, she hoped Meg wouldn't succumb. But she feared Meg would go back to him, try yet again to salvage the amorphous thing she called 'my marriage'.

'Shit,' said Shelly. 'Why now? After all that time of Meg desperate for a letter, and he didn't have the decency to write even to tell her he was alive. Why now?'

'Return address is their house, not that that means he's there,' said C.C., climbing up the steps of the porch.

'What about the postmark?' Shelly asked, sliding over and making room for C.C. on the swing.

C.C. sat, looked at the envelope, squinting, twisting slightly to get full sunlight on it. 'Wisataukee.' She let out a long, slow breath. 'He's home,' she said in a flat, desolate voice.

The sound of a car approaching from up the road made Shelly turn and look. 'It's Meg! What should we do? Should we hide it?' She felt like hiding herself. She glanced over her shoulder again. The car was coming up on Hatch's place.

'We can't hide it, Shel,' said C.C. 'That would be wrong, not to mention illegal. But I don't want to just give it to her either. Not blindside her with it, anyway. Not when everything's just turned around for her.' She chewed on her lip a moment, then slapped the letter across her knee. 'Damn! This is about as expected as snow in July. And a lot less welcome.'

They both jumped up as Meg's little red car pulled into the driveway, laden with lumber strapped to the top, the tires crunching over the gravel, a cheery beep-beep in greeting. Meg's tanned arm stuck out the window, waving. The ancient, jangly phone rang inside the house. Still, even after several weeks of being hooked up, a foreign sound to them all. The rare calls they got were mostly wrong numbers.

'Crimeny!' said C.C. 'Why is it everything happens at once?' She showed the letter to Shelly, then tucked it inside the stack of other mail. 'I'll just leave the mail on the table, where I always do. If she checks, she checks. Otherwise, we'll tell her on the weekend, when Azaad goes to his other job.'

Shelly nodded, smiling. She knew that Meg had long since stopped checking the mail. They would have till the weekend.

The phone continued to ring. 'I'll get that, you help them with the stuff,' said C.C., trotting for the door.

Shelly nodded again, picking up her glass. She stepped down the stairs in her bare feet, watching for splinters as she did, then for thistles as she stepped onto the wild lawn. She was halfway around the house when it occurred to her how their roles had shifted. Here *she*, Shelly, was, asking questions, not only letting C.C. tell her what to do, but grateful for it. Meg was gallivanting around town with a younger man. C.C., always the one to follow, acquiesce, had assumed her place as the rightful belle of her southern home.

Who'd a thunk it? Shelly thought, rounding the huge rosemary bush. 'Hey,' she called to them. 'What took y'all so long?' She wouldn't have admitted it to anyone, but she had started to worry. Meg, out of the car, but with her hand still on the door handle, turned. She looked both surprised and amused.

'I thought you were C.C.!' said Meg. 'You did it again. You said "y'all".'

'I did not say "y'all",' said Shelly.

Meg and Azaad exchanged nods and smiles, and Meg looked back at Shelly. 'Yah-huh!' she said, a light laugh bubbling out of her. 'Ow-ahh deah Shelly hay-ahs been southern-ahhhized!'

'I did not! *Have not!*' said Shelly. She could feel her face burning. To her annoyance, she thought she may actually have said it this time. 'Come on, let's unload and get back to work,' she said sternly, walking past them as they began to untie the lumber from the top of the car, maddening smiles still on their faces.

Shelly set her glass on the back steps then walked over the gravel, impressed at how her own feet had toughened up. She began untying a knot, opposite them. Without looking up she said, 'Y'all shore-lee did take y'all's time. We've been waitin' a possum's age for y'all t' get back heahh.' Shelly felt triumphant when even Azaad burst out laughing.

⋆　　⋆　　⋆

The lumber neatly stowed on the porch, the three walked inside the front door. The house was remarkably cool, a refreshing change from outside. Meg led the way down the hall, Azaad following, Shelly behind him. While the other two had been in town, she and C.C. had taken up all the runners prior to replacing the trim in the hall today. The walnut floor felt cool, smooth and familiar on Shelly's hot feet. She stopped, placed her hand on the balustrade of the stairs, lingering, smiling. She felt at home here, finally. In a strange yet deeply satisfying way.

'C.C.?' Meg's panicked voice rang out from the far end of the living room. 'Are you okay? *What's wrong?*'

Shelly turned, bolted toward the sound. 'Ceece, talk to me,' came Meg's voice again. She wasn't shouting, but there was no mistaking the urgency in her voice. Shelly pushed past Azaad, who was standing to the side of the doorway, looking frightened and uncertain. She ran down the length of the living room.

C.C. was on the floor, the phone on her lap, one hand still on the receiver in its cradle, the other on the carpet, fingers digging into the fibers of the beautiful rug. Her face was pale. She was staring straight ahead, her eyes unseeing, her cheeks wet with tears. Shelly and Meg sat on either side of her, very close, their arms around her. Shelly glanced up, wondering if Azaad was still in the doorway. He had left, giving them privacy.

A thought per second ran through Shelly's mind: something's happened to Lucy. Or Kathryn. Or maybe Purdy called and said— She actually hoped for the last one. The others were too horrible to contemplate.

'Honey? Please, talk to us,' Meg said, touching her knuckles gently to C.C.'s cheek, wiping her tears as they came. C.C.'s eyes remained vacant.

'It was—' began C.C. Shelly and Meg both held her, waiting. C.C. closed her eyes. She breathed, shuddery and ineffective. She opened her eyes, but stared straight ahead. When she finally spoke, her voice was quiet, level. 'It . . . was . . . the doctor. It appears I have ovarian cancer.' She closed her eyes again, shook her head slowly side to side.

Shelly couldn't help the gasp that came out of her. Meg let out a small cry. 'They want to do more tests,' said C.C. 'Tomorrow. I'm supposed to go to a clinic in Nashville. But the doctor says he's pretty sure. They just need to find out how bad.'

'*Shit*,' Shelly whispered, before she even knew the word was on her lips.

'Oh, Ceece,' said Meg, sounding like a small piece of her was drifting away. 'No.'

Shelly was aware of movement in the hall. Azaad had appeared again, but he was standing to the side, barely visible. He didn't enter. Shelly watched as he bent, his hands lowering Dollop to the ground. Dollop trotted into the room, crawled up on Meg's lap. But he didn't curl up, he simply stood there, seeming to know that something was very wrong. Shelly carefully reached over and lifted the phone off C.C.'s lap. Meg lifted Dollop into its place. C.C. folded down, her arms around Dollop, and began to cry, big keening sobs, while Shelly and Meg held her from either side, like book ends.

The next morning Shelly got up before anyone, at six a.m. Meg would be driving C.C. to Nashville; they had to be at the clinic at eight a.m. The plan they'd made the night before was to rise at six thirty and leave the house by seven. But Shelly wanted to have breakfast ready by the time they came downstairs. She'd set her alarm, tiptoed downstairs, and made flapjacks, from a box. But none of them could eat a single one. So Shelly had poured some orange juice into a Thermos, threw a couple of granola bars and bananas into a bag, and hugged them each goodbye, smiling, assuring both those worry-warts that it would be okay. It would. She'd stood on the porch waving confidently till the dust had settled at the far end of Raven Road. Then, crumpling onto the steps of the porch, she allowed herself to cry again.

She didn't know how long she sat there. She rose like a zombie, wandering aimlessly around the house. Dollop followed her for a while, crying for Meg, or maybe for all of them. Finally, he went back to his bed, the old couch pillow in the kitchen. Shelly walked from room to room, not even really seeing, just touching things, random things. Until she walked into the dining room. There, on the table by the window, neatly tucked between the phone and a small lamp, she saw the mail from yesterday. She reached for the letters. Slowly, she sorted them. There were two bills on top, a couple of pieces of junk mail, then C.C.'s two letters, one from Purdy, one from Lucy. Oh God. How would they tell them? Kathryn? She threw the letters at the table, and ran from the room, crying again.

She stopped at the front door only long enough to shove her feet quickly into a pair of Georgie's hard rubber gardening clogs. Then she burst out the door, ran across the porch, down the steps. She ran down the front path, the big shoes catching slightly on the lumpy grass veins. She slammed her fist into the mailbox as she passed, denting it slightly, welcoming the pain in her hand. She turned left, onto Raven Road, running toward – she didn't know what. The end of the road. The only way they could drive or walk or run from Dogs' Wood. The sweat was already dripping down her sides. She remembered the day she'd met Richter out here, so short, yet so long ago. How he'd scared the bejeezers out of her, then turned out to be her friend. As she ran past Hatch's house, she brushed her tears away, glanced over her shoulder, hoping Richter might be following her, as he often did when she passed by. But he was nowhere in sight. Already, a stitch burned in her side. She grabbed at it, but kept running. Past the house that had had the pretty bulbs when they'd first arrived. All gone now, replaced by petunias of every color. She ran past without looking. She didn't want to see anything pretty, nothing that trumpeted life. Halfway down the road she could hardly breathe, she was just lifting her legs and putting them down as fast as she could. Finally, she reached the end, where Raven met County Road Twenty. She leaned over, put her hands on her knees, trying to catch her breath. Some saliva hung from her lips, a hard, metallic taste in her mouth, like blood. She spat, wiped her mouth on the back of her wrist, angry at the saliva, angry at the taste, angry at her inability to carry herself as fast or as far as she needed. She righted herself, started running again. She ran diagonally across CR-20, no idea where she was going, not caring. There were no cars, no people. As she had complained many times, they were miles from anything out here, miles from civilization. Miles from home.

Home. Cancer had found C.C. at her childhood home, as if it had been waiting here for her. C.C. had lost too much already in her life. Shelly lengthened her stride in order to step hard on a crumpled 7-Eleven cup on the side of the road. She ran past the big barn, past the little chapel, past the falling-down house. Her legs felt spent, undependable, but she forced herself on, the physical pain only just beginning to do its work of nudging out the emotional pain. She felt palsied; and though she tried not to think about it, she remembered seeing the end of a marathon on TV where, at the very end, a lone woman crossed the finish line on will alone, her body long since given out. Just before the finish line, she buckled, like she was nothing more than the clothes she was wearing. She crawled across, losing control of every bodily function. At the time, watching, it had both mystified and horrified Shelly that anyone would push beyond their limits that way. Now she found herself actually aiming for that level of physical pain. Maybe then, her body numb and useless, her mind and heart would also release their grip.

Maybe it was the image of that woman that caused her to turn her toe in. Or maybe the image was a warning that her legs could not, should not, be trusted any longer. Later, she would only remember that right after she thought of that woman, she felt the toe of her right shoe catch on the heel of her left. If she hadn't been wearing those clunky rubber clogs, if she hadn't been so tired, her muscles so exhausted and quivery, she might have caught herself, merely stumbled. But it was all she could do to stretch her hand out before she hit the asphalt.

She first felt the burn on her wrist, the skin scraping off, then the scouring of the tender underside of her forearm. Then her knee hit, then almost simultaneously, her upper body smashed against her arm, as the ground flew up into her. She heard the snap of bone, felt the screaming pain, as if the stitch in her side had slid into her arm and exploded. She didn't even feel the skin on her knee break open. She turned her head, just before her face hit, small stones grinding into her cheek, dirt into her eye. Then, nothing.

A dog. Barking in the distance. Richter? She lay motionless, willed him to find her. The wind had been knocked out of her. She was trying to breathe, get some oxygen; she couldn't call out for him. But she needed help. *Help. Richter.* She could only think the words, still gulping ineffectually for air. Pain rippled out from her arm trapped under her, a concentric throbbing, spreading into her ribs, then outward across her entire body. As she came to fully, finally sucking in ragged breaths, there wasn't anything that didn't hurt. Then she thought of C.C., and moaned.

Suddenly there was a touch, very gentle. Someone's hand on her shoulder. A voice, low, deep, resonant. ''S okay, ma'am. I gots you. I gots you.' A pause. 'Ma'am?'

She raised her head, saw him, but it hurt and she lowered her head, turning, resting her other cheek back on the road. He put his face near hers, his hand still lightly on her shoulder, and she stared at him, his black skin with large pores, his wiry gray hair, like a cap on his head, the whites of his eyes, bloodshot and slightly yellow. His teeth were also yellow, one front one chipped on an angle.

'Y'all took a bad spill, ma'am. Mebee you ought just stay put. I'll call for hep.' She blinked. He was blurry. *Hep.* She wasn't sure she understood him, his accent, his chopped speech.

'My arm,' she said, her voice sounding distant and separate from her. 'I think it's broken.'

'I best call for an ambew-lance,' he said, straightening.

'No!' Shelly said, her head clearing with the surge of adrenalin. 'I don't have . . . insurance. I can't . . .' She started to cry, like a child. 'I can't . . . afford . . . an ambulance.' She let the tears come.

He stared at her, his gray eyebrows up, then down. ''S okay, ma'am. Don' chu worry, now. Old Bix's here. He take ker you.' She wondered if Bix was the dog she'd heard barking, how a dog was going to take care of her. As well as anything, she decided. 'Kin you walk, ma'am?'

Shelly took a quick mental inventory. 'I think so.' Her head hurt nearly as much as her arm. But, except for a burning sensation on her knee, her legs seemed okay.

He helped her up, careful to hold only her left arm. Still, she winced with nearly every movement. 'You okay, ma'am?' he asked her several times.

They were standing, but Shelly was waiting for things to stop spinning. Finally, they did.

He asked again. 'Ma'am? Kin you walk?'

She opened her eyes. 'Yes. I'm okay. I can walk now.'

He was staring at her feet. 'Uh, ma'am? Y'all have *two* shoes? Prior?'

She looked down. She saw only the left green gardening clog on her foot. Her right foot was bare. She looked around.

'Ah! Yonder,' said the man, pointing behind her several feet. The shoe lay in the grass, on the side of the road. 'It got isself flung good as you!' Shelly almost smiled, but tasted the blood in her mouth. She swallowed, not trusting herself to be able to spit with her banged-up mouth. She looked down, saw her ruined tank top, smears of dirt and blood on it.

When they reached her shoe, he bent, keeping his arm outstretched, maintaining his touch on her. As if that small touch would prevent her from toppling over. But it did.

'Here y'be,' he said, squatting in front of her like a parent helping a toddler, one arm still up, fingers on her good elbow, the other holding her shoe. She slipped her foot in. He was a dear man.

'I live just there, behind the chapel. I takes care the grounds. Kin you make it back there? Or do you want to sit a spell, in the chapel? Be dark and cool in there, but ain't nothin' to clean you up with. I gots peroxide back the house.'

Shelly stared at him, his words marching into her brain as if they were animated but sluggish creatures, crawling one by one, sometimes one over another, her brain lifting them, deciding where they belonged, then slowly putting them together. She did not want to sit in any sort of house of God. 'Your house. If you don't mind.'

'Not t'all,' he said. "Bout ready to break for a glassa anyways. I'm Bix. I won't bother you by shakin' yo hand. Bixby Fordham. But ever'one jes calls me Bix.'

'Shelly Kostens,' she said, concentrating on her steps as they made their way across the manicured lawn. She cradled her right arm in her left hand, watching the ground ahead. She walked like a soldier would walk, knowing there were land-mines. Somewhere. Everywhere.

She blinked, focused, refocused. It was surreal. It was beautiful. All across the grounds were little islands of flowers, some with rocks, some with statuary. It seemed every tree they passed was a different kind, each with a small marker at its base. Although churches of all kinds, even the grounds, had always unnerved Shelly, this shady, cool park-like garden felt like a sanctuary.

She sat in Bix's small house at a half-round wooden table, chipped and dented but looking fairly recently painted white. It was pushed up against the wall, under a small clean window with no curtain. A jar of flowers on the table. He helped her into a chair.

'You okay?' She nodded. He scurried off to a back room. She stared at the bouquet. A bell jar, looking impossibly clean, the water impossibly clear. The flowers were slightly wild-looking, several different varieties and colors, but their stems had been carefully placed in the jar so that their colorful heads arched in a graceful mound above.

The man returned with a folded towel, a box of tissues, a brown bottle of peroxide.

'Z'er someone I kin call, ma'am? Mebee your husband?' he asked her, gently dabbing peroxide on her cheek. She couldn't respond, to his words or the sting on her cheek. She wasn't sure why. She just kept looking at that water. 'I kin clean your face up a bit, but you gots to see a doctor at some point, ma'am. You gots dirt in yo cheek, heeah. You gots to git that arm set. And I caint drive, or I would. Kin I call friends? You gots family heah?'

She stared at him, then shook her head. There was no one to call. No one in the world. No family. No husband. Not C.C., not Meg. Azaad couldn't help her, with just his bicycle.

She shook her head miserably.

Bix finished dabbing at her cheek. He put the folded towel on the table in front of her. Shelly carefully set her arm on it, crying out. She could see it was misshapen, a small, pointed bulge pressed her skin out mid-way between her wrist and her elbow. The pain was intense, hot, especially when she'd lifted it to set it on the towel.

But the longer she sat still, completely still, the

more the pain slowly ebbed. Bix left to dispose of the bloody tissues. Shelly closed her eyes and barely breathed. She sat more still than maybe she ever had in her life. She felt suddenly, oddly calm in this small, tidy house with its hopeful jar of flowers on the table. Without moving, she dropped her eyes to her arm, to the bulge, thinking about all that was broken. Dazed still, she looked up again, at the dome of colorful flowers, the water in the jar, the green stems at criss-cross angles, magnified, leaning against one another. It looked hodgepodge from below, but nearly every stem seemed to be supporting a neighboring stem, and its flower above at its perfect angle.

'Call Jack Hatch,' she said quietly when Bix returned. 'He's our neighbor, on Raven Road. But I don't know his number.'

'Eh, if'n I fetch you the book, kin you find the number, ma'am? I know it hurts for yeh t'move, but, if you kin just search out the number, read it 'loud t'me, I kin dial. I, I . . .' He turned his head slightly, like a dog that had done something wrong, or thought it had.

'Sure,' she said. 'I can look it up.' He stepped away and quickly returned with a phone book and a cordless phone. He set both on the table in front of her arm. She looked at his face, his kind, smiling face. She supposed he couldn't read. Maybe he knew the numbers zero through nine, enough to dial the phone, but not letters. She opened the phone book to the Hs. Then she didn't know whether to laugh or cry. She couldn't read the small print of the phone book. Not even close. Without her reading glasses, she was just as illiterate as he was. But worse, even without looking, she suspected that Hatch would have an unlisted number. Of course he would. It was only because of them that he had a connected phone line at all. But maybe he was listed under another name. Hell, maybe Jack Hatch was just his pen name. She had had a client in New York, a well-known film director, who had listed himself as Stewart Garcia in the phone book, an homage to his two favorite musicians. His friends knew to look him up under that name. But what would Hatch use? One of his book characters? She couldn't possibly remember them all. Besides, that would be too straightforward for Jack Hatch. He was far too conniving for that.

Shelly sighed, looked up at dear Bix, wondering how to break it to him that he was going to have to take a long walk down Raven Road, to Hatch's house, if he wanted to help her.

Dear Bix.

Dear. Alias. Dear. Deere. John Deere.

'Bix? Do you have anything like a magnifying glass?' she asked. He nodded, stepped away again. She licked her finger, awkwardly using her left hand, flipping the pages of the phone book backwards. She got to the Ds as Bix returned. He handed her an old, round magnifying glass with a thick, beveled black handle. Jet or maybe obsidian, Shelly thought.

'It was my daddy's,' said Bix. 'To study seeds, roots, tree rings, and the like. Y'all want some sweet tea?' He took a tentative step toward the tiny kitchen, looking at her hopefully. She nodded, said thank you. As he stepped away, she quickly ran the magnifying glass over the page, scanning names. *Deeb. Deemer. Deen, Deep. Deere!* There were two Deeres. But neither one on Raven Road. She blew out a frustrated breath. But John Deere was his alias! He'd told her! The mower, that's what he'd said. 'Meet my alias.'

'Ohhh, you sneaky bastard,' she said under her breath, suddenly moving the magnifying glass to the left-hand page. That would be so like that man, to have an alias of an alias! She ran the glass over the columns of names. *Deal, Dean . . .*

Bix returned and set two glasses of tea on the table, and sat down. Shelly didn't look up. *Deane, Deangells, Deany, Dear!* John Dear, 503 Raven Road.

'Gottcha!' said Shelly, pounding the phone book with her good fist, which immediately sent a shooting pain into her broken arm, making her flinch. 'Ow!' Bix laughed.

'Aint you had nuff of hurtin' yo'self, ma'am?'

Shelly smiled, nodded. Then, taking great care with her uncoordinated left hand, poked at the buttons of the phone as it lay on the table. She lifted it to her ear, closed her eyes, praying that Jack Hatch, a.k.a. John Dear, was not out pacing by his tent.

CHAPTER 37

PURDY

The black wall phone rang loudly, making Purdy jump in his chair. 'Damn,' he said, relieved to see that Mrs D'Blatt's bad ear was toward him. He had thought that his startle response was nearly gone. But his phone didn't often ring midday, so he chalked it up to that. The phone rang again. He excused himself from the table, patting the old woman's hand to get her attention. Mrs D'Blatt was having a good day. She'd been regaling the regulars with stories from her self-proclaimed 'sidewinder youth'.

'Have to go answer the phone,' Purdy nearly shouted to her. She nodded, said, 'Shoo!' Purdy smiled, turned and strode toward the bar. He slipped his hand into the pocket of his apron, touching the most recent letter from C.C.

He felt downright jaunty as he walked across the restaurant. The letter in his pocket was the twenty-first he'd received from C.C. It was nearly a week and a half old, no doubt due to a lag in the mail delivery. Sometimes he wouldn't get a letter from her for several days, then he'd get three or four on one day. But this letter was maybe the most treasured of all of them; it contained what he'd been hoping for for so long: an invitation. C.C. had asked him to come down for the Fourth of July, for a long weekend. As she said in the letter, 'It's still a ways off,' but she'd wanted to give him time to think about it, knew he'd have to make lots of arrangements for his businesses and his bees, *if* he decided to come. As if he needed to think about it! But she was right; he did need to make arrangements. He'd bunched up every task and delivery he could think of in the coming weeks, to free up that weekend. Before he left he would make a week's worth of soup for Mrs D'Blatt, and let everyone else know that the restaurant would be closed. Mick would look after his bees.

Mick. Purdy smiled as he stepped behind the bar. As soon as he had read C.C.'s invitation, Purdy had run across the street to tell his son. But Mick had his own news. He had met a lady of his own, from Chicago, on one of those online things. Father and son had chatted like a couple of boys about their girlfriends! Purdy had also told Mrs D'Blatt about C.C., several times, but having never met her, the old woman kept forgetting who C.C. was. And Purdy had to admit, it was a little hard to explain, this woman he was in love with, and was becoming more and more sure she loved him back, their entire courtship having taken place through letters.

The phone rang again and he stopped in his tracks, just as he reached the bar.

It suddenly occurred to him that it might be C.C. calling, that maybe she'd finally given up her prohibition about phones, wanted to talk to him 'live' before they made plans to visit in person. Of course! That's why she hadn't written for a while. He was suddenly paralyzed. What would he say? Did they *really* know each other? He and Keppie had exchanged letters, but when he came back and they got married so quickly, he found he really didn't know her.

With the phone ringing a fourth time, he did his breathing exercises, tapped his elbows, then let his hand dip back into his pocket. He pulled the letter out, saw the familiar loopy hand-writing, touched the sharp corner of the envelope, then the stamp. A ribbon of calm ran through him. Oh, he knew C.C. so much better than that, maybe even better than he had *ever* known Keppie, rest her soul. He knew Ms Caroline Camilla Tucker Prentiss Byrd as well as he knew himself. She'd poured herself and her life out into those letters, as he had. He tucked the letter back into the pocket. The phone rang again, sounding more insistent, though he knew that was just him. His hand was nearly upon the black receiver, and suddenly he was sure of it. It was her.

'Hello!' he said, his heart pounding, sweat on his brow, but trying valiantly to sound jovial.

'Is this, uh, Purdy?' It was a man's voice. 'Shit. I don't know your first name. Shelly only told me that everyone called you by your last name.'

Purdy shook his head. 'Excuse me? This is Purdy. Mick Purdy, Senior. Who is this?'

'Hatch.'

Purdy's mind scrambled to make sense of that single word, and the fact that he'd said 'Shelly'. It had to be C.C.'s Shelly. Hatch, *Hatch* . . . It was familiar, but . . . 'I'm sorry, do I know you?' he asked.

A pause, then the man's voice, not gruff exactly, but . . . 'No. I'm the neighbor. I live next door to Georgie's old house, now C.C.'s—'

'Oh, right! Down there in Tennessee.' Purdy's frown of concentration relaxed into a grin again, remembering now. C.C. had mentioned Hatch in several letters. He was the writer who had burst in when the gals broke that water pipe. He chuckled, just remembering how C.C. had written about it.

Purdy stopped smiling. Why would C.C.'s neighbor be calling? His insides squeezed, the ribbon of calm gone.

'Is everything okay?' Purdy turned his back to the restaurant, leaned on the wall near the phone. He put his finger in his open ear and repeated himself. 'Is everything okay?'

'Oh, well . . . Man. Shit. I wish it was.'

Purdy sat on the stool. 'Tell me.' He took his finger from his ear; it only amplified the echoy pounding of his pulse.

'I – I'm. Look, I don't know how to say it, but things aren't so good down here. For the ladies. Especially C.C.'

Purdy tried to swallow before speaking, but a whole world was in his throat. 'C.C.?' he asked finally.

'Look, I'm sorry, man. I guess the best way is just to come out with it: she's got cancer. I think it might be bad.'

Purdy heard the blades. Chopper blades. The same roar, the same thundering of the ground beneath him, shaking him. 'Cancer?'

'Yeah, a, uh – a ladies' cancer.' The engines of trucks, then the loud, staccato popping of automatic weapons. He looked up, breathless, terrified. It was just a delivery truck, idling outside; Joe Spurn's footsteps, walking across the tile floor to the restroom. He closed his eyes, held the phone between his ear and shoulder, tapped his elbows with his fingers again.

'Ladies' cancer?' he repeated to Hatch.

'Yeah. Meg went with her to Nashville yesterday, and then Shelly went running off like a fool, and she broke her arm. Messed herself up pretty good. And the poor Indian kid, or whatever the hell he is, he just has a bicycle and a hammer and doesn't know what the hell to do, so he's just hammering on that house day and night. Except for when he's outside, doing some kind hoojywoojy dance, or meditating or whatever the hell he does . . . What? Yoyo? Yogurt? Oh, Shelly says it's yoga. Anyway,

470

I've got Shelly staying over here with me, and the little dog, but I think C.C. could use your support. And Shelly said C.C. has a daughter up north. I'm supposed to call her next. Oh, and . . . a *what*? Hang on, Purdy. A gray grogger? What the hell is a gray grogger? *Granddaughter?* Are you saying granddaughter?'

Purdy waited, impatience flaming inside him.

'Shelly says a granddaughter, too. But I'm not sure about that. Doesn't seem like C.C.'s old enough to have a granddaughter. Shelly's had some dental work done so she's hard to understand. That, and she's also on painkillers so she's a little dopey. Ow! I didn't mean it like that. Just read your damn magazine! Let me talk to the man, would you?'

Purdy's head was spinning. *Of course* C.C. has a daughter! And a granddaughter! In Wisataukee. Kathryn and Lucy. He had never met them, but he felt he knew them. He knew them.

'I'm coming down,' said Purdy. 'I'll . . . I'll leave today.' Awareness plunged down on him. All his preparations, the deliveries, the rescheduling. All coming up in the next couple of weeks so that he could be away on the Fourth. And Mick was gone this week, in Chicago. 'No, I'll need . . . I don't know, a few days anyway. To get things squared away here. I'll come as soon as I can.' He reached for a pen and pad. The tapping had helped. Having something to do helped. 'Where is she exactly? The clinic?'

'Now hold on,' said Hatch. 'Like I said, C.C.'s in Nashville, at the hospital there. But I've arranged for her to go to a specialty cancer clinic in Atlanta. Meg's going to drive her down in another day or two, stay in the family quarters there. But I think you should come here first. To the house. . . . *Oh, for Pete's sake, woman!* Hang on, Purdy. Shelly's writing on a pad now. Oh geeze. She has to write with her left hand and it's a mess. I think she wants me to ask you to call the girls, C.C.'s girls, her daughter. I guess she thinks it'd be better coming from you than me.'

'Yes, I'll call,' said Purdy, standing now, writing on a pad: 'Pack – ask Della to cover – have Mick check car.' Then, speaking as much to himself as to Hatch, Purdy said, 'I'll call Kathryn right now.'

'Hang on,' said Hatch again, irritation in his voice. 'Shelly's saying something *more*.' Purdy listened to muffled voices. He waited, repeatedly and impatiently pressing the heel of his hand into the side of the bar. 'She thinks she knows where C.C.'s address book is, over at the house. I can go over and look for that if you want. For Kathryn's number.'

'No!' said Purdy, more harshly than he'd meant. 'I'll just call information. If I have trouble, I'll call you back. What's your number?' Purdy nodded as he wrote down the number, then repeated back to Hatch, just to be certain. He was too agitated, too frightened, and didn't want to risk making a stupid mistake.

Hatch sighed dramatically. '*Christ, woman!* I can't very well have a phone conversation if you keep wanting to have it for me. *Now* what?' There was a pause nearly longer than Purdy could stand; he thought about hanging up, but he reminded himself that it was Shelly trying to talk to him, about C.C.

'She says the daughter's last name is Puhenis, Prenna, something like that. Wait, she's writing—'

'PRENTISS!' shouted Purdy. 'I *know* that. Thanks. I'm sorry.' He calmed himself. 'Thanks a lot, Hatch. I'll be in touch.'

'No problem. But, Purdy? I just want to say one more thing.'

Purdy felt like he might explode.

'C.C. didn't want you to know. You or Kathryn. About the cancer. She made Meg and Shelly promise not to call. But not me, and I'll take full responsibility. C.C's going to need all the support she can get. So take it easy, man. Driving down here. C.C. needs you here in one piece.'

Purdy only nodded before he hung up the phone. Hatch's brusque tone going soft suddenly, on top of everything else, had made it impossible for him to speak.

As he drove north, the highway seemed particularly dark and lonely at nearly four in the morning. Purdy thought about his phone call to Kathryn, thought about meeting her. He wondered what they would talk about on the long

473

drive south. The three of them were all connected by C.C., but sight unseen. He knew there was a rift between Kathryn and her mother. He suspected that was why C.C. didn't want them to know, either him or Kathryn: she didn't want fear bringing them to her. Purdy had mixed feelings. On the one hand, he didn't like going behind C.C.'s back like this; on the other, he couldn't imagine not seeing her, especially now. It wasn't just the illness bringing them to her. It was C.C. herself.

On the phone, Kathryn had sounded shocked, of course. But she hadn't cried, just gotten very quiet. Until she told him that her car didn't work, that she'd recently resigned from her job, and she hadn't found new work yet, and she needed to get her car fixed, and – then she'd wept. When she'd calmed down, he'd offered to drive up, come get her and Lucy, drive them all down, which had sent her into more sobbing. But finally she'd gotten control. She had thanked him profusely, and they'd agreed on the day and time. Wednesday, early morning. Kathryn said they'd be ready and waiting.

Purdy sighed, rubbing his palm over the leather steering wheel. He had been counting the days till he could drive down and visit C.C. How many times had he wished he could push the date up? But not like this. Not like this.

Everything felt backwards: he was rushing to the side of the woman he loved by heading in exactly the wrong direction. Backwards, yet somehow right. He was honored to be able to bring C.C.'s family to her now. As much as he wanted to be the one she most needed to see, he knew that wasn't the case.

A bus passed him going the other way, a few small reading lights inside revealed some of the sleeping, reading or just staring passengers.

Kathryn had offered to bus down to Tupper, or even Chicago, but he'd said that wouldn't be necessary. He didn't tell her, but he hated to think of her and little Lucy, so scared and worried about their mom and grandma, sitting on the bus, so alone among strangers. No, he'd insisted, he would come for them. He had left Tupper a little before three a.m., a small suitcase in the trunk of the old Audi, a car he would never have bought for himself. But when Mick got a deal on it, and replaced the engine, he'd bought it from him after driving it only once. It was a great highway car, very solid. Thick, dark leather seats. The big back seat would be great for little Lucy to sleep on. He looked at the two Thermoses he'd prepared, lying in the seat next to him, where Kathryn would soon be sitting. One of coffee, strong and hot, for the adults. One of apple juice, chilled, for the little girl.

Purdy tried to take a deep breath, but he was too nervous, too frightened. He had *so* looked forward to meeting them, but not like this. Not like this.

The lights got his attention before the siren. He caught the blue and red in his rear-view mirror. He instinctively lifted his foot off the accelerator, checked his speed. As it gained on him, he heard the siren. Closer, louder. His heart was racing; he'd felt the shot of adrenalin right away. He braked, too quickly and his seat belt locked against his chest as the car lurched. He pulled over, skidding slightly as he came to a stop. It was dark, there were no streetlights. He felt out of control, too many sounds. He thought of C.C. Of Kathryn and Lucy. Slowly, he unclenched his hands from the steering wheel, began tapping his elbows, calming his breathing. The ambulance blew by in a rush of speed, light and sound. Then, deathly quiet. He turned on the radio, a DJ announcing the station, then *Fairfield's Favorite Oldies*. Then the song started. *The Beatles? A golden oldie?* It didn't seem right. He hummed quietly with the music as he waited for the one set of car headlights coming up the dark road behind him to pass, then he pulled forward, and accelerated up to highway speed again. Let it be. Indeed.

The apartment complex was small, old, forgotten. Several small, old, forgotten cars were scattered across the parking lot, which was not twenty yards from train tracks. He walked up the steps, found number 219, and knocked lightly. He waited, then rapped again. The door opened and there . . . was

C.C., only younger, thinner. It took his breath away. They stared at each other. Finally, she spoke, very quietly. It was still very early.

'Mr Purdy?' He could see tears forming in her eyes.

'Just Purdy.' He held out his hand. 'So pleased to meet you. I just wish the circumstances were different.' Kathryn bit her lip, nodded, shaking his hand. She stepped to the side and he saw Lucy, just before the little girl stepped back behind her mother's leg. 'This is Lucy,' said Kathryn. Lucy shyly peeked out again, and he gave her a little wave, not wanting to scare her. When he looked back at Kathryn, she was crying. He didn't know what to do. What would Lenny have done? If only he were here, instead of him. But Lenny wasn't here.

'I'm here, honey,' Purdy said softly. She fell into him and he put his arms around her, patted her back. 'I've got you.' And as soon as he said it, he realized she had him, too.

After a minute, she slowly pulled away, wiping her tears on her sleeve, giving him a weak smile. 'I can't begin to thank you enough, for coming to get us, taking us down.'

'Not at all, not at all.'

'We're ready. This is it.' She pointed to two suitcases, one a largish gray, and a smaller pink, wheeled one, with Hello Kitty on it. Purdy nodded. 'Oh, and the things from the kitchen. I'll be right back,' said Kathryn. She disappeared, and he stood there, not sure if he should take their cases to the car, or wait. Lucy had stayed where she was, staring at him, her face mostly hidden behind her blue teddy bear, so he waited. Kathryn returned with a large Thermos, and a full, canvas grocery bag. 'Coffee, and food for the road, for all of us. So we don't have to stop.'

'That's nice of you. Thank you,' said Purdy, nodding. They were still talking in that quiet, careful way people do in the very early morning, when events have pressed in on the normal boundaries of time and space and all that is routine. He was glad she'd packed food, couldn't believe he hadn't. He had only brought a fried egg sandwich, which had been his breakfast on the road, eaten as he crossed the border into Iowa.

They loaded up the car, then Kathryn tucked Lucy into the back seat with her blanket, a big pillow, and the blue teddy bear. 'The Dramamine is going to make us both sleepy, okay, honey? So just try to sleep as much as you can.' She was little more than whispering. 'But let me know right away if you feel sick.' Purdy blinked, but said nothing. Kathryn buckled the little girl's seat belt, kissed her, then climbed in front, buckled herself in.

'Ready, then?' he asked quietly, glancing at one, then the other. It was after six now, and a few people had emerged to collect a paper, or walk a dog. But the world still felt unoccupied. Hushed and fragile, like something that needed to be held very, very carefully.

Kathryn took a deep breath, then nodded. Purdy started the engine, drove out of the parking lot, and headed south.

CHAPTER 38

MEG

Meg sat in the coffee shop across the street from the clinic, drawing lines down her Styrofoam cup with her thumbnail. Numbers and phrases from doctors, brochures, the internet swarmed like angry insects, taking turns dive-bombing her. '*Her CA-125 levels are . . . We suspect Stage 2 but . . . The ultrasound indicates several tumors . . . Family history of cancer . . . Ovarian cancer . . . silent killer.*'

Meg ran her hand through her hair. It was oily, her clothes wrinkled. She was exhausted. Everything had happened so fast. It felt like one minute she had been standing at the kitchen sink at Dogs' Wood, playing with lentils, and the next she was driving C.C. to Nashville, then Atlanta. Both trips had been as silent and full of fear and portent as when she had driven C.C. home from the hospital after Len died; or when she'd driven her to and from his funeral; or when C.C. had sat next to her as Meg had driven aimlessly for miles, after she'd realized that Grant had left her. Not like their trip down to Tennessee, which was supposed to be their escape, their new beginning. And it had been. Till now.

Meg took a small sip of the coffee, made a face. It was awful. She looked out the window at the empty street, the sky grayish pink in the new morning light. Dawn and dusk seemed to be the waiting hours. She swallowed another cold, bitter gulp of her coffee, then shoved the cup to the middle of her table so she wouldn't mindlessly sip any more of it. She didn't even drink coffee. She didn't know why she'd ordered it.

She glanced at her watch. The rounds would start in about an hour, and C.C. had asked her to be there. She was almost two weeks post-op, and three days into the chemo. She hadn't wanted to discuss any other options. So, the day after they'd arrived, she'd had surgery. Then started chemo as soon as possible. She questioned nothing, complied with everything. She was immobilized far more by her fear than her surgery.

Meg closed her eyes. She wished she knew how to be strong for her. While it was true that C.C. demurred to most people, with a grin or a laugh – or worse, an apology – it wasn't like she, Meg, was any pillar of strength. Especially after Grant left her. She would have been just as immobilized, sitting alone in her empty house, had it not been for her friends. Maybe Shelly should have driven C.C. to Atlanta instead. Shelly was tough. But no, Shelly was no good with drama like this. As evidenced by her actions the day she and C.C. had left for Nashville. Meg shook her head. Oh, Shelly. A broken arm. Stitches inside her mouth.

She'd literally had to make her inner pain a physical pain. Thank God for Hatch.

Meg wished she could talk to Shelly, but when she'd tried, from the payphone at the clinic, Shelly was mostly unintelligible. Meg had just cried when Hatch took the phone, so they'd hung up. C.C. didn't know; Meg wasn't going to tell her.

She clasped the cup of coffee again, wrapped her hands around it, hoping for warmth that was no longer there. She closed her eyes, her head dropping, fatigue and worry weighing her down. She sat like that for several minutes, her mind mostly blank. She did briefly wonder if the older, unshaven man in the dirty sport coat sitting three empty booths away from her might think that she was praying. She almost felt a need to correct him, just in case he had that mistaken impression. But she didn't think she could lift her head up now, much less her body. Instead, she used what little energy she had to think of C.C., send love and strength from every fiber of her being, like two small birds, flying out of the coffee shop, across the street, and up into room 441 of the Gynecological Wing of the Levey-Penning Cancer Care Center. And as she did, it occurred to her that that might be a prayer of some sort after all.

Meg stood at the door to C.C.'s room. Her hand on the big silver knob, she stopped herself, double-checked the number, 441, then the card next to it: 'C. Byrd, fem., age 49'. The halls in the hospital had all begun to look alike, the doors in the halls also identical. She had even mistaken nurse Judy for nurse Terry. Stupid, really. Judy had brown hair, Terry, red. But they both wore blue scrubs, both were about the same height, both pleasant, competent. Though Judy was a bit less friendly, and noisier. She pulled the sheets with a snap, closed the sliding cabinet under C.C.'s bed with a bang. Mary seemed to be perpetually smiling, her green eyes sparkling. She had a gentle touch and, without fail, before she left the room, she always asked C.C., 'Now, anything else I can do for you, Ms Byrd?'

Meg squared her shoulders, took a deep breath, put on her smile, not too big, not overly cheery, just right.

C.C. was sitting up against several pillows, the sheet and thin blanket rumpled around her hips. She had her black reading glasses on, some sort of booklet or newsprint magazine in her hands, which she let fall on her legs as Meg entered. She smiled, peering over her black half-frames, her hair sticking out every which way from her little pony-tail, her roots showing. It was all Meg could do not to burst into tears.

'How's my girl?' Meg said, chipper as a bird, breaking her own rule of evenness and restraint. C.C. would see right through it, see it for the worry it was. 'What can I get you? Another pillow?' The questions came out too rapid-fire, she knew, with too much enthusiasm. But it was either that or tears, so there it was. She strode over to C.C.'s bedside, gave her arm a gentle squeeze, then lifted the mostly empty glass of ginger ale on the bed table. 'Something else to drink?'

'Oh, stop fussin' over me, Meg! I declare, you're like a momma hen!'

Meg smiled, tugged C.C.'s covers up under her arms, folded the top sheet, smoothed her hand over the fold, all the while softly clucking. C.C. laughed, first swatting at her, then grabbing and kissing her hand.

'Whatcha got there?' Meg asked, nodding to the book.

C.C. lifted it, showing her, but also seeming to study it curiously herself, as if she wasn't quite sure. 'Crosswords,' she said, almost questioningly. 'I don't know why. Terry brought it when I finished that novel. But I'm terrible at these.' She jerked the booklet upward, then smiled. 'But you're the crossword queen. Wanna help me?'

Meg nodded, pulled her own glasses out of her purse. C.C. scooted over, patted the side of the bed and Meg sat, sliding her glasses on. She put her finger on the page and read aloud: 'Seven across: Late night icon. Six letters.'

'O'Brien?' asked C.C.

Meg stared at her. 'He's hardly an icon.' Was C.C. really that much younger than she was? Could six years make that big a difference in their cultural knowledge?

'Carson!' said C.C. Meg smiled.

They worked on the puzzle for a while, till Meg noticed C.C.'s eyelids drifting down. 'You want to rest for a bit?' she asked her. 'Before the doc gets here?' C.C. didn't answer, simply slid down, pulling a pillow with her, tucking it under her head. Meg carefully pulled C.C.'s glasses off, folding them. She set them on the bedside table, then put her own next to them. She eased the extra pillows out from behind her head, so C.C.'s neck wouldn't be bent at that odd angle. She clicked off the light, then pulled the sheet and blanket up to C.C.'s shoulders, smoothed the fold again. She stood over C.C., for several long minutes, just her fingertips resting on her sleeping friend's shoulder.

Finally, Meg moved across the room, closed the blinds slowly, quietly. Then she sat, upright, on the edge of the blue upholstered chair in the corner. She stared at the silhouette of her hands, nested in her lap in the darkened room. She mind-lessly stroked her fingers. After a few minutes, she realized she was feeling for the band of indented skin on her left ring finger. It wasn't there. She inhaled deeply, clasped her hands together and kept them motionless. Even in the dark, she knew that the faint band of white skin that had persisted there for so long was gone now too.

CHAPTER 39

SHELLY

'Okay, now it says to fold the flour into the wet mixture,' said Shelly. She had to keep her head down, not look at him in that frilly apron, or she'd burst out in painful laughter again.

'Oh, of all the fool— How the hell do I do that? How in God's name would a person *fold* flour? Next you're going to tell me to iron the sugar.'

That did it. Shelly was laughing again, her head resting on the cookbook. At least this time she hadn't almost fallen off the stool. Hatch was entirely too entertaining, though in certain ways he might not be intending. As if the sight of him in what was clearly a woman's apron wasn't enough, he now had flour on his eyebrow and chin, not to mention pretty much the entirety of his kitchen. And, his endless complaining was getting more and more creative, and amusing. She was just glad the stitches in her mouth had dissolved.

'Ohhh,' Shelly moaned. She adjusted herself on the seat of the stool at the long green marble bar that divided the kitchen from his huge living room.

She sat up, repositioned her casted arm on the counter. 'Hatch, you gotta stop. You're killin' me here.' She looked at him as sternly as she could, with not very much success. His mouth was open, his eyebrows raised innocently. He pointed the handle-end of the wooden spoon at himself, then at her, back and forth, a silent, accusatory, '*I'm killin' you?*'

'Listen, honey, this was your lame-brained idea, to bake.' He changed his voice to a falsetto: '*Please, Hatch! Please help me bake a cake.*' He was curt-sying with his apron in one hand, the bowl of flour still in his other arm, batting his eyes at her. Shelly felt the pain in her rib cage before the laugh even came out. '*No! I mean TWO cakes,*' he continued in his high-pitched voice. '*One for C.C., and one for the gardener who saved my fool ass when I tried to run away from home.*'

'Stop!' she gasped. Hatch, obviously barely containing his own smile, was looking at her over the tops of his reading glasses. Even though about the only thing she could do to participate in the 'baking' was to read the recipe, he still insisted on checking nearly every part she read to him, trot-ting around the bar and leaning in next to her, or over her shoulder. Each time he did, she could smell his aftershave, feel his breath on her hair.

'Okay!' said Shelly. 'Okay. Seriously, now. Be good. Did you get all the eggshell out of the egg mixture?'

Hatch stared into the smaller bowl on the

counter, moved the whisk that was in it slowly around. 'No eggshells in there.' He looked up at her, over his glasses again. 'Should I put some more in?'

Shelly looked around for something to throw at him. There was a dishtowel near her so she grabbed that, balled it up, and awkwardly threw it at him, left-handed. He easily sidestepped the slow-moving missile.

She was nearly bursting with joy. This was unabashed flirting, but innocent, like she hadn't done since . . . ever. There was an easiness to this. It felt lighthearted and completely free of expectation. They were neighbors. Maybe even friends. No doubt she was already indebted to this goofy, odd man. Not just for her, but for what he had done for C.C. That had been incredibly generous.

She had been a complete mess when he'd come for her at Bix's house. Climbed into his Volvo, sobbing. Sobbed the entire way to the hospital. Again when he'd given his name as the person financially responsible for her bill. And much of the drive home. His home. He had settled her on his huge sectional in his living room with a cup of lumpy powdered cocoa. (Cocoa! in June! He must have thought it the most comforting thing, since she couldn't have alcohol with her pain medication.) Then he had run upstairs, actually running, to fix up a room, grunting every other step. She'd been afraid he'd have a heart attack. He had fussed up there for twenty minutes. She'd dozed on the couch, once or twice pulled from her drugged state by a loud thud, clatter, or string of curses coming from upstairs. Finally, he'd reappeared, perspiration shining on his wide, tanned forehead. He offered her his arm to help her off the couch, then up the stairs, one at a time. He got her settled in one of his many guest rooms, complete with hot-water bottle, ice bag, TV, books, magazines and a little bell. Then he'd gone downstairs again to fix her some dinner, which he brought up on a tray. Canned tomato soup and a little one-serving plastic tub of butterscotch pudding. She had three stitches in her mouth and was really not interested in eating, but she had one spoon of both soup and pudding, and thanked him. For the food, the bed, the care. The bill. She said she'd pay him back, every cent. Then she started crying again. It was like every tear she'd held in for years had broken through some dam. It was awful. But Hatch had been great. Although he'd looked as embarrassed as she felt, he'd just sat there, patting her good hand.

She looked at him now, wielding the wooden spoon like a scepter, peering at her over his glasses, taking small predatory steps toward her. She felt that fluttery giddiness of being playfully stalked. She glanced around, looking for something else to pitch at him. She knew it was juvenile. Knew it was what girls did when they were young, and that they did it because they wanted to kiss, and be kissed, but were in no way ready for that. So they threw things at the boys they liked. She, Shelly Kostens, not ready for a kiss. But she wasn't. Not at all. She had a brief thought that what worked in fifth grade should not necessarily be used in one's fifties, but, feeling trapped by inaction, she looked left and right, almost panicked with the need to hurl something. There was a jar of pens at the end of the counter, but they were out of reach. She looked at the cookbook in front of her, but decided that would be too heavy: she couldn't lift it with one arm. She almost laughed out loud that her first thought was that it would be too heavy for her, never mind that it might knock him silly. She screamed. He had rounded the end of the bar and he had her locked in his predatory gaze. There was nothing within reach to throw! As a desperate last resort, she threw something heavier than the cookbook. With her uncoordinated but uninjured left hand, she threw him a kiss.

He stopped. He just stared at her, for too long. She immediately regretted what she'd done. She dropped her gaze to the book, pretending to use her finger to find her place, and felt as trapped by her action as she had by her inaction.

'Backatcha,' he said finally. Shelly wouldn't look up, but her heart felt like a small, wadded-up piece of paper, making small quivering movements as tiny parts opened on their own.

'Now do something useful and look up "fold" in that damn book,' he said, rounding the corner, returning to the kitchen.

She thumbed through the pages. 'If Meg were here, I bet she'd know how to fold flour. Maybe even C.C.' That stopped her again. Just mentioning her name was enough to sober the moment. She wished she could do something more constructive than baking a cake. She checked herself: *vaguely helping* to bake a cake.

Constructive. Construction was the thing that was most needed. And it was the *last* thing she could do now. She'd found online that there was to be a Parade of Homes Tour of recently remodeled homes in the area. If they could get on that tour, the prestige would allow them to raise the asking price when it went on the market, *and* be good advance publicity, get people through the home. She just didn't know if it was going to be possible, in terms of their progress. Or, if C.C. would be in any shape to endure that. But maybe she could come over here, to Hatch's house, for some of her convalescence. Hatch was pretty good at it.

Shelly made a mental note to wander next door later, check on things and see if Azaad needed anything. She was up to that much anyway. Hatch had kept her strictly indoors, afraid, he'd said, that she'd run off again and break her other arm. He told her that he'd gone over and filled Azaad in, just after he'd tucked her into bed that first day, and had continued keeping him advised of things like when to expect Purdy and Kathryn and Lucy. Hatch had told Shelly he'd helped Azaad with a new window. But Shelly got the feeling that the two of them felt pretty uncomfortable around each other. Azaad was so shy, and Hatch was so . . . Hatch.

'Hatch?'

He turned, again peering over his reading glasses at her. 'Hmm?'

'I want to go to Atlanta, be with C.C. I can't bear being here anymore.'

Hatch put the bowl down again, took his glasses off. 'It's that bad here, eh?'

'No! I'm sorry. I didn't mean that. Of course not. You have been . . . great. Beyond generous. I really do appreciate everything.' She smiled, then as she felt the flush in her cheeks, quickly resumed looking for directions on how to fold flour.

'It's been good for me too,' Hatch said quietly. He cleared his throat, adding loudly, 'Helluvan excuse not to write. Best I ever had, I think.'

'Hey!' Shelly said, sitting up suddenly. 'Maybe a change of venue would be good for you too! We could do a road trip, to Atlanta, stay in a hotel—' Damn it. She couldn't afford a hotel. Plus, it came out all wrong. Like she wanted . . . That *wasn't* what she wanted. She suddenly felt overwhelmed, like she'd done too much today. She rested her head back on the counter.

'Hey,' he said softly, suddenly next to her again, not touching her, not leaning into her. That *hey* was all he said, and standing there was all he did. But it was enough.

★　　★　　★

'Knock, knock! Bix? Helloo! It's me, Shelly. The lady you helped?'

'Lady?' asked Hatch, standing just behind her, holding the frosted cake on a paper plate. She elbowed him with her casted arm in its dark blue hospital sling, then listened, rapping again on the door with her left hand. No one answered. Shelly looked at Hatch. He seemed agitated, kept looking around nervously.

'What in the world is wrong with you? Are you afraid someone will question your manhood because you're holding a cake?'

He made a face at her. 'No. It's just . . . nothing. Forget it.'

'What?'

He looked at her, judging, then leaned in, his mouth near her shoulder. He whispered, 'Churches give me the willies.'

'Really? You too? Same here! Even synagogues. But especially, don't tell C.C. this, Catholic churches. They *try* to make those places scary. I'm sure of it. But –' Shelly glanced around with exaggerated furtiveness. She lowered her voice to a whisper – 'umm, Hatch? We're not actually *in* a church. Just so you know.' She turned back around, pulled Bix's door closed with her left hand. 'Well, I guess we struck out. He's not here.' They were walking back to the Volvo, parked on the side of the road, when a voice called out behind them.

'Hey, y'all!'

Shelly turned. 'Bix! Where'd you come from?'

He brightened when he saw it was her. 'Oh, hey! It's the runnin' lady.' He motioned over his shoulder. 'I was back yonder, turnin' the compost.'

'You remember Hatch?' Shelly said, gently touching his elbow.

Bix nodded. 'How do, suh?' Hatch nodded back.

'We brought you this. It's a lemon cake.' She gestured to the cake. 'We made it for you. To say thanks.'

Bix stared, his face alight with pleasure. 'For me, now? Y'don't say! Well, can y'all c'mon in and have a piece wit me?'

Shelly looked at Hatch. He shrugged, then nodded. They followed Bix back to his house.

They sat at the table and made small talk, in between bites of lemon cake and sips of tea. Shelly was surprised how good the cake was, sweet, tart, moist. But the small talk was painful for her, and clearly for Hatch too. But not for Bix. He told them about his father, chatted about people in Fleurville, activities of the church. Then, suddenly, he asked Shelly where she'd been going when she'd taken the fall on the road. 'Dint seem like you was jogging exactly. Not in them beaver shoes you was wearing.'

Shelly smiled, thinking 'beaver shoes' was a good name for the large, wide-toed rubber clogs. 'No, not jogging, exactly. More just . . . running . . .' She tipped her head side to side, opting not even to try to explain.

Bix looked at her thoughtfully, then nodded. She knew he understood the omitted word. To change the subject, Shelly asked him what *he'd* been doing that morning when he'd seen her, how he happened to be out there. And the simple response of 'tending to a tree up front' was merely the opening of a conversational door that Bix marched through with enthusiasm. He told them about the trees 'up front'. From there he slid easily into bark wounds and root care and natural insect control. Good seasons and bad. The ages of different trees on the property. Shelly was waiting for any crack into which she could wedge a comment about needing to head home, when Bix himself offered them a perfect segue for a quick getaway. 'The kerria just started blooming few days back. Y'all want to see her?'

While she found Bix sweet and his passion heartfelt, and even vaguely interesting, she was ready to go home, have a nap. She nodded. 'Sure. We can look on our way back to the car.' She sounded tired even to herself.

As they stood, Bix stepped past them and out the door. Hatch touched her back, very gently.

'You okay?'

Shelly nodded. She whispered, 'But ready to go home.'

Hatch nodded, whispering back. 'He's a nice old guy. Probably knows every damn thing about anything that grows in dirt. But unless we make a break, we're going to learn it all too.'

Bix was waiting for them when they stepped into the bright sunshine. 'She's right over here,' he said, pointing to a brick wall, next to which was a tall flowering shrub, vivid yellow flowers spilling over its gracefully arching branches. Shelly touched a fingertip to the edge of a petal. They were joyful, like blooming sunshine. They made her think of C.C.

'Beautiful,' she whispered to no one, almost swallowing the last syllable. She looked away, across the grounds. Hatch put his hand on her back again, and it steadied her.

He said to Bix, 'I think we'd better be going. I need to get this one back for some rest.'

'Yes, suh. I expect so. She been right through it.'

'Bix, it's been so good to see you,' said Shelly, and she meant it. 'Thank you again so much for all you did for me. I hope we'll see you again sometime. I'd love for my friends to meet you.' She stopped, her mouth open. She couldn't believe she hadn't thought of this before. 'Hey, Bix? How long have you been the gardener here?'

'Oh, near 'bout m'whole life! My daddy was groundsman before me. I growed up with soma these gals.' He nodded to the trees on the grounds.

'Did you know C.C. Tucker?'

He ran his hand over his chin and seemed to look up at the sky. 'Tucker sounds familiar.'

'Uh, her whole name is Caroline Camilla Tucker, her aunt Georgie lived right over there, on Raven.'

'Oh!' said Bix, brightening. 'Now, I shorely'

member her! Miss Georgie, she was a fine artist. And C.C., was she the cute little thing with blonde hair, came to live with Miss Georgie?' His face darkened. 'Tucker. She the poor soul lost her momma and daddy in a car wreck, way back.'

Shelly nodded. 'And her sister. She lost her sister too.'

'Yeah. I more'n once found her sitting by herself in the chapel. Near 'bout broke my heart, ever' time.'

Shelly nodded, her heart near about breaking too.

'She living heah now, again?' Shelly nodded. 'Tell her t'come by, see ole Bix!'

Shelly nodded again, but couldn't speak. Hatch spoke for her. 'She's away, for a bit. But I'm sure she'll be stopping by the chapel, maybe in a couple weeks, and will come see you.'

'Well, that'd be fine. Jes fine.'

Shelly held her hand out, then stepped forward, guarding her broken arm, turning and awkwardly wrapping her good arm around Bix's shoulders. He patted her back.

'Y'all take care now, heah? No mo' runnin' away, heah?'

Bix was smiling, so Shelly did too. But she was dead serious when she said, 'Yes, sir.'

CHAPTER 40

HATCH

Driving the convertible again, with a woman next to him, the air blowing past him – life felt almost good. Yeah. It was good. He felt like barnacles of gloom were blowing off him. And to think, he had been nearly ready to pack it in.

His left elbow was parked on top of the rolled-down window, and as they roared along I-40, the wind flew up the short sleeve of his Hawaiian shirt, then ruffled through the torso of the shirt, making it look like a huge heart was beating wildly underneath. It made him laugh.

There was some guilt involved in feeling this good, what with C.C.'s illness, and Shelly's anxiety. C.C. was trying to keep her illness from her family, and trying to keep everyone but Meg away, so as not to worry them. Thing was, he knew everyone was far more worried being kept at bay than if they could just see her. He thought it would be good for her, too, if they kept their visit brief. He and Shelly had talked it over, several times, and decided that it might just be necessary to surprise her, so she wouldn't fret about it.

He glanced at Shelly in the seat next to him, smiled. He'd told her to wear a scarf if she didn't want her hairdo blown to bits. She'd found an old-lady type scarf, green with yellow polka dots, probably one of Georgie's, and tied it on her head, under her chin. The scarf aged her some, sure, but in an interesting, retro kind of way. With those big sunglasses of hers, she looked like a fifties pin-up girl.

When they'd left Bix's house, Shelly had asked him to drive her to Nashville, to a temple there. But she'd been virtually silent on the drive over, other than to tell him that Fleurville didn't have a temple, Nashville was the closest. How she knew this, he didn't ask, but he suspected it was one of many things she'd been researching on his computer since she'd been at his house. Nor did he ask why she wanted to go. He'd just driven her there, dropped her off, then bought a novel at a nearby drug store.

The drug store had had a meager selection, but he was desperate for something to read, and so damn tired of the newspapers, with their stories about guns and shootings and wars and man's inhumanity to man, that he thought if he had to read another he'd go out and buy a gun himself and shoot the next newspaper stand he saw. So he'd bought a thin novel, written by a man, but clearly for women. He'd found a diner and sat drinking coffee, eating toast with apple butter, and reading the novel. He'd been so embarrassed by the cover art that he'd folded two napkins into a make-shift book cover. But the waitress pretty much let him be, and every other time she asked if she could get him something else, he'd order more toast, and more apple butter.

Shelly called his cellphone nearly two hours later, saying she was done. Standing out in front of the temple as he pulled up, he'd been struck by her. Not a classic beauty, but a strong, formidable woman. So much life behind those eyes. But when she climbed into the car, he could see her red, swollen eyes behind her sunglasses, her bruised and battered face from her fall, her broken arm. All he could think was: this is a wounded woman. Without a word she'd fastened her seat belt, then reclined her seat. Before they'd driven out of Nashville proper, she was asleep. Or pretending to be.

But that was days ago, and now they were in the car again, but this time the convertible, heading the opposite direction, a bright sunny day. With her head turned, he couldn't see her scabbed cheek, only her soft, unmarred one, and the tiny bit of color she'd placed on her cheekbone. She'd also put on some lipstick, a light shade, barely darker than the natural color of her lips. Her seat wasn't reclined, nor was she asleep or pretending to be. But she might as well be. She sat still, silent, staring at the side of the highway, watching it all go by. What was she looking at out there, he wondered. Maybe the litter, or looking for the odd, lone shoe that seemed to find its way to every highway he'd ever driven on. Maybe the rapidly increasing signs as they approached the city. He didn't know what. She'd clammed up pretty good, for over a week now, ever since her long talk with the rabbi. A woman rabbi, she'd told him. Shelly had spent the past several days sleeping a lot, and writing in a little notebook she'd collected from Dogs' Wood, and sometimes surfing the web on his old desktop computer. Hatch had left her pretty much alone, missing her, which surprised him, since she was right there, living in his house. But she was elsewhere. On a mission, he knew not what. He'd strolled by several times, bringing her coffee or soup or mashed potatoes, and sneaking glances at the screen. It seemed there wasn't anything she wasn't studying: ovarian cancer, Judaism, Catholicism, the local real-estate market, something about a giant lizard. Recipes with chocolate in them.

As the highway curved, he glanced in the rear-view mirror, checking on the cake. It was the second of the two they'd baked, taken from the freezer last night, frosted this morning. It sat on the back seat in a plastic cake container Shelly had bought just for the purpose, and the coats they'd wedged up against either side were doing the job and keeping it from sliding.

Hatch returned his attention to the road. He ran his hand through his hair, just to move and stretch a bit. Meg had given him a great cut, but he was

501

due for another. He thought about Meg, her quiet ways, her calm certainty. Her simple gesture to him had probably been the first step of him coming out of . . . He sighed. He had to accept that he'd probably been clinically depressed. Maybe suffering one peculiar to writers. That attempted denial of the outside world, the real world, interfering with his interior world. Especially when it wasn't going well. And it had not been going well for so long. There wasn't even much satisfaction in the fact that he was writing again. He'd pretty much accepted that he'd run out of juice. His insides seized just thinking about the dreck he'd written so far.

'How 'bout some music?' he asked Shelly. 'That might take your mind off . . . things.'

She looked over at him like she was coming out of a trance. 'I'm not sure I want my mind taken off of it.' She turned back away, looked to the side again, briefly, then turned toward him again. He watched her, watched the road, back and forth. She looked very serious. 'I still don't know what I'm going to say to her. I'm really not good in these situations.'

He nodded, offered his right hand to her, palm up. She put her left hand in his. She turned away from him again, but held on.

Meg had initiated his rescue with the haircut and the talks and walks, and C.C. had been like a buoyant life preserver with her good humor and near-constant smile. But there was no doubt that

Shelly had been his deliverance, in the end. This brassy, tough, smart broad had fallen deep enough into her own hole of pain and self-doubt, and then literal injury, that she'd somehow landed next to him. They seemed to be finding their way out of the hole together. Odd, how helping someone else can lead to your own salvation.

Hatch noted the exit numbers. He gave Shelly's hand, still in his, a small squeeze, then let go, taking the steering wheel in two hands and straightening in his seat. He looked over his shoulder, then merged into the right lane. 'Better get the map, Shel. I think our exit might be coming up here soon.'

She opened the glove box, removed the map she'd printed from his computer, studied it, then looked up. 'We want Charlotte Road. Exit two-twelve.' He nodded. Shelly sat heavily back in her seat. She took a deep breath. 'There it is. Already.'

'Here we go, then.' Hatch put on the turn indicator, turned the wheel slightly, slowing, and they left the highway. 'Where to from here?'

'Um, left up here. That'll put us on Charlotte. Then stay right.' Out of the corner of his eye he could see Shelly put her hand on her chest. 'God. My heart's beating a mile a minute.' She took deep breaths. 'Okay, right, up here, on Henley.' Her hand shot out and lightly grabbed his knee. 'What if . . . ? What if they've moved her? What if she doesn't want to see me?'

'Well, we'll deal. But I bet she'll want to see you. And why would they move her?'

'Well, if . . . if . . . Hell! *I* don't know.'

He patted her knee. 'Easy, old girl. Think positive. Y'know?' He turned the car onto Henley.

Shelly answered with more directions. 'Next will be a right on Cumberland, but it's about four miles up.' She was nervously making small tears along the side of the papers in her lap.

'Okey-dokey,' said Hatch, trying to lighten the tension that had mystifyingly gotten trapped in the open convertible.

They drove for another few minutes, then Shelly called out, 'There! See the sign? Slow down.' He slowed below the speed limit, willing to do almost anything for her at this moment. 'There! It says Visitor Parking to the left.' She was leaning forward, like a child.

Hatch parked the car in the shade of a big tree, far from the entrance. There were much closer spaces, but he wanted to be in the shade while he waited. Plus, he thought the longer walk would do Shelly good, maybe let her calm herself before she went in. He glanced at his watch: 11.09. They'd made good time. He clasped his hands in his lap, staring forward. He listened to a mockingbird calling in the distance. Then to the clicking sounds of the cooling engine. He pushed his thumb against the cuticle of his index finger. He knew she'd go when she was ready. He didn't want to rush her, so he sat, without looking at her.

With Shelly, he needed to take everything slow.

He wanted to take it slow. Unlike with other women, of whom he wanted pretty much all that he could get as soon as he could get it. With every other woman, though, even his wives – *especially* his wives – it was a given that they were not interested in him beyond a certain level, either. His money, yes. His fame, often. But himself? Never. He supposed he'd chosen them for just that reason. He'd always liked women who were . . . what? Self-absorbed. Women who were not interested in pulling apart the knot that was Jack Hatch. Exactly how he'd wanted it.

He glanced to his right finally. She was still staring ahead. What about the knot that was Shelly Kostens? He quickly looked forward again.

Suddenly her hand was on the door, pushing it open, hard. She nearly jumped out of the car. She was ready, apparently.

'I can do this, right?' she asked him quietly, standing by her open door.

He nodded. She closed her door. He climbed out of his side, closed the door, walked to the end of the car, then stopped abruptly. 'Hey, what about the cake?'

'Oh! Shit. *Shoot*,' she said, glancing over her shoulder.

Hatch laughed. 'You think they have swear patrol here or something?'

It filled him up that he'd made her smile. She reached into the open convertible, grabbed the cake. 'I think it was a good idea you had, to bring this.

Thanks. I feel better, y'know, having something. Can we make another, to take to—'

'Oy!' said Hatch, interrupting, and imitating her. 'I think I've been there, done that with the baking thing.' He walked around the end of the car. 'Maybe we can just *buy* one?' She met him there, the cake held in front of her. She nodded, seemed almost to smile, but looked down at the top of the cake container. He hoped she knew he wasn't taking liberties with the plan, wasn't going to attempt to come with her. He couldn't quite read her, still wrapped in the scarf and behind those glasses. He just wanted – what? He wasn't sure.

He pointed to his head. 'Um, did you want to take the scarf off?'

'Oh God! Shit – *shoot*!' She pulled at the knot with her free hand, the other holding the cake container against her, but the knot was too tight. He reached over, undid it for her, handed it to her. His heart was beating ridiculously. He took a step away from her. She went to stuff the scarf into her pocket, realized she didn't have one. He reached for it; she handed it to him. Slowly, she removed her sunglasses, held them in her hand, staring at them. 'Thank you,' she said quietly. She looked up. Her green eyes were intense, equal parts determination and dread. She had a respectable shiner under her right eye. And an ugly scab from where the docs had scrubbed the gravel and dirt out of her cheek. He wondered if his shirt was flapping again, despite the still air.

'You're welcome. It was a nice day for a drive.'

Oh, he could kick himself! He should have stopped at you're welcome. It wasn't about the drive, it was about her. He had been thrilled to drive her, accompany her. But he couldn't bring himself to say that. The banter, the verbal sparring with her, was one thing. But at some point, they seemed to have stepped over a line. But he wasn't sure a line of what.

He looked at her. The muscles in his arms seemed to be twitching. His brain was sending mixed signals. Hug. Don't hug. He debated more consciously. It might be too much. It would.

'Good luck,' he said, wondering if that wasn't an entirely inappropriate thing to say.

He stuck out his right hand, then quickly switched to his left, remembering she had only her left. But she didn't grip his hand in a handshake; she took just his fingers, held them for a moment, her unblinking eyes still on him. Then those emerald eyes closed, and she brought his hand to her face, pulling him toward her slightly. She pressed his knuckles lightly to her uninjured cheek. Then she opened her eyes, and slowly lowered and let go of his hand. She smiled, turned and walked away.

He watched her walk across the parking lot, her white pants slightly wrinkled in the back, her sheer green blouse, worn like a jacket, untucked and unbuttoned over her tank top, fluttering behind her. She cut across the expansive lawn, and finally down the wide sidewalk, with only her short, midday shadow accompanying her. She paused with her hand on the door. Then she pulled it open in one fluid motion, and disappeared inside.

He wished he could do more for her. But he knew the best he could do for Shelly was to help C.C. receive the care she was getting at one of the finest cancer facilities in the country. And though he would never tell Shelly, or any of them, he had extended himself dangerously to do that. Last year he'd finally had to send back the huge advance he'd gotten, after three years had passed with not a word, much less a novel, sent to his editor. The synopsis and sample chapters he'd just sent to his editor last month was a bad rehashing of his seventh, and most successful, book – a guy escaping another guy, a third guy after them both, the woman, the other woman, the twist, the turn, the flip. Instead of a small-town lawyer, a small-town insurance agent. Instead of the mob, corporate scandal. Instead of a blonde, a brunette. He just hoped he could stand to write the thing. The partial had been enough to secure the – much smaller – advance, and more importantly, been enough to cover C.C.'s initial care. She might have to sell a couple more of Georgie's paintings to see her through till she sold the house, but she'd be okay. Financially.

Hatch paced in the parking lot, looking at the door Shelly had entered. He wiped his clammy palms on his trousers. Shelly had gotten *him* nervous, for God's sake! A dog barked in the distance. A big dog, low and deep. He thought of Richter. Azaad had both dogs; he would give them dinner if they weren't home in time. Hatch looked at his watch. Barely five minutes.

He looked toward the entrance again. Was she with her yet, he wondered. Probably. *Man!* It had to be hard. For both of them. He thumped his closed hand lightly against his chest, sending Shelly – what? Whatever she needed. Whatever he had. His stomach churned, he resumed his pacing.

He wished he could call Meg; she'd talk him down from his nerves. He smiled, thinking about her, about C.C. Shelly. So grateful that all three had landed next door, and in his life. Pictures, like photos, clicked through his mind: their night arrival, his watching them, angry at first that they'd intruded on his isolation. Skulking around watching them, listening to them. Then he laughed out loud. Him, with the baseball bat. Them, soaked and screaming. How he'd inadvertently frightened them. How they'd thought he was . . .

Hatch stopped pacing, his breath caught somewhere inside. Everything stopped. A silence descended, enveloping him. He stared ahead, at nothing, but seeing so much. *What if . . . ?*

He resumed pacing, cognizant now of what was happening. It had been so long since he'd felt this electric pulse, this flow, like a restored connection to some invisible river of inspiration. The exterior world going quiet, an interior world revealing itself.

This was a whole different story.
But his editor wouldn't care, as long as it was good.
This could be such fun to write!

The Trio, they called themselves. Well, he had a different name for them.

Muse.

He looked up, saw the sign, a half-wall of white adobe in the thick lawn, the sunlight dappled on it from a nearby craggy apple tree. Why were these places always white, sterile-looking? They should try harder with their appearance. It might make people feel less scared. He imagined Shelly sitting with her now, sitting next to her, talking softly.

He ran to the car, pulled the yellow legal pad and a pen out of the briefcase he'd tossed in the back, just in case he could make himself work. He tore the top few pages of writing off and stuffed them into the briefcase, grateful not to work on that piece of crap. He ran to the lawn, to the white adobe wall. It was shady there. Quiet. He had to adjust, move slightly, to lean back between the words, where the iron letters on the sign wouldn't dig into his back.

He almost laughed out loud again. Here, of all places, leaning against words, words on a wall. He turned slightly, looking at them. They were, like all printed words, mute. Yet there was an undeniable shout to these: The Sisters of Jude Abbey. He would never in a million years have pictured himself writing on the lawn of a religious institution. But here he was. And inside somewhere was Shelly, with her sister. The Sister.

Hatch uncapped his pen, grinning at the irony. He still didn't believe in God. But, if he wasn't mistaken, he was pretty sure he had faith in Meg, C.C. and Shelly.

He wrote two words on the top of the pad: Chapter One. His pen was poised for only a moment above the page, then his thoughts came so furiously he could hardly make his pen keep pace, flipping the pages over fast, one, then another, his breathing rapid, urgent. When he stopped finally, on page six, he rested his head back against the wall, closed his eyes, took a deep breath. The mockingbird was gone, but he could hear the soft, unafraid chatter of a squirrel, maybe two, nearby. He felt empty, and utterly filled. It occurred to him that it was possible, *possible*, that he might also have found a little bit of faith in himself again.

CHAPTER 41

AZAAD

Azaad heard a car in the driveway. That would be Purdy and Kathryn and Lucy. He stood up, slowly. He'd been hammering the thin finishing nails into the floor molding and his legs were tired and cramped. In fact, there wasn't much on him that wasn't stiff or sore. He stretched, pressed his hands into his lower back, leaning backward. Then he reached upward, took a deep breath, then dropped forward, legs straight, placing his palms on the floor, stretching his hamstrings. It was the window that had really taken the toll. He'd had to balance the heavy thing by himself. Hatch had helped him carry it in, but Azaad was so intimidated by the guy that he had installed it by himself.

He checked his watch. It was two thirty. They were late. They'd called Hatch, who had relayed the message to him, that they'd decided not to make the ten-hour drive in one day, and had spent last night at a motel. But they were going to get an early start and thought they'd arrive late morning, noon latest. They must have run into heavy traffic.

He walked to the kitchen and met them coming in the back door. Or at least, he met the little girl, who burst in at a run through the mudroom, then stopped when she saw him. She blanched, twining her legs together in unmistakable need, and hugging a blue teddy bear close to her chest. Without looking at her, he said quietly, 'Bathroom's right down that hallway there, at the end.' She ran past him.

He heard someone else come in through the mudroom. He turned, and did a double-take. It wasn't just that she was pretty, it was that she was a young C.C. Her face anyway. She was taller, thinner. And she wore her hair long and loose. But her button nose, her small pointed chin, the same blue eyes, so like C.C.'s. She had her hands tucked in the back pockets of her blue jeans, a sleeveless, white, sort of peasant blouse hung past her slim hips. The shirt might have been crisp that morning, but now it looked wrinkled and tired-looking. In fact, Azaad saw that the woman herself looked beyond tired, with shadows under her eyes. He realized he'd been staring. Embarrassed, he looked down.

'Hi,' she said, extending her hand. 'I'm Kathryn Prentiss, C.C.'s daughter.'

'Azaad,' he said, his mouth feeling dry, his hand moist. 'Dubois,' he said, pressing his palm on his jeans several times before taking her hand. 'I, uh, I'm sorry about your mom.' He gave her hand a small shake, then let go. He turned, looking over his shoulder at the direction the little girl had run.

'That was my daughter, Lucy,' Kathryn said. He looked at her. 'There.' She nodded her head, gesturing behind him. He turned back again. In the doorway was the little girl, mostly hiding behind the wall.

'Hi,' he said, feeling his face flame. He couldn't control it. Seeing her shyness brought out his own.

'Hi,' she said quickly, then pulled herself back behind the door frame.

'Did you wash your hands, Lucy?' her mother asked. Lucy poked her head out and nodded. Azaad glanced back and forth between them as they spoke, then at the floor again when silence descended.

Finally, he made himself look at Kathryn again, briefly, then away. If only he didn't get so tongue-tied, meeting new people. Especially women. He took a deep breath. 'Uh, where's, um . . .' Oh crap. He couldn't remember the man's name. He'd known it just a moment ago! This is what shyness did; it robbed him of speech, memory, manners.

'They're in the car, both sound asleep.'

They're? Both? Azaad thought back to his conversation with Hatch. The guy from Illinois, C.C.'s . . . what? Boyfriend? Could you call a sixty-year-old man a *boy*friend? He was going to bring C.C.'s daughter and granddaughter down, the three would stay here with him . . . Purdy! That was his name! Purdy, Kathryn and Lucy. Three. That's all Hatch had said.

'I'm sorry,' said Azaad, scratching his hand, looking at the sink. 'They?'

He made himself very quickly glance at her again; he knew from painful experience that his shyness could sometimes be construed as rudeness. Kathryn was smiling, but thankfully she was looking at her daughter.

'Yeah, we picked up a hitchhiker, right?' she said, winking at Lucy, who ran to her side. She hid herself behind her mother, and hid her grin behind her teddy bear. She nodded. He looked at the sink again. *A hitchhiker?* This house was turning into a kind of hostel. Oh well, Azaad thought. He didn't think C.C. would mind; she was always open to new people. He was a perfect example.

He fidgeted where he stood. He didn't know what to say.

Thankfully, Lucy tapped her mother, whispered in her ear. Then she began pulling her mother by the hand to the door.

'Wait, please,' said Kathryn. Lucy stopped. 'I don't want to wake them, or at least not Purdy. The poor man did most of the driving.' She looked at Azaad and it was all he could do to force himself not to look away. Kathryn tipped her head to the side, her hands out of her pockets now, held out to her sides. 'He insisted. Kind of an old-fashioned guy.' She smiled. Beautifully. It made him look at the floor again. Kathryn hastily added, 'But he's

515

a very nice man. I finally wore him down, made him let me drive the last bit. Actually, I told him I really wanted to drive an Audi, which is true. Nice car. But he also looked exhausted.'

Azaad kept nodding as she talked, so she'd know he was listening, but always briefly. He knew she was talking to ease the awkwardness, and he was grateful.

'I think he was out cold about a minute after I took the wheel.' She laughed lightly. 'We couldn't bear to wake him when we pulled in, could we, Luce?' The little girl shook her head, smiled at him, then hid her face behind her mother's thigh again. Then her other hand emerged, still clutching the teddy bear, and tapped her mother's shoulder. Her mother bent, and Lucy whispered again.

Kathryn smiled, nodded. 'Can you ask him?' Lucy looked at him, then her mother. She blushed, and nodded shyly. Not looking at him, she said, 'Mr Zazahd, you want to see?' He smiled.

'His name is Azaad, honey,' Kathryn said. It sounded so nice, the way she said it. 'That's his first name. Ah-zahd. Can you say that?'

'Uh-zahd.'

'Good!'

Kathryn turned to him again. 'Would that be okay?' He buried his hands in his pockets, looked at the toes of his shoes, then up again, his eyes on hers. He might have been staring at the sun for how painful it was. But he did it. Briefly. He nodded, head down again.

Lucy pulled her mother into the mudroom and Azaad followed them out the door, down the steps and over to the Audi. It was parked in the shade, all four windows open. The driver's door and the one behind it were slightly ajar. He felt his crooked smile, imagining Kathryn whispering to Lucy to be very quiet and to not close the doors so as not to wake Purdy, and he guessed the hitchhiker, also asleep.

Loud snores reverberated from the car, cartoon snores, big snuffly inhalations, even bigger cheek-vibrating exhalations. It sounded like just one person, so the hitchhiker must be a quiet – and sound – sleeper, he thought.

Lucy grinned at him, put her finger to her lips. As they quietly approached, Azaad could see a portly, bald man, asleep in the partially reclined passenger seat. His head was on the headrest, turned toward the window, his mouth partially open. The slanted afternoon light filtered through the leaves of the big maple, dappling the front seat. But most of the interior of the car looked cool and darkened by shade.

Lucy handed her teddy bear to her mother, then tiptoed over and beckoned to Azaad. As he drew up next to the car, he glanced at the empty back seat. Lucy held her hand high, one finger pointing downward. Azaad looked down, in the man's lap. He saw Purdy's thick forearms and beefy hands wrapped protectively around something in his lap. He took a step closer, and grinned. It was a skinny

517

little dog. Bigger than Dollop, but not by a lot. He watched the little dog's chest rise and fall, almost in time to Purdy's snores.

Azaad raised his eyebrows at Lucy, and they both smiled. Lucy grabbed Azaad's hand and pulled him back toward the house. Kathryn was already standing on the top step, holding the door open. She smiled at Azaad, her eyes sparkling. And damn if he wasn't able to smile back at her, his hand still tightly clutched in her daughter's.

The three of them sat at the breakfast nook. Azaad had gotten everyone drinks, sweet tea for Lucy, the Rooiboos tea for him and Kathryn. He'd also found some of Meg's good, grainy cookies, and put those on a plate on the table. Lucy was on her second one.

'I've never tried this,' said Kathryn, taking another sip of her bright red tea. 'It's good. And very pretty.'

'I like this,' said Lucy, holding up her sweet tea. She looked down, her long eyelashes covering her eyes, suddenly shy again. She took another small bite of her cookie, as she rubbed her finger on her bear's nose.

'So,' said Azaad. 'Is that your dog or, um . . . Purdy's?' He still felt awkward, saying the man's name when he hadn't even met him. Especially having spied on him sleeping in the car.

'You don't know about M.J.?' Kathryn asked. He shook his head. 'Wow. Okay. Well, it's a kind of long story. But, on their drive down here, Mom and Meg and Shelly, they were asked to take her to her home in Kentucky.'

'Oh! Wait. I do remember,' said Azaad. 'The little runaway dog. Yeah, Meg mentioned that. But . . . how . . . ?'

'. . . do we have her?' finished Kathryn. Azaad nodded. 'Well, because of Lucy.' Lucy beamed. 'We were driving along, and when we passed the "Welcome to Kentucky" sign, I pointed it out to Lucy, told her that Tennessee would be next. That's when she—'

'Can I tell?' Lucy asked quietly.

'You bet! You tell.' Kathryn looked at Azaad, a kind of surprise in her eyes, but also undeniable pride.

'I said, "Kentucky! That's where M.J. lives!"' said Lucy. 'And Mom said, "That's right," and so I said, "Let's go get her!" and Mom said we couldn't.'

'Well, I didn't exactly say we couldn't . . .' said Kathryn.

Lucy jumped in again. 'Well, you said that the lady who owned her wouldn't let us have her, that Meemaw and Aunt Meg and Shelly had already tried to buy M.J. But I said that maybe if that lady knew that Meemaw was sick, then she'd let us buy her dog.' Lucy went on, in an explaining voice, 'Meemaw told me in a letter that the lady had lots and lots of dogs. And boy! She does!' Azaad almost laughed. Lucy had come alive, like

519

someone had plugged her in. Azaad had immediately recognized that she was as shy as he was, at least initially. He wondered if her mother's surprised look earlier was that Lucy had warmed up to Azaad so quickly. Shy recognizes shy, he knew. He grinned at Lucy and she told him earnestly: 'She has, like, about a *hundred* dogs!'

'Well, maybe not one hundred,' said Kathryn, laughing.

'Almost!'

'Anyway,' said Kathryn, picking up the story, 'when Lucy said that, about me telling her about Mom being sick, I turned to Purdy and looked at him. He pulled the car over, right there on the highway. He looks at me and he says, "Out of the mouths of babes." We got downright giddy about the possibility. So Purdy called his son, Mick—'

'And he told us how to get there, and we did!' said Lucy, triumphantly.

'We explained the situation, about Mom, and we again offered to buy—'

'And she *gave* M.J. to us!' Lucy blurted out, now kneeling on her chair.

Kathryn nodded but got suddenly quiet, a somber expression taking the place of the broad smile that had been there.

Lucy looked at her mother and somehow understood. Quietly, the little girl repeated, 'She *gave* M.J. to us.' Then, in a whisper, Lucy added, 'She had the cancer, too.'

Kathryn's eyes welled up with tears. She looked

like she wanted to explain to Azaad, but didn't trust her voice. She stared at her tea, both hands wrapped around her glass.

'Candy's a surbiver,' explained Lucy, sitting in her chair again. 'Right, Mom?' She stroked her mother's hand.

Kathryn nodded, wiped a finger under each eye, blinking her eyes. She patted Lucy's hand. 'That's right, sweetie,' Kathryn said. Then she turned to Azaad. 'She's a six-year breast cancer survivor. So, here we were, all prepared to give her just about any amount of money we could afford, me and Purdy together—'

'And me *too*!' said Lucy, her face pinched in mild indignation.

'That's right,' said Kathryn. 'Absolutely. Lucy was going to give us the rest of her trip money, *and* her piggy bank.'

'But she just *gave* M.J. to us!' said Lucy, back on her knees again. '*And* she gave us M.J.'s *bed*, and a *big* bag of dog food, and some special *biscuits* . . .' She put her finger on her mouth, eyes darting up to the ceiling, thinking, recalling. 'Oh! And this little coat she said M.J. would need for the cold winters up north. For when we go back. It's sooo cute! Wait till you see it, uh, uh, Uh-zahd! And she's the best dog in the whole world! Can I go get her, Mom? Please? I won't wake Mr Purdy. I'll just—'

'Knock, knock,' said a voice, followed by a rapping on the back door.

'C'mon in, Purdy!' yelled Kathryn, jumping up. 'We're in the kitchen.'

Purdy walked into the kitchen, the dog in his arms. He set M.J. gently on the floor and she stood there, her legs looking bizarrely thin, and, frankly, at the moment, none too sturdy. Both the man and the dog had that disoriented look of the recently wakened. 'How long have we been asleep out there?' he asked, blinking his eyes. He rubbed his hands vigorously on his cheeks, making a burbling sound that made Lucy giggle. 'Golly! I'd still be snoozing away out there if it weren't for M.J. here nudging me awake. She did her business outside, by the way,' he said, looking at Azaad.

'I'm sorry. Purdy, this is Azaad. Azaad, this is Purdy.' They met each other halfway, near Kathryn, and shook hands.

'You were only out there maybe fifteen minutes or so,' said Kathryn, answering Purdy's question. 'Twenty, maybe. We didn't have the heart to wake you. Either of you.' She gestured to the table, to her and Azaad's empty chairs. 'Purdy, have a seat. Let us get you something to eat. It's lunchtime.'

'Aw, that's okay,' he said, clearly trying to be polite. He patted his belly. 'Wouldn't hurt me to skip lunch.'

'*Sit!*' said Kathryn with affectionate force.

When M.J. promptly and obediently sat down in the middle of the kitchen floor, everyone laughed, especially Lucy.

CHAPTER 42

KATHRYN

Lucy's bony elbow was digging into Kathryn's thigh as the long van turned left, then right, then left again. Finally, they were going to see her mom. They'd waited till the first two rounds of chemo were over, and they hadn't told her they were coming. Meg had said she thought a visit would do C.C. good, but that if asked, she would say no. So they were going to surprise her. All of them. Kathryn hoped it was the right thing. She just knew she didn't want to wait any longer to see her mother.

But at the moment, the elbow, the motion sickness threatening already, her roiling emotions, all made Kathryn feel like she might explode. One way or another.

She glanced at Lucy. She had forgotten the Dramamine till after the van had pulled up. She'd quickly run in and dosed them both, but it wasn't enough in advance. Clearly. Lucy had that pale, unfocused look she recognized all too well. And they'd only just begun the long drive to Atlanta. And, except for Shelly, Kathryn had only just met every single one of these people. Tossing cookies was not the first impression she wanted to make.

She took a slow, shaky breath, tried to fix on a point on the far horizon out the van window. But looking out the side window, even the far horizon kept changing. She tried again to concentrate on her breathing, but she felt hot, which could be carsickness, or not. She'd been carrying the fear about her mother like a fever in her own body since she'd gotten the phone call from Purdy. *Cancer.* And her mother didn't want her to know. But she was grateful for one thing: that she'd already quit her job. She'd left on her terms, not because of her mother. Thank God she had quit already.

She knew that, without Jack, she might not have gotten the chance to set things right with her mother. What if her mom . . . No. She wouldn't go there. She would not let her fear push her into dark comers. Never had she been so scared, but she couldn't even allow herself to think beyond getting to her mother, seeing her, and holding her. Telling her that she loved her.

And though she felt guilty even admitting it to herself, yet another emotion tangled up around the others. Kathryn could not deny, nor did she want to suppress, a thread of exhilaration about her own life. For the first time in a long time, she felt a sense of possibility. She had loved working on the house the past few days. Azaad kept commenting how good she was. He didn't even add, 'for a woman'. The physical labor was a relief, a joy to her. And seeing something in shambles, then building it, piecing it together, making something strong and sure was deeply satisfying. She had never contemplated the beauty of perfectly angled trim, meeting in the corner nearly seamlessly. Or the satisfaction of running a bead of caulk along a line of tile, timing it just right, fast enough so that it didn't dry, slow enough to keep it uniform, then running her wet finger over it to smooth it. She couldn't learn from Azaad fast enough. Now, if she could only find gainful employment doing something even half as satisfying.

And Azaad had offered an explanation for something else too. When they were replacing the big window in the living room, and watching Lucy playing outside with the dogs, Kathryn had told Azaad about how difficult school was for Lucy. That she couldn't really read yet, and writing seemed to be physically difficult. He'd stopped working, listened attentively, then said one word: dyslexia. He'd told her that he was dyslexic and he suspected Lucy might be too. He said getting her tested would be the first step, then there were all kinds of learning programs that could really help. He confided in her that he had been bullied all his school years because of his undiagnosed learning disability. Kathryn realized that that was probably why he was so shy. But he seemed more and more comfortable around her, because of work, and because of Lucy. Those two had hit it off from the get-go.

Kathryn closed her eyes as the van bumped over a big dip, not sure if her lurching stomach was caused by the movement, or her turbulent thoughts. To have quit her job and sublet her apartment (Matt had been thrilled to take over the lease and move out from his parents' house) was earth-shaking enough. But to have withdrawn Lucy from school – permanently, before she had to face the humiliation of starting the same grade over – was the most shocking and momentous, and *liberating* move she'd ever made. For Lucy, and for her. Terrifying, yes, but for the first time in her life she felt like she was something other than adrift in her own life. She wasn't just letting the current take her wherever it would. For once, she was going to paddle. Chart a course. *Rig a sail!*

Kathryn's stomach lurched again and her hands clenched into fists. Wrong metaphor. No need to add seasickness to carsickness. The van leaned left, then right, barreling toward the interstate. She should definitely have asked Shelly for the front seat. She'd thought about it, but it seemed only appropriate that Shelly should be co-pilot.

Kathryn looked out the window, forward this time, but saw with dread that they were heading onto a broad, curving interchange loop. 'Hold on,' she whispered to Lucy, who was looking worse too. Around and around the van went, pushing

Kathryn hard to the right. She held on, fighting the G forces. The van climbed up and around, feeling like it might tip onto two wheels at any moment. Oh God. Lucy looked green.

'Shelly?' Kathryn spoke quietly but was still surprised at how loud her voice sounded in the quiet van. And how even talking made the queasiness worse. 'Any chance we could change seats with you? Both Lucy and I are feeling a little car sick.'

'Absolutely!' Shelly was out of her seat instantly, before the van had fully merged onto I-24. Kathryn held Lucy's hand, towing her as they made their way up the narrow center aisle. Shelly stepped in near Azaad to let them pass. He stood, helped her maneuver around without bumping her broken arm. Then he offered Kathryn his hand for balance as she stepped up and dropped into the front seat, Lucy in her lap.

She rolled down the window, grateful for the blast of fresh air.

'Very common for people with dyslexia to suffer from motion sickness.' It was Azaad, whispering up to her. 'I've got something here that might help.' Kathryn didn't dare turn, but heard rustling in the seat behind her.

'You doing better now, with the air?' she asked Lucy quietly. Lucy didn't speak, just looked balefully at her.

Azaad's arm suddenly appeared next to her, reaching up from behind. 'Here, try this,' he said.

'One for each of you. It's candied ginger. It really helps. Just take tiny bites, or just suck on it.' Kathryn took them from him, handed one to Lucy. It was a misshapen disc, about the size of a quarter, translucent gold, coated in sugar crystals. The last thing in the world Kathryn wanted right now was to put something – anything – in her mouth. But she nibbled on the edge.

Surprisingly, it did not make her feel worse. At first it was pleasantly sweet, then the strong ginger taste came through. It did seem calming to her stomach and head. She took the tiniest bites possible, rolling it inside her mouth with her tongue. They drove in silence for a half-hour, and whether from sitting up front, the fresh air, the ginger, or the Dramamine kicking in, the nausea slowly receded. Lucy's color came back to normal and her eyes brightened. She tapped on Kathryn's leg. 'I'm okay now, Mom,' she said. 'Can I go sit with Azaad?'

'If it's okay with him.'

'Sure,' he said, and Lucy scooted around to the seat behind. Kathryn buckled her own seat belt and she heard Azaad helping Lucy with hers. She listened to Azaad and Lucy talking, a soft murmur behind her.

She suspected Purdy had dozed off. She wondered if Shelly and Jack were sitting together, but she didn't dare turn, or the motion sickness would get the better of her. She was dying to know what was going on with those two. Shelly called him Hatch, never by his first name, and half the time she spoke of him or to him, it was somewhat derisively. And vice versa. But she was pretty sure there was affection there too. And several times she'd caught their eyes meeting, lingering. Once, a brush of their hands in passing. And Shelly often spent the night over at Hatch's, but Kathryn knew she had her own bedroom over at his house; she'd seen it. It was a head-scratcher. She could hear the clicking of Jack's laptop in the back of the van. She shook her head; for her to attempt that in a moving vehicle would do her in.

What a disparate group they were! She had to go over it in her mind again, pinning down all the names and faces, human and canine, and all the connections. And the reason they all now found themselves traveling south in this big van, having come together from far-flung places: C.C. Prentiss Tucker Byrd. Her mother. The woman she mostly thought of as her goofy, sometimes even ditzy – and meddling – mother.

But listening to bits of conversation over these past few days, she had come to see her mother through their eyes. She had been surprised, even incredulous at first, hearing the personal impressions and details of their conversations, letters, adventures with her mother. C.C. Byrd was warm, compassionate, bright, thoughtful, funny, delightful, a great storyteller. A great and true friend. Kathryn would not have known it was her mother Purdy was describing on the drive to Tennessee. But there was no doubt that, from all their letters, he had come to know her mother very well. Better than *she* did. Kathryn leaned her head back on the headrest. She had never wanted anything so much as she now wanted to know this woman.

She let her head roll to the right on the headrest, glancing out the window to the world rushing by outside. A test. Yes, she was okay; the Dramamine was kicking in, she could feel the drowsiness coming over her. She watched the long morning shadow of the van, rushing along on the edge of the highway beside them. A van full of people who cared about her mother.

She hoped the surprise of all of them coming down would be good for her mom. Kathryn worried, though. This was a lot of surprises. Her mother had made her wishes clear; she didn't want anyone to know she was ill. Not Purdy, not her. She knew it was her mother's way of protecting them, not putting anyone in any discomfort. Her mother's way. Kathryn sighed. She couldn't help but wonder now if her mother's near-constant smile, all that caring for others, protecting, holding in over the years, had somehow led to this cancer. She watched the shadow of the van, undulating over the fast-moving ground, as if racing them to get there first.

Her thoughts stalled, the hum of the engine like a lullaby. She stretched, yawned, rolled her window all the way up, set her head against it. Suddenly there was something between her head and the window. A rolled jacket. Denim. Azaad's. She smiled, murmured her thanks, again without turning. She kneaded the jacket till it cradled her head just right. She felt a thread of strain being pulled out of her, a tension unraveling. She felt held, by the van, by all these people, even the dogs. They'd somehow thrown in their lot together. And at the center was her mother. She became aware only of her breathing, and the comforting, woody, spicy smell of the jacket.

The sound of the engine gearing down woke her. She figured they were pulling off for gas. She rubbed her face, stretched, blinked and then saw the sign: Levey-Penning Cancer Care Center.

She felt like she had been beamed aboard from a different galaxy. 'We're here? Already? Geeze, that took no time at all.' Someone chuckled. It smelled like Chinese food in the van.

'Nothing like a nice long nap to make the time fly, eh!'

Kathryn nodded. They wound through the parking lot, following signs for areas for larger vehicles. 'We stopped for take-out at a Chinese restaurant, and asked for directions. Atlanta is a beautiful city but mercy! Every other street in the downtown area is Peachtree something! Anyway, you were so sound asleep, we didn't want to wake you. We got you some stir-fried rice, if you're hungry. In the back.'

Kathryn shook her head, said no thank you. She

never had much appetite upon waking. It made breakfast the hardest meal for her. She turned around, feeling safe from motion sickness since they were just slowly trolling through the parking lot. Jack was on the back seat, tapping away on his laptop, his face scrunched in concentration. A large, grease-stained bag with 'Chang's Chinese Take-Out' on it, sat next to him. Shelly was also sitting on the back seat, but at the opposite end. She was talking on Jack's cellphone. With Meg, Kathryn realized. They were discussing logistics, who should go when. Purdy had a sleeping little dog on either side of him, his arms lightly curled around each. Lucy was also asleep, her head on Azaad's shoulder. 'Thank you,' Kathryn mouthed to Azaad, who nodded, blushing slightly. She tapped her daughter's knee.

'Wake up, honey. We're here. Wake up, Lucy.' Lucy lifted her head, rubbed her fists in her eyes and looked around, blinking. Kathryn handed Azaad his jacket. 'Thank you so much, for the pillow. Both of us, actually,' she said, smiling. Azaad nodded, smiled again, then looked down, folding his jacket rather precisely in his lap.

As soon as the van was parked, Shelly clapped her hands. 'Okay,' she said, leaning down and pulling up a cloth bag from between her feet. 'Here are your letters.' She pulled differently-shaped and colored envelopes one at a time from the bag, passed them to the appropriate person. 'Now,' she said, grinning, 'here's how we're going to do this.'

CHAPTER 43

C.C.

C.C. adjusted herself in the bed, peered over her reading glasses, stared at Meg. There was something wrong. She was leaving and returning to the room too many times for one morning. And she seemed to be avoiding eye contact with her. Even when she was reading her book, over in the chair, C.C. would glance up from her magazine and more often than not, she found that Meg was watching *her*. But then she'd quickly lower her eyes to her book, *Exploring Buddhism*, opened to the same page for too long now.

'Good book?' C.C. asked, testing.

'It is good,' said Meg. 'I'm just having a hard time focusing at the moment, though. My mind's wandering.' Meg rubbed her tired-looking eyes, but she gave C.C. a smile.

Meg did look tired. But C.C. was still a little worried that it smelled in the room – the chemo side effects – and that maybe that was what was distracting Meg. Even though the nurses, bless their hearts, were very good about cleaning up right away, spritzing that nice orange air freshener.

And she sympathized with Meg, not feeling compelled by what she was reading: C.C. was also having trouble maintaining interest in the magazine in her hands. She no longer cared about four-hundred-dollar shoes, or the jackets and coats the stars would be wearing this fall. The hairstyle page was downright depressing. She touched her thin ponytail atop her head; she'd lost a lot of hair already. Maybe she should tear out the pictures of the ones she liked. Maybe she could try to find a wig to match.

A knock on the door saved her from an article comparing the longevity of eleven different lipsticks. It was a soft knock, not like the doctors' and nurses' two loud raps before they pushed right on in. It grieved C.C.'s southern sense of decorum that their knock was never accompanied by its mate: waiting to be invited to enter.

The knock sounded again, a little louder, seven or eight in a row, but not insistent, tentative. Must be another volunteer. They always waited to be invited in. A whole network of cancer survivors, all women, so far. It helped to talk to them.

C.C. straightened her bed covers. 'C'mon in,' she said.

The door opened slowly, a crack, then more, till—

A nun! Just her head, or rather, her face, tightly wrapped in her wimple. C.C. had a moment of panic. She'd asked to speak with the clinic priest just once, when she'd first arrived, and she'd been frank with him about her questions, what felt like her dwindling faith. Had they sent a nun here to bolster her? Condemn her?

'Hello,' C.C. said, hoping it didn't sound guilty. But the nun still hadn't even stepped in. In fact, only her head poked in, the rest of her remained behind the door. Her bright eyes glanced around, landed on C.C. 'Good afternoon!' she said finally. 'I'm Sister Margaret James, and I'm doing pet therapy visits today. I've got a little canine volunteer here with me, if you're interested.'

C.C. grinned. Hallelujah! The opposite of G-o-d! Something about the nun looked familiar. Her eyes? Maybe she looked a little like that actress in that movie, the one with the two divorced women, she had a British accent . . . Oh hell. *Heck!* C.C. quickly corrected her thoughts in front of the nun. But she couldn't remember the name; her memory was worse than ever. But one thing she could identify: the nun had the soft southern accent of a northern transplant who has been here a long time.

'Sure,' said C.C. 'Please come in. I love dogs!' She pushed herself into a more upright sitting position, cleared her IV tubing out of the way. Meg stepped over to her bedside. Meg was making odd sounds, little high-pitched wheezing sounds. 'Are you okay?' C.C. asked quietly, concerned.

'Fine! Fine,' said Meg, unconvincingly. The stress of all this was wearing on her, clearly. C.C. should insist she go back to Dogs' Wood for a while, send Shelly down. If she still wanted to come. She missed Shelly, and Meg clearly needed a break. She would suggest it after the nun's visit. 'Just excited to see a dog,' Meg said. 'I miss Dollop.'

Oh. Of course. C.C. felt guilty again. She was keeping Meg from her beloved Dollop.

Meg nodded toward the door.

The nun was walking across the room. C.C. smiled, first politely at the nun, then at the little black nose and one back paw protruding from under the nun's big sleeves. She wondered if the dog was shy. Or else the nun was just careless with her big sleeves. C.C. wanted to reach for the dog, rescue it from the fabric. But she wasn't going to grab a dog from a nun's arms.

The nun smiled at her. 'How do you do?' she said. 'I'm Sister Margaret James,' she repeated. C.C. nodded, then, flustered, said, 'Oh! Forgive me. I'm C.C. Byrd. Pleased to meet you. And that's Meg Bartholomew.'

The nun smiled at each of them, then began to pull her sleeves away from the dog. 'And this is—' Its snout and face were caught in the sleeve opening.

'Oh, Meg! Look! Doesn't it . . . he? she?' she asked the nun.

'She,' replied the nun, smiling. She pulled the dog free from her sleeve, but kept it facing her, not C.C.

'Oh, Meg! Doesn't she look *just like her*?' C.C. said, sitting forward in bed, amazed.

'Like who?' asked Meg.

C.C. stared at her, stunned. 'Who? *M.J.!*'

The dog turned its head, grew almost rigid, her eyes locked on C.C.'s face. As the nun released her, she jumped, in one fluid movement, landing on C.C., her front paws on her chest, whining, licking at her chin, her tail wagging furiously. C.C. saw the white tip, waving like a flag, the precise white toe socks on her front feet.

'*No,*' she whispered. 'No! It isn't . . . It couldn't be.' C.C. was crying. '*M.J.?*' The little dog switched to high speed, as if she intended to consume C.C.'s ear by the licking method.

Meg and the nun were laughing. 'Is it really you?' C.C. asked, hugging and kissing M.J., knowing it was her, recognizing her with every sense, the sleek lines and unique markings, her sweet doggy breath, the small whining noises she made, the feel of her little manic tongue. C.C. glanced up. 'It's her?' she asked weakly.

'Yes!' came the unison reply.

'Oh, Sister. Oh,' whispered C.C., choked up. 'This is a true miracle.' If this was their plan to get her back into the Catholic fold, it was working. She looked at Meg. 'But how . . . ?' She abandoned the question. The room was filled with a potent new air, and she just wanted to breathe. She held M.J. close.

'Does Candy— Did— I mean—' She couldn't untangle the joy from the surprise from the confusion. Then a question formed all too easily: 'She's just here for a visit, right?' She wanted to pull the question back, leave it unasked. But another knock on the door interrupted any answer. C.C. looked at the door, blinking, then laughed. To the nun she said, 'The doctors and nurses are through here like it's Grand Central station. Excuse me.' Again, she waited for them to push through. Instead, the knock repeated. 'Come in?' said C.C., perplexed.

Again, the door opened just a crack. Then nothing. C.C. was about to call out again, louder, when red hair appeared. Just . . . red hair. Red hair with gray . . .

'Shelly?' said C.C.

'How's my girl?' Shelly said, flinging the door open. She ran to the bed, wrapping her arms around both C.C. and M.J.

'Aren't *you* a sight for sore eyes!' C.C. wrapped her free arm around Shelly's neck, breathed in the familiar scent of her old friend. 'How'd you get down here?!' C.C. asked, then suddenly realized that Shelly had hugged her one-armed too. She stared at the blue sling, the purple cast peeking out over her wrist and fingers.

'Jesus, Mary and Joseph! What did you do to yourself?'

'Well said, my dear Ceece!' said Shelly. 'Exactly right. Look what I *did to myself*,' she said, raising her broken arm. 'I . . . fell. Um, out for a . . . jog. Let's just say it was due to inadequate shoes.' Meg laughed, and she and Shelly stepped toward each other and they too embraced. They looked

538

at each other, beaming. Shelly nodded, almost imperceptibly. C.C. was stunned to see *Shelly*, not Meg, wipe a tear from her eye. Shelly turned to C.C. 'So, I see you've been reunited with your little friend.'

'Were you in on this?' She pressed her cheek against M.J., then buried her nose in her thin neck, reveling in her familiar smell. A sort of furry apple bread, C.C. thought.

'Ahhh,' said Shelly, looking around the room, meeting all the eyes. 'Long story, but, yes, sort of. You might say, I was a bit of a catalyst.'

'Might?' asked C.C. 'You've been a catalyst your whole life!' Meg burst out laughing, nodding. And so did the nun! C.C. couldn't believe it, but she thought Shelly was blushing! Shelly ran her fingers through her hair. It had gotten so long. It looked good.

Suddenly self-conscious, C.C. remembered her own hair, already so much gone. She touched her thin, top-of-the-head ponytail, her standard 'style' now, so it wouldn't cramp her neck when she napped. To her own eye, she looked like Pebbles Flintstone. All she needed was a bone up there. She was embarrassed that she was embarrassed about her hair. But she was.

'So, how did M.J. get to . . . come for a visit?' C.C. asked.

Shelly sat on the edge of the bed. 'Well, I guess I'd have to say the answer to that is somewhat of a miracle. Maybe several. But, sweetie?' C.C. was struck by how serious Shelly looked, again. 'M.J. is yours. She's *yours*. Forever.'

C.C. held M.J. tight against her, staring at Shelly, then the nun, then Meg. They were all smiling at her. 'Thank you, Jesus! And everybody!' Tears rolled down her cheeks. 'How? What about *Candy*?'

'Yes. I'll – I'll tell you later.' Shelly was dabbing at her eyes again. Amazing. C.C. laughed, dried her own tears. She leaned back against her pillows. Shelly looked different. Thinner? Maybe. C.C. stared hard at her, unable to figure out what, besides the broken arm, was different about her. One thing for sure, she wasn't used to hearing Shelly talk about miracles. Or, seeing her all misty-eyed.

'Hon? Did you hit your head in that fall?' C.C. asked quietly, touching, very gently, the remnants of a scab on her cheek.

The nun, Shelly and Meg all burst out laughing again. '*Yes!* Fortunately!' said Shelly, picking up C.C.'s hand and kissing it, then affectionately jiggling it. '*You* look *good*, Ceece.'

C.C. waved at her. 'Oh, *please*.' She looked down, stroked M.J., who had finally settled herself into her little round life-preserver shape on C.C.'s lap. Shelly touched her ponytail. 'I mean it. Way better than I expected. Your hair like this is cute. Simple, clean. Shows off your gorgeous face. It's like . . . pure you.'

C.C. changed the subject. 'But really, how'd you

540

get down here? And M.J.? And Sister, are you in . . . on . . . on . . . ?' C.C. stared at her. She looked at Shelly. Nun. Shelly. Shelly, nun. Freckles. Eyes. Voice.

'*Oh . . . my . . . God!*' C.C. put her hand over her mouth. 'Are you . . . ? The sister? I mean, *her* sister?' Breathy laughter filled the room. C.C. kept staring at the two of them, the same exact smile. Green eyes.

'C.C. Byrd, I'd like you to meet my sister, The Sister. Pah-dum-dum,' said Shelly, adding a little foot riff on the shiny linoleum floor. 'A.k.a., Sister Margaret James.' Shelly's voice and expression softened slightly as she added, 'F.k.a., . . . Nina. We, uh, reconnected. Hatch kind of rescued me, then— Oh, sweetie, it's a long story. And I'll tell you every juicy detail later. Okay?'

Regardless of what had transpired to bring them together, C.C. saw it was still very hard for Shelly to say her sister's name from a past life, the name that undoubtedly was still a bridge to the pain between them. She was having trouble absorbing it. Sister Margaret James extended her hand. 'Pleased to meet you, C.C. *Very* pleased. You might even say it's the answer to my prayers.' Yes, Shelly's *exact* smile.

'So!' said Shelly, clearly needing to move along, past the myriad currents of emotion flowing around the room. She patted M.J. on the head. 'Anee-wayyy! M.J. isn't the only delivery. *You*, dear lady, got so much mail at the house, that it was either bring all the cards and letters down here to you, or move out of Dogs' Wood altogether to make room for it all.'

C.C. grinned. 'Oh, I doubt *that*!' C.C. tipped her head back onto the mound of pillows behind her, exhausted, but happy.

'I bet you'd like to see some of that mail, huh?' Shelly asked her.

'Oh, that can wait. I want to see *you*. I can't believe you're really *here*.' She grabbed Shelly's hand. 'And your sister. The Sister!'

'Yeah, like that's never going to be a joke again!' said Shelly, grinning. 'But, I need to bring your mail in now. You see, I had to get a little bit of help carrying all the letters.'

The doorknob turned. C.C. waited, smiling, confused. Then, with a growing dread. Had they brought Azaad down here? Her hand went to her little ponytail again, then her makeup-less face. The door cracked open. She waited, her full heart beating hard.

'Hello? Come in,' said C.C., looking at Meg, then Shelly, uncertain, nervous.

All at once a small hand poked through the crack, holding a square blue envelope, waving it in the air. C.C.'s heart nearly burst with joy. She recognized the envelope. And she would know that little hand anywhere!

'*Lucy?* Honey?' Lucy pushed open the door, flew across the room. Shelly barely had time to step aside as Lucy threw herself on the edge of the bed, making M.J. jump up.

'Meemaw!'

C.C. reached for her with both arms, pulling the IV tubing taut. 'Oh, my sweet piece-a-pie! How in the world did *you* get here?' Lucy pulled away slightly, looked at C.C., then Meg. '*She* drove us,' she said, pointing to Sister Margaret James.

'Wha . . . ?' asked C.C. But there was another knock at the door. Another familiar hand stuck through, waving a letter. '*Kathryn Marie Theresa Prentiss!*' cried C.C. 'If that is you, honey, you better get your butt in here right this minute!'

Her daughter stepped into the room, but stopped, pressing her letter against her chest. C.C. could see her chin quivering. Suddenly she ran toward C.C., falling to her knees beside the bed, her face in her mother's hands. She said just one word, barely audible. But C.C. heard it. And it was the word she most needed to hear.

'*Momma.*'

CHAPTER 44

MEG

Meg was laughing and crying all at once at the sight of C.C. hugging her daughter and granddaughter, little M.J. on her lap, quivering. Meg was sure M.J.'s response was a mix of delight and confusion at all the commotion. But the way the little dog kept gazing up at C.C., then snuggling in close again, it was clear she knew she was home.

Another knock at the door made everyone wipe their tears and take a breath. The room was getting crowded, but Meg smiled encouragement at C.C. when she looked at her, her eyes full of questions. And fatigue? Meg suddenly worried that it was too much, that C.C. was already overwhelmed. Normally, C.C. was the ultimate, more-the-merrier social butterfly. But these were not normal circumstances. Nothing about their lives fell even within shouting distance of normal, for so long now. But maybe this was what normal was going to be now. Meg sat, almost collapsing into the chair in which she'd spent so many hours, staying close to C.C. She scanned the room, grateful for every face, every connection. It felt better than almost any family gathering she'd ever experienced.

Family. What was that, really, if not a rather small word for a very large concept. You're born into one, perhaps from some mix of chance and fate. Or you fall together, through some mix of chance and fate.

The knock came again. C.C. looked at Meg.

Meg smiled reassuringly. She tipped her head toward the door.

'Come in?' said C.C., her voice rising with a note of apprehension.

A small, colorful bouquet of flowers in a yellow ceramic teapot came through the crack in the door, eliciting soft laughter from the group. There was no mistaking the brown hand clutching it. Meg glanced at C.C., saw the small panic cross her face, her hand going to her hair again. Oh, Ceece, thought Meg. Your beauty is so deep; please see that. C.C. slunk down in her bed slightly. She looked suddenly pale and small. She pulled the sheet up nearly to her chin, sliding M.J. up along with it.

Azaad stepped into the room, his eyes on the floor, his handsome brown face tinged with more crimson than usual, his dark curls falling forward in a curtain around his eyes. He held the flowers in front of him. Meg felt awful. This was torture for shy Azaad, torture for C.C. Each was clearly soldiering on for the other. Meg was trying to think what to say, to anyone, to stop the parade of visitors, when C.C. suddenly sat up. She looked at Kathryn, then to Azaad, then back to Kathryn, her eyes lighting up. Meg looked at Kathryn and they gave each other a knowing grin.

'Hello, Azaad. Well, c'mon in and join the crowd. The more the merrier.'

Azaad smiled shyly, standing a good distance from C.C., still holding the flowers. He seemed suddenly to remember, and lurched forward, setting them on the table next to C.C. 'These are for you.'

'Thank you, darlin'. How sweet. You've met everyone here?' There was no mistaking her glance at her daughter again. Azaad nodded. 'So I take it you're all co-conspirators?' Azaad nodded again, then walked over to the sink, next to Sister Margaret James, and leaned back against the wall, tucking his hands behind him.

Another knock.

'No. Mercy!' said C.C. 'Surely not. Who's left?'

On cue, the door opened slightly. This time, just a bare hand waved exuberantly, as if in a puppet show. Everyone laughed, then Hatch stepped into the room.

'Jack,' said C.C. flatly. 'Thank God.' Meg couldn't tell if C.C. was relieved or disappointed.

'Hey, babe!' Hatch said, flashing a grin.

'Hey, neighbor,' C.C. said, her hand again smoothing her hair.

Hatch took C.C.'s hand in his, sweeping his other grandly behind his back as he kissed her knuckles. He awkwardly kneeled. It took him a few seconds to balance properly, then, finally, he spoke.

'Lady C.C.,' he began dramatically. Lucy let loose a high-pitched giggle and everyone, even C.C., laughed at that. Hatch resumed his sober countenance quickly. 'I have taken certain liberties, madam, and I beg your forgiveness. But I have found strong medicine for thee. I have come a great distance to bring you this strong medicine, riding among angels in, you could say, a chariot of God.' Laughter from around the room; what a ham, thought Meg, grinning. Hatch continued, the energy rising in his voice. 'Yea, but though we were sore afraid and were nearly lost in the evil labyrinth of Peachtree Road, Peachtree Boulevard, Peachtree Circle, Peachtree Drive, Peachtree Parkway, and – deep inhale – Peachtree Lane, for what we thought surely would be all eternity, and yea, but for Chang's Chinese Take-Out, were we delivered of both hunger and confusion. Finally, we have arrived thusly, here in your temporary domain, bearing our gifts of love and well wishes.' He waved his arm grandly around the room, took another deep breath. 'So, by your leave, dear lady, may I exit and return with said Strong Medicine?' C.C., laughing, gestured for Hatch to rise, and the room applauded.

Hatch put his hand on the floor, pushed and tried to stand, but yelped, sounding, finally, like Hatch. 'Ow! Damn. My knee! Ohhh. Gimme a hand, would you?' He gestured toward Azaad, but following Shelly's lead, the assembled group gave him a hearty round of applause.

'Okay. Fine,' said Hatch, his head hanging for the briefest of moments. 'I deserved that. But really. I can't get up. Someone help me.'

Instantly hands were extended to him, but it was Azaad who pulled him to his feet. Hatch looked at C.C., held up one finger to her. 'I'll be right back!' He spun on his heel and disappeared out the door before any word came out of C.C.'s slightly opened mouth. The room took a collective sigh.

'My! Someone's feeling his oats today,' said C.C., eyeing Shelly, who blushed.

The door opened and Hatch stepped in again, quickly closing the door behind him. Holding the knob, he said quietly 'Madam C.C.? I present, Strong Medicine.' He pulled the door open.

Purdy was peering over an enormous flowering plant, the pot held in both his hands against his round stomach. Meg thought he almost seemed to be hiding behind it. His white eyebrows looked even whiter against his crimson face. His eyes looked full and shiny as they met C.C.'s.

'Enter, my good man,' Hatch said. Purdy took a tentative step into the room, then stopped.

Meg, along with everyone else, looked from Purdy to C.C. And as one, their smiles fell.

C.C. was crying, and it didn't look like happy tears. She slumped down, rolled her back to the door, carefully cupping M.J. near her stomach. Meg stepped close to the bed, squatting, her face near C.C.'s, gently touching her shoulder, feeling a crushing responsibility inside.

'Ceece?' she said. 'Honey?'

C.C. pressed her face to M.J., her fur already wet with her tears. C.C. looked beseechingly at Meg. 'Please,' she whispered, '*please, no*. Tell him to go.'

Helpless, Meg looked at C.C. Had she misjudged this that badly? C.C. had told her of her strong feelings for Purdy, that courting by letter had been deeper and more revealing and entrancing than in person. That being 'a certain age' helped cut to the essentials, allowed them to see they were a 'match made in heaven'. C.C. had told her she *couldn't wait* to see Purdy, first when they were going to head back north, then when their plans changed and they stayed and she had asked him to come visit. She'd been so excited to show him Dogs' Wood.

But that was before, Meg knew. Before her world shattered, yet again. Meg looked at Shelly, who had come close and was patting C.C.'s leg, but she looked as bewildered as Meg felt. The room was silent, except for C.C.'s quiet crying. Finally, Meg looked up, toward the door. But Purdy was already gone.

CHAPTER 45

C.C.

C.C. looked at the book in her lap, closed it. She was tired of reading. But she was happy to be out of bed, at least for a while. She felt slightly less 'the patient' in Dogs' Wood, and especially in the now-lovely living room. She looked out the window, at the namesake trees, their blossoms long gone. But they were still beautiful, even in the July heat. The lawn looked slightly better; Bix was helping, but he said it would take time, that he could do more in the fall. At least it was neatly mown, some new flowers, mostly petunias, in around the porch, just for show.

C.C. looked out the window. The air was wavery in the midday heat. She'd given Shelly the okay to sell a couple more of Georgie's paintings, and they'd installed central air conditioning. Good thing. July. Longer than they'd anticipated staying, yet not nearly long enough. But they'd soon be heading back. It could all go very quickly from here, if they passed inspection.

Shelly had bargained and cajoled to get the Parade of Homes committee to allow them an extension, since the deadline for applications and inspections had long since passed. She had finally succeeded, as only Shelly could. Now, if Dogs' Wood passed, and it became part of the tour, they could significantly boost the asking price, according to Shelly. And therefore, she'd said, they shouldn't wait. They should put the house on the market right away, strike while the iron was hot and they had all that free advertising.

So now everyone was madly working upstairs – everyone except for her, and Hatch, who was madly working on his novel. But Azaad, Kathryn, Shelly, Meg, and even little Lucy were upstairs, painting the second-floor bedrooms, or hanging new curtains or light fixtures. She could hear the radio playing, often several of them singing along.

Meg had told her this morning that they might have to cut some corners, strategically place some furniture in front of unpainted trim, things like that. There was so much more that should be done on the house, top to bottom, but they had to just go for cosmetic touch-ups at this point. The timing couldn't be any tighter. The committee was coming tomorrow.

They hadn't done a thing to the third-floor bedrooms, nor the basement. The bathrooms needed more work. Shelly had assured her that the Parade people had said they could close off certain areas of the home, as long as the main living areas were on display. And C.C. had hoped to do so much more with the landscaping outside.

But wasn't there always more to do? Wasn't it always the case that things were left half finished before . . .

She forced a deep breath. She had to let go. Whoever bought it would make it their own anyway. She'd find a place in Wisataukee, make it her own. Maybe with Meg. When Dogs' Wood sold, she'd be financially independent; Meg and Shelly would benefit too. Kathryn had reluctantly made arrangements to reclaim her apartment. Azaad had posted another sign at the co-op. Shelly, who they would have voted least likely to adopt the South, had done just that, and would move into Hatch's house, but into her own room, and paying rent (Kostens Interiors was growing, and she'd even begun payments to creditors). Shelly insisted they were just friends, but it was clear to all it was a special friendship. It was official: the Trio was splitting up.

C.C. felt the tears welling so she looked around the living room, trying to distract herself. It was beautiful. Wait till the committee saw this room. Azaad and Kathryn had pushed to get it finished before she came home. The new windows, trim, stonework, even a new lintel over the doorway that Azaad had carved himself: dogwood flowers. The big mirror from Georgie's bedroom now hung above the mantel. It had looked heavy and almost Gothic in the bedroom upstairs, but here it looked grand, even majestic above the fireplace. She wished she could see it with a fire there, with

Christmas decorations around it. The tree would go in the corner, over there; you'd be able to see the reflection in the mirror, and maybe some—

She looked at her reflection. 'C.C. Tucker Prentiss Byrd. Look at you now,' she said softly. She adjusted her colorful turban, a large silk scarf from Georgie's collection, wrapped around her bald head. She continued surveying the room. They'd brought a large painting of Georgie's from the carriage house, hung it on the far wall. A large version of the one in Shelly's bedroom. Flowers in a slender vase. It was beautiful. It was the *pièce de résistance* of this room. In fact, Georgie's paintings were responsible for much of this room. And so much more. Sell a painting, buy paint. Sell a painting, put in central AC. Sell a painting, pay Jack back for much of the clinic care. There would be more – more paintings, more bills. At first, selling the artwork had been hard. But there were so many, and she'd come to feel Georgie's presence up there in the studio with her, that her old aunt was pleased, thrilled even, at the climbing sales prices. The high bidder on the last one had been the Memphis Art Museum. C.C. hoped she'd get to go visit it before they headed back to Iowa. It would be a thrill and an honor to see Georgie's painting hanging in the Tennessee Artists Room.

C.C. looked at herself in the mirror again. Well, she finally looked thin, maybe all the more so with the huge mound of pillows behind her; whenever anyone walked by, they seemed to want to stuff a pillow behind her. She shook her head, the bleak irony of her weight loss placing a sad smile on her lips. It was not the first time she'd had the thought. What she would have given, before, to be this thin. But she hadn't so much lost the weight as had it stolen from her. Cancer had stolen so much. The worst, her faith – in life, in God, in her hopes for the future. Especially any notion of romantic love.

She had been mortified to see Purdy, there in Atlanta. Then ashamed at her outburst. But it was as it should be. He had returned to Illinois, his home. He'd sent her two letters since, but she refused to open them, insisting Meg take them away. She had nothing to offer Purdy, other than the dark and looming unknown that lay before her. She would not do that to any man, but especially not Purdy, who had been through so much in his life, and was still so recently a widower.

C.C. stared at her nearly eyebrowless face, looking alien and expressionless. Her eyes began to fill again. She turned away. Blinking, she opened the novel she'd been reading, trying to find her place, not even halfway through. But once again, she just stared at the words. Her eyes drifted to the mirror; she couldn't help it. Then the nausea rose up, like an angry wave. She took one of Azaad's sugared ginger pieces from the small plate on the table next to her, nibbled on the edge; they did seem to help. But one thing calmed her even more: she rested her palm on M.J., as always, by her side. She was currently giving herself a leisurely bath. C.C. watched her pulling her chin in, stroking her little tongue along the swirling line of fur down the center of her chest. M.J. still quivered when excited or frightened, and she was both with Richter. But when she was next to C.C., she was calm, content. As was C.C. with her. She had sent Candy Suddle a small painting of Georgie's, a landscape that reminded C.C. of the Kentucky horse farms. A gift from the heart, to thank her for her gift from the heart.

C.C. continued watching her dog. She still could hardly believe it: *her dog*.

'Hiya, Duckie!' said Shelly, suddenly standing in the doorway. Her hair was covered with a red kerchief, and a good thing. It had a big splotch of dark green paint on it. She had a matching smear on her chin. She held a small pillow by its corner. She stopped, just past the entryway, surveying the room admiringly. 'Damn but this room turned out well! Don't you think? It's really gorgeous in here!' She strode across the room, pillow in hand, went to tuck it in behind C.C.

'No!' said C.C. Shelly looked taken aback. 'I mean, yes, the room is gorgeous, but no more pillows back there! Here, put it under my knees.' Shelly tucked it under her legs and C.C. adjusted it. 'Thank you.'

Shelly looked at the door, then out the window, anywhere but at C.C. 'What can I get you?' she asked, still not looking at her. Not *everything* had changed. But C.C. thought

Shelly seemed especially tense at the moment. Things were not going well upstairs, she guessed. She didn't want to know; they wouldn't tell her anyway. Everyone tiptoed around her since she'd come back from Atlanta.

'Nothing, thanks,' C.C. said. 'I'm fine.'

Shelly cocked her head slightly. 'You sure?'

C.C. nodded. 'Back to work with you.' She waved her hand toward the hall.

''Kay. Lucy and I are almost done painting the hallway up there. She's a great kid. We've got the radio on, some kid station but it's got some good tunes. We're rocking out up there, painting letters, then painting over them. Azaad's idea. When we're done, it's on to my bedroom.'

C.C. nodded. They were all working so hard, trying to finish in time. 'G'wan!' she said, waving Shelly back upstairs.

Shelly bent, kissed her cheek, then turned and ran upstairs.

C.C. didn't even have time to pretend to look at her book again.

'Hi, Ceece,' chirped Meg, brushing by Shelly. 'Need anything?'

C.C. smiled, shook her head.

'You want me to bring in the Mac?' Jack had loaned them one of his laptops; it could play DVDs.

'No thank you. I can't make it through a whole movie. They put me to sleep.'

'Did you watch that disk on Buddhism that I gave you?'

C.C. sighed. Never in a million years would she have guessed that Meg would be the one preaching religion to *her*. 'Yeah. That one was short enough that it didn't put me to sleep, but it sure made me have to pee. All those water metaphors!'

Meg laughed. 'But doesn't it just make so much *sense*?' C.C. shrugged, nodded. 'So are you a Buddhist now?' Meg asked, eyebrows wiggling good-naturedly.

C.C. laughed. 'Not hardly. But I liked it. That idea that we're all energy, flowing from one to another, all connected. And that it was short, twenty minutes or something.'

Meg nodded again, but looked dismayed. 'That's what you liked about it? That it was short?'

C.C. stroked M.J.'s head with one finger. 'No. It's just that, well, Meg, honey, I just don't know what I'm a part of, at the moment. You know?'

'That's just it!' said Meg. 'You are a part of everything, Ceece! We all are.'

M.J. stretched, rolled to her side and let a tiny, breezy fart. C.C. smiled, hoping Meg hadn't heard.

'I've got something for you,' said Meg quietly. Uh-oh, thought C.C. Another book or something about Buddhism. Meg stood, but reached into the back pocket of her jeans. She handed C.C. an envelope.

C.C. stared at it, but didn't take it. She recognized the handwriting immediately, but something looked different about it. It took her a few seconds, then she registered. It had no stamp, no postmark. She felt the shot of adrenalin course through her weak body.

She looked questioningly at Meg, who stepped close, still holding the letter out to her. C.C. shook her head.

'Ceece,' said Meg. 'Please?' C.C wouldn't look at her. Meg set it on her lap and C.C. saw something more alarming than the lack of stamp. The return address was c/o Jack Hatch.

Her heart seemed to go into some unnatural rhythm. M.J. looked up at her. C.C. looked at Meg. 'He's here? At Jack's?' She couldn't help the feeling of panic. She handed the letter back to Meg. 'Take it. Put it with the others.' She slumped against her mound of pillows, knocking one to the floor. Meg picked it up, held it to her chest. She set the letter on C.C.'s lap again. C.C. turned her head, pretended to look out the window.

'C.C.,' Meg said softly, 'at least see the man. He's come all the way down here. Twice, now. Have the respect to talk to him, end it in person, if that's what you really want. But I don't think that's what you really want.'

C.C. couldn't look at her. 'I can't. I'm afraid, Meg. I can't see him. And I sure can't— I'm afraid to do something so hopeful as falling in love. Now. It's like some part of me knows that if I don't, it can't be taken.' It took all she had to get the words out. 'So much has been taken in my life. And I don't want to be the one doing the taking, either.

The man was *just* widowed, Meg.' Finally, she looked at her, and Meg opened her mouth, but C.C. stopped her. 'I know you're going to say what the doctors said, that my prognosis is good, that they believe they got all the cancer. But you and I both know that this cancer is like a mean horse that's kicked you, and is just waiting on you to walk round the other end so it can sink its teeth into you.'

'That is *not* what I was going to say,' Meg said gently. C.C. looked away again. 'I was going to say, follow your heart. Just sit with M.J., get calm, get quiet so you can hear what your heart has to say about Purdy. You know how Buddhism defines love?' C.C. rolled her eyes, but Meg either didn't see or ignored her. 'Love is wanting others to be happy. That's all.' Meg reached for M.J.; joined C.C. in stroking her. Neither of them spoke for a long minute.

'Meg?'

'Yes?'

'You know why I finally called the doctor, made that initial appointment?'

'Because of Purdy?'

'No. Because of M.J.'

'M.J.? She wasn't even here then.'

'No, but I thought about her a lot. And one morning, I was lying in bed and I had this really strong thought of her. I was remembering holding her at the fortune-teller, and it was like I could feel her on me, her bony legs, her little tail, her cool nose. Then I remembered how Janet, the fortune-teller, told us that M.J. might be saying something was wrong with her, with her health, and y'all laughed. But I was so worried about M.J. And then, lying there in bed, I suddenly remembered that conversation we had, the three of us, in that bathroom at the gas station. Do you remember?'

Meg shook her head no.

'About how dogs can sense things?' C.C. explained. 'Shelly said they helped people with heart conditions, epilepsy. You mentioned they could smell cancer.'

'Right. I remember now,' said Meg, sitting on the edge of the couch, C.C. making room for her.

'Anyway, it just suddenly dawned on me: What if M.J. was saying that there was something wrong with *me*? With *my* health?'

'Oh my God, C.C.,' whispered Meg, looking stunned. She reached over and stroked M.J. thoughtfully. 'Directly or indirectly, M.J. saved your life.'

'I really believe she did.'

Meg stood. 'Then ask M.J. about Purdy.' C.C. laughed. 'I'm completely serious,' said Meg. 'She's a smart little dog. Just try to be still with her, present in the moment. Detach from everything as much as you can, and see what's left.' Meg kissed C.C.'s cheek, then walked out of the room.

'Dern Buddhist,' C.C. whispered affectionately. But she had to admit, it seemed to be taking Meg places, good places. She was like a new woman. Still, C.C. had half a mind to make Meg drive her up to the Crown of Thorns chapel one of these Sundays, and make her sit through a hellfire and brimstone service, just to get back at her for all her Buddhism lectures.

C.C. didn't even realize she'd stuck her hand into the pocket of her robe, but started when her hand bumped against it. Her rosary. She pulled it out, closed her eyes, moved her fingers along it, slowly, bead by bead. Saying her rosary, no matter what, was always like coming home. She put it back in her pocket, and touched the letter, brushing M.J. as she did. M.J. stretched again, this time her paw pushing against C.C.'s arm, as if she was pushing it away from the letter. C.C. smiled, patted her. 'Not you too? Pushy little dog! Everyone's telling me what to do.' M.J. wagged her tail, stood up, climbed off her lap, turned around, and lay back down in her tight little circle near C.C.'s knees. 'Well, what's *that* supposed to mean?' she asked, laughing. M.J. wagged her tail again, then closed her eyes. C.C. shook her head. She could make everything and nothing from what M.J. had just done. Maybe M.J. was telling her she was on her own with this one.

C.C. stared at the letter again, then carefully slid her finger under the barely sealed flap. She lifted out the folded pages, two, the even handwriting a bit smeared on the left side of each page. C.C. touched one of the smears, feeling a surprising tenderness: he hadn't written this with one of his quick-drying pens. She could picture his hand, his left hand, curled over the top of each page, writing the words, maybe not caring that they smeared a bit.

She took a breath, put on her reading glasses, and lifted the pages.

My dearest C.C.,

I don't know what to say. Or rather, what to write. After all the letters, I guess I'm out of words.

But I'm not. I have so many words left. Not to mention your words, which I'm going to give back to you here in a minute. But I have to tell you first, I blame myself for not seeing the position we were putting you in, there in Atlanta. It was too much, family, friends, and M.J., and then me. How does a body hold all that surprise and emotion and whatnot? After everything you've been through. And I, of all people, should have known. You've been through trauma after trauma, and with all of us there like that, especially me, well, it was just the wrong way to do it. We were all so eager to see you. And all I could think about was holding you. I'm sorry, C.C. I am truly sorry.

As I have said before in my letters, I am as in love with you as a person can be, considering I have never even held you. But we both agreed it's possible, right? If love at first sight is possible, then surely love after a few thousand words is possible! I'll never forget that one letter you wrote to me, I think it was the tenth or so. (I just checked – it was the twelfth. I brought the shoebox I keep them in with me. Do you know it's almost full?!) Anyway, now I'm going to give you your own words, words you wrote to me:

'There's something about seeing the way you've written my name on the envelope, and your own in the corner, me in the middle here, you in the corner, up there. And yet, there we both are, on the envelope, together somehow. Then when I slit the envelope open and see your writing, your words and sentences, sometimes neat and even, so careful, and nervous, maybe? Then some-times flowing and tilting, as if your thoughts and excitement are a horse, trotting away with you! It's like I can read your letters before I even read the words. I love our letters, Purdy. Don't you think we've all lost something in the rushed pace of emails and cellphones? Don't you think you and I have gained something, corresponding this way? Meg calls letter-writing "careful, considered discourse". (Doesn't that sound *just like her*?! Well, maybe you don't know her well enough yet, but let me tell you, that's the English teacher for you!) All I know is, I surely never would have believed that two people could get to know each other so well by writing to each other. But I think we have, don't you, Purdy? We've shared so much. Our life stories, our past, and our present. And maybe it does, as you said in your letter, say something about our future.'

You wrote those words, darling C.C. Can't you still feel that way? Please tell me that you can.

Meg told me (and forgive her, she loves you like a sister, which you know) that you told her that you couldn't pursue anything with me due to your illness. Please, darling C.C.! I took some sort of vow with you long ago, probably after only a few letters.

C.C. – none of us knows how much time we have here on earth, let alone to spend with someone else. I don't mean to sound too philosophical now, but what is time? Maybe it should be measured by the love we give and receive, not by the clock or calendar.

You can't tell from the words on this page, but I stopped writing up there. I needed to think, so I took that big ole dog of Jack's for a walk. Or rather, he took me. I think it's best not to put that fella on a leash. Anyway, I had to think about whether to ask you this. I decided I would. I hope you understand what I'm getting at. Here's what I want to say: I know how much you loved Lenny. And I know he loved you. So, C.C., if you could have another few years, or months, or even days with Lenny, wouldn't you jump at that chance?

I did not have that kind of love with my Keppie, as you know. But I am a better person for my life with her; she had to put up with a lot with me, especially after I got back from the war.

As you now know, I have taken Jack up on the offer to stay with him for a few days, so I am as close as ever I have been to you, yet I've never felt so far away. I am nearly stir-crazy over here, especially knowing all the bustling that's going on over there, getting ready for that inspection thing. I'm handy with a hammer! I could help!

Okay. I've rambled on long enough. It's just, isn't it true that none of us knows the future? Ever? But C.C., if I did, if I knew I had five minutes left on this earth, I'd want to spend four of them holding your hand, looking into those beautiful blue eyes. And if you were willing, the last minute I'd be kissing you, on into eternity.

Darling, please say yes. Please let me be your

Purdy

C.C. wiped her tears with the corner of the throw, laughed at herself for crying, and at nearly the same minute, was wishing every woman in the world could receive a letter like this. It was different from his other letters, more poetic and romantic. She couldn't help but wonder if maybe Jack had helped him with it, just a little. She didn't care; she knew even if all the words hadn't come from him, the feelings had.

She was just about to call for Meg, tell her to go get Purdy, when the doorbell rang. M.J. stood up on C.C.'s lap, put her front paws on the back of the couch, and let out three sharp barks. C.C.'s heart did a quickstep. She smiled, knowing it must be Purdy. He had hurried over on the heels of his letter, unable to wait for her reply. She was glad. Glad for his persistence. Glad for his eagerness. Sorry for her stubbornness. Sorry for wasting precious days and minutes. Her reply was yes, would always be yes.

C.C. remained sitting, knowing someone would run to the door momentarily. They practically tackled her if she made so much as a move to get up off the couch. She glanced at herself in the mirror again, used both hands to straighten her turban on her head, used another part of the throw to dab away any lingering wetness from under her eyes. She smiled at her reflection. She guessed she didn't look too bad, considering.

She righted herself on the couch, neatened the throw. Waited. Then, she couldn't resist peeking.

She leaned over, onto the back of the couch, peering out the window.

She let out a breath of disappointment. It was a man, but it wasn't Purdy. This man was tall, narrow-hipped and relatively broad-shouldered. Definitely not Purdy. He was dressed in a button-down shirt, tucked into jeans, an unbuttoned sport coat over cowboy boots on the bottom, baseball cap on the top. The Tennessee man's formal attire. She was straining to see him better, but he turned away, looking like he was surveying the property. C.C.'s heart seized: the inspection committee. This guy had gotten the date wrong! He turned back around, but was gazing upward. He must be checking out the ceiling of the porch roof. C.C. wished they'd had time to paint the outside of the house.

No. No she didn't! She suddenly felt angry. He wasn't even here on the right day! She wasn't going to apologize for anything. She looked back out, scowling. Well, she'd be damned if she was going to let him in! He'd just have to come back tomorrow. They'd see Dogs' Wood's potential.

She started crying. Her emotions were so close to the surface, and at the moment, there were just too many of them. She didn't want the inspectors, any of them, to see Dogs' Wood's potential. She didn't want them in her house at all. She wished someone would get the door, tell this man to go away. Tell him to tell the committee not to come tomorrow, either. Or ever. She followed the man's gaze along the front path, to the mailbox, and—

His car.

Her heart nearly stopped. Parked by the mailbox was that old, orangish BMW. Unmistakable. She looked at him again, fear gripping her as he leaned forward and pressed the doorbell again. She saw the logo on the front of the cap. She saw his face.

Jesus, Mary and Joseph. What was Grant Bartholomew doing here at Dogs' Wood?

CHAPTER 46

MEG

Meg was lying on the floor, on her side, painting the trim in her bedroom, when she heard Shelly running up the stairs, her steps loud and at full speed. She must have run right to the radio, because it suddenly stopped. Then she heard Shelly calling to her even before she came in the room, a strained, urgent whisper. '*Meg! Grant! Here! Grant is downstairs!*'

Meg jumped up, the brush full of paint falling on the plastic-covered floor. She grabbed Shelly's arms. 'What? *Are you kidding me?*' The thought of her husband standing downstairs shook her to her core. 'Why? Why now?' She started turning half-circles, not knowing what to do.

Shelly grabbed her. 'Look, you wash up, get changed, I'll go talk to him. *Shit*. The guy doesn't write, he just shows up. The least he could have done was let you know—' Shelly cut herself off. She looked at Meg, her eyes wide. '*Oh my God!* Meg. The letter. He *did* write you. I completely forgot.'

'Shelly! What are you saying?' asked Meg, grabbing her.

'*From Grant!* Oh my God. Where's the letter?' Shelly was staring at her, but unseeing.

'What letter?' Meg demanded.

But at that instant Shelly's face refocused and she headed into the hall. '*Wait.* Wait right here.' As Shelly ran downstairs, Meg snapped into action. She hurriedly changed her clothes, brushed her teeth, hair, put on some lipstick. She felt alternately ill and agitated.

Shelly stepped tentatively back into the room, a dusty, creased envelope in her hand. 'Honest to God, Meg, we didn't hide it from you. It came the same day C.C. got the call, from the doctor.' Shelly leaned down over her knees, catching her breath, then rose again. 'You remember the call, how we found her in the living room, all collapsed? She'd just brought in the mail, but it . . . overtook us, that news. And when you two left for the clinic, and I was here, and I found the stack of mail where C.C. had left it, I saw letters to her from Lucy and Purdy.' Shelly was almost breathless, her expression pleading. 'The whole world seemed to be falling apart and I remember throwing the letters down on the table and then taking off running and then I fell and . . .' She caught her breath. 'Just now, a minute ago, I realized what must have happened. Some of the mail went under the couch. This, and a utility bill. Hidden by that damn ruffle. I swear to you, I – it was an accident. Meg, I didn't mean to hide it from you.'

Meg took the letter, touched where it was

addressed to her, then slowly moved her finger to the return address: Grant. At home. In Iowa.

'Of course I believe you,' she said, disbelieving only of the letter, not of Shelly. But her brain was on overload. *Grant was here. Now.* He *had* written to her, probably wanted her to come home. But she'd never answered. Because she'd never received his letter. His one letter to her dozen. But maybe one was enough. It was what she'd wanted from the beginning, for him to write to her. It was beyond her dreams that he would drive down to find her. She thought about tearing into the letter, but didn't want to in front of Shelly. She would see him first, talk to him. She grabbed her purse from under the plastic covering the dresser, tucked in the letter.

'Again, Meg, I'm really sorry.'

'It's okay. It's okay,' said Meg. She set her purse on the plastic over the dresser, staring at her fingers resting on it. She reached under the plastic again, took the thin gold band from a dish there, slipped it on.

'I'll go tell him you're on your way.'

Meg nodded. She stood alone, trying to stop her mind, the room, her world from spinning. She walked to the door of the bedroom, her hand on the knob, but stopped. She stared at herself in the long mirror on the back of the door. She stepped away, assessing herself. She'd done it a million times in her life, though she had never been one to spend too long in front of mirrors, just long enough to make sure everything was more or less in its place, zippers up, two earrings, no spinach on the teeth. But now she was struck by her own reflection, how her hair, newly cut and almost pure silver now, framed a face filled with fear. She couldn't seem to stop backing away, watching herself literally shrinking before her eyes, until she nearly bumped into the dresser. Startled, she grabbed her purse, and headed downstairs. She clenched the handrail, in her chest what felt like the frantic beating of the wings of a bird, trying to escape.

Neither she nor Grant seemed to know whether to shake hands, embrace or do nothing. They defaulted to the latter. Meg suggested they go somewhere, alone. Grant nodded, and they left. Meg walked behind him across the veranda, then down the path. She never turned around, but she knew C.C. and Shelly's worried faces were at the window, watching her, each fortifying her with their own unique brands of silent prayers and admonitions.

When they were both in his parked car, Grant handed her three additional letters. 'I sent these from the road. I guess you must have given me the wrong address. Found them when I got home and picked up our mail.' She said nothing, just took them, stared at the address. '*713 Raisin Road*', they were addressed. She was awash in confusion. He *had* written to her. All this time . . . If she'd known, she . . . She opened her mouth, but had too many questions. She gave him the wrong address? Where had he been? Why had he . . . ? When did . . . ? How?

Should she read his letters now?

As Grant started the car, his left hand atop the steering wheel, she noticed he wasn't wearing his ring. No tan line. She sucked in a tight breath, found the envelope with the most dated postmark and slid her finger carefully under the flap. It gave her something to do. Plus, she figured he wouldn't have handed them to her now if he didn't want her to know what he'd written, before they talked. She pulled out the single piece of paper, aware, even with this distraction, how very odd and uncomfortable it felt to be riding in his car again. A passenger again. Like a child riding with a friend's uncle, feeling alone and small, not knowing quite if she was safe. Then, as she read, she realized that feeling was warranted. Finishing one letter, she opened the next, then the next, a perverse need to read every hurtful word.

The three letters were all short, but the words and sentences were like gunshots. They made her flinch; she felt them penetrating, as she was sure they were meant to. She felt herself shrinking in her seat as she read. They were exactly the opposite of the letters he'd written to her in college. They weren't letters so much as litanies, of her flaws and faults, worded differently in each one, but each amounted to his complaints about her: she'd been too wrapped up in the kids, or her job;

she was rigid, controlling and unadventurous. Sex with her was rote. He'd stopped loving her a long time ago. And then, the final blast: she made him feel old. He had come right out and said that. The letters also contained a brief summary of his needs and wants, again, worded differently in each, but what amounted to the opposite of everything he saw in her: he needed freedom, for once in his life he didn't want *any* constraints: no work, no schedules, no commitments. He wanted new pursuits, new adventures. One line she remembered verbatim: *I need to explore sexually, before it's too late.*

But maybe worst of all, each of those first three letters had ended with a couple of token sightseeing notes thrown in, pseudo-literary descriptions of Devil's Tower in Wyoming, Glacier National Park in Montana, Garden of the Gods in Colorado. They were incongruous, tacked-on. As if it made all the insults okay. *I haven't loved you in a long time and you make me feel old, but hey, let me tell you about these great, red rocks in Colorado!* As if she cared what he was doing, seeing.

Except she *had* cared. She had.

She angrily slid her finger under the flap of the last letter, the dusty one, the only one correctly addressed. The paper sliced into her knuckle. A drop of blood appeared and she stared at it, then wiped it on the back of the envelope, leaving a red smear. Reading, she calmed slightly. It was more somber, far less accusatory, though not contrite. He'd explained that he had returned home, found her letters to him, and his to her, unopened, undelivered. He'd only then realized he'd had the wrong address. He'd gotten something important from his travels, he'd written, and perhaps gotten something out of his system, and he 'was ready for her to come home'.

It seemed a sudden, dramatic turnaround from his other letters and Meg couldn't help but be curious about what had forced it. And why he'd felt compelled to bring the earlier, hurtful letters to Tennessee for her to read. She sucked her finger, tasting the blood, swallowing it. They sat in silence for the rest of the short drive, Grant glancing over at her only once, to ask, 'Left here?' to which she nodded.

Nor did they speak as they pulled into the parking lot of Hickory Pete's, nor as they exited the car, nor as they walked across the parking lot. He held the door for her, but only as an afterthought. She stepped past him, forced closer than she would have liked. She could smell his aftershave, then the smells of the diner. She felt suddenly dizzy, ill. She stumbled slightly entering, but caught herself.

It was well past the lunch rush so they were immediately seated at a small, tippy table in the center of the diner. The waitress took their order: coffee for Grant, regular, non-sweet iced tea for Meg. As soon as she left, Grant bent down, the instability of the table evidently bothering him too much to ignore. She glanced under; he was trying to push sugar packets under the short leg. She sat up, stared ahead, wishing she did not feel embarrassed.

With Grant grunting under the table arranging sugar packets, Meg's brain seemed to click into thesaurus mode. She thought about all the words he might have used in that last letter, but hadn't. *Reconcile. Resolve. Reunite. Get back together. Patch things up. Work it out.* But no. Nothing close. He'd just said he was 'ready for her to come home'.

Grant sat up finally. The table now rocked in the opposite direction. He had made it worse. One sugar pack would have done it, she thought. Grant grabbed two more sugar packets and leaned down, toward the other leg. 'Please, Grant. Just leave it,' she said softly.

He sat up, tossed the packets toward the rectangular container. They skidded to a stop in front of the metal napkin holder. Meg started to reach for them, to put them back where he'd gotten them, but stopped herself.

Grant excused himself to the restroom and she watched him, the walk she knew so well, the back of that Yankees cap. He was almost more familiar to her from behind than from the front. She noticed that most of the roomful of scattered diners were also watching him, and she realized why. He was wearing his hat. Hats off inside was mandatory in Fleurville. He should have been able to figure that out just by looking around: hats on tables, hanging on chairs, held protectively in laps. Was he just being obstinate? Oblivious? He disappeared into the men's room and Meg breathed, for what felt like the first time.

Grant is here. She still hadn't wrapped her mind around it, didn't know what it meant, to him, to her. To them. She'd wished for it a thousand times, but now . . . She felt like she'd had a recent near-drowning, had somehow managed to swim to safety, and now, suddenly and unexpectedly, felt herself in the grip of another fierce undertow.

It was the letters. Especially the letter from under the couch. The one letter, of all of them, that had been correctly addressed and delivered. But never to her. Meg shook her head slightly. What were the chances? What if she *had* gotten that one letter, not the others? She leafed through the letters in her lap, three addressed to '713 Raisin Road'. What could have been amusing instead made her angry. Raisin instead of Raven. How in the world had he gotten that? Back at the kitchen table, before the trip, him listening to the radio, scribbling notes, as she was trying to talk to him. He hadn't cared enough to even listen, to know where she'd be on this earth. 'You must have given me the wrong address,' he'd said. No. She had not. She most certainly had not.

But . . . She took a deep breath, calmed herself.

He *had* written to her. She remembered the fortune-teller. Was *this* her miracle? She lifted one of the letters, staring at the way he'd addressed it:

'To: Mrs Grant Bartholomew, 713 Raisin Road, Fleurville, Tennessee'. Then, to the side, a blue stamp from the Post Office, in bold blocky letters: 'Address Unknown: Return to Sender'. Meg shook her head. Like some bad sixties song.

Grant returned, sat down again, then leaned down. Meg was afraid he was going after the table leg again, but he merely pulled one leg of his jeans down around his boot. It was a new look for him. He must have picked it up in his travels. Sort of urban cowboy. It made him seem all the more foreign.

She glanced at him, hoping he'd start their conversation. He was running a thumbnail up and down the curve of his mug handle, looking into his coffee. She didn't know what to say, where to start and, apparently, neither did he. She almost wished that they'd gone to a bar to talk. She could use a drink. But she'd wanted to stay close to the house, and she knew she had to remain sober for this. After all this time, she was not prepared for Grant wanting to reconcile, especially after his previous literary invective. How in the world had he moved back toward her, as surely as she had moved away?

When he finally spoke, Meg startled. He stopped, laughed a little, then continued. 'So, here we are.' She nodded. 'I got lonely after a while, Meg. Out on the road. I guess that's what it took. And it wasn't the same, out there. With other women. Women are different nowadays. Demanding.

Insistent. Rude, even.' He laughed again. 'And I thought *you* were a little set in your ways.'

Meg tried to breathe. She felt her chest squeezing in on itself. He'd never been very eloquent, but now it was like he was just blurting things out, as if it was not she, Meg, his wife, he was talking to. Like his letters, he was being completely careless about how his words might affect her, as though she were some dispassionate listener. She wondered if she always had been.

She had a bitter taste in her mouth. She wished she'd ordered sweet tea after all. *Other women.* She was speechless, but not without words. In fact, too many were flying around her head: *Betrayal. Infidelity. Temerity. Bastard. Thirty years.* She stared angrily at him, watched his smile change to confusion, then something approaching concern, but only fleetingly. Then that steely-faced expression that she knew was his armor against her anger. She realized she'd been glaring at him.

She closed her eyes, just tried to breathe. Then she looked at him, spoke evenly, but not dispassionate. 'You . . . saw other women, slept with them?' If he couldn't hear it, she could feel the sharp edge, the glinting blade of her question.

Grant fidgeted, then flushed, then grinned. 'Well, yeah.' He saw her anger, maybe even saw her eyeing the napkin holder. 'Really now, Meg. We were separated, you and I, and . . .' He rubbed his hand over his face, looking frustrated, irritated.

'Separated?' she said, a bizarre calm surrounding

her, like a thick, quieting blanket of snow. 'That's what you call driving off with your things, never talking to me, never telling me you were going to leave, much less telling me that you were even *thinking* about leaving?' She lowered her voice, almost to a whisper, and annunciated each word. 'Grant, you left me a *note* under Buster's *hidden* urn. You could not have left me more alone and unknowing if you'd tried. In fact, I think you did try. I think you tried to make it as awful and frightening and deserting as you could. Maybe not consciously, but that's still what you did.'

'Well, you left first. Or, I mean, you were going to leave. On this trip of yours. Look,' he exhaled noisily, 'I just want you to come home, work on . . . this.' He gestured to the letters.

The incredulity flamed up, melting her calm. His stupid, petulant 'you left first' sounded like a ten-year-old boy. Gesturing to the letters. He wanted her to come home, work on all those flaws of hers. She stared at him, but saw a complete lack of cognition in his eyes. He really didn't understand. He thought that he could just drive down here, bring those hurtful, hateful letters, and she would accept and acknowledge her many faults, vow to work on them, jump into his arms, and let him whisk her back to Iowa.

Iowa. Her lungs, of their own accord, pulled in a tremulous breath. 'So, just to confirm what's what here,' she said evenly, 'you had an affair, or several, while you were on the road. Because *you* had left *me*. We were over, in your mind, so therefore you were free to – how shall we put this? – explore, sexually?'

'Well, I wouldn't call them affairs, exactly,' he said. 'It's not like they were ongoing things, y'know? It was just like when we were in college. You meet someone, go home with them. Meg, it was freedom. I desperately needed freedom.' He seemed relieved that she finally understood.

She realized that she had been slowly and perceptibly nodding her head. Oh, how she understood. How she finally understood. She sat back in her chair, just breathing. Then, quite suddenly, none of it mattered. That, in itself, was sad. But it was true. 'Yeah, me too, Grant. Me too.'

'You . . . you? What do you mean? Who . . . ? What do you mean, Meg?' His stammering, then shock, then anger was not infuriating. It was heartbreaking. She had meant freedom, that she too needed freedom. But he clearly had assumed she'd meant that she had had an affair, or maybe was involved with a man now. That hadn't even dawned on him, before now. The possibility of that. It was all about him.

She watched his emotions banging around inside like so many balls in a pinball machine, every flapper possible whacking away at them. The objective was, had always been, to keep those flinging, rolling emotions from getting through, slipping down the gap in his psyche, where he might have to acknowledge, deal with, and God forbid, express what he was feeling. She'd had more heartfelt talks with Hatch, and even Azaad.

'Look, Meg. This isn't going how I expected – wanted. This isn't . . .' He looked irritated again. Her fault this wasn't going well.

How did they get here? Only a small, rocking table separating them, but as far apart from each other as they'd ever been, and she accepted now that they'd been pretty far apart for a long time.

Meg looked at her hands around her glass of tea. Her left hand. She moved her hands to her lap, slid the ring off. She discreetly tucked it in her pants pocket. Then she put her clasped hands in her lap, one hand holding the other, like a friend would.

'Y'know, this is funny, you'll appreciate this story! Heh-heh.' A new tack. She was beginning to hate that small laugh of his, that artificial smile. Like he was trying to pick her up in a bar. Probably just like he'd done with women when he was on the road. Turn on the charm. Tilt your head a little. Give that easy smile. 'So, I get home, and you're not there, and I see the whole letter fiasco thing, and I write the last letter. That one.' He touched the top letter of the stack, now sitting next to the napkin holder. 'Anyway, so there I am, by myself. I've been home, I dunno, a few days, and I'm sitting eating a TV dinner in front of the tube, watching that reality show about trading your wife in,' again, that laugh, 'and I realize I could do a lot worse! A lot!' He looked down briefly, then coyly at her. 'Then, the news came on and, and, it was like, bam! They said, "Happy Father's Day" and, I mean, wow. You know, it was nice enough at first to have the house to myself, not to have all the schedules and expectations. But at that moment, the picture of it, of me, sitting there with my packaged dinner on a TV tray . . .' He smiled at her, shrugged his shoulders. 'Truth be told, the picture struck me as a little pathetic. I got up and closed the curtains.' That laugh again.

She was beyond any emotion. She felt like a cultural anthropologist, observing, studying this specimen, the male of the species. Had he always done that? The coy looks, the little boy charm? Had he always been able to flick some switch somewhere, turn on that smile, move her on to a different topic or spin the angle like a deft PR person? How in the world could she not know the answer to that question, after thirty years of marriage? She had no idea who he was.

'So, Grant, you want to reconcile because . . . you missed me on Father's Day? For dinner?'

Grant's eyes opened, then he smiled again. 'Well, I didn't mean *that*, exactly.'

'No, you're right. Excuse me. You said it was the *picture* of yourself, sitting alone on Father's Day. You said that, quote, "seemed a little pathetic". As if you would have been embarrassed had anyone seen you.'

'Well, y'know, I *would* have. I would have been

embarrassed that I had no idea where my wife was—'

'*Wait a minute.*' Meg had to control her voice. No more dispassionate observation. The table was sharp on her fingers where she gripped the edges. 'You *knew* where *I* was. In Fleurville, Tennessee. Not my fault you had the name of the street wrong. It was you who had no interest when I tried to tell you the address. *Raisin Road!* For crying out loud, Grant! Who lives on Raisin Road?' Meg felt panicky, like she'd jumped into cold water and it was sucking the breath and reason out of her. Not here. Not at Hickory Pete's. She closed her eyes, tried to picture a beach, a meadow, anything to calm herself. Then she saw Dollop's face, and almost started crying. She wished he was in her lap, protecting her from the ravages of love, the almost visual collapse of her marriage, right in front of her. But it wasn't, really. It was just the same old wreckage that she hadn't seen till now.

Dollop. She wanted to race home to him, to a love that was steady, pure, unconditional and certain. Home. To Dogs' Wood.

She wiped a betraying tear with the back of her hand. 'Grant, you were the one who walked out on me. It was me who had no idea where you were, except by one lousy postmark before I left Iowa, which only told me you were on the road. You *meant* to leave me hanging.'

Grant looked around the restaurant, his face

flushed, smiling at all the people he clearly assumed were looking. His smile fell when he saw the diner was empty; the staff busy with dinner prep in back. Their waitress had refilled their drinks once, then had politely left them alone. Meg stared at Grant, awed by the extent to which he placed himself at the center of all things.

'Meg. I . . .' He hung his head. 'You're right. Of course you're right. I'm sorry, Meg. But can't you see that I needed this time away? That I needed to spend some time alone to see that alone wasn't the way I wanted to be.'

'Alone?' She hadn't wanted to speak at all, but the word, the single word just slipped out.

His voice quieted. 'Yes. Even when I was with another woman, I was alone, Meg. Trust me on that. And please, let me tell you this. I've been trying, here. Something happened. On my trip. When I was in Montana, I stayed on the road a little late. I must have dozed off. Behind the wheel.'

Meg gasped a little, wishing she hadn't.

'I know!' he said, brightening. 'The car grazed the guard rail, then it overcorrected and veered across the highway, and cars were honking and swerving. It was just a miracle no one hit me. It was a miracle I didn't die that day. And all that night, I was thinking of you.'

Meg was utterly still. She was aware of something inside her, in the core of her being. If one was able to feel the moment of conception, the union of two disparate things, the splitting and building of cells, to feel the spark as it crested the hill approaching the realm of life, this, this feeling in her now, was the opposite of that. Something small and tiny and undernourished finally bowed its tiny head and died inside her. Not because Grant could have died, though she was immeasurably glad that no harm had come to him, or to anyone else. She didn't hate him, didn't want him hurt. But also, if he had died, she would not have had the clarity of this moment. The sharp, ringing clarity of Grant Bartholomew's narcissism. Had she just looked past it all these years? Did she just not let herself see it? Or had she immersed herself in her kids, her job, ordered things neatly around him just so . . .

She looked at him, tenderly at first, then somberly, certain that the sadness she felt was also on her face. Quietly, she asked, 'The *car* over-corrected? You're glad that . . . that no one hit *you*? Don't you mean, Grant, thank God *you* didn't hit anyone? That you didn't *kill* anyone? Maybe a child?'

He opened his mouth, closed it, his angry eyebrows pressing in. 'Look, Meg. I drove all the way down here to . . . because you didn't answer any of my letters. You *asked* me to write to you and I did. I did. I . . . I want you back home, Meg. Enough of this. Let's just go home. I mean, think about it, especially with C.C. and all. Do you want to die like that? Alone?'

586

Meg stared at him for a long minute, then looked at her hands in her lap again. She stretched her fingers out across her jeans, thought about her hands on the steering wheel of her car, her hands grasping and swinging a sledgehammer into a wall, the same hands lifting and carrying lumber, holding a hammer, pounding a nail, cupping handfuls of lentils, stroking Dollop, rubbing Shelly's shoulder, holding C.C.'s hand.

She looked at Grant again. She couldn't even contemplate all that he did not grasp. This, above all else, how could he not understand? How could he think, even for a minute, that C.C. would ever die alone? *Not in a million years.*

'Just come home, Meg. You just need to come home now.'

'I am home, Grant.' She looked at him, gently, but with deep conviction. 'And I understand. I really do. And you need to understand that my life is here, at least for now. Maybe, for a while. When C.C. sells the house, I want to find a place here, in Fleurville. Maybe I'll go back to teaching. Or . . . I don't know. But I need to be here for now.'

Grant glared at her. His jaw was tight, flexing. 'There's someone else, isn't there?'

She looked at him, wondering if there would ever come a time when he might accept her honest answer to that question. She thought now was as good a time as ever to try. 'Yes,' she said. 'Me.'

* * *

Meg sat on a chair pulled near the couch, near C.C. C.C. had her knees up, making room for Shelly at her feet. They had long since watched the taillights of the BMW pull away, up Raven Road, then gone. Meg was surprised at the sadness she'd felt, but knew it was inevitable, appropriate. They would talk again, she and Grant, maybe by phone. Or maybe they would write letters.

The three of them had been talking for hours, and then just sitting. Dusk was handing the last of itself over to dark outside. No one had turned lights on in the living room, but because it had come so gradually, they could still see each other – the outline of their faces, or where some hidden pocket of light caught a cheekbone or eye or smile. C.C.'s pale face stood out the most.

'Girls?' asked C.C.

'Yes?' they said together.

'I have a favor to ask.'

'Anything.'

'Anything.'

'I've asked Purdy to stay a while, so we might have to do some . . . rearranging.'

'Wonderful!'

'Excellent!' Meg bumped into Shelly as both bent to hug C.C., laughing as they grabbed on in a fumbling group hug in the dark.

'I have to tell you one thing he said, after we talked,' said C.C. She spoke quietly, but Meg could hear amusement in her voice. 'He said that if things worked out like he thought they would, then one day we might want to get married.' C.C. giggled, then continued. 'He said there was only one thing, a sort of condition, if we were to ever get married.' C.C. paused for a long minute, making Meg smile. *C.C., ever the storyteller, teasing out the dramatic effect.* 'He said he just couldn't see being married to someone and not sharing a last name, even though, he said, having different last names is the modern thing to do.' She giggled again. 'That's what he said: "the modern thing to do"! Isn't that sweet? Anyway, he said he would never ask me to give up Lenny's last name, but that he simply couldn't take that name either.' C.C. was having a time of it trying to not laugh. 'He was so serious when he said this, but . . .' She laughed and snorted. Meg wondered how many of her pills she'd taken. But her laugh, as always, was infectious. 'He said he just couldn't be . . . Purdy Byrd!' The three fell on each other, the giggles and snorts and little gasping shrieks filling the room.

Then, inexplicably, Meg started to cry. At first she thought it was from laughing so hard, then she realized it wasn't. But they weren't really tears of sadness either. She simply was overflowing, immersed in this kindred moment, her spirit once again steeping and blending with these two women. She wiped her eyes with the backs of her wrists. She left her eyes closed – there was very little difference now, it was so dark. She breathed in all the lush ingredients of the moment. She wanted to say something, to somehow capture it all, thank these two women, with whom she'd shared so much. But she found she couldn't speak.

Finally, C.C. did, her voice serious. 'Girls, I have something else to tell you. And it might upset you.' Meg could hear her taking a deep breath.

Had she heard from the doctor? More test results?

'I called off the inspection,' said C.C. 'For tomorrow.'

No one spoke. Meg, flooded with relief that it wasn't about her health, was simply curious. But she worried that Shelly was upset. She couldn't see her face, but she could feel an unmistakable tension.

'I'm staying,' C.C. continued. 'For a while, anyway. Purdy and I are going to take it day by day. He's not making any decision about his property up north, though he says he thinks it would do him a lot of good to move. He's very eager for a new start. But either way, I've made a decision. I'm not selling Dogs' Wood.' The room was as quiet as it was dark.

'But—' Shelly began, then stopped.

C.C. jumped in, spoke fast. 'I'd really love it if you would both stay on, keep working on the old gal. She's only half finished.'

Meg heard what sounded like a small grunt from Shelly. The tone was impossible to discern. A moan? Exasperated sigh?

'Ceece?' asked Shelly. 'Just which old gal are you saying is half finished?'

C.C. burst out laughing again. 'All of us, girl-friend. All of us!'

'Amen to that!' said Meg. She felt someone grab her hand; she couldn't tell whose it was before another grabbed, and then there they were, a clutching clump of six hands. Meg looked out the big new window, into the dark night. She remembered cleaning the old windows, the broken panes, with C.C. that day, to better see the beautiful dogwood blossoms. All she could see was blackness now. If a moon was coming, it was not up yet. But she imagined what was there: the porch, the path, the mailbox, the three dogwood trees. But at the moment, the world beyond that window was a black, blank slate. If the weather held, thought Meg, it would be perfect for watching the fireworks, just two days away. C.C. said they'd have a pretty good view from right there in the living room, better from the veranda. Meg had never been a fan of fireworks, especially up close, what with the noise and smoke. But she thought watching from the porch, with Azaad and Kathryn and Lucy and Purdy and Hatch, and these two women to whom she was now in every way attached, would be perfect.

And then she had them, the words she couldn't think of earlier, to wrap around the moment. 'Well, ladies, it's going to be an Independence Day like none other, isn't it?' Someone said 'Amen!' again, with a slight southern accent. Surprisingly, Meg couldn't tell who.

'Look. Outside.' That was C.C.

Meg looked, saw nothing. Then, a small, fleeting spark, then blackness again. Another, low in the grass. Then nothing. Then another, farther away, halfway to the mailbox. Then two more, in the lawn still, but nearer the porch. Then more and more, till suddenly the black night was punctuated in dozens of spots by dots of light, hovering near the ground. Meg grinned, watching the tiny, living lanterns.

'I love lightning bugs,' C.C. whispered with gentle reverence. 'Momma used to say they were a reminder that God's light is in every living thing.'

Still holding hands, the three women silently watched the fireflies in their nightly dance, small blinking beacons, slowly floating up from the grass.

'Like early fireworks,' said Shelly.

More like little stars, thought Meg. Like little fallen stars, rising up, taking their place, if not in the heavens, then somewhere between heaven and earth, hovering there, together.

C.C.'s Southern Sweet Tea

This is authentic US Southern sweet tea. It is <u>very</u> sweet!

2 litres cold water
8–10 tea bags
400–600g sugar
A small pinch of bicarbonate of soda (baking soda)

Pour the water into a saucepan and add all other ingredients (tea bags, sugar, soda) and put on a high heat. Stir occasionally with a wooden spoon, and heat until just boiling, then immediately remove from heat and place lid on pan so mixture can steep. When cooled slightly (10–20 minutes), remove tea bags and pour tea over pitcher of ice, and serve into glasses of ice.
Serves 8 glasses.

Meg's Rooibos Sun Te

Purchase good quality Rooibos tea bags. Place 8–10 bags in a large glass pitcher (approx. 2 litres). Fill pitcher with cold, fresh water. Place pitcher in sunny area (indoors or out) for 2–4 hours. The sun will 'brew' the tea. Check on it regularly to appreciate its ever-growing beautiful deep ruby color. When brewed, serve over ice. To sweeten, use small amount of Stevia (available at natural food stores). Fruit slices (peaches, strawberries, oranges, etc.) may be added for presentation, sweetening, and flavor. May be made by using hot water brewing method, but you will miss the taste of the sun!
Serves 8 glasses.

Fleurville Co-op Portobello Mushroom Sandwich

8 large Portobello mushrooms, stems removed, caps cleaned with moist towel
2 cloves garlic, minced
8 slices 100% whole wheat bread
2 tbsp. mayonnaise
4 tbsp. softened goat's cheese
approx. 2 tbsp. sun dried tomato pieces; or slices, chopped coarsely
2 packs of bean sprouts
salt and pepper to taste

Mix mayonnaise, goat's cheese and sun dried tomatoes with a fork, mix well, till warm and spreadable. Set aside. Remove stems from mushrooms and clean 4 large Portobello mushroom caps. Brush with olive oil and grill, or slice thickly and sauté in 2–4 tbsp. of olive oil, with the minced garlic. Stir often and turn when slices are slightly darkened. Put bread in toaster so it will be ready when the mushrooms are done. Continue cooking until mushrooms are just tender, not limp. Sprinkle with dash of salt and pepper, to taste, but mindful that the salt brings out the flavor of the mushrooms.

As soon as the toast is done, immediately spread a layer of goat's cheese mixture on each slice of toast, dividing evenly among the 8 slices. Pile hot mushroom slices on one slice, top with hefty mound of bean sprouts and then add the remaining slice of toast. Cut diagonally and serve immediately, while warm. Makes four fat sandwiches.

Hatch and Shelly's Lemon Cake

200g sugar plus 200g caster sugar
130g plain flour
2 pinches of salt
5 large eggs, room temperature and separated – whites into large non-metal bowl, yolks into medium bowl.

Two medium, very ripe (bright yellow) lemons
Icing sugar
Water
9–inch (23 cm) round cake tin
1 6–hole muffin tin

The night before, wash one lemon under cold water. With a sharp knife, cut into very thin slices, set aside. Boil 110ml water with 100g of sugar and bring to boil and continue to boil till it thickens slightly. Turn off heat and place lemon slices in immediately and cover with tight lid. Leave to stand overnight.

Next day: drain lemon slices (you can save the liquid and use to sweeten plain iced tea or other drinks). Set slices on plate and sprinkle liberally with caster sugar and set aside. Wash other lemon, cut in half, juice each half into small bowl. With zester tool, or grater, zest the entire peel into the juice.

Preheat oven to 175°c, gas mark 4. Grease (cooking spray works well) and dust a round cake tin with flour. With paper towel, wipe *edges only* clean of flour and grease. Batter will need to 'climb up' edges and it can't if greased.

Measure flour and salt into a small bowl, set aside.

Beat the egg yolks until they turn pale yellow in color. Set aside.

Clean the beaters of your mixer thoroughly, and dry completely. If there is foreign matter on the beaters the egg whites may not perform properly. Beat egg whites on high speed until they are glossy but not dry. Stop as soon as stiff (but not dry) peaks form. Now <u>very</u> <u>slowly</u> pour in one cup 200g caster sugar while mixing. When sugar is incorporated, add lemon juice and zest and mix.

Gently fold yolks into whites, then immediately fold flour into egg mixture till the flour is completely incorporated. Do not stir or use mixer or you will lose the air which allows your cake to rise.

Pour into the prepared cake tin till about ⅔ full. Divide the remaining batter evenly among the muffin cups. There should be enough to fill six tins half way up.

Place both on center rack of oven and bake, about 20 minutes for cupcakes, about 30–35 minutes for cake, checking frequently but without opening the oven which can make the cake fall. When top is lightly golden, cake is done. You can check by inserting cake tester or sharp knife. Stick in center of cake and remove. It should come out clean.

Cool cake on rack for 15 minutes, then carefully slide knife around edges and lift with spatula to remove. Place on serving plate and cool for ten more minutes, then dust with icing sugar, and decorate with candied lemon slices on top. Cup cakes may be left plain, dusted with icing, or frosting.

Cake will yield 6–8 slices, perfect for your book club or meeting, and the cupcakes make sure the family isn't left out!